Three sizzling, intense romances by
favourite Mills & Boon authors

New Year
Fireworks

Praise for the authors:

Merline Lovelace
'With *The Duke's New Year's Resolution*,
Merline Lovelace writes a terrifically edgy, yet
hopeful, story about two wounded souls.'
—*RT Book Reviews*

Diana Hamilton
'Diana Hamilton creates a pleasant story with
well-rounded characters and strong
story development.'
—*RT Book Reviews* on *The Faithful Wife*

Catherine Spencer
'On New Year's Eve, the attraction between
Cassandra Wilde and Benedict Constantino
reached a boiling point…'
—*RT Book Reviews*

NEW YEAR Fireworks

MERLINE
LOVELACE

DIANA
HAMILTON

CATHERINE
SPENCER

MILLS &
BOON

Mills & Boon, an imprint of Harlequin (UK) Limited, Eton House, 18-24 Paradise Road, Richmond, Surrey TW9 1SR

NEW YEAR FIREWORKS © Harlequin Books S.A. 2013

The publisher acknowledges the copyright holders of the individual works as follows:

The Duke's New Year's Resolution © Merline Lovelace 2008
The Faithful Wife © Diana Hamilton 1997
Constantino's Pregnant Bride © Kathy Garner 2003

ISBN: 978 0 263 90247-1

010-0113

Harlequin (UK) policy is to use papers that are natural, renewable and recyclable products and made from wood grown in sustainable forests. The logging and manufacturing processes conform to the legal environmental regulations of the country of origin.

Printed and bound in Spain
by Blackprint CPI, Barcelona

The Duke's New Year's Resolution

**MERLINE
LOVELACE**

A retired Air Force officer, **Merline Lovelace** served at bases all over the world, including tours in Taiwan, Vietnam and at the Pentagon. When she hung up her uniform for the last time, she decided to combine her love of adventure with her flair for storytelling, basing many of her tales on her experiences in the service.

Since then, she's produced more than seventy-five action-packed novels, many of which have made bestseller lists. Over nine million copies of her works are in print in thirty-one countries. Named Oklahoma's Writer of the Year and the Oklahoma Female Veteran of the Year, Merline is also a recipient of Romance Writers of America's prestigious RITA® Award.

When she's not glued to her keyboard, she and her husband enjoy traveling and chasing little white balls around the fairways of Oklahoma. Check her website at www.merlinelovelace.com for news, contests and information about upcoming releases.

To our traveling buds, Sue & Pat, who shared
the glories of the Amalfi Coast with us despite
the knuckle-biting roads and one sprained ankle.
Next stop—the Pyramids! And very special
thanks to Elizabeth Jennings, doyen of Italy's
fabulous Women's Fiction Festival and the kind,
patient fellow author who straightened out
my mangled Italian.

One

Sabrina Russo got only a few seconds' warning before disaster struck.

The powerful roar of a vehicle rounding the hairpin curve behind her carried clearly on the late December air. Cursing, she kicked herself for parking her rental car in a turnout a good ten yards back. The roads on this portion of Italy's Amalfi coast were narrow and treacherous at best. Walls of sheer rock hedged the pavement on one side, thousand-foot drops on the other. But, like the worst kind of numbnuts tourist, she'd *had* to leave the protection of the turnout and inch along this narrow, pebble-strewn verge to snap a picture of the colorful village spilling down the steep mountainside to the blue-green Mediterranean below.

The slick leather soles of her boots provided only marginal traction as she scrambled back toward the turnout. She was still trying to reach its protective guardrail when a flame-red Ferrari convertible swept around the curve.

Sabrina caught a glimpse of the driver—just a glimpse. Her frantic mind registered dark hair, wide shoulders encased in a buckskin-tan-colored jacket, and a startled expression on a face so strong and chiseled it might have been sculpted by Michelangelo. Then the Ferrari was aiming right for her.

"Hey!"

Yelping, she leaped back. She knew she was in trouble when her left boot heel came down on empty air. Faced with the choice of throwing herself forward, under the Ferrari's tires, or toppling down the steep precipice behind her, she opted for the tumble.

She didn't fall far, but she hit hard. The cell phone she'd been using to shoot the photos flew out of her hands. A rocky outcropping slammed into her hip. Her gray wool slacks and matching, hip-length jacket protected her from the stony, serrated edges. The wool provided little buffer, however, when she crashed into a stunted, wind-tortured tree that clung to the cliffside with stubborn tenacity.

Pain shot from her ankle to her hip in white-hot waves. The achingly blue Mediterranean sky blurred around the edges.

* * *

"Signorina! Signorina! Mi sente?"

A deep, compelling voice pierced the gray haze. Sabrina fought the agony shooting through her and turned her head.

"Ecco, brava. Apra gli' occhi."

Slowly, so slowly, a face swam into view.

"Wh—what happened?"

"Siete…" He gave a quick shake of his head and shifted to flawless English. "You fell from the road above. Luckily, this cypress broke your descent."

Sabrina blinked, and a twisted tree trunk came into focus. Its thin branches and silvery-green leaves formed a backdrop for the face hovering over her. Even dazed and confused, she felt its sensual impact.

The man was certifiably gorgeous! Whiskers darkened his cheeks and strong, square chin. His mouth could tempt a saint to sin, and Sabrina was certainly no candidate for canonization. His short, black hair had just a hint of curl, and his skin was tanned to warm oak.

But it was his eyes that mesmerized her. Dark and compelling, they stared into hers. For an absurd moment, she had the ridiculous notion he was looking into her soul.

Then more of her haze cleared and she recognized the driver of the Ferrari. Anger spiked through her, overriding the pain.

"You almost hit me!"

She planted a hand against the tree trunk and

tried to sit up. The attempt produced two immediate reactions. The first was a searing jolt that lanced from her ankle to her hip. The second was a big hand splayed against her shoulder, accompanied by a sharp order.

"Be still! You're not bleeding from any external wounds, but you may have sustained a concussion or internal injuries. Tell me, do you hurt when you breathe?"

She drew in a cautious breath. "No."

"Can you move your head?"

She tried a tentative tilt. "Yes."

"Lie still while I check for broken bones."

"Hey! Watch where you put those hands, pal!"

Impatience stamped across his classic features. "I am a doctor."

Good excuse to cop a feel, Sabrina thought, too pissed to appreciate his gentle touch.

"You have no business taking these hairpin turns so fast," she informed him. "Especially when there's no guardrail. I had nowhere to go but down. If I hadn't hit this tree I could have... Ow!"

She clenched her teeth against the agony when he ran his hands down her calf to her ankle.

Frowning, the doc sat back on his heels. "With your boot on, I can't tell if the ankle is broken or merely sprained. We must get you to the hospital for X-rays."

He glanced from her to the road above and back again.

"My cell phone is in the car. I can call an ambulance. Unfortunately, the closest will have to come from the town of Amalfi, thirty kilometers from here."

Terrific! Thirty kilometers of narrow, winding roads with blind curves and snaking switchbacks. She'd be down here all day, clinging to this friggin' tree.

"It's better if we get you to the car and I drive you to the hospital myself."

Sabrina eyed the slope doubtfully. "I don't think I'm up for a climb."

"I'll carry you."

He said it with such self-assurance that she almost believed he could. He had the shoulders for it. They looked wide and solid under his suede bomber jacket.

Sabrina was no lightweight, however. She kept in shape with daily workouts, but her five-eight height and lush curves added up to more pounds than she cared to admit in polite company.

"Thanks, anyway, but I'll wait for the ambulance."

"You could black out again or go into shock." Pushing to his feet, he braced himself at an angle on the slope and issued a brusque order. "Take my hand."

The imperious command rubbed her exactly the wrong way. She'd spent a turbulent childhood and her even more tempestuous college years rebelling against her cold, autocratic father. She'd paid the price for her revolt many times over, but she still didn't take orders well.

"Anyone ever tell you that you need to work on your bedside manner, Doc? It pretty well sucks."

His dark brows snapped together in a way that clearly said he wasn't used to being taken to task by his patients. She answered with a bland smile. After a short staring contest, his scowl relaxed into a reluctant grin.

"I believe that has been mentioned to me before."

The air left Sabrina's lungs a second time. The man was seriously hot without that crooked grin. With it, he made breathing a lost cause.

"Shall we start again?" he suggested in a less impatient tone. "I am Marco Calvetti. And you are?"

"Sabrina Russo."

"Allow me to help you up to the car." He reached down a hand. "If you please, Signorina Russo."

It was either wait for the ambulance or take him up on his offer. No choice, really. Sabrina needed to get her ankle looked at and be on her way. She had business to take care of. Important business that could put the fledgling company she'd started with her two best friends into the black for the first time since they'd launched it.

She laid her hand in his, her nerves jumping when his fingers folded around hers. Loose stones rattled and skittered down the slope as she levered up and onto her uninjured leg. Once vertical, she got a good look at the sheer precipice only a few yards beyond her tree.

"Oh, God!"

"Don't look down. Put your arm around my neck."

When she complied, he lifted her and hooked an elbow under her knees. She could feel the muscles go taut under the buttery suede as he made his careful way up the slope. Determined not to look down, she kept her gaze locked on his profile.

The dark bristles sprouting on his cheeks and chin only accentuated his rugged good looks. He had a Roman nose, she decided, straight and strong and proud. His eyes were a clear, liquid brown. And was that a sprinkling of silver at his temple?

Interesting man. When he wasn't trying to run people down, that is. The black skid marks leading to the convertible nosed onto the narrow verge made Sabrina bristle again.

"You came around that corner way too fast. If I hadn't jumped backward, you would have hit me."

"You should not have left the safety of the turnout," he countered. "Why did you do something so foolish?"

She hated to admit she'd been mesmerized by the incredible view and was snapping pictures like an awestruck tourist, but she had no other excuse short of an outright lie. Sabrina had committed more than her share of sins in her colorful past. Lying wasn't one of them.

"I was taking pictures. For my business," she added, as if that would lessen the idiocy.

He didn't roll his eyes but he came damned close. "What business is that?"

"My company provides travel, translation and executive support services for Americans doing business in Europe. I'm here to scout locations for a high-level conference for one of our clients."

He nodded, but made no comment as they approached the red convertible. Raising a knee, he balanced her on a hard, muscled thigh and reached down to open the passenger door. Despite her efforts to protect her ankle, Sabrina was gritting her teeth by the time he'd jockeyed her into the seat.

"My purse," she ground out. "It's in the rental car."

He did the almost-eye-roll thing again.

Okay, so leaving her purse unattended in Italy— or anywhere else!—wasn't the smartest thing to do. She certainly wouldn't have done so under normal circumstances. But this was such an isolated stretch of road and she'd kept her rental car in view the whole time. Except when she'd nose-dived over the side of the cliff, of course.

Good thing she *didn't* have her purse with her then. If she had, it might have gone the way of her cell phone. God knew where that was right now. One thing's for sure, she wasn't crawling back down the slope to look for it.

"I locked your car," the doc informed her when he returned with her purse and the keys. "I'll send someone back for it while you're being attended to."

He folded his muscular frame behind the wheel with practiced ease and keyed the Ferrari's ignition. It came to life with a well-mannered growl.

"I'll take you to the clinic in Positano. It's small but well equipped."

"How far is that?"

"Just there." He indicated the cluster of colorful buildings clinging to the side of the cliff. "The place you were photographing," he added on a dry note.

Sabrina was too preoccupied at the moment to respond. Navigating these narrow, twisting roads in the driver's seat was nerve-racking enough. Sitting in the passenger seat, with a perpendicular drop-off mere inches away, it was a life-altering experience.

Stiff-armed, she braced her palms against the edge of her seat. Her uninjured leg instinctively thumped the floorboards, searching for the nonexistent brake on every turn. She sucked air whenever the Ferrari took a curve but gradually, grudgingly, had to admit the doc handled his powerful machine with unerring skill. Which didn't explain why he'd seemed to aim right for her a while ago.

She must have startled him as much as he had her. Obviously, he hadn't expected to encounter a pedestrian on that narrow curve. He wouldn't encounter this one again, Sabrina vowed as the convertible hugged the asphalt on another switchback turn. She'd learned her lesson. No more excursions beyond the protection of the guardrails.

Dragging her attention from the sheer precipices, she pinned it on the driver. "Your name and accent are Italian, but your English has a touch of New York City in it."

"You have a good ear. I did a three-year neuro-surgical residency at Mount Sinai. I still consult there and fly over two or three times a year." He sent a swift glance in her direction. "Are you a New Yorker?"

"I was once," she got out, her uninjured foot stomping the floorboard again. "How about you keep your eyes on the road, Doc?"

She didn't draw a full breath until the road cut away from the cliffs and buildings began to spring up on her side of the car.

Positano turned out to be a small town but one that obviously catered to the tourist trade during the regular season. This late in the year, many of the shops and restaurants were shuttered. Those still open displayed windows filled with glazed pottery and bottles of the region's famous limoncello liqueur.

The town's main street led straight down to a round-domed church and a piazza overlooking the sea, then straight up again. Since it was only two days past Christmas, the piazza was still decorated with festive garlands. A life-size nativity scene held the place of honor outside the church. Sabrina caught a glimpse of colorful fishing boats pulled up on a slice of rocky beach just before the doc made a sharp left and pulled into a small courtyard.

Killing the engine, he came around to the passenger side of the Ferrari. Once again she looped her arm around his neck. Her cheek brushed his when he lifted her. The bristles set the nerves just under her skin to dancing as he carried her toward a set of double glass doors.

The doors swished open at their approach. The nurse at the counter glanced up, her eyes widening in surprise.

"Sua Eccellenza!"

Sabrina's German and French were much better than her Italian, but she was fairly certain nurses didn't routinely accord physicians the title of Your Excellency. The rest of their conversation was so machine-gun fast, however, she didn't have time to figure that one out before the nurse rushed forward with a wheelchair.

"Rafaela will take you to X-ray," the doc said as he lowered her into the chair. "I'll speak with you after I review the films."

She must look like she'd just fallen off a cliff, Sabrina thought ruefully. The nurse gave her a fish-eyed stare until a sharp order from the doc put her in motion. With a squeak of the chair's rubber wheels, she propelled Sabrina through another set of double doors.

Marco remained in the reception area for a long time after the doors swished shut. He couldn't blame Rafaela for gaping at this woman, this Sabrina Russo. The resemblance was incredible.

So incredible, he'd almost lost control of his car when he'd spotted her back there on that narrow road. Thank the Lord instinct had taken over from his shocked brain! Without thinking, he'd cut back into the proper lane and jammed on the brakes.

Then his only concern was getting to her, making sure she'd survived the fall. But now…

Now there was nothing to keep him reliving those terrifying seconds just before she fell. One thought and one thought only hammered into his skull.

He might have killed her. Again.

His jaw clenched so tight his back teeth ground together. Unseeing, Marco stared at the double doors. A phone buzzed somewhere in the distance. Outside, a horn honked with typical Italian impatience.

He heard nothing, saw nothing but the image of the woman who'd disappeared behind the doors. Her face, her features remained vivid in his mind as he reached into the inside pocket of his jacket.

The picture he drew out of his wallet was old and dog-eared. It was the only snapshot he hadn't been able to bring himself to pack away. His throat tight, he stared down at the laughing couple.

He'd been in his early twenties, a premed student at the University of Milan. Gianetta was three years younger. She looked so vibrant, so alive in this faded picture that a fist seemed to reach into Marco's chest and rip out his beating, bleeding heart.

How young they'd been then. How blinded by lust. So sure their passion would stand the test of time. So heedless of the words of caution both his family and hers felt compelled to voice.

He should have listened, Marco thought savagely. He'd been premed, for God's sake! He should have recognized the signs. The soaring highs. The sudden lows. The wild exuberance he'd ascribed to the mindless energy of youth. The seeds had been there, though. He could see them now in the laughing face turned up to the camera.

A face that was almost the mirror image of Sabrina Russo's.

She could be Gianetta's sister. Her twin. They had the same sun-streaked blond hair. The same slanting brown eyes. The same stubborn chin.

Or...

His stomach knotting, Marco echoed the irrational, improbable thought that had leaped into his mind when he'd glimpsed the woman in the road.

She could be his wife.

Gianetta, who had insisted on launching the sailboat despite the weather warnings.

Gianetta, whose frantic radio call for help still haunted his dreams.

Gianetta, whose body had never been recovered from the sea.

With a muttered oath, Marco shook his head. He'd been working too hard. Performing too many difficult surgeries. The long hours and unrelenting pace had gotten to him. How absurd to fantasize for so much as a single second that this American, this Sabrina Russo, could be his dead wife!

He was glad now his surgical team had pleaded

with him to take a long-overdue break between Christmas and New Year's. Obviously, he needed it.

With another impatient shake of his head, he pushed through the double doors and strode down the hall toward X-ray.

Two

Wincing, Sabina swung her legs off the X-ray table and sat up on the edge. The remains of the boot they'd had to cut off lay discarded beside the table.

"Allow me to assist you, Ms. Russo."

Rafaela nudged the wheelchair closer. After a somewhat graceless transfer, the nurse got Sabrina settled into the chair.

"I shall take you to an exam room, yes? Dr. Calvetti will review the X-rays and consult with you there."

"You called him something else when we first came in," Sabrina commented as she was wheeled into the corridor. "*Eccellenza,* wasn't it?"

"*Si.*"

"What's with that?"

"He prefers to use his medical title here at the clinic, but I forget myself sometimes. My mother cooks and cleans for him when he's in residence at his villa, you see."

"Not really. Who is he?"

"His Excellency Don Marco Antonio Sonestra di Calvetti, twelfth Duke of San Giovanti, fourteenth Marquis of Caprielle, ninth Marquis d'Almalfi, Count Palatine, sixteenth Baron of Ravenna…" She paused. "Or is it the seventeenth Baron Ravenna?"

"You got me."

"There are more titles. Many more." Smiling, Rafaela steered her patient into an exam room and set the brake. "Mama can recite the entire list without taking a breath. She has worked for the Calvetti family since she was a young girl."

Okay, Sabrina was impressed. So the doc was also a duke. Not to mention a world-class hunk. The combination was almost enough to make her forget how close His Excellency had come to flattening her into roadkill.

But not quite enough to keep her from scowling when he delivered the good news/bad news.

"The X-rays show no sign of concussion or fractured bones in your ankle. However, you may have damaged or torn a ligament. We won't know for sure until we perform a stress test."

"Where and when do we do that?"

"It's a simple test. A manipulation of the foot and ankle. I'll do it now if you can stand the pain."

Uh-oh! That didn't sound good.

"Once we are done, I will prescribe painkillers. But you must be alert for the manipulation, so you can tell me when I hurt you."

When, not if. That sounded even worse.

"Okay, Doc, let's get this over with. Or should I say duke?"

"Either will suffice." Those dark eyes held hers. "Given the circumstances, perhaps we should dispense with titles altogether."

She wasn't sure exactly what circumstances he referred to but had no problem with a more egalitarian approach. "That's fine with me."

"Good. You must call me Marco. And may I call you Sabrina?"

She granted the polite request with a regal nod. "You may."

"Very well, Sabrina. Rafaela and I will help you onto the exam table."

She managed it with their assistance and a couple of hops. Once they had her in place, Rafaela rolled up the hem of the wool slacks. The bruised, inflated sausage she revealed made Sabrina grimace.

"Lovely," she muttered.

"It will get worse before it gets better," the doc—duke—Marco warned.

He washed his hands at the sink in the exam room. The scent of antibacterial soap came with him as he rolled a stool close to the table, seated himself and cupped her heel. His touch was gentle, lulling Sabrina into a false sense of security. That lasted only until he flattened his other hand against her shin and applied pressure. The pain almost brought her off the table.

"Okay, okay," she gasped. "You found the not-so-sweet spot."

He relieved the frontal pressure and applied it sideways. More prepared this time, Sabrina merely gritted her teeth.

"It is not as bad as I feared," he said when he'd completed the test.

"Easy for you to say!"

"I don't believe you've torn the ligaments, merely strained them. We will wrap the ankle in a compression bandage. Then you must stay off your feet, apply ice and take the painkillers I will prescribe."

"Stay off my feet for how long?"

"As a minimum, until the swelling goes down and the pain lessens. After that, you may require crutches for a few days to a week."

"A week!"

Sabrina swallowed a groan. Her tight schedule was disintegrating before her eyes. She'd already re-arranged it once to spend Christmas Day in Austria with her two best friends and business partners.

Sabrina, Devon McShay and Caroline Walters had met years ago while spending their junior year studying at the University of Salzburg. Filled with the dreams and enthusiasm of youth, the three coeds had formed a fast friendship. They'd maintained that friendship long distance in the years that followed. Until last May, when they'd met for a minireunion.

After acknowledging that their lives hadn't lived up to their dreams, they'd decided to pool resources. Two months later, they'd quit their respective jobs and launched European Business Services, Incorporated. EBS for short. Specializing in arranging transportation, hotels, conference facilities, translation and other support services for busy executives.

Now Devon McShay, the former history professor, Caroline Walters, the quiet, introverted librarian, and Sabrina the one-time rebel and good-time girl were hard-nosed businesswomen. They had an office and a small staff in a Washington, D.C., suburb and had spent megabucks on advertising. They'd landed a few jobs, but nothing big until aerospace mogul Cal Logan hired EBS to work his short-notice trip to Germany.

Sabrina had done most of the frantic prep work for Logan's five-day, three-city blitz, but came down with the flu the day before she was supposed to fly to Germany. Devon took the trip instead, with some interesting results. Sexy Cal Logan had made it plain he wanted to merge more than business interests with Devon.

Dev was now scrambling to put together a conference for high-level Logan Aerospace executives while Caroline and Sabrina divided forces to scout locations for the lucrative new contract they'd just landed with Global Security International.

Their client wanted to hold the conference the second week in February in either Italy or Spain. Caro and Sabrina had jumped on the computer to find locations with sufficient available rooms and conference facilities on such short notice.

Their choices narrowed to a handful of potential sites, Caro flew into Barcelona to physically inspect those along Spain's Costa Bravo. Sabrina was supposed to check the possibilities here, on Italy's Amalfi Coast. They had less than two weeks to put together an acceptable proposal, and Sabrina wasn't about to let a little thing like a sprained ankle deter her.

There was another side to her determination. One that went deeper and struck at what she was. Or what she used to be. She'd struggled too long to get out of her father's shadow...and taken too much crap from him and his lawyers when she'd resigned from the board of the Russo Foundation to go into business with her two friends. Sabrina fully intended to make it on her own *and* make a success of EBS, which meant hopping off this exam table and getting her butt in gear.

She aimed her best smile at the doc/duke. "Bring on the ace bandage and painkillers, and I'll be on my way."

"Your way to where?"

"I'm booked in a hotel in Ravello tonight. I'm scouting it as a possible conference site."

According to Sabrina's research, the picturesque

mountaintop resort was only a short distance from Positano as the crow flew. Too bad she couldn't sprout wings. The trip would take forever on these tortuous roads.

"You cannot drive to Ravello if you take prescription narcotics," the doc countered firmly. "Or anywhere else, for that matter. Under Italian law you cannot drive at all."

"Great!" She blew out a frustrated breath. "Okay, forget the drugs. Just bandage me up, throw in a set of crutches and I'll gimp on down the coast."

Marco hesitated. He was tempted to comply with her request—extremely tempted. The woman's resemblance to Gianetta had shaken him more than he cared to admit. He would like nothing more than to send Sabrina Russo on her way and slam the door on the memories she'd stirred.

Unfortunately, his personal preferences conflicted with the oath he'd taken as a physician and the knowledge that he was at least partially responsibility for this woman's injury.

"I'm afraid you don't appreciate the seriousness of your sprain," he told his reluctant patient. "It will heal itself in time if you're careful. If you bring the wrong pressure to bear on your ankle, however, you could cause more serious damage that might require surgery to repair. Or leave you with a permanent limp."

She paled a little at that. Satisfied that he had her attention, Marco pressed on.

"I should like you to remain in Positano tonight.

I'll tend to your ankle and, if your condition allows, you may continue your journey tomorrow."

She gave in grudgingly. "I guess I have no choice."

"Very well. Rafaela, a pressure bandage, please."

The nurse had anticipated the request and had a rolled bandage in hand. She was every bit as efficient as her mama, Marco thought, pleased all over again that he'd paid her tuition to nursing school.

When he moved his stool closer and propped Sabrina's foot on his knee, her breath hissed in. Marco used his gentlest touch to wrap the ankle. The skin around the injured joint was distended, the bruising already vicious.

The calf above, however, was long and smooth and shapely. As he cupped the firm flesh, a jolt went through him. This time the shock had nothing to do with seeing what appeared to be the ghost of his dead wife. This time it was lust, hard and fast and hot.

Gesù! What possessed him today? Disgusted with himself, he caught only the tail end of his patient's question to Rafaela.

"...recommend a good hotel?"

"The tourist season is over, Signorina Russo. We have only one hotel still open. The five-star Le Sireneuse. It's quite elegant and very popular with film stars and visiting dignitaries. Their rooms are usually booked a year or more in advance, but I'll call and see if they have anything available, yes?"

"Thanks."

Rafaela slid out the cell phone clipped to her waist and made the quick call.

"It's as I feared, Signorina. The hotel is fully booked. I'll try The Neptune. It's just outside town and may still be open."

Marco brought the bandage under a delicate arch and waged a fierce internal debate. His gut told him to say nothing, to let this woman find her own accommodations. She disturbed him in too many ways. Yet the sense of responsibility bred into him with his name and title would not allow him to ignore the fact he had contributed to her present predicament. Then there was that haunting resemblance to Gianetta...

"There's no need to call another hotel. You must stay at my villa tonight."

"Thanks, but I wouldn't want to impose."

"It is no imposition, I assure you. The villa is small, merely a vacation home, but has several guest suites. I should prefer to keep a watch on you to make sure you don't suffer any residual effects from the accident. And," he added with a smile for the nurse, "Rafaela's mama will cook for us. Rafaela will tell you her mama serves the best grilled swordfish on the Amalfi coast."

"It's true, Signorina. Mama's *pesce spada* will make you weep with joy." The young nurse kissed her fingertips in tribute to her mother's skills. "You will taste nothing like it."

"Well..."

"Good," Marco said. "It is settled. How does the bandage feel? Not too tight?"

His patient tried a tentative wiggle. "It's fine."

After securing the bandage with a Velcro strap, he carefully lowered her foot and rose. "Before I give you something for the pain, please tell me if you have ever experienced an adverse reaction to drugs or have a medical condition I should be aware of."

"No to both."

Marco considered the range of drugs available at the small clinic and wrote an order for an opiate that would provide swift relief with the fewest side effects. While he waited for Rafaela to return with the medication, he flipped up his cell phone and arranged to have Sabrina's rental car delivered to his villa.

"We will leave the keys here at the clinic. Ah, here are your pills. They are very strong," he warned.

After she downed the correct dosage, Marco helped her into the wheelchair again. They made a stop at the woman's washroom, where Sabrina hopped in with Rafaela's assistance and out again a few moments later.

When he wheeled her out of the clinic and scooped her into his arms for the transfer to the Ferrari, he could tell she was already starting to feel the effects of the fast-acting medication. Her body was pliant in his arms, her breasts soft against his ribs. While he held her, she turned her face up to his.

"Thanks for taping me up, Doc. Duke. Marco."

Her smile was wide and natural. Nothing like Gianetta's teasing pout. He hadn't noticed the dimples before, perhaps because Sabrina Russo hadn't relaxed and smiled at him until this point. And her eyes were a warmer, richer brown than he'd first thought.

Holding her this close, her mouth just a whisper from his, Marco noted other differences, as well. Her breasts were fuller, her hips rounder and she had the long, sleek legs of a thoroughbred. She was much a woman, this American. Very much a woman.

Marco was more prepared this time when his groin went tight. Nevertheless, the punch hit hard and forced a reminder that this woman was his patient and would be a guest in his home. Willing his rebellious body to behave, he lowered her into the passenger seat and reached across her for the shoulder harness.

He smells like antiseptic soap, Sabrina thought, feeling more than a little woozy. Soap and suede and some subtle, tangy aftershave she'd only now noticed. She'd been too shaken—or too pissed—to sniff his neck before.

"How far is it to your villa?" she asked when he'd backed the convertible out of the clinic's courtyard.

"Not far. About five kilometers."

"Oh, boy! On these roads, that means we'll get there when? Midnight?"

"I promise, you'll arrive in plenty of time for a nap before dinner."

"I may zonk out before then," she warned as her head lolled against the seat back.

"I hope so." One corner of his mouth tipped up. "That will save much wear and tear on the floorboards!"

Despite the lethargy creeping through her, Sabrina registered the impact of that crooked grin. Holy crap! The man should come with a warning label. When he dropped his brusque me Doctor/you Jane attitude and let himself be human, His Excellency was downright dangerous.

"I'll try to restrain myself," she replied.

And not just her thumping foot, she admonished herself sternly. She couldn't let herself be distracted by sexy Italians right now. Caroline was depending on her for input into the megaproposal they had to submit by the end of next week. Sprain or nor sprain, crutches or no crutches, Sabrina intended to provide the required info.

For now, though, she'd just rest her head against the back of the seat and let the cool December air play with her hair. The loose tendrils fluttered around her face as the Ferrari maneuvered through the narrow streets of Positano.

The village was practically vertical. Pastel-painted shops and homes stair-stepped down the mountainside seemingly right on top of each other. At the bottom of the incline, dominating the piazza, was the cathedral. Beyond the church was the pebbly shore lined with colorful fishing boats.

As Sabrina had noted on the way into town, many of the small hotels and restaurants were shut-

tered. Umbrellas were folded and chairs neatly
stacked on the terraces of open-air restaurants. Yet
a few hardy tourists huffed up the steep, cobbled
street, guidebooks in hand.

A momentary worry threaded through her as she
wondered how the heck she'd handle streets like this
on crutches, but she pushed the thought aside with
a drug-induced optimism. She'd manage. Somehow.

When they left the town, the road once again
became a narrow slice of pavement cut out of sheer
rock. Rather than look down, Sabrina slumped in
her seat and closed her eyes.

The next thing she heard was Marco's deep voice
murmuring in her ear. "We're here. Don't stir. I'll
carry you to your room."

She felt his arm slide under her knees. His other
went around her waist. As if it was the most natural
thing in the world, she wrapped an arm around his
neck.

He lifted her easily. She could get used to this
mode of transportation, she thought as she snuggled
against his chest and buried her nose in the warm
skin of his jaw.

"You need a shave," she complained sleepily.

"So I do. My apologies, Signorina. I'm on vacation, you see, and had not thought I would get this
close to such a beautiful woman."

She nuzzled closer. "'S okay. You look good with
bristles. You look good, period."

"Grazie."

She formed a hazy impression of a vine-covered arch, whitewashed walls, the sound of the sea slapping against rocks. Then a door opened and a gray-haired woman bustled out. Rafaela's mom, Sabrina thought as the woman greeted Marco in a torrent of Italian.

She heard him respond with her name, say something about ice. Mere moments later he lowered her onto sheets that smelled of sunshine and starch. His hands were gentle as he removed her one remaining boot. She was asleep almost before he propped a cushion under her injured ankle to elevate it.

Three

Food. She needed food.

The thought dragged Sabrina from a deep sleep. Or maybe it was the scents teasing her nostrils. Eyes closed, mind still only half engaged, she sniffed the air. The tantalizing aromas of garlic and onions sizzling in olive oil competed with something sweet and yeasty and fresh baked.

A loud rumble emanated from the vicinity of her stomach, reminding Sabrina she hadn't eaten since the roll and a cup of coffee she grabbed at the airport before claiming her rental car and driving south toward the Amalfi coast. She'd planned to stop at a restaurant along the way and lunch on the region's incredible seafood.

Instead, she remembered with a sudden jolt, she'd almost become food for the fishes!

The memory of how close she'd come to tumbling off a cliff and plunging into the sea brought her lids up. She blinked, confused for a moment by the unfamiliar surroundings, then the haze cleared.

She was in a bedroom. In Marco Calvetti's villa. Stretched out on a king-size bed. With her left leg stuck up at a thirty-degree angle and pillows propped under her knee and ankle. A cold compress was draped over the swollen joint.

She wiggled a bit to get comfortable and surveyed the room with more interest. It was a perfect blend of Mediterranean and modern, with Moorish arches and stucco walls painted a warm terra-cotta. An exquisitely carved antique chest stood against one wall. A flat-screen plasma TV hung on another.

But it was the view through the arches that held Sabrina spellbound. It gave onto a long, narrow terrace. Potted geraniums, hibiscus and trailing vines added splashes of color to an otherwise unbroken vista of sea and sky.

"Holy cow!"

Was that faint blur in the distance Capri? Sicily? Sabrina wasn't sure what part of the coast she was on or which direction the windows faced. She itched to get out onto the terrace for a better look and was gingerly lowering her foot when a soft knock sounded on the door behind her.

"*Si*," she called. "*Entri*."

"Good," Marco said when he opened the door. "You are awake."

"Barely."

She struggled to sit up as he came into the room. The first thing she noticed was that he was carrying a set of aluminum crutches. The second, that his sexy whiskers were gone.

Clean-shaven, his hair damp and slicked back, his broad shoulders molded by a cream-colored, V-neck sweater, he still looked good enough to eat.

Which reminded her...

"Please tell me that's Rafaela's mama's cooking I smell."

"It is indeed. I came to ask if you would like a tray here. Or are you feeling up to dinner on the main terrace? It is heated, so we'd be quite comfortable."

"You have another terrace with a view like this?"

"Several, actually. The villa is like the others along this stretch of coast. More vertical than horizontal, I'm afraid. But you don't need to worry about navigating stairs," he assured her. "I had an elevator installed when the place was built. The lift is very useful for Signora Bertaldi—Rafaela's mama. And for my own when she comes over from Naples for a visit."

"Then dinner on the terrace it is."

Now that she'd recovered from the shock of the accident and wooziness caused by the pills, Sabrina found herself intensely curious about the sexy doc.

"Does your mother visit often?" she asked as she pushed off the bed and onto her one good foot.

"Not often." He kept a firm grip on her arm while she experimented with the lightweight crutches. "Nor do I, for that matter. This is only my second time this year."

That surprised her. This bedroom didn't have an unused feel to it. The oversize marble tiles showed not a single dust bunny and light flooded through sparkling windowpanes. Rafaela's mama must have a squad of maids at her disposal to keep everything so fresh smelling and spotless.

"So where do you spend the rest of the year?"

"In Rome. That's where I have my practice."

Interesting. She knew now he had a mother in Naples and a practice in Rome. There were still some significant gaps in her database, however. Like whether there was a Mrs. Doc/Duke somewhere in the picture. Never shy, Sabrina figured there was only one way to find out.

"What about your wife? She must love coming down to this beautiful villa."

"My wife died three years ago."

"Oh, I'm sorry."

"So am I. Come, let's test your skill with these crutches."

His tone didn't invite further questions or expressions of sympathy. Sabrina swallowed her curiosity and clumped a few tentative steps.

"Be careful not to put too much pressure on your

armpits. You don't want to compress the nerves there. Use the foam handgrips to support yourself as much as possible."

He stayed close by her side her while she made a circuit of the spacious suite.

"Your rental car has been delivered," he said when he was satisfied she could maneuver. "Your cases are just outside, in the hall. Would you like me to bring them in so you can freshen up before we eat?"

"Yes, please."

She felt like she'd rolled in dirt, then gone to sleep in her clothes. Oh, wait! That's exactly what she had done.

"Can you manage alone, or shall I have Signora Bernaldi come help you?"

"I can manage."

"Very well."

He set her roller bag and briefcase on an upholstered bench at the foot of the bed and carried her smaller tote into the adjoining bathroom.

"There's a phone on the vanity and one by the toilet. Press one-six if you require assistance."

"One-six. Got it."

"I'll wait for you in the hall."

Sabrina fished in her suitcase for a black, ankle-length crinkle skirt and a velvet jacket trimmed with lace, then hobbled into the bath. The oval whirlpool tub drew a look of intense longing but she suspected she couldn't climb in without having to call for help climbing out.

Not that she'd mind getting naked with the doc. Especially now that she knew he was single.

Not single, she amended. *A widower.*

The thought of what he must have suffered sobered her.

She'd never lost a spouse, but had come close to losing her father when he was diagnosed with cancer several years ago. Foolishly, Sabrina had thought his illness might finally breach the walls between them. Instead it had left Dominic Russo more determined than ever to mold his only child into the woman he thought she should be.

She'd resisted his determined efforts for most of her life. With her mother watching helplessly from the sidelines, she and her father had engaged in a running battle of wills. Sabrina's warfare had taken the form of outrageous pranks and, later, wild parties.

His illness had sobered her, though. Shaken by his near brush with death, Sabrina had abandoned her own career as a top buyer for Saks Fifth Avenue and agreed to serve as the executive director of the Russo Foundation.

Big mistake. Huge. Her father couldn't give up an ounce of control. He'd questioned her decisions, countered her orders and generally made her life a living hell. She'd stuck it out, trying to make it work, until she finally admitted she could never fit the mold he'd designed for her.

Shaking her head at the memory of their titanic clashes, she thumped over to the vanity and sank down on a tufted stool. After stripping off her slacks and sweater, she went to work with a washcloth and lemon-scented soap before dragging a brush through her hair and reapplying her makeup.

The black crinkle skirt went over her head easily and dropped down to hide most of her bandaged ankle. The velvet jacket buttoned up the front, with a froth of ivory-colored lace swirling around the scooped neckline.

Feeling like a new woman, Sabrina dug in her suitcase for a pair of black, beaded ballet flats. She could only get one on, but its nonslip rubber sole provided an extra measure of security on the tiles as she crutched her way to the door.

Marco was waiting in the hall, as promised. Like the guest suite, the long, sunlit corridor sported graceful Moorish arches and a spectacular view of the sea. A magnificent Ming vase with a spray of fresh gladioli added to the fragrance of furniture polish and sunshine.

"The elevator's just here," he said, gesturing to a small alcove. "It will take us up to the dining room."

Up being the operative word, Sabrina saw when the door swished shut. The control panel indicated the villa was built on four levels. According to the neatly labeled buttons, the garage and main salon occupied the top floor. Below that were the library, the dining room and kitchen. Then came the bedroom level and, finally, the spa and stairs to what she presumed was a private beach.

"You weren't kidding about vertical," she commented as the elevator glided upward with silent efficiency.

"It is the price one pays for building where the mountains drop straight into the sea. Ah, here we are."

The elevator opened onto the library. It was a dream of a room, one Sabrina could happily have spent days or weeks in. Shelves filled with books and art objects lined three walls. The fourth wall was solid glass and gave onto another terrace with dizzying views of the ocean. Her crutches sank into a Turkish carpet at least an inch thick as she maneuvered around a leather sofa with a matching, man-size armchair and ottoman. What caught her attention, though, was the sleek laptop sitting atop a trestle table that looked like it might have once graced a medieval palace.

"Do you have wireless here?" she asked hopefully.

"I do."

"Mind if I use my laptop to log on?"

"Not at all. Here, I'll write the password for you."

He stopped at the table and jotted down a sequence of numbers and letters. Sabrina tucked the folded paper into the pocket of her jacket.

"Thanks. I think I mentioned I'm in Italy on business. I have several appointments I need to confirm. I also need to contact my partners. We're working a project with a very tight deadline."

"I understand. But first we eat, yes?"

"Yes!"

The mouthwatering scent of garlic and onions grew more pronounced as they entered the dining room. Like the library, this room, too, looked out on the sea. The table was a beautiful burnished oak and long enough to seat twelve comfortably. A smaller table had been set with china and crystal out on the terrace. It was tucked in a corner that protected it from the sea breezes and warmed by a tall, umbrella-like patio heater.

Lemon trees in ceramic pots provided splashes of color. Despite the lateness of the season, flowering bougainvillea climbed the walls. Enchanted, Sabrina passed the crutches to Marcos and eased into the chair he pulled out for her.

"I'll tell Signora Bertaldi we're ready," he said. "I would offer you an aperitif, but you should not combine alcohol with the drug I prescribed for you."

"No problem. The view alone is enough to get me high."

While Marco went inside, she breathed in a lungful of salty air and leaned forward to peer over the terrace wall.

Yikes! Good thing she wasn't acrophobic. She was sitting suspended in seemingly thin air, with only the wave-splashed rocks a hundred or so feet below.

Her host returned a few moments later with Rafaela's mama. "This is Signora Bertaldi. She runs this house—and me—with a most skilled hand."

The older woman blushed at the compliment. "His Excellency, he exaggerates."

Her eyes were dark and keen and set in a web of fine wrinkles. They stayed locked with disconcerting intensity on Sabrina's face.

"Please to excuse my English, Signorina Russo. It is not so good."

"It's better than my Italian. I met your daughter this afternoon, by the way. She says your *pesce spada* will make me weep with joy."

The strange intensity gave way to a wide smile. "Then it is good I cook the fish for you tonight, *si?*"

"*Si.*"

"Please to sit, Excellency. I will bring the olives and antipasto."

Marco complied and stretched his long legs out. "So, Sabrina. Tell me more about this business that brings you to Italy."

She couldn't have scripted a more perfect finish to a day that had edged so close to disaster.

The sunset was glorious. The grilled swordfish was everything Rafaela had promised. The cappuccino came topped with sweet, creamy foam. The company...

Okay, she could admit it. She was seriously in lust with His Excellency, Don Marco Antonio d'Whatever. She'd always been a sucker for a man with smooth, polished manners and linebacker's shoulders. Not to mention tastes that ranged from opera to water polo to the succulent jerk-chicken skewers cooked up by New York City sidewalk vendors. And let's not forget eyes that crinkled at the corners when he smiled.

Still, she didn't deliberately plan her grimace as she got to her feet after their leisurely meal. Or her clumsy stumble when she tried to get the crutches under her. But she certainly didn't object when Marco muttered an oath and swept her into his arms.

"You're in pain, aren't you?"

"A little."

"I shouldn't have kept you up so long. You need to rest and elevate your ankle."

To hell with her ankle. A far more urgent need gripped Sabrina. With his mouth only inches from hers, she ached to brush her lips over his. She could almost taste their silky heat.

She didn't realize how transparent her thoughts were until they were in the elevator and he bent to press the button to take them to the lower level. When he straightened, he wore his doctor's face. Cool, assessing, concerned...until his gaze snagged hers.

Gesù!

Marco smothered the oath, but he couldn't hold back the hunger that punched through him, hot and swift and fierce. He wanted this woman. Wanted to taste her, touch her, hear her moan with pleasure as his mouth and hands roamed her lush, seductive curves.

The hours they'd spent together since their near calamitous meeting had erased his initial, absurd notion she might be Gianetta's twin. Or even, God help him, her ghost.

Sabrina Russo was nothing like his temperamental, tempestuous wife. Her laugh was spontaneous and natural, without a hint of frenzy lurking just under the surface. Her lively mind challenged his. And her mouth... Sweet Jesus, her mouth!

The elevator glided to a stop and the door slid open, but Marco made no move to exit. He knew he shouldn't yield to the urge to kiss this woman. She was his patient, a guest in his home. An American entrepreneur, impatient to be on her way and complete the tasks that had brought her to Italy. They were casual acquaintances at best. Strangers who would say goodbye in the morning.

The stern lecture proved completely ineffectual against the heat that raced through his veins. Only by an exercise of iron will could he hold off until he was sure she understood his intent. He saw it in the quick flare of her eyes. Heard it in the sudden rasp of her breath. With a low growl, Marco bent his head and took her mouth with his.

She tasted of dark coffee and sweet, rich cream. He angled his mouth, wanting more of her. Her arms locked around his neck. Her head tipped. She opened her lips, welcoming him, answering hunger with hunger.

He shifted her in his arms, his blood firing when her full breasts flattened against his chest. His body was so taut and straining with need he almost missed it when she gave a small jerk. He whipped up his head and caught her trying to cover a wince.

"Christ! I hurt you."

"No!" Her cheeks were flushed, her breathing ragged. "I banged my foot. The elevator…it's so small."

Shame and disgust hammered at him with vicious blows. Calling himself all kinds of a pig, Marco angled her injured foot away from the elevator wall.

"To kiss you like that was inexcusable of me," he ground out as he carried her into the corridor. His footsteps echoing on the tiles, he strode toward the guest suite. "I'm sorry, Sabrina."

The flush faded as her mouth tipped into a smile. "I'm not."

Still thoroughly disgusted with his lack of control, Marco shook his head. "I don't usually assault injured women."

"You don't, huh?" Amusement danced in her eyes. "How about those who aren't injured?"

"You tease, but that was no way for me—for anyone!—to treat a guest."

"Hey, you can't take all the credit, Doc. I was giving as good as I got back there in the elevator." She cocked a brow. "Or was I?"

He couldn't help but grin. "You were, Ms. Russo. You most definitely were."

That was still no excuse for his behavior. It took a fierce effort of will, but Marco managed to block the all-too-vivid feel of her mouth hot and eager under his and shouldered open the door to the guest suite. Signora Bertaldi had come down to straighten the room while he and Sabrina lingered over cappuccino. The bed was turned back, the sheets smoothed, the pillows plumped and ready.

Firmly suppressing the erotic and highly inappropriate thoughts that jumped into his head, Marco tugged down the top sheet and lowered his burden.

"We left the crutches upstairs. I'll ask Signora Bertaldi to bring them to you. She waited to help you prepare for bed before she left for the evening."

"Sure you don't want to tuck me in yourself?"

Laughter lurked behind her all-too-innocent expression. She was teasing him again. He knew it, but the knowledge didn't keep the gates from springing open and the mental images he'd just suppressed from pouring through. He could see her stretched out on those smooth sheets, one arm curled above her head, her lips parted in invitation...

Dammit!

"No," he admitted with brutal honesty. "I am not at all sure. But I'll send Rafaela's mama to you."

Marco was sweating when he left the guest suite. Shunning the elevator, he took the stairs to the upper floor. What the devil was wrong with him? Why did this woman stir such intense, erotic fantasies?

He hadn't remained completely celibate after his wife's death. He was a man. He had normal appetites, the usual physical needs. There were women in Rome, sophisticated women who played the game of flirtation and seduction with practiced charm. Yet none of them had roused him like this long-limbed American beauty.

Now he had to decide what the devil he would do about it.

Four

Four

"Oh, yuck! Your ankle looks like an overcooked bratwurst."

Grinning at her friend's apt description, Sabrina swung the laptop propped on her stomach around. Its built-in camera made a dizzying sweep of the guest bedroom before her face was once again displayed on the screen alongside those of her two partners. How the heck had the world survived before videoconferencing?

"It is pretty gross," she agreed with a glance at her garish, yellow-and-purple lower limb. She'd unbandaged the ankle to let it breathe for a while. Before wrapping it up again and crawling under the covers for the night, she'd decided to try and contact her partners.

She'd caught Devon in Germany, where she was working frantically to set up the premerger meeting of executives from Logan Aerospace and Hauptmann Metal Works. Caroline, like Sabrina, was scouting sites for the job that had unexpectedly dropped into their laps last week.

"You need to stay off that ankle," Caro insisted, her heart-shaped face showing genuine concern. "Hole up at your hotel for the next few days and do not, I repeat, *DO NOT* even think about checking out those conference sites. I'll finish here and zip over to Italy. I can be there Thursday. Friday at the latest."

Devon countered with an alternate plan. "Don't cut your schedule short, Caro. I'll put things on hold here and fly down tomorrow. I can play nurse to 'Rina and scope out sites at the same time."

"Guys. Really. No need for either of you to charge to the rescue. I'll manage just fine."

"Sure you will," Devon scoffed. Her warm brown eyes held a combination of affection and concern. "I've been to the Amalfi coast. I know it's straight up and down. I also remember you mentioning that the hotel in Ravello had a lot of stairs and terraces."

"Actually, I'm not staying at the hotel. The doc who almost hit me offered to put me up at his villa tonight. He wants to check my ankle tomorrow to make sure I'm good to go before I take to the road again."

"That's the least the jerk can do," Dev huffed.

"Hey, did I mention that the jerk is a duke as well as a doc?"

Judging by their expressions, her partners weren't impressed.

"He's also seriously hot," Sabrina added nonchalantly.

The too-casual comment didn't fool either of her friends. They'd known her too long. They knew, as well, the good-time-girl reputation she'd worked so hard to maintain during her rebellious teen and college years.

Sabrina still enjoyed a good time. She wasn't particularly vain, but she recognized that her long legs and seductive curves attracted as many men as her family name and her father's wealth once had. As a consequence, she maintained a wide circle of male friends. Several had pushed to become more than friends. After so many years of resisting her father's attempts to dominate her, though, Sabrina was in no hurry to give up the freedom she'd struggled so hard to achieve.

That didn't mean she couldn't appreciate a real hottie when one almost ran her over. Especially one who could kiss like Marco Calvetti. She could still feel the delicious aftershocks of their session in the elevator.

"Uh-oh." Devon squinted into the camera at her end of the connection. "You've got that look on your face."

"What look?"

"The one that says your doc is fair game."

"Well, he is. His wife died a few years ago. I may be reading between the lines, but I think he's buried himself in his work since then. You wouldn't believe how gorgeous his villa is, yet this is only the second time this year he's driven down from Rome."

She chewed on her lower lip for a moment, mulling over her impressions of her host.

"He's really charming, guys, but also rather intense. It wouldn't hurt him to loosen up a little."

Devon and Caroline exchanged knowing, computer-generated glances.

"If anyone can loosen the man up," Dev drawled, "you can. Just remember you're now one of the walking wounded. Go easy on that ankle."

"And don't worry about scouting conference sites," Caro added. "Worst-case scenario, we can give Global Security fewer options."

"Absolutely not." Her professional pride stung; Sabrina was adamant. "This contract is too important. We're not scaling back our proposal. I'll be good to go tomorrow," she said firmly.

Which wouldn't give her time to loosen up the doc, she thought with real regret. Too bad. She could think of any number of inventive ways to follow up on that kiss.

Desire rippled through her as she said goodnight to her friends, shut down her laptop, and rewrapped her ankle. The damned thing still throbbed, but the ache was bearable so she decided against the pills sitting on the bedside table. Instead, she let the restless murmur of the sea surging against the rocks lull her to sleep.

She was up and dressed by eight the next morning. The faint scent of yeasty, fresh-baked rolls told her Signora Bertaldi was already at work in the kitchen.

Thankfully, Sabrina had stuffed a pair of merino wool palazzo pants in her suitcase at the last minute. The wide legs made getting them on over her still-swollen ankle a breeze. She teamed the oyster-colored slacks with a lightweight red sweater and a Versace scarf in a riot of colors. The rubber-soled beaded ballet slippers provided nonskid traction as she made her way along the tiled hall to the elevator.

She fully intended to hold the doc to his promise to check the sprain before she left. First, though, she intended to hold Signora Bertaldi to *her* promise of a goat cheese frittata for breakfast. If the frittata came anywhere close to the woman's grilled sword-fish, heaven awaited on the floor above.

So did Marco, she discovered when she thumped into the library. He put aside the newspaper he'd been reading and sprang to his feet.

"You should have rung for help."

"I didn't need it," she replied when she recovered from the sight of the doc in well-washed jeans that hugged his muscular thighs and a silky black pullover that showed off some *very* impressive pecs.

Raising a crutch, she waved the tip in an airy circle. "I'm getting the hang of these things. What I *do* need, though, is coffee. Hot. Thick. Sweet."

"Of course." His assessing glance dropped to her foot. "But first, how is your ankle this morning?"

"Still fat and ugly, but it doesn't ache as much."

"Good. I'll look at it after we eat. Shall we have breakfast here in the library or on the terrace?"

"The terrace, please. I want to soak in every last ounce of your incredible view before I hit the road."

"I've been thinking about that." He matched his step to hers as they crossed through the dining room and went out on the spacious terrace. "I have a proposal for you to consider. Before I put it to you, let me fetch your coffee and tell Signora Bertaldi you are up and about."

Amused, Sabrina sank into the chair he held out for her and turned her face to the sun. She could get used to being waited on by a duke. Not that Marco fit her notions of royalty as shaped by her previous contacts.

She'd dated the playboy son of a Saudi sheik once. Just once. It was an eye-opening and not particularly pleasant experience. She'd also attended a couple of parties in London where Prince Harry popped in. He was great fun but way too young for her. Marco, on the other hand, was just the right age, height, size and shape.

Regret flickered through her. Too bad she was working against such a tight deadline. She wouldn't have minded a few more days with the sexy doc.

Maybe she could extend her stay in Italy after she finished checking out conference sites. Or arrange a return visit once they had the Global Security contract firmed up.

She was considering the possibilities when Marco returned with two cups of espresso topped with frothy cream. As he passed her one of the cups, he sprang the proposal he'd mentioned earlier.

"I think you should stay here for the rest of your time on the Amalfi coast. Use this villa as a home base and make day trips to the locations you want to check out."

The suggestion dovetailed so closely with Sabrina's thoughts she almost choked on her first sip of the thick, sweetened coffee. Her startled glance met Marco's calm gaze. If there was more than mere courtesy behind the invitation, he hid it well.

Her first instinct was to jump on the offer. Excitement pulsed through her at the thought of another session or two of close body contact with this intriguing man. Unfortunately, the road map she hastily conjured up in her mind quashed that quiver of excitement. The distances involved weren't all that great but she'd have to navigate them on tortuous roads, then gimp around on crutches.

"Thanks for the offer," she said with genuine regret. "It's very tempting, but I don't think I'm up to driving out and back each day on these roads."

"You don't need to drive them. I'll be your chauffeur."

"You?"

"*Si.*" A smile crept into his dark eyes. "Or don't you trust my driving? I would remind you that your foot did not thump the floorboards once during the drive from the clinic to the villa. Then again, you were out cold for most of that trip."

"You must have better things to do than transport me up and down the coast."

"Actually, I don't. I'm on vacation until January fifth. My surgical team has threatened to resign en masse if I return before that date. I have nothing on my schedule until then except a mandatory appearance at the ball my mother gives each year to celebrate La Fiesta di San Silvestro."

"That's on New Year's Eve, isn't it?"

"It is. So I'm at loose ends, you see. You would save me from utter boredom."

She didn't believe that for a minute. Someone with Marco's varied interests could easily fill up every minute of his vacation. His library alone could surely keep him occupied for weeks.

Sabrina hesitated, torn between the urge to spend more time with this man and the uncertainty of where it might lead. She didn't have time for personal entanglements right now. Caro and Dev were depending on her to provide the necessary input for the new contract proposal.

Which would be a lot easier to accomplish with someone who knew the area at the wheel, her traitorous mind pointed out.

That was a rationalization. She knew it. But what the heck. If the man wanted to spend his precious vacation time helping her nail down prospective conference sites, who was she to argue?

"If you're sure you have nothing more pressing to do," she said slowly, giving him a last out.

"I'm sure. And if you remain over until New Year's Eve," he added, "you must accompany me to the ball. It's really rather spectacular."

Okay, now she was hooked. What woman in her right mind would pass up the chance to attend a fancy-dress ball with someone like Marco Calvetti? The thought flashed into her mind that it was strange he didn't already have a date. The man was rich, cultured and a widower. But why look a gift hunk in the mouth?

"I'd planned to wrap up my business and fly home on the thirtieth," she told Marco. "I'll have to check on whether I can change my tickets. And get in some serious shopping. And…"

Signora Bertaldi's arrival with a loaded tray interrupted Sabrina's hasty revisions to her schedule. Tantalized by the mingled scents of broiled tomatoes, basil and melted goat cheese, she returned the older woman's greeting.

"Signorina Russo will be staying with us for a while longer," Marco informed her, speaking in English for the benefit of his guest. "You have additional help coming in from the village this morning, *si?*"

"Si, Excellenza." Signora Bertaldi placed the tray on the table. "The two who always assist me when you are in residence."

"Bring in more if you need them."

"I will," she promised as she positioned a heaping platter before Sabrina.

Marco himself poured fresh-squeezed orange juice from a carafe on the tray. The offerings also included a basket of fresh-baked rolls, a ramekin of creamy butter and an assortment of jams. Wishing them *buon appetito,* Signora Bertaldi left them to the dazzling sunshine and the sumptuous breakfast.

After breakfast Marco examined Sabrina's ankle. He had her sink into the soft leather of the sofa in the library and carefully unwrapped the Ace bandage. The swelling had gone down considerably but the skin was mottled with ugly purple-yellow bruises.

He rotated her foot gently, frowning when she fought to hide a grimace. "You really should stay off this today. It requires more ice and elevation."

"No can do. I need to get to work. How about I stretch out on the backseat of your Ferrari with an ice pack draped over my ankle?"

The prospect of driving around the Amalfi coast with a bandaged foot sticking out the rear window of his lean, mean machine didn't seem to particularly faze him, but he came up with an alternate suggestion.

"I have a better idea. My mother keeps a small fleet of vehicles at her home in Naples. I'll call and ask to borrow a sedan. It will give you more room and comfort."

"You're brave enough to tackle these hairpin turns in a big, honkin' sedan?"

"I've done it many times, I assure you."

"It will take you forever to get to Naples and back," Sabrina protested, remembering her own meandering journey after she left the interstate just south of the city.

"I'll have the car delivered. It will take an hour, two at most. During that time you will rest here on the sofa, with your foot up."

The command sounded so much like the ones her father used to issue that Sabrina bristled instinctively. Common sense kicked in a second or two later.

"Deal."

He rewrapped her ankle and helped her stretch out on the soft leather. Propping a pillow under her foot, he straightened and gestured toward the speakers attached to a high-tech iPod dock.

"Would you like to listen to some music while I fetch ice and make my calls?"

"What have you got on there?"

"Everything from Andrew Lloyd Weber to Zucchero."

Sabrina opted for show tunes over Italian pop rock. While Sarah Brightman and Steve Barton blended their voices in the haunting love duet from

The Phantom, she let her gaze roam the library. Until now she'd caught only brief glimpses of the room as she and Marco passed through it.

She took her time now, seeking clues to the personality of the man who fascinated her more by the moment. She couldn't make out the titles of the books in the shelves lining three walls and itched for a closer look. She settled for studying the treasures interspersed among the volumes.

That bust of a Roman matron looked as though it might have been carved while Pompeii was still a thriving metropolis. And that small oil painting on an ornate stand was either a Caravaggio or a damned good copy. A caduceus carved from translucent alabaster occupied place of honor amid a collection of objects that looked more like medieval torture implements than medical instruments. On the shelf next to the caduceus was a chess set with tall, elaborately decorated pieces in ivory and red.

Not until her gaze had made a complete circuit of the library did something begin to nag her. She couldn't put a finger on it right away. Frowning, Sabrina made another sweep of the bookcases before glancing at the long table that served as Marco's desk.

A maroon leather paper tray and blotter sat squarely in the center of the slab of polished oak. A gold Mont Blanc pen jutted from its holder beside the blotter. Next to it was his sleek laptop and a cordless phone propped up in its charger.

What was missing, Sabrina realized after another puzzled moment, were photographs. Most desks contained at least one, framed and positioned for optimal viewing. Usually of the owner's spouse or family.

Intensely curious now, she glanced around again. Nope. No snapshots. No formal portraits. Not even one of those cartoonlike caricatures sketched by the street artists who plied every piazza in Rome.

Apparently Marco didn't choose to surround himself with visible reminders of the wife he'd lost three years ago. Was her death still so painful?

Although intensely curious, Sabrina wouldn't poke her nose into his past. God knew enough people had poked into hers over the years.

Maybe he'd open up a little when they knew each other better. The prospect of spending the next few days getting to know the handsome doc had Sabrina humming along with Sarah Brightman.

Five

"You invited one of your patients to recuperate in your villa? An American?"

Marco smiled at the sniff that came through the phone. A Neapolitan born and bred, his mother had a native's disdain of foreigners. That included Sicilians, Sardinians and Corsicans as well as everyone west of the Apennines and north of the Abruzzi.

"Who is this woman?"

"Her name is Sabrina Russo. She's in Italy on business. Since I was partially responsible for her injury, I felt I should offer the hospitality of my home."

That touched on another sore spot. His mother understood why Marco preferred to stay at his own villa during his infrequent trips down from Rome instead of the palazzo in Naples his family had called home for generations. He still had apartments there, an entire floor. He and Gianetta had occupied the apartment most of their marriage, until Marco had accepted his current position as chief of neurosurgery at Rome's prestigious *Bambino Gesù* Children's Hospital.

Palazzo d'Calvetti was still his home, but these days he preferred the simple solitude of this villa he'd had constructed after Gianetta's death. His mother understood, but she didn't like it.

Marco dined with her regularly, which mollified her somewhat. And dutiful son that he was, he made the requisite appearances at her numerous charity and social events, including the big New Year's Eve gala. That reminded him…

"If Ms. Russo is still in Italy on the Feast of St. Silvestro, I'd like to bring her to your ball."

The request produced a startled silence. Marco understood his mother's surprise. He hadn't escorted any woman to the ball since Gianetta. With good reason.

The media had gone into a feeding frenzy after Gianetta's death. Even now the paparazzi hounded him mercilessly, and one disgusting rag insisted on trumpeting him as Italy's most eligible bachelor. He preferred to keep his private life private and was careful to avoid the appearance of anything more than casual friendship with the women he dated. Until now, that had meant *not* escorting any of them to the ball so steeped in his family's history and tradition.

Marco could rationalize the break with his long-standing policy without much difficulty. Sabrina would be in Italy for a short time. Her life and her business interests were on the other side of the Atlantic. At best, the attraction sizzling between them could spark only a brief affair.

But spark it would.

He'd already decided that.

He'd gone to bed last night hungry for this long-limbed American with the sun-kissed blonde hair and laughing eyes. The hunger hadn't abated after a restless night's sleep. Just the sight of her limping into the library this morning had given him an un-expected jolt.

She wanted him, as well. He'd seen it in her flushed cheeks and heard it in the flutter of her breath after their kiss in the elevator last night.

The memory of that urgent fumbling made him shake his head. He would handle her with more finesse next time, with more care for her injured ankle. He was plotting his moves when his mother recovered from her surprise.

"Yes, of course you may bring her. I'll have my secretary add her to the guest list. What is her name again?"

"Russo. Sabrina Russo."

"Russo." His mother sniffed again. "Her ancestors must have come from northern Italy. In the south, she would be Rossi."

"I don't know where her ancestors came from."

In fact, Marco realized, he knew very little about her other than she was in business with her two friends and in Italy to scout locations for a conference.

"Bring her to dinner," the duchess ordered. "Tomorrow. I want to meet her."

He returned a noncommittal reply. "I'll see if she's available and get back to you. *Ciao,* Mama."

"Tomorrow," his loving mama repeated sternly before hanging up.

He had to smile at the autocratic command. Maria di Chivari had married into her title more than forty years ago. Since then it had become as much a part of her nature as her generous heart and fierce loyalty to those she loved.

He reentered the library some moments later with a cold compress. Sabrina was lying on the sofa as ordered, her foot elevated, humming off-key to the mournful solo coming from the iPod. Mr. Mistoffelees, Marco identified absently, from the hit show *Cats.*

"The car is on the way," he said as he draped the compress over her ankle, "but I'm afraid I may have opened a Pandora's box. My mother wants to me to bring you to dinner tomorrow night."

"Is that bad?"

He answered with a rueful smile. "Only if you object to someone probing for every detail of your life, past and present. She has an insatiable curiosity about people."

"People in general? Or the women you invite to stay at your villa?"

Marco hesitated a few seconds before replying. "Other than a professional colleague or two, you're the first woman I've invited to stay."

He could see that surprised her. Shrugging, he offered an explanation.

"This place is my escape. My refuge. I had it constructed after my wife died. Unfortunately, I don't get down here often, and then only for short stays."

Her expression altered, and Marco kicked himself for mentioning Gianetta.

His guest didn't use the reference as a springboard to probe, but the question was there, in her eyes. He could hardly refuse to answer it, given the heat that had flared between him and this woman last night. He moved a little away from the sofa and shoved his hands in the pockets of his jeans.

"Before we moved to Rome, Gianetta and I lived in Naples. We kept a boat at the marina there. A twenty-four-foot sloop. She took it out one afternoon and a storm blew up."

His gaze went to the library's tall windows. The bright sky and sparkling sunshine outside seemed to mock his dark memories.

"Searchers found pieces of the wreckage, but her body was never recovered."

"Oh, no!"

The soft exclamation eased some of tension holding Marco in its iron grip. He'd heard so many platitudes, so many heartfelt expressions of sympathy, that they'd lost their meaning. Sabrina's soft cry was all the more genuine for being so restrained.

Inexplicably, he felt himself responding to it. With the haunting strains of Mr. Mistoffelees's lament in the background, he forced the memories.

"Gianetta loved to sail. Her family had made their living from the sea for generations. I used to joke she had more salt than water in her blood. She was—she was almost insatiable in her need to feel the wind on her face and hear the sails snap above her."

She had craved other thrills, as well. Downhill skiing on some of the Alps's most treacherous slopes. Fast cars. The drugs she'd flatly denied taking even after Marco discovered her stash.

At his insistence she'd gone through rehab. Twice. She swore she was clean, swore she'd kicked her habit. Yet he knew in his heart she'd driven down from Rome that last, fatal weekend to escape his vigilance. To escape him.

"I had a difficult surgery scheduled that week. A two-year-old child with a brain tumor several other neurosurgeons had deemed inoperable."

He'd been exhausted after the long surgery, mentally and physically, and wanted only to fall into bed. Gianetta flatly refused to cancel her planned trip to the coast. She'd been cooped up in the city too long. She needed the wind, the sea, the salt spray.

"I stayed in Rome until the boy was out of danger and in recovery, then drove down to join my wife for the weekend."

To this day Marco blamed himself for what followed. If he'd postponed the surgery... If he'd paid as much attention to his wife as he had his patients...

"I could see the storm clouds piling up when I hit the coast. I called Gianetta on my cell phone and begged her not to take the boat out."

Begged, cajoled, ordered, pleaded...and sweated blood when he arrived to find she'd disregarded his pleas and launched the sloop.

"As soon as I reached the marina, I contacted her by radio. By then she was battling twenty-four-foot swells and the boat was taking on water."

He could still hear her shrill panic, still remember the utter desperation and helplessness that had ripped through him. He could save the life of a two-year-old, but he couldn't save his wife.

"The last time I heard her voice was when she sent out an urgent S.O.S. The radio went dead in midbroadcast."

"How sad," Sabrina whispered. "You never got to say goodbye."

He flashed her a quick look, startled by her insight. For all their ups and downs, all the arguments and hot, angry exchanges, he'd never stopped loving his passionate, temperamental Gianetta. He'd sell his soul to be able to tell her so.

"You remind me of her," he said after a long moment. "You have the same color hair, the same eyes. Yesterday morning, on the road... For a second or two I thought perhaps I was seeing a ghost."

"So that's why you almost ran me over!"

Sabrina struggled upright on the sofa. She wasn't sure she liked being mistaken for a poltergeist, even briefly. And now that she thought about it, she realized Marco wasn't the only one who'd made that mistake.

"Now I know why Rafaela gaped at me at the clinic. Why her mama stared at me when I first arrived. Do I look that much like your Gianetta?"

His gaze roamed her face. "The resemblance is startling at first glance, but I assure you it's merely superficial. As I've discovered in the course of our brief acquaintance, Ms. Russo, you are very much your own woman."

"You got that right."

His slow smile banished the ghosts. "And very, very desirable."

Well! That was better. Mollified, Sabrina sank back against the cushions. She would have liked to draw Marco out a little more about his wife but she sensed his need for a shift in both subject and mood.

A quick glance at her watch indicated they still had some time to kill before the car arrived. She *should* get on her laptop. She needed to reconfirm her appointments for the next few days and update Devon and Caroline on the latest developments in her changing-by-the-minute schedule.

With Marco standing so close, though, Sabrina couldn't force her mind into work mode. Instead she nodded to the small, square table in the corner.

"I see you have a chessboard set up. We still have some time before the car arrives. Do you want to take me on?"

"You play?"

"Occasionally. When I do," she warned, "I usually draw blood."

"Ha!" He crossed to the table, lifting it with ease, and moved it into position beside the sofa. "We shall see."

Seen up close, the pieces drew a gasp of delight from Sabrina. They were medieval warriors from the time of the Crusades, with armor and weaponry depicted in exquisite detail. The Christian bishops carried the shields of fierce Knights Templar. The Muslim king was mounted on an Arabian steed. Even the queens wore armored breastplates below their circlets and veils.

"White or red?" Marco asked.

She chose white and saw that that the box containing the pieces also included a timer.

"The game will go faster if we play speed chess. How about two minutes max per move?"

When Marco nodded, she hit the timer to start the clock and moved a pawn in the slightly unconventional Bird's Opening, named for the nineteenth-century English master, Henry Bird.

Marco glanced up, his eyes narrowed, and countered with From's Gambit. Four moves later, Sabrina put him in check and had to bite her lip to keep from laughing at his stunned expression.

"You weren't joking about drawing blood. Who taught you to play like this?"

"My father. Chess is about the only thing we share a common interest in."

He lifted his gaze from the board. Sabrina deflected the curiosity she saw in his eyes by tapping the button on the timer.

"The clock's ticking. Your move, fella."

Frowning, he moved his rook to protect his king. She smothered a grin and countered with her knight.

"Checkmate."

Marco's brows snapped together. He scowled at the board, searching for another move, but she had him boxed in.

"I demand a rematch."

Sabrina took him three games to two and was about to put him in check again when the notes of a door chime cascaded through the intercom.

"That must be my mother's chauffeur. We'll finish this game when we return."

"Some folks are just gluttons for punishment."

While he went to trade car keys with the driver, Sabrina descended to the guest suite to slip on her jacket and grab her briefcase. The briefcase thumped awkwardly against her crutch as she hit the elevator again.

Marco was waiting when she emerged on the top floor. He'd pulled on his buttery suede bomber jacket and hooked a pair of mirrored aviator sunglasses in the neck of his black sweater.

Oh, man! Oh, man, oh, man, oh, man!

Suddenly, avidly eager to complete her business and get back to the villa, Sabrina let him take the briefcase and went through the door he held open for her.

She stopped just over the threshold. Her eyes widened when she took in the gleaming Rolls parked under the portico. "This is your mother's sedan?"

"One of them," Marco answered calmly as he opened the passenger door of the chrome-plated behemoth. "She likes to travel in comfort."

Sabrina was no stranger to limos or Rolls Royces. Her father never drove anywhere when he could be driven. This baby, however, was a classic. With its massive grill, elongated body and top folded down into an oversize trunk, it had been crafted before the automobile industry cared about such minutia as weight and fuel efficiency.

The prospect of taking the narrow, hairpin turns in this monster made Sabrina gulp. Resolutely, she quashed her nervousness and handed Marco the crutches.

"Do you have enough room?" he asked when she sank into cloud-soft leather.

"More than enough." She waved an imperious hand. "Drive on, McDuff."

Tourists of all nationalities had made the arduous ascent to the mountaintop town of Ravello for centuries. First by donkey cart, then by motorized vehicles, they climbed roads so steep and narrow that traffic had to back up in both directions to let a tour bus pass.

The views alone were worth the nerve-bending trip and the reason Ravello had drawn so many artists over the years. Their ranks had included D. H. Lawrence, who wrote *Lady Chatterley's Lover* while ensconced in a villa overlooking the sea, and composer Richard Wagner. Wagner's works had become the centerpiece of the town's annual music festival. The festival now drew thousands, according to the research Sabrina had done on the site.

Throughout the climb she caught awe-inspiring glimpses of sky and sea and rugged, rocky coast. The higher they went, the more stunning the vistas. Finally, Marco nosed the Rolls around the last steep curve and she caught her first view of the town itself. The twin towers of its cathedral dominated the jumble of whitewashed buildings perched high atop the cliff. Red-tile roofs and a profusion of flowering vines and trees added bright spots of color.

A sign indicated the town was closed to all vehicles except those belonging to residents and hotel guests. Another sign directed visitors to a parking lot at the base of the town walls. Marco bypassed the visitor lot and made for the main square. The Rolls bumped across the cobbled plaza crowded with tiny cafés, gelato stands and shops displaying beautifully crafted pottery.

The hotel Sabrina wanted to visit sat smack in the historic center of the town, almost in the shadow of the cathedral. When Marco pulled up at a facade adorned with weathered arches and belfry towers roofed in red tiles, a valet rushed forward to open Sabrina's door.

"Good morning. Are you checking in?"

"No, we're not staying," she replied in her shaky Italian. "I'm Sabrina Russo. I have an appointment with your hotel manager."

The well-trained valet switched to English as she swung out of the car. "Ah, yes. Mr. Donati, he says to expect you."

He supported her while she balanced on one foot, waiting for Marco to retrieve her briefcase and the crutches from the backseat.

"Do you wish a wheelchair, madam? I have one, just here."

"Thank you, but these are fine."

When she had the crutches under her arms, he tugged open the hotel's ornately carved door. "Please to go in and be comfortable. I'll call Mr. Donati to tell him you have arrived."

With Marco carrying her briefcase, Sabrina entered a lobby filled with light and terrazzo tiles and arches that opened on three sides to a courtyard with a magnificent view of the sea. In the center of the yard was a splashing fountain surrounded by lush greenery and tall palms nourished by the warm Mediterranean breezes.

They'd crossed only half of the lobby when a thin individual in a business suit and red-silk tie hurried out to greet her. He stopped short when he saw the man at Sabrina's side.

"Your Excellency! I didn't know... I wasn't aware..."

Flustered, he smoothed a hand down his tie and bowed at the waist.

"Please allow me to reintroduce myself. I am Roberto Donati, manager of this hotel. We met several years ago, when you and your most gracious mother opened Ravello's summer music festival."

"So we did. And this is Ms. Russo. She's come to survey your excellent establishment."

Donati took the hand Sabrina extended, obviously wondering how an American businesswoman had hooked up with the local gentry.

"Would you care for an espresso or cappuccino before we begin?"

"Perhaps later," she replied. "May I leave my coat and briefcase in your office while we tour the conference facilities?"

"But of course. Allow me to take them for you. And yours, Your Excellency."

Before handing over the briefcase, Sabrina extracted a pen and notepad. She skimmed her notes on Global Security's conference requirements and was ready when Donati returned with a folder.

"This contains our catering menus and the floor plans of our guest rooms and meeting facilities."

Marco took the folder. "You have your hands full, Sabrina. I'll carry this for you."

"Thanks."

With the men adjusting their pace to hers, she let Donati escort them across the open courtyard.

"Luckily, February is our off-season," the manager commented. "I indicated in my initial e-mail that we have fifty-three rooms available the week you specified. We've had several cancellations, so the number is now fifty-six. I have assurances from the hotel across the square that they can accommodate the remainder of your conference attendees."

"I'll want to see those rooms, too, before I leave."

"Of course. Once we finalize the meal plans, I'll provide a revised estimate incorporating those room rates."

"Hold on, I need to make a note of the numbers."

When she fumbled with the pen and pad, Marco stepped forward. "Let me do that for you."

She had to grin. "Doc, duke, chauffeur and secretary. You're a man of many talents."

His dark eyes smiled into hers. "Ah, but wait until I present my bill."

Damn! The man could melt her into a puddle of want without half trying.

Heat spreading through her veins, Sabrina handed him the pad and glanced up to catch the manager watching them. His goggle-eyed stare gave way to a combination of speculation and calculation.

Uh-oh! Maybe arriving at the hotel in a vintage Rolls with His Excellency in tow wasn't such a smart move. Good thing she had Donati's original estimate in writing. He'd better not try to pad the final figure. Sabrina would hold his feet to the fire.

She and Marco departed the hotel after lunch on a gorgeously landscaped terrace overlooking the sea. During the drive back down to the coast, she mulled over the revised estimate Donati had provided.

"How does it look?" Marco asked.

"The numbers seem high at first glance. I'll have to compare them to the final estimates from the other hotels."

"I'll call Donati and see if he can do better."

"No!"

Her sharp negative drew a surprised glance.

"Thanks," Sabrina said, tempering her tone, "but I prefer to handle these negotiations myself."

"My apologies. I merely wished to help."

She winced at the ice-coated reply. When he wanted to, the doc could wield one hell of a scalpel.

"Now it's my turn to apologize. It's just…"

She paused, chewing on her lower lip. The stubborn need to assert her independence had driven her for so long. She couldn't shake it, even now.

"My father doesn't believe I can make it on my own," she said finally. "I'm determined to prove him wrong."

"I see." Marco thought about that for a moment. "This is the father who taught you to play chess?"

"One and the same."

"He underestimates your killer instinct. I have your measure now, however. You won't win this evening as easily as you did this morning."

She couldn't resist the challenge. "Maybe we should up the stakes."

"Maybe we should. What do you suggest?"

Laughing, she waggled her brows. "Ever play strip chess?"

She was kidding. Mostly. And completely unprepared when Marco dug into his jacket pocket.

One handed, he flipped up his cell phone and punched a speed-dial button. His conversation was in Italian, but Sabrina caught enough to experience a sudden shortness of breath.

"The meeting took longer than anticipated," he informed his housekeeper. "There's no need for you to wait for our return."

He listened a moment and nodded.

"That will be fine. Thank you. I'll see you tomorrow. *Ciao.*"

The phone went back into his jacket pocket. The slow, predatory smile he gave Sabrina told her the night ahead could prove extremely interesting!

Six

Marco lost one of his loafers in the first game. He forfeited its mate in the second.

"I've never seen such unorthodox moves," he protested. "You sacrificed a queen *and* a knight to gain a pawn."

"Thus opening the back door for my bishop. Stop whining and pay up."

He gave a huff of laughter and kicked off the loafer. As they reset the chess pieces for the next game, Sabrina calculated how many additional wins she'd have to score before she had him naked.

Socks, two.

Jeans, one pair.

One each belt, silky black pullover and, presumably, briefs.

Good thing they'd cut the two-minutes-per-move time limit down to one. Anticipation was putting her into a fast burn.

Anticipation, and the fact that they were alone in the villa. Stretched out on the plush Turkish rug in the library. With one of Vivaldi's violin concerti coming through the speakers and glasses of wine within easy reach. Since she hadn't had to resort to the painkillers after that first, powerful dose yesterday afternoon, she was enjoying the full-bodied red made from grapes grown in the Irpinia hills outside Naples.

They'd dispensed with the table and placed the chessboard on the carpet. Sabrina sat with her back against the sofa and her foot propped on a folded cushion. Marco sat cross-legged opposite her. He'd raked his fingers through his hair after one of her more outrageous moves. No longer neat and combed straight back, it showed more curl in the dark, disordered waves.

She itched to reach across the board and comb her hand through those waves. Or feather a finger along the dark sweep of his eyebrow. Or…

"Your move."

With a start, she saw he'd opened with queen's knight to a6. She advanced her king's pawn and the hunt was on.

* * *

She lost that game and paid with one of her beaded ballet slippers. They played to a draw on the next. Then Marco claimed her other shoe and she retaliated in the next game by crushing him with five moves.

"Ha! Take that!"

She expected him to peel off a sock or yield his belt. Instead, he dragged his black pullover over his head.

Sabrina's throat went bone dry. She'd snuggled against that broad chest each time Marco had carried her. Snuggling was good. She'd enjoyed snuggling. Seeing his upper half naked and in the flesh was better.

Her heart hammering, she let her gaze roam over the wide shoulders, the muscled pecs, the scattering of dark hair that swirled around his nipples and arrowed down toward his flat belly.

She didn't realize he'd deliberately sabotaged her concentration until she lost the next two games in a row. In the first, she forfeited her Versace scarf. She debated for several moments after the second.

What to surrender? Her slacks? Her red sweater? Or… Hmm. Her gaze dropped to the Ace bandage wrapped around her ankle.

"Don't even think it."

The amused warning brought her head up with a snap. Marco was watching her with the satisfied smile of a hunter who's cornered his prey. Her skin prickled everywhere his gaze touched.

"The bandage would be cheating."

"All's fair in love and strip chess, fella."

"In that case…"

With a quick sweep of his arm, he shoved the board out of the way. Sabrina started to protest the careless treatment of such beautiful pieces. The protest got stuck in her throat when Marco caught her elbow and slowly, inexorably, drew her down until she lay beside him on the silky carpet.

"Now, my beautiful Sabrina, I will claim my prize."

He slid a hand under the hem of her sweater. Her belly hollowed at the feel of his warm palm against her skin. Then his hand moved upward, tugging the sweater with it.

Cool air kissed her exposed flesh. So did Marco. She quivered as his mouth grazed her midriff, over the lace of her demibra, the mounds of her breasts. He tugged the sweater higher, and Sabrina raised her arms. The red knit came off, was flung aside. The hunger in his eyes stirred her to near fever pitch.

"I imagined you like this," he said, his voice rough. "Stretched out beneath me. Your arms above your head. Your mouth mine to take."

Suiting his actions to his words, he covered her mouth with his.

A flash fire ignited in Sabrina's blood. Her tongue met his. Her hands planed over his shoulders, his back, down the track of his spine. His skin felt smooth and hot over taut muscle and corded tendons.

They were both breathing fast when he fumbled for the front fastening on her bra. Sabrina retained just enough rational thought to gasp out a protest.

"You… You haven't won that yet."

"All's fair," he retorted with a wolfish grin.

The fastening gave and her bra went the way of her sweater. Marco's grin morphed into a look of such raw hunger that Sabrina's nipples tightened even before he bent to take one in his mouth. His teeth rasped the sensitive bud. His tongue soothed it. His teeth tormented her again.

Pleasure streaked from Sabrina's breast to her belly. Her back arched. She was hot and wet and ready long before he reached for the side zipper on her slacks.

He had her naked in less than a minute. When he rose to peel off his own clothing, her already erratic pulse went berserk. She almost licked her lips at the sight of his lean flanks and flat stomach. His sex, she saw with a jolt of fierce, primal elation, was hard and erect.

She reached for him, eager to wrap her hand around the steely shaft, but he turned away to drag the cushions off the sofa.

"We must take care, eh?" His accent thickening, he positioned her atop the cushions. "Your ankle…"

Sabrina was more concerned about other body parts at the moment. Like the aching tips of her breasts. And the spasms deep in her belly. And the wet heat between her thighs.

"Please tell me you have a condom somewhere close at hand," she begged.

The hunger in his dark eyes gave way to a flash of genuine amusement. "I'm Italian. What do you think?"

"I think," she panted, "we'd better stop talking and get the damned thing on."

He dragged his jeans over and extracted a packet from his wallet. *"Ecco."*

Sabrina snatched it out of his hands. "Let me."

He was all hard ridges and hot steel. So hard, she would have taken him in her mouth if she hadn't been desperate to take him into her body. So hot, she barely got the condom on before he jerked out of her hand and eased her back down onto the cushions.

Their first time was slow and careful.

Sabrina almost went mad at Marco's deliberate pace. In, out, in. Each insertion stretched her eager flesh. Every withdrawal left her panting for more.

She could feel her climax building. Feel the sensations spiraling outward from her core. Wanting to take him with her, she hooked her good leg around his thigh and clenched her vaginal muscles.

Every cord and tendon in his body went rigid. He gave a low grunt, but refused to thrust harder or faster. Instead, he wedged his hand between their straining bodies and pressed his thumb against her pulsing flesh.

Sabrina exploded in a flash of pleasure so intense the whole room seemed to rock. Marco whipped his hand away and surged into her. His body locked with hers, he rode her climax to his own.

Gradually, the room stopped spinning. Air rushed back into Sabrina's lungs. She looked up into the face a few inches from her own and gave a breathless laugh.

"Wow."

His mouth curved into a smug grin. "I think so, too."

They made love the second time in the shower.

Marco was afraid she might slip on the slick tiles and insisted on accompanying her into the spacious, walk-in enclosure.

He also insisted on soaping her down, front and back. She returned the favor. Mere moments later he had his shoulder blades planted against the tiles and Sabrina's thighs locked around his waist.

The third time came later, well past midnight.

Driven by a different kind of hunger, they invaded the kitchen. Sabrina was naked under the cashmere robe Marco had draped around her. He'd pulled on his jeans but hadn't bothered with a shirt or shoes.

She perched on a high swivel stool. Her elbows were propped on a counter made of tiles decorated with grape vines and baskets of lemons. Marco got out the seafood au gratin casserole Signora Bertaldi, bless her, had left in the fridge and slid it into the oven.

While they waited for the casserole to bubble, Sabrina munched on olives and tore pieces from a crusty loaf of bread to dip in oil and balsamic vinaigrette. Marco got out a corkscrew and another bottle of wine.

"Here."

She held up a fat black olive. Corkscrew and bottle in hand, he leaned forward, so she could pop it into his mouth. His strong white teeth just missed crunching down on her fingers.

"Mmm, good."

He set the bottle aside and dipped a crust of bread through the vinegar and oil mixture. Teasing, taunting, he drew the crust along her lower lip. Her eyes held his as she swiped her tongue over her lips and licked the drops of oil and sweet, tart vinegar.

His gaze locked on her mouth, Marco rounded the counter. Sabrina's borrowed robe gaped at her knees. He opened it further by the simple expedient of easing his hips between her thighs.

The next thing either of them knew, the oven was smoking and the seafood au gratin was bubbling over the sides of its dish in fat, sizzling splats.

Sabrina woke in Marco's arms the next morning. To her relief, she found the ache in her ankle had subsided to an occasional twinge and the swelling had almost completely disappeared. Gleefully, she abandoned the Ace bandage and traded the crutches for the cane Marco had delivered from the pharmacy in Positano.

While he showered, she slipped into a lacy camisole and a lightweight wool Emanuel Ungaro pantsuit, both in misty blue. Her ballet flats didn't do a whole lot for the outfit but she knew she wasn't ready for the three-inch heels on her only other pair of shoes.

They left shortly after breakfast for Sorrento and the first of the two facilities she intended to check out that day. The bustling harbor city had been a favored vacation spot since the days of Pompeii. Warm Mediterranean breezes made for streets lined with palm trees and a jumble of outdoor cafes. The balmy atmosphere provided an exotic backdrop for the colorful Christmas decorations still displayed in the streets and shop windows.

Sabrina craned her neck to take in the elegant nineteenth century facades of the hotels that had drawn so many visitors to this seaside resort. Only one had the available rooms and conference facilities to meet her client's needs.

The Excelsior Vittoria Grand Hotel sat high on the cliff once occupied by the Emperor Augustus's villa. With its fin de siècle buildings and magnificent views of Mount Vesuvius and the Bay of Naples, the hotel had played host to kings and queens as well as a long list of celebrities that in-

cluded Enrico Caruso, Jack Lemmon, Marilyn
Monroe and Sophia Loren.

Marco pulled up at its impressive portico and
turned the car keys over to the parking valet. Sabrina
had taken a lesson from the experience at Ravello.
Concerned his presence might jack up the cost estimates, she asked him to enjoy a cup of cappuccino
in the hotel's terrace café while she met with the assistant manager.

"Are you sure you don't wish me to help you take
notes?" he asked, clearly amused by her stubborn
determination to handle matters herself.

She countered with another question. "Have you
attended any functions at the Excelsior?"

"Several," he admitted.

"Go." She waved a dismissive hand. "Relax.
Have a cup of coffee."

"Very well. I'll wait for you on the terrace."

She met with the assistant manager in his office
before taking a tour of the hotel's facilities. She
had the quote he'd sent in response to her initial
e-mail. After viewing the conference setup and fi-
nalizing meal selections, she bargained hard to
get him to knock another ten percent off his
bottom line.

Flushed with victory, she joined Marco on the
sun-drenched terrace. He rose and slid his sunglasses down to the tip of his nose.

"I take it your negotiations went well."

"They did."

"Congratulations."

"Two sites down; two to go. At this rate, I'll have the information I need in plenty of time to prepare our final submission."

"I'm glad," he said, relieving her of her briefcase. "I was worried the accident may have impacted your ability to make your scheduled meetings."

"It would have," Sabrina admitted. "I couldn't have negotiated these roads or found my way around nearly as well without your help. Thank you."

"It's my pleasure."

His slow smile raised goose bumps up and down her spine.

"Very much my pleasure."

The day's second site survey required a trip by hydrofoil to the Isle of Capri. Like Sorrento, it had been a popular vacation destination since the time of the ancient Greeks. Its rocky cliffs rose from an azure bay, with resort hotels strung out along both sea level and the heights.

Sabrina had visited Capri's fabled Blue Grotto only once and would have loved to make a return trip. Unfortunately, they didn't have time to transfer to a small boat and ride the choppy waves into the cave. Her appointment with the manager of the hotel high on the cliffs overlooking the bay was set for two o'clock.

Marco accompanied her on the *funicolare* ride to the top of the cliffs. Good-naturedly he once again agreed to wait at a café in Piazza Umberto I. Sabrina wasn't as successful in her negotiations this time and almost wished she'd brought His Excellency along for additional firepower. Still, she left with a quote that was considerably under the one provided to her by the hotel in Ravello.

"Too bad," she commented to Marco on the hydrofoil back to Sorrento. "Ravello would have been my first choice. I liked the size of their break-out rooms and their audiovisual set up. Once I have the last estimate in hand, I might call Donati and see if he'll cut another five percent off his bottom line."

Stuffing her notes into her briefcase, she gave herself up to the vibrating hum of the boat's engine and the simple pleasure of Marco's arm draped over the back of her seat.

They'd left the Rolls parked at the ferry terminal. Marco held the passenger door for her and leaned down, his hand propped on the open door frame.

"How's your ankle holding up?"

"Good."

"Can you manage another stop?"

"Sure. Where?"

"My mother commanded me to bring you for dinner," he reminded her with a wry smile. "I can beg off if you wish."

"I'm fine. Really."

"Are you certain? I love my mother dearly, but she can be a bit overwhelming at times."

"Trust me. I learned at an early age to hold my own against overwhelming *and* overbearing."

He settled in the driver's seat and gave her a thoughtful glance as he buckled his seat belt. "You must tell me about this father of yours sometime."

"I will. Sometime."

But not with the sun sinking toward the sea and the early December dusk gathering on the hills. Right now Sabrina wanted to drink in the spectacular views of the Bay of Naples and enjoy the company of this intriguing, complex man.

"I'd rather you tell me about yours. I'd like to know a little about your background before I meet your mother."

"My father died when I was four. I barely remember him. I have a sister, AnnaMaria. She's an artist. She works mainly in bronzes and lives in Paris with her husband, also an artist. Perhaps you've heard of him? Etienne Girard?"

"I have! I attended an exhibit of his work a few years ago. His sculptures are, ah, very intense."

"Very," Marco agreed with a grin. "I'm still learning to interpret the message in rusted iron and neon."

"And your mother?"

"Ah, Mama." His smile turned affectionate and rueful at the same time. "She's Neapolitan born and bred. She has the blood of our history in her veins—Greek, Roman, Byzantine, Norman, Bourbon. Her father fought against the German military occupation during World War II and helped the city win its freedom in 1943. He was later elected to parliament, but was murdered by the Camorra because of his vigorous efforts to stamp out organized crime. They gunned him down on the front steps of his home."

His family had certainly suffered their share of tragedy. Like the Kennedys, Sabrina thought.

"After his death, my mother took up the fight herself. She, too, served in parliament until she married my father. Since then, she's used her title and her influence to help any number of causes."

"She sounds like a remarkable woman."

"She is."

Sabrina settled back in her seat, eager to meet the mother and learn more about the son who fascinated her more every hour she spent in his company.

Seven

As Marco explained during the short drive from the ferry dock, the original seat of the Dukes of San Giovanti was a hilltop fort north of Naples. The first duke received his title in 1523, along with his charter to guard the approaches to the rich trading port.

The present seat was a palazzo in the very heart of the city. To reach it, Marco negotiated the traffic-clogged harbor drive with a patience born of long familiarity. Sabrina didn't mind the slow crawl. It gave her plenty of opportunity to gawk at the massive fortress guarding the harbor. Begun by the Angevins in the eleventh century and added to by the Spanish in subsequent centuries, the castle served as royal residences for a long succession of kings.

She also got glimpses of the famous Quartieri Spagnoli—the Spanish Quarter, laid out by Spanish soldiers in the seventeenth century. The teeming, densely populated area was quintessential Napoli.

Tall, multistory stucco buildings crowded so close together that the balconies on one side of the street almost touched those on the opposite side, completely blocking out the sun. Washing flapped from the balconies like bright pennants. The colorful Christmas decorations strung across the narrow alleys added to the chaotic scene.

Sabrina spotted a crew taking down the Christmas decorations and replacing them with a banner announcing a massive fireworks display and rock concert to celebrate the coming Fiesta di San Silvestro.

"I bet the Spanish Quarter rocks on New Year's Eve."

Marco flicked a glance at the dark tunnel of streets. "You don't want to wander into the Quarter at night. Especially the night of San Silvestro. Some Neapolitans still practice the tradition of throwing broken furniture out the window to show they're ready for a fresh start."

"Out with the old, in with the new, huh?"

"Exactly." He maneuvered around a traffic circle and turned onto a wide boulevard. "We have another tradition you may want to consider, however. Wearing red underwear on New Year's Eve is supposed to bring good luck."

His smile was slow and wicked.

"I would enjoy seeing you in red underwear. I would enjoy even more getting you out of it."

"Then I'll have to hit the shops," Sabrina said, laughing. "Red panties and a dress for your mother's New Year's Ball. *If* I get everything done I need to and can change my airline reservations."

"We will get it done."

"We have New Year's traditions in the States, too," she commented as the boulevard sloped up toward the magnificent baroque cathedral dominating the city's skyline. "When you did your residency in New York, do you remember champagne toasts and black-eyed peas on New Year's Day?"

"I remember more the nonstop football games. Or what you American's call football."

"What about resolutions? Do you make 'em and break 'em like we do?"

"That's an all-American tradition." He threw her a quick look. "Have you made yours for the coming year?"

"Not yet. I'll have to think about it."

She didn't have to think long.

She'd intended to fly home late tomorrow evening. Even if she changed her ticket, she would gain only a few more days in Italy. Marco had to return to Rome by January fifth and she needed to be back in the States by then, working furiously with Caroline to put their final proposal together for the Global Security conference.

She wouldn't think about the ticking clock, Sabrina resolved. She'd enjoy the time she had left in Italy. She'd scout the last hotel, stuff herself on Signora Bertaldi's cooking, go to a ball and make love morning, noon and/or night to her handsome doc.

With that delicious resolution firmly in mind, she craned her neck for a better view of a fat, white moon rising above the cathedral's spires.

Sabrina fell instantly in love with the Palazzo d'Calvetti.

Three stories tall and at least eight bays wide, its facade featured different window frames and pediments on each level. She could see the Moorish influence in some, the Italian Renaissance in others. A crowning cornice topped by statues of various saints ran the length of the facade.

Marco parked under a central portico supported by marble columns and escorted Sabrina up the shallow front steps. They were met at the door by a butler who welcomed His Excellency home with genuine warmth.

"*Grazie,* Phillippo. This is Ms. Russo, my guest."

The butler blinked in surprise but recovered quickly. "*Buona sera,* madam."

Sabrina was starting to get used to these double takes and answered with a smile. "*Buona sera.*"

"Is my mother in the main salon?" Marco asked.

"She is, Your Excellency, but she wished me to

let her know the moment you arrived and she will come down."

While he pressed a buzzer on the intercom panel, Sabrina took in the magnificent barrel-vaulted main hall lavishly decorated with hand-painted Majolica tiles. A grand staircase bisected the hall in dead center and led in sweeping twin spirals to the upper floors.

She was still absorbing the rich architectural detail when a door slammed on the second floor. A moment later, a slim, silver-haired woman in tailored slacks and a mink-trimmed sweater hurried down the stairs.

"Marco!"

"Buona sera, Mama." Bending, he kissed her on both cheeks. *"Come sta?"*

"Bene. Multo bene."

The affection between the two was genuine and readily apparent, but when the duchess turned to his guest her warm smile vaporized.

"Madre del Dio!"

Sabrina suppressed a sigh. Marco had assured her the resemblance to his dead wife was merely superficial. She was beginning to wonder. He covered the awkward moment with an introduction.

"Sabrina, may I present my mother, Donna Maria di Chivari Calvetti. Mama, this is my guest, Sabrina Russo."

"Forgive me for staring," the duchess apologized in musically accented English. "It's just… You look much like…"

"Like Gianetta," her son finished calmly. "At first glance, I thought so, too. But you will find, as I have, it is only a trick of the eye."

An odd expression flickered across his mother's face. It came and went so quickly Sabrina couldn't interpret it. She had no difficulty interpreting the cool comment that followed, though.

"I will admit I was surprised when my son told me he had a guest staying at his villa." She raked a glance at said guest from her windblown hair to the tip of her cane. "I hope you're recovering from your unfortunate accident?"

The question was polite, but the slight if unmistakable emphasis on the last word almost made *Sabrina* do a double take.

Good grief! Did the woman think she'd tumbled down a cliff in a deliberate attempt to snare her rich, handsome son? Had that—or some similar ploy—been tried before? She'd have to ask Marco later.

"I'm recovering quite well, Your Excellency. Your son has taken excellent care of me."

She would have loved to add that his bedside manner was improving every day, too. Wisely, she refrained.

"Indeed."

With a regal nod, the duchess led the way past the marble staircase to the west wing of the palazzo.

"I wasn't sure you'd be able to mount the stairs so I've ordered an aperitif tray to be set up in the Green

Salon. It's on this floor and there's a water closet just there, across the hall, if you wish to use it."

"Thank you, I do."

"We'll wait for you in the salon," Marco said. "It's the third room on the left."

Sabrina didn't dawdle. Her lip gloss and hair restored to order, she left the powder room and counted the rooms as she passed them. The first looked like it might have been once been the palazzo's armory and now served as a museum for antique weapons displayed in locked cases. The second was an office of sorts, with glass-fronted cabinets containing tall, leather-bound volumes of documents. Sabrina's partner, Devon the history buff, would salivate at the sight of those musty volumes.

"...do you know about her?"

The duchess's sharp question came through the open door of the third room, as did Marco's reply.

"I know enough, Mama."

The exchange was in Italian but clear enough for Sabrina to follow easily. She took another step before she realized her soft-soled flats and the rubber tip of her cane masked her approach.

"You say she's in Italy on business?"

"She and her partners provide travel and support services for executives doing business in Europe. She's scouting conference sites."

Time to announce her presence, Sabrina thought. She lifted the cane, intending to thump it on the parquet floor. The duchess's next comment stopped her cold.

"If half the articles my secretary pulled off the Internet about this woman are true, she's scouting more than conference sites."

"What do you mean?"

"She's the daughter of Dominic Russo, the American telecommunications giant. He put her on the board of the foundation that oversees his charitable interests, but subsequently removed her. The rumor is he's disinherited her. Cut her off without a cent."

"Ah," Marco murmured. "So that's why she's so determined to make it on her own."

"Perhaps, perhaps not. Don't you think it's just a little too coincidental that she fell right at your feet?"

Sabrina had heard enough. Bringing the cane down with a loud thud, she entered the salon.

Marco stood behind a tray holding an array of bottles, a silver martini shaker in his hand. His mother was seated in a tall-backed armchair and had the grace to appear chagrined for a moment. But only for a moment. Her chin lifted as Sabrina gave her a breezy smile.

"Your information's accurate, Your Excellency, except for one point. My father didn't remove me from the board of the Russo Foundation. I quit. Are those martinis in that shaker, Marco?" she asked with cheerful insouciance. "If so, I'll take two olives in mine."

"Two olives it is," he confirmed with a gleam of approval in his dark eyes.

His mother was less admiring. "I'm sorry if I offended you, Ms. Russo," she said coolly. "I wish only to watch out for my son's welfare."

"I understand, Your Excellency. No offense taken."

"I'm perfectly capable of watching out for my own welfare," Marco drawled as he handed his mother a tall-stemmed martini glass. "But I thank you for your concern."

The duchess merely sniffed.

She unbent a little over dinner served in a glass-enclosed conservatory that looked out over the lights of the city.

"Have you visited this part of Italy before, Ms. Russo?"

"Only once, when I was a student at the University of Salzburg. One of my roommates was a history major. We drove down from Austria one weekend to explore the ruins at Pompeii and Herculaneum."

"So you've not spent time in Napoli."

"No, Your Excellency."

"You must call me Donna Maria."

Sabrina's lips twitched at the royal command. "Certainly. And please, call me Sabrina."

"We have a painting by Lorenzo de Caro in the gallery. It depicts the city as it was in the early eighteenth century. You must let me show it to you after dinner."

The rest of the meal passed with polite queries concerning Sabrina's year in Salzburg and her current business. Not until she and the duchess had made their way to the galley, leaving Marco to look over a document his mother wanted his opinion on, did she learn the ulterior motive behind the invitation to view de Caro's masterpiece.

The painting was small, only about twelve by eighteen inches, but so luminous that it instantly drew the eye. Lost in the exquisitely detailed scene of a tall-masted ship tied up at wharf beside the fortress, Sabrina almost missed Donna Maria's quiet question.

"How much has my son told you about his wife?"

"Only that she died in a tragic boating accident. If Marco wants me to know more," she added pointedly, "I'm sure he'll tell me."

The duchess hiked a brow. "You are a very direct young woman."

"I try to be, Donna Maria."

"Then I will tell you bluntly that I love my son very much and don't wish to see him hurt again."

"I don't plan to hurt him."

"Not intentionally, perhaps." Her forehead creasing, the duchess studied her guest's face. "But this resemblance to Gianetta…"

"It can't be that remarkable," Sabrina said with some exasperation.

"Come and judge for yourself."

Donna Maria led the way to the opposite wing

of the gallery. It was lined with portraits of men and women in every form of dress from the late Middle Ages onward. Cardinals. Princesses. Dukes and duchesses in coronets trimmed with fur and capped with royal red.

"These are my parents." She stopped in front of a portrait depicting a willowy blond and a stern-looking man in a uniform dripping with medals. "And here are my husband and I in our wedding finery."

The painter had captured the couple in the bloom of youth. There was no mistaking the love in the young Donna Maria's eyes or the pride in her husband's as he gazed down at her.

"How happy you both look."

"We were," the duchess said softly.

Her gaze lingered on the portrait for a long moment before moving to another. This one showed her seated on a garden bench with her two children standing beside her.

"This is Marco at the age of eight, and my daughter AnnaMaria at age six."

Sabrina could see the man Marco would become in the boy's erect posture and intelligent eyes.

"And this is Gianetta," the duchess said, her tone hardening. "Marco had this painted shortly after they were married."

Unlike the other portraits in the gallery, this one was an informal collage of sky and sea and sail. At its center was a windblown, laughing woman manning the helm of a sleek boat. The colors were vivid, the strokes bold slashes of sunlight on shadow.

Disconcerted, Sabrina leaned forward for a closer look. She might have been looking at a portrait of herself in her younger, wilder days. The hair, the eyes, the angle of the chin... No wonder everyone close to Marco gawked when they saw his houseguest!

"She was beautiful," the duchess said, making no effort to disguise her bitterness. "So beautiful and charming and unpredictable that everyone fell all over themselves to find excuses for her erratic behavior. Everyone except me. I could never... I *will* never forgive her for putting my son through such hell."

Whoa! That was a little more information than Sabrina had anticipated. Donna Maria didn't give her time to process it before zeroing in for a direct attack.

"Is the resemblance between you and Gianetta more than physical, Ms. Russo? Are those other stories my secretary pulled from the Internet true?"

Sabrina's eyes narrowed. "As I said earlier, you shouldn't believe everything posted on the Internet."

The duchess refused to be fobbed off. Like a lioness protecting her cub, she went straight for the jugular.

"Which story isn't true? The one that claims you seduced the son of a sheik? The one that says you like to party until dawn at nightclubs in New York and Buenos Aires and London?"

The gloves were off now, Sabrina thought grimly.

Like they'd been so many times with her father. Well, she was older and a whole lot wiser this time around. The body blows didn't hit as hard or hurt as badly as they did when her father threw them.

"Sorry, Your Excellency." Her shrug was deliberately careless. "I'm well past the age of having to defend my actions. To you or anyone else. Shall we join Marco for coffee?"

With Sabrina's ankle so improved, Marco returned his mother's Rolls and reclaimed his Ferrari. The powerful sports car ate up the miles between Naples and his seaside villa in less than an hour.

Sabrina was quiet for most of the trip, more shaken than she wanted to admit by the exchange with his mother. Her past had come back to haunt her with a vengeance. All those wild parties... All those torrid affairs... She couldn't deny them and was damned if she'd try.

She wondered whether the duchess had poured the juicy stories into her son's ears. Marco gave no sign of it when he accompanied her to the guest suite.

Or when he took her in his arms.

Or when his mouth came down on hers.

The heat was instant and so intense Sabrina knew she was in trouble. Her bones had never liquefied like this. Her blood had never bubbled and boiled. She wanted this man more with each breath she took but, somehow, found the strength to ease out of his embrace.

"Your mother showed me Gianetta's portrait. She looked so vibrant. So full of life."

"She was," he said simply. "I loved her with all the passion of my youth."

Sabrina hugged her waist. She'd tasted passion, too. Many times. But with the brutal clarity of hindsight, she saw that she'd never truly loved. Not the way Marco described.

She could love this man, though. She knew it, deep in her heart. She was already halfway there.

She was still dealing with that disconcerting realization when he unbelted the jacket of her pantsuit and undid the buttons, one by one.

"Ah, Sabrina."

He dipped his head and kissed her nose, her mouth, her chin, the swell of her breasts above the lacy chemise.

"You enchant me," he murmured in Italian, his voice low and rough. "You enthrall me. You make me feel alive again."

Eight

"He said that?"

Amusement rippled across Caroline's heart-shaped face, displayed next to Sabrina's on the laptop's screen.

"You enthrall him?"

"It didn't sound as corny in Italian."

Sabrina scooted up a little higher and balanced the computer on her bent knees. She'd decided to laze amid the rumpled sheets and duvet while Marco showered. After the night just past, she wasn't sure she'd have enough strength to roll out of bed and take her turn.

At least she'd managed to reach over the side of the mattress for his discarded shirt and pull it on before powering up the computer. She could smell the faint tang of his aftershave mingling with the scent of their lovemaking as she queried her partner.

"Are you sure you don't mind if I stay in Italy until January fourth, Caroline? That's the first day I can get out on a new ticket."

It was also the *last* day she could spend with Marco before he headed back to Rome. Sabrina shoved that nasty thought aside. They still had today and the Feast of San Silvestro tomorrow and New Year's Day and...

Caroline interrupted her mental count. "Of course I don't mind. I won't get home until late on the third myself. Zap me your estimates and I'll send you mine. We can do the comparative analysis by e-mail and work up the final proposal when we get home."

"Will do. I just have one more site to check out. Marco and I are going to hit it today. Then I have to do some serious shopping."

"For?"

"A ball gown."

"You're going to a ball?"

"Yep. We're going to celebrate the New Year in style."

"Answer me this, my friend. How will you dance on that ankle?"

Sabrina raised her leg and examined the joint in question.

"The swelling's gone. I can actually see the bones again. They're still covered in ugly green and purple, but what the heck. Here, have a look."

She swiveled the laptop around and aimed the built-in camera at her foot.

"The pain is gone, too," she said, wiggling her toes. "If I take it easy and use the cane today, I ought to be able to manage at least one waltz tomorrow night. Although…"

She repositioned the laptop and saw her own face screwed up in a grimace.

"I was pretty ambivalent about attending the big bash after meeting Her Excellency yesterday."

"What changed your mind?"

The grimace morphed into a catlike grin. "Marco. The man can be pretty convincing when he wants to."

Her partner smiled but still had doubts. "From what you told me about his mother, I have to say she sounds rather formidable."

"She is."

Caroline bit her lip. She and Devon knew all too well the scars Sabrina had acquired over the years in her fierce battles with her father.

"You've spent a good part of your life fighting to hold your own against a domineering parent. Are you sure you want to enter into battle with another?"

"I'm not engaging in a protracted battle. I'm just attending a party with my studly doc-slash-duke, after which we'll go our separate ways."

She shrugged aside the disconcerting twinge that caused and cocked her head.

"The shower just cut off in the bathroom. Gotta go, Caro. I need to confirm the ticket change, get dressed and hit the road. I'll e-mail a spreadsheet with the final cost estimates for the sites here in Italy as soon as I nail down the last one."

"Okay. I'll do the same for the sites in Spain."

"*Ciao* for now, girl."

She ended the videoconference and sent her fingers flying over the keyboard. She'd have to pay a hundred and eighty dollar differential in airfare plus another hundred in penalties for changing her ticket. Add in the cost of a gown and the necessary accessories, and this was turning out to be an expensive stopover.

Since these weren't business-related expenses, Sabrina intended to cover them from her personal account. Good thing she'd built up a healthy savings before walking away from the board of the Russo Foundation.

Marco emerged from the bathroom just as she clicked the confirm button to purchase the new ticket. "It's done. I've changed my... Yowza!"

She froze with her fingers still curved over the keyboard, speechless at the sight of six foot one of nearly naked male.

He had a towel draped around his hips. Above the fluffy cotton his chest hair gleamed dark and damp. Below, his muscular thighs narrowed down to strong calves and disgustingly healthy ankles. With his bronzed skin and short, curling hair, he could leave a string of broken hearts from Naples to Nashville to Nepal.

"You should give a girl some warning before you stroll into a room looking like that! I almost swallowed my tongue."

"Tongue swallowing could be symptomatic of a serious medical condition," he said solemnly. "You'd better let me have a look."

He had to drop the towel in order to make the necessary examination. For some reason, he also had to peel off Sabrina's borrowed shirt.

The laptop got shoved onto the bedside table. The duvet slithered over the side of the mattress. Marco curled his hands under her thighs and tugged her down until she was stretched out under him.

"Open your mouth and say ah."

"Now that," Sabrina gasped when they came up for air some time later, "was what I call a thorough examination. I might have to hire you as my personal physician."

Marco rolled onto his side and propped his head in his hand. Christ, she was beautiful. With her tangle of tawny hair and her long, supple body lying limp beside his, she made him feel smug and sated and hungry, all at the same time.

"It would be difficult for me to make house calls to the States. You'd have to stay here, in Italy."

He said it with a lazy smile but as soon as the words were out the idea took hold. Suddenly thoughtful, he let his gaze drop to her mouth, still swollen from his kisses, and brought it up to meet hers again.

"Why *not* stay longer, Sabrina?"

"I wish I could. Unfortunately, my partners and I have a company to run."

Marco curled a tendril of tawny gold around his finger and feathered the ends with his thumb. Just a few days ago he'd driven down from Rome with nothing more than a week of rest and relaxation in mind. Then this woman had dropped into his life. They'd spent less than a week together, but all he had to do was look at her to know he wanted more.

"Since your company provides support for executives doing business in Europe," he said slowly, "perhaps you should consider the cost effectiveness of establishing a forward operating location in, say, Rome."

Chuckling, she dropped a kiss on his chest. "That would certainly make house calls more convenient for my personal physician. Now I suggest we postpone any further doctor/patient consultation until later. We gotta get it in gear, fella."

Marco let the subject drop, but the idea of keeping Sabrina in Italy remained fixed in his mind during the drive to the last conference site on her list, a resort some forty kilometers south of Salerno.

The Villa d'Este sat all by itself on a rocky promontory jutting into the sea. It was a new condo/time share/vacation resort that had been constructed for guests who wanted to avoid the bustle of the more popular tourist locales. The facilities were top rate and the prices comparable to the other sites Sabrina had scouted, but she left ready to cross the place off her list.

"Too isolated and difficult to get to," she commented as the Ferrari slowed for a truck spewing a black cloud of diesel fumes. "Good thing I made a previsit. On paper, the resort looked perfect."

With a blind curve ahead, Marco couldn't pass. He dropped back, his nostrils flaring at the noxious fumes.

"So, which of the other three locales tops your list?"

She flipped through her notes. "I really liked the facilities and unique setting in Ravello, but that estimate came in considerably higher than either Sorrento or Capri. I e-mailed Signor Donati yesterday and asked him to take another look at his catering costs."

Marco didn't offer to weigh in with Donati. He'd made that mistake once, and felt the bite of Sabrina's prickly independence. Yet he knew one phone call from him could resolve the issue.

The knowledge bothered him. He wasn't used to sitting back while someone else took the lead. He headed a highly skilled surgical team with unquestioned authority. He made life and death decisions daily in the operating theater, and made them fast. In addition to chairing the neurosurgery department at his hospital, he sat on the board of directors for the International Pediatric Neurosurgical Association and the Gamma Radioknife Institute. He routinely loaned his name, his title and his reputation to any number of charitable enterprises. That combination carried as much weight here in southern Italy as it did in Rome.

At Sabrina's specific request, however, he'd stayed in the background while she met with the hotel personnel in Capri, Sorrento and at the Villa d'Este. He'd shrugged off her stubborn determination to handle matters herself at the time. Now it put a decided dent in his ego. She was foolish not to use his influence, he thought as the truck in front of them belched another wave of noxious fumes.

Muttering a curse, Marco pulled out to pass. A long line of oncoming cars forced him to cut back.

"At this rate, we'll eat his exhaust all the way back to Salerno."

The irritated comment drew a quick glance from the woman beside him. She stuffed her notes in her briefcase with a rueful smile.

"I told you before, but I'll tell you again. I really appreciate you playing chauffer for me this week."

Marco didn't want her appreciation. He wanted her. The more he thought about keeping her in Italy, the more determined he was to make it happen.

He needed to lay some groundwork first, and he couldn't do that with this damned truck spewing fumes in his face. He caught sight of a brown sign ahead denoting the turnoff for a place of historical interest.

"Have you been to the Temple of Poseidon at Paestum?" he asked as the sign flashed by.

"No."

"It's too close by for you to miss."

"Marco, we don't have a lot of time for sightseeing. It's almost three o'clock now and we're still several hours from home."

He slowed for the turn and cut the wheel. "This won't take long."

Sabrina stifled a dart of annoyance. After his good-natured chauffeuring, she could hardly insist they save Paestum for another day.

Still, she couldn't help thinking of all she needed to get done. At the top of the list was putting her notes in order and e-mailing Caroline the results of her site surveys. When she received the input from Caro's surveys, she'd have to get to work on a comparative analysis. And sometime before the ball tomorrow night she needed to squeeze in a few hours of shopping. The last thing she was interested in right now was a side trip to view some ruins.

Her minor annoyance evaporated at her first glimpse of the temples. The three massive Doric structures rose from a grassy plain dotted with the scattered remnants of the ancient city built by the Greeks around 600 B.C.

"The one in the center is as large as the Parthenon!" she gasped. "And so beautifully restored."

She got a better view of the main temple when they pulled into the visitor's parking lot. Awed, she let her gaze roam the starkly beautiful rows of columns topped by an elaborate frieze and a pitched roof. Marco hooked an arm over the steering wheel, content to sit for a few moments while she absorbed the incredible sight.

"The center temple was dedicated to Poseidon," he told her. "The god of the sea. He was known as Neptune to the Romans, who took the city from the Greeks and occupied it until well into the ninth century."

"Why did they leave?"

"Some say it was malaria, some believe it was a Saracen assault. That's the Temple of Hera on the right. On the left is the Temple of Ceres, goddess of agriculture. Are you up to walking in for a closer view?"

"Most definitely."

Her ankle had barely given her a twinge all day, but she was more than willing to tuck her arm in Marco's for the short stroll to the temples. Her fingers curled into the sleeve of his jacket. She was developing a real attachment to this soft suede. A cold breeze came in off the sea, bringing with it wispy fingers of fog and making her glad she'd worn a black cashmere sweater under *her* jacket.

She spotted only two other visitors in the distance, wandering among the ruins of a small amphitheater. With a little thrill, she saw that she and Marco had the temples to themselves. They approached slowly and mounted the steps at the entrance. Their footsteps echoed on the marble floor. Standing amid columns that had tumbled and been rebuilt gave her the eerie sensation of being part of man's unceasing battle against time and the forces of nature.

"I can almost see a procession of white-robed priests and priestesses," she murmured. "They must have made offerings to Poseidon in hopes he would fill their nets with fish...then wondered how the heck they'd offended him when a storm blew up and sank their ships."

"Something I've wondered, too."

Stricken, she glanced up the man beside her. "Oh, Marco, I'm sorry. I didn't mean to evoke unhappy memories."

"You don't need to apologize." His gaze drifted around the ring of inner columns. "The people who worshipped here thousands of years ago recognized the capriciousness of the gods. That's as good an explanation for Gianetta's drowning as any I've been able to come up with."

The quiet comment mirrored Sabrina's thoughts of a few moments ago. Somehow, putting his wife's death in such a timeless historical context made it a little more understandable. But only a little.

When they exited the temple, Sabrina hugged his arm tight against her side.

"Shall we sit for a moment?" he asked, steering her toward a stone bench strategically positioned for contemplation of the decorative frieze. "I want to follow up on our conversation this morning."

"Which one?" A mischievous smile tugged at her lips. "The one where you told me to open up and say ah? Or the one where we discussed making you my personal physician?"

"The possibility isn't as remote as it sounds. I think you should consider my suggestion of setting up a forward operating location in Rome."

Surprised, she twisted around to face him. "Are you serious?"

"Very much so. Think of the cost savings if you and your partners didn't have to fly back and forth from the States to survey locales or provide an on-site presence for your clients."

The calm reply left Sabrina scrambling for breath. She'd thought they were just indulging in postcoital banter this morning. She had no idea he considered the forward location a viable possibility.

"Caroline and Devon and I just started European Business Services six months ago," she explained. "We don't have the contracts or the resources yet to open an office in Rome."

"I could help. I have a great many connections within the medical community. I also belong to a number of professional associations. Each of these associations rotates their annual conference to various countries."

Her brow creased. "You're offering to steer business my way?"

"If it will keep you in Italy, yes." He held up a palm to forestall her instinctive protest. "I know, I know. You're determined to make a success of EBS on your own. You also don't want me meddling in your negotiations. But entrepreneurs exploit their personal and professional contacts all the time. You're shooting yourself in the foot by not taking advantage of my connections, my so lovely, so enchanting Sabrina."

She couldn't argue with that. EBS had landed their first really big contract because one of men she'd dated in her wilder years had referred his old college buddy. The fact that his buddy just happened to be Cal Logan, CEO of Logan Aerospace, had made for a nice chunk of change.

She wasn't sure why she kept resisting the idea of using Marco's influence. At first, she'd worried his title and obvious wealth would affect her negotiations with the hotel managers she'd come to meet with. Now...

Now she worried her hunger for this man might well be clouding her judgment. All he had to do was toss out the idea of setting up an office in Rome and she was ready to sign a lease!

The thought of staying close to him, of letting this undeniable attraction sizzle into something even hotter, made her heart skip a few beats. Then her gaze shifted to the temple looming just over his shoulder.

Their brief conversation about his dead wife leaped into her head. So did an almost photographic image of the portrait the duchess had shown her.

Gianetta, the beautiful. Gianetta, the tragic. Gianetta, Marco's lost love.

He swore the resemblance was only skin deep. His mother seemed to think otherwise. At this moment, Sabrina didn't know who was closer to the truth.

As if sensing that he'd thrown her a curve ball, Marco lifted her hand and brushed a kiss across her knuckles. "I'm not asking you to decide right this moment. We have until the fourth of January together. Use the days ahead to think about my proposal, yes?"

Right. Uh-huh. Sure.

Like she was going to think of anything else?

Nine

The next morning they kicked off their New Year's Eve celebrations with a slow, delicious session between the sheets.

Sabrina couldn't think of *any* better way to end the old year and get ready to ring in the new—until she joined Marco on the terrace for breakfast. Signora Bertaldi's cappuccino and fresh-baked brioche had her salivating even before she greeted the older woman.

"*Buon mattina,* signora."

"*Buon mattina.*" Beaming, Marco's housekeeper placed a foam-topped porcelain cup before Sabrina. "I don't cook the lentils and sausage this morning because you will eat them tonight, at Palazzo d'Calvetti, yes?"

"I, uh, think so."

Sabrina looked to Marco for guidance. His nod confirmed lentils and sausage were on the menu.

"You must be sure to have both," the cook instructed. "For luck."

"I will."

When she went into the kitchen for the plates she'd kept warming in the oven, Sabrina turned to Marco.

"What's the schedule of events for this evening?"

He leaned back in his chair, looking good enough to eat in tan slacks, a sky-blue oxford shirt with the cuffs rolled up and a white sweater knotted loosely over his shoulders.

"Plan on a long night. Dinner at seven, with thirty or so close family and friends. The ball begins at ten."

"How many attend that?"

"The guest list usually runs to about four hundred. At midnight, we'll watch the fireworks displays from the terrace, with more music and dancing to follow. Those with enough staying power usually try to greet the dawn. But don't feel you have to stay up all night. Your ankle gives us a built-in excuse to go upstairs any time we wish."

"Upstairs?"

"I usually remain in town over Fiesta di San Silvestro and Il Capodanno. It's easier than fighting the crowds jamming the streets. I was going to tell you this morning to pack a few overnight things."

Sabrina wasn't so sure about this sleepover. She could handle a dinner for thirty or so and easily get lost in the crowd of four hundred at the ball, but the prospect of facing the duchess across a breakfast table didn't exactly light her jets.

"Are you sure I won't be intruding on your mother's hospitality?"

"Not at all. I have my own apartments in a separate wing of the palazzo."

That issue resolved, Sabrina addressed a more pressing one.

"We'll have to drive into Naples early enough for me to hit the shops. I need a gown for tonight."

"And some red underwear," he reminded her with a grin that sent little shivers down her back.

Oh, boy! Less than a half hour out of Marco's bed and she wanted back in it. She had it bad, Sabrina realized. *Reeeally* bad.

"And some red underwear," she confirmed with a catch in her breath.

"You might find something to suit you in Positano. A friend of mine owns a boutique that caters to the guests at La Sirenuse."

La Sirenuse, Sabrina recalled, was the five-star hotel with rooms booked a year in advance by movie stars and oil tycoons. If the boutique was good enough for them, it was certainly good enough for her.

"It's worth a shot."

"I'll call Lucia and tell her we'll stop by on our way to Naples. If you don't find something there, I know several good shops in the city."

Two minutes after walking through the front door of Lucia Salvatore's elegant boutique Sabrina knew she'd struck gold. Forewarned by Marco's call, the vivacious owner had three fabulous gowns ready for Sabrina to try on.

She swept out of the dressing area to model each gown for Marco. He heartily approved of the strapless black taffeta with a full skirt that rustled when she walked. He was even more enthusiastic over the shimmering emerald satin that hugged her breasts and waist before exploding into rainbow-colored layers of chiffon. But the gold lamé body sheath won his vote, hands down.

The slinky fabric clung to Sabrina's every curve, shooting off pinpoints of light with each step. The diagonally cut bodice narrowed to a slender strap and was clasped with a jeweled leopard that draped over her left shoulder. The skirt was slit to the thigh on the right side.

"That one," Marco pronounced. "It must be that one."

Sabrina had to agree, especially when Lucia produced a pair of gold sandals with manageable heels.

"Don Marco said you have hurt your ankle and

must take care how you walk. It's good that you are so tall. These should work well for you."

The thong sandals worked very well. Sabrina took a practice turn around the dressing area and didn't wobble once.

"You will need long gloves," Lucia announced. "And for your hair…" She tapped a finger against her lower lip and surveyed her customer with a connoisseur's eye. "You will wear it up to show off our little pet, yes?"

Sabrina swept up her hair with both arms and angled around until the glittering leopard draped over her shoulder caught the light.

"Oh, yes," she murmured to the jeweled beast. "We have to show you off."

"I have just what you need." The boutique owner unlocked a glass case and slid out a hair comb. "It is antique and perhaps a little expensive, but the golden topaz stones are perfect with this dress."

A glimpse at the price tag indicated it was more than a *little* expensive. But Sabrina knew she had to have it the moment she twisted her heavy mane atop her head and anchored it with the comb.

"I'll take it. Now please tell me you have some red briefs in stock."

"Briefs?"

"Briefs, bikinis, hipsters…I'll take whatever you have as long as they're red."

"But do you not wish for ecru with this dress? Or

perhaps…" She stopped, laughing as the light dawned. "Ah, yes. You must wear red for luck."

"That's what I've been told."

"Come with me."

Moments later, the gown went into a zippered bag. Shoes, long gloves, comb and flame-red hipsters went into a tissue-lined tote. Pleased with her purchases, Sabrina dug out her American Express card.

"Oh, no, Ms. Russo."

"You don't take American Express? No problem. We can put it on Visa."

"No, no." The brunette flashed a quick look at the man waiting patiently in the front room of the boutique. "When Don Marco called, I assumed… That is, he told me…"

"Told you what?"

"He said you were his guest and instructed me to send the bill for whatever you purchased to his villa."

Sabrina stiffened, but kept her smile firmly in place. "He's a real sweetie pie, isn't he? Just go ahead and charge the items to my card."

The shop owner looked taken aback at hearing His Excellency referred to as a sweetie pie, but she ran the AmEx card without further discussion. Sabrina signed the ticket and sailed out with her purchases in hand.

"All set."

"Good. Let me take those."

She waited until they were in the Ferrari and on the narrow, winding road out of town to let loose with both barrels.

"Lucia said you told her to send the bills for my purchases to the villa. Do *not* embarrass me like that again."

"Embarrass you?" He looked honestly bewildered. "How does that embarrass you?"

"Oh, come on! Why don't you just take out a billboard ad saying we're lovers?"

His brows snapped together. "I wasn't aware you wanted to disguise the fact."

"I don't! But neither do I want you to pay for my underwear."

With a muttered curse, he pulled the Ferrari into a turnout. Ironically, it was the same turnout where Sabrina had left her rental car to snap pictures of the picturesque town spilling down the cliffs to the sea.

The car halted with a jerk, its nose pointed toward the restless sea. Marco shoved the gearshift into park, set the emergency brake and twisted the key in the ignition before slewing around in his seat. Anger blazed from his eyes.

"I'm not allowed to buy you a gift?"

"A ceramic bowl is a gift. A bottle of perfume is a gift. Two thousand dollars worth of clothing and lingerie crosses the line."

"Who set these rules?" he demanded, his accent thickening with his anger. "One hundred dollars for perfume, *si*. Two thousand dollars for clothing, no."

Thoroughly irritated, Sabrina fell back on the only argument she could. "There are no set rules. Just logic and common sense."

"This may sound logical to you," he retorted. "It doesn't to me."

She scrubbed her forehead with the heel of her hand, hating this argument, hating the memories it brought back of all the times she'd locked horns with her father in an effort to assert her independence, financially and otherwise.

"It's… It's not so much the amount that matters as the way you handled it. You should have consulted me before making an arbitrary decision to foot the bill."

"I ask again. I need to be clear on this, you understand. You want me to consult with you before I buy you any gift, large or small?"

"Yes. No."

He lifted one brow sardonically, and Sabrina gave a frustrated huff.

"Oh, hell, now I don't know what I want."

Her obvious frustration took the edge from Marco's anger. With a visible effort, he reined in his temper.

"We're new to each other," he said in a more even tone. "Still learning this intricate dance. Two steps forward, one back, like a waltz. We're bound to miss a step or two until we perfect our rhythm."

He let his glance shift to the sea. The churning waves held his gaze for long moments. When he turned to her again, all trace of anger was gone.

"I loved one woman and lost her. I don't know yet where we will go, you and I. Neither of us can know at this point. But I *do* know one thing with absolute certainty. I don't want to lose you, Sabrina *mia*."

Now that was hitting below the belt! She could go nose to nose with her father any day, matching his hardheaded stubbornness with her own. Marco's quiet declaration took every ounce of fight out of her. Worse, the tender endearment he attached to her name turned her insides to mush.

"I don't want to lose you, either."

He framed her face with his palms. "One step forward, my darling."

It was easy, so easy, to take that step. Sighing, she tipped her chin for his kiss.

She had no idea how long they might have sat there, practicing their steps, if a tour bus hadn't pulled into the turnout. The tourists piled out, oohing and ahhing over the incredible view. Their cameras were already clicking when Marco keyed the ignition.

They stopped for a late lunch in Torre Annunziata, a small town in the shadow of brooding Mt. Vesuvius, then had to battle horrendous traffic in Naples. Every other street, it seemed, was blocked in preparation for the night's festivities.

They finally pulled up at Palazzo d'Calvetti a little after five. The butler greeted Marco with the same warmth he'd showed on their previous visit. Bowing to Sabrina, he informed the duke that his mother and sister were in the upstairs salon.

"*Grazie,* Phillippo. Our bags are in the car. Will you have them taken to my apartments?"

"Of course, Your Excellency."

Marco took Sabrina's elbow to help her up the broad staircase and escorted her to a sitting room rich with antiques and bright sunlight. Donna Maria was seated at a gilt trimmed desk with reading glasses perched on the end of her nose, skimming what Sabrina guessed was a last-minute to-do list.

She looked up at their entrance. Pleasure flooded her face at the sight of her son. "Marco! I was beginning to think you would not arrive in time for dinner."

He bent to kiss her on both cheeks. "Traffic was a nightmare, Mama."

The duchess welcomed Sabrina with a voice that was a few degrees warmer than on her previous visit but stopped well short of gushing.

Marco's sister, on the other hand, more than made up her mother's reserve. She was a slender brunette in orange-striped leggings and an eye-popping electric-blue tunic that echoed the blue streak in her short, spiky black hair. With a yelp of delight, she threw herself into her brother's arms for an exuberant reunion.

Laughing, Marco had to cut into her torrent of Italian. "AnnaMaria, be still long enough for me to introduce to my houseguest."

"So this is your American, eh?" She turned in the circle of his arms and raked Sabrina from head to foot with the critical eye of an artist. "Mama told me you look much like Gia. I think... The hair, yes.

The eyes, a little. But not the mouth. Or the bones. Those wonderful bones are yours."

Sabrina could have kissed her!

"Ah, here is Etienne and my beautiful bambinos. Come meet Marco's American."

The burly French sculptor carried a doe-eyed little girl in one arm. A boy of four or five swung like a mischievous chimp from the other. The boy let go only long enough for his father to engulf Sabrina's hand in a thorny palm.

"A pleasure to meet you, Ms. Russo."

"And I, you. I attended an exhibit of your work at New York's Metropolitan Museum of Art a few years ago."

"Ah, *oui*. The Paris au Printemps Exhibition."

He didn't ask her opinion of his work but the question came through in a quizzically raised brow. Sabrina responded with a warm smile.

"I was especially intrigued by one piece. I think it was titled *An Afternoon in Montmartre*. I was amazed at how you captured the quarter's vibrancy in two pieces of twisted metal and a rope of flickering neon."

"AnnaMaria! Take charge of these monkeys! I want to go out on the terrace and speak more with this so very intelligent and charming woman."

"You have no time for flirting, Etienne. If Mama is done with me, we need to feed and bathe the children before we dress for dinner."

"An entire house full of servants," the sculptor

complained with a good-natured grin, "and she insists we feed, scrub and tuck these two in ourselves."

"Go!" the duchess instructed her daughter and son-in-law. "See to your children."

"What can we do to help?" Marco asked his mother.

"Nothing. Everything is as well ordered as it's going to be. But I hope you and Sabrina will excuse me if I, too, go rest a bit before dinner."

"We'll go up, as well. We can unpack and have an aperitif before the hoards arrive."

He and Sabrina accompanied the duchess up the grand staircase and parted company on the third floor.

"You'd best be downstairs by a quarter to seven to greet our guests," she told her son.

"We will."

She turned toward the east wing, hesitated. Her glance flicked from her son to Sabrina and back again. "Have you warned her about the paparazzi?"

"Not yet."

"They could be…difficult."

"We'll don our armor before we come downstairs."

"*Bene.*"

Sabrina contained her curiosity until Marco escorted her into his suite of rooms in the east wing. She caught a glimpse of their bags set side by side on a padded bench in a cavernous bedroom before demanding an explanation.

"What was that about?"

"You're not the only one who has fed the beasts,"

he commented with a dry reference to the articles his mother had pulled off the Internet about her. "They attacked like sharks after Gianetta's death. One tabloid even hinted I had somehow sabotaged the sailboat."

"Dear God! Why would you do that?"

"The usual reasons. Jealousy, anger, to rid myself of an inconvenient wife so I could marry my mistress."

Shrugging, he opened the doors of a parquetry chest to display a well-stocked bar.

"It didn't seem to matter that I *had* no mistress. What would you like to drink?"

"It's going to be a long night. I'd better stick with something nonalcoholic for now."

Marco chinked ice into two glasses and twisted off the lid on a bottle of Chinotto. The dark liquid fizzed like a carbonated drink and had a unique taste that combined bitter and sweet at the same time.

"We always allow a few members of press to take photographs at the ball. Be warned, they'll have an avid interest in you."

"Because I resemble Gianetta?"

His dark eyes held hers. "Because you will be the first woman I've invited to the ball *since* Gianetta."

Ohh-kaay.

Sabrina took another sip of the fizzing soft drink and willed her heart to stop hammering against her ribs. The waltz Marco had described so beautifully earlier suddenly seemed to have picked up in tempo. She couldn't shake the feeling she'd just been swept into a sultry tango.

The tempo kicked up yet again a little over an hour later.

Gowned, gloved, her hair anchored high on her head with the topaz-studded comb, she swept out of the bedroom in a glitter of gold. Two paces into the sitting room she caught sight of Marco and stopped dead.

Her jaw sagged. Her breath got stuck somewhere in the middle of her throat. The best she could manage was a breathless whisper.

"Wow."

"My sentiments exactly," he answered in a low growl. "You look magnificent, Sabrina *mia*."

His eyes devoured her as he crossed the room. Hers drank in the snowy white tie and pleated shirt, the black tails, the jeweled insignia of some royal order pinned to the red sash that slashed across his chest.

Tonight, Sabrina realized as her heart drummed out a wild beat, her handsome doc was every inch a duke.

Ten

Marco wasn't the only one rigged out in royal splendor for the night's festivities.

His mother was stunning in a gown of white satin and a diamond tiara studded with emeralds the size of pigeon eggs. More emeralds cascaded from her ears and throat.

His sister and brother-in-law somehow managed to look both dignified and unconventional, Anna-Maria in a shimmering cobalt gown that highlighted the blue streak in her hair, Etienne in a black cut-away and a jaunty white silk scarf looped over one shoulder in place of a tie.

With everyone dressed so formally, Sabrina expected dinner to be a stiff affair. Instead, the

guests were lively and the meal a gastronomical
delight that included the expected lentils and savory
stuffed sausage.

"For richness of life in the coming year," the
retired admiral seated next to Sabrina informed her
as he speared a piece of sausage.

She'd already discovered he was Marco's great
uncle on his mother's side and a real character. He
wore his navy uniform, with thick gold ropes at both
shoulders and a chest covered with medals. Bushy
white whiskers sprouted from his cheeks and an eye
patch covered one eye. His other eye kept trying to
get a good look down the front of Sabrina's gown.

Like when he shooed away the hovering waiter
and insisted on refilling her wine glass himself.

"Allow me, Signorina."

She rewarded his determined efforts by hunching
her shoulders to display a teeeeeny bit more cleavage.

"Ahh," the admiral murmured, his whiskers
twitching. *"Bellisima."*

She glanced up in time to catch Marco observing the byplay. Grinning, he lifted his goblet in a
silent toast. She responded with a wink.

The mischievous wink hit Marco with almost
the same impact as the sight of Sabrina in glowing
candlelight. His fingers tightened on the stem of his
goblet as he drank in the sight of her.

Until this moment, he'd wanted her with a hunger
that seemed to multiply with each passing hour.

Seeing her now, her face framed by those loose, careless tendrils, her eyes alight with laughter, turned hunger into something deeper, something richer. Something that made his heart constrict.

Marco hadn't missed the startled glances Sabrina had drawn when the dinner crowd had first assembled. Most of them had known Gianetta, some well enough to have experienced her wild, almost frenetic highs on occasions like this. But Sabrina's ready smile and genuineness had soon charmed them out of their initial uncertainty.

Nor did she falter during the long, lively banquet. Despite Uncle Pietro's ogling and the fact that most of the conversation was in Italian, she held her own easily with young and old. Not surprising given her privileged background, Marco supposed. As Dominic Russo's only child, she'd no doubt attended many functions like this. Yet Marco felt himself falling a little more in love each time she responded to a question with her less than idiomatic Italian or flashed him a laughing glance.

When her guests had finished their brandy-flamed lemon gateau and after-dinner coffee, the duchess nodded to her son. Marco rose with her.

"We have a half hour before the guests will begin to arrive for the ball," Donna Maria announced. "Please use the time to refresh yourselves or enjoy drinks in the main salon while we do our duty downstairs."

Marco used the loud scrape of chairs and general exodus to explain the drill to Sabrina.

"Mother traditionally grants interviews to society editors and entertainment TV reporters before the ball. It's a good opportunity for her to push her favorite charities and latest projects. Unfortunately, it's become a command performance for Anna-Maria and me, as well. Will you be all right if I desert you for a half hour?"

"I'll be fine." Her eyes twinkled. "Your uncle has offered to show me the gardens by moonlight."

"The old goat!" Curling a knuckle, he brushed it over her cheek. "If I were you, I'd stick to the lighted paths."

"I will," she promised, laughing.

Her rippling amusement stayed with Marco as he joined Etienne to escort the duchess and AnnaMaria down the grand staircase. He couldn't remember the last time he'd taken such delight in the sound of a woman's laugh. Or such intense pleasure from the simple act of touching her.

The aftershocks from that touch were still with him when his mother and AnnaMaria seated themselves on a stiff-backed sofa in the green salon. Marco and Etienne took up places behind them.

Donna Maria's ever efficient secretary had furnished a copy of the guest list to the various papers and TV networks weeks ago. They in turn had submitted their requests for interviews with particular celebrities, which had been coordinated with the individuals involved. Those interviews would be conducted when the guests arrived for the ball. This session focused strictly on the family whose roots went so deep into Neapolitan society.

Donna Maria presented brief prepared remarks before graciously inviting questions. Most concerned the drive she'd just launched on behalf of the victims of the floods that had devastated the village of Camposta. AnnaMaria and Etienne were asked about their latest exhibits. Marco fielded several questions concerning the seventeen-hour surgery he'd performed last month to separate twins conjoined at the base of their skulls.

He was beginning to believe they'd escape the session relatively unscathed with a reporter at the back of the room raised her hand.

"Sophia Ricci here. I have a question for His Excellency, Don Marco."

"Yes?"

The reporter edged to the front of the gathering. She was in her early thirties, with a thin, attractive face and black hair razored into uneven lengths.

"I see a name has been added to the guest list. Ms. Sabrina Russo, of Arlington, Virginia."

When she paused and let a small silence spin out, Marco lifted a brow. "Is that your question?"

"No, Your Excellency. I would like to know if Ms. Russo is the woman you were spotted with yesterday, disembarking from the ferry in Sorrento?"

A stir of palpable interest flowed through the reporters, and Marco smothered a curse. The hounds had picked up the scent sooner than he'd expected.

"She is," he replied.

Pens clicked. Notebook pages flipped. While her rivals scribbled furiously, Ricci's eyes gleamed with the triumph of having scooped them all.

"The same woman my sources tell me is currently staying at your villa?" she asked slyly.

He'd learned long ago the futility of attempting to deny the facts. "That's correct."

"May I ask how you met?"

"Quite by accident. Ms. Russo fell and sprained her ankle. Luckily, I was close by and was able to treat the injury. She's been recuperating at my villa."

"So is she your patient?" Ricci asked with dogged persistence. "Or your lover?"

Donna Maria's head snapped up. AnnaMaria let out a little hiss. Marco forestalled their instinctive responses and answered with the authority bred into him by his heritage and his demanding profession.

"Ms. Russo is my *guest,*" he said coldly. "Now you must excuse us. We've kept her and our other guests waiting long enough."

Ricci was no more immune to his icy stare than first-year residents at the hospital. She stepped back, momentarily cowed, as Marco offered the duchess his arm. Etienne did the same for AnnaMaria.

"That woman will be at her desk all night," Donna Maria predicted grimly as they mounted the grand staircase. "You'd best warn Sabrina to expect the worst."

"I will."

"You know how they flayed Gianetta."

His jaw set. "I know."

How could he not? He'd had to force his way through them, protecting his shuddering, sobbing wife with his body the last time she checked into a rehab clinic.

"Sabrina is stronger than Gia. And…"

He searched for the right word to describe her.

"…and truer to herself," he finished slowly. "She'd have to be, to resist Dominic Russo's attempts to break her."

The duchess halted halfway up the stairs. Marco met her frowning gaze with a steady one of his own. After a long moment his mother blew out a long breath.

"So it's that way, is it?"

"It is for me."

"And for her?"

The tension knotting the cords in his neck eased. "I'm working on that," he said with a wry smile.

The duchess tapped the toe of her jeweled shoe. "You'd better ask her to stand beside you in the receiving line. That might spike the worst of their guns."

Two steps down, AnnaMaria's eyes widened. "Mama! You wouldn't let Etienne stand with us to greet the guests until he made a respectable woman of me."

Her loving husband snorted. "And whose fault was that? You wouldn't agree to marry me until you were well into your ninth month. Have you forgotten how your water broke at the altar?"

"Please!" A pained expression crossed the duchess's face. "Do not remind us. Marco, go find Sabrina."

He located her in a circle that included three of his cousins and a long-time friend of his sister.

The all-female group was hunched forward in their chairs and deep in a discussion of last year's American presidential elections. Not surprisingly, Sabrina heartily agreed with her European counterparts that a woman was more than capable of leading either the U.S. *or* Italy.

"I'm sorry but I need to steal you away," he said with a smile.

She excused herself from her new friends and rose. The long column of her gown shimmered like molten gold as she hooked her arm through his.

"How's your ankle?" Marco asked.

"Good. Except for a *very* short stroll with Uncle Pietro, I've kept off it."

"Can you take a little extra duty? The ball guests are about to arrive. I'd like you to join me in the receiving line."

She slanted him a surprised glance. "You told me this is the first time you've brought a woman to the ball since your wife died. Won't it add fuel to the speculative fire if I'm included in the receiving line?"

"Unfortunately, the fire has already been fueled. One of the reporters downstairs asked about the woman I was spotted with in Sorrento yesterday. She found out you're staying at my villa and wanted to know if we're lovers."

"She asked you that? In front of your mother?"

"She did."

"How did you respond?"

"I told her you were my guest. We left it at that."

Lips pursed, she shook her head. "I seriously doubt it will stay left."

"Probably not. As you Americans say, however, the best offense is a good defense. Or is it the other way around?"

"Beats me."

"No matter. We'll put ourselves in plain sight and let everyone think what they will."

She wasn't convinced. "Don't you think you should clear this with the duchess first?"

"It was her suggestion."

"You're *kidding!*"

He had to smile at her thunderstruck expression. "No, Sabrina *mia,* I am not."

"Well, in that case..." Squaring her shoulders, she pasted on a brilliant smile. "Lead on, McDuff."

Sabrina knew darn well her presence in the receiving line would generate all kinds of speculation.

Sure enough, the guests who streamed into the grand ballroom regarded her with expressions that ranged from mild interest to avid curiosity.

Marco introduced her simply as his guest from America, in Italy on business. But the possessive hand he kept at the small of her back didn't go unnoticed. Nor did the private smiles he gave her between introductions.

Once most of the guests had been received, Marco officially opened the festivities by leading his mother out for the first waltz. Head high, her emerald-and-diamond tiara sparkling in the light, Donna Maria moved with regal grace in her son's arms.

Her next partner was one of the guests of honor—the mayor of the city of Naples—leaving Marco free to cross the parquet floor and hold out a gloved hand to Sabrina.

"Shall we?"

Either by luck or by design, the song was a slow, dreamy Italian love song. Marco held her close. Too close for ballroom protocol, judging by the glimpses Sabrina caught of raised eyebrows. She knew darn well the tight arm around her waist was intended to take most of the strain off her ankle. That didn't stop her from reveling in its hard, muscled strength or delighting in the brush of Marco's lips at her temple.

He was too well mannered to dance only with Sabrina, and far too solicitous of her injury. But before doing his duty with his mother's other guests, he made sure she was comfortably seated in one of the chairs lining the long ballroom. An assortment of his friends and acquaintances were detailed to keep her entertained.

The group included a wiry professional soccer player, who swore he owed the hump in the bridge of his nose from a kick Marco delivered when they were boys, and a sixtyish socialite arrayed in diamonds who regaled them all with stories from her days as stripper. She had everyone in the group helpless with laughter when a young couple caught Sabrina's eye. They stood at the edge of the gathering, hesitant to intrude, until she smiled an invitation.

"Please," she urged. "Join us."

"No, no, Signorina." Keeping an arm curled around his wife's shoulders, the young man demurred. "We come only to wish you happy on this Feast of San Silvestro."

"Thank you. The same to you."

"We see you with His Excellency," his wife said shyly. "We want to tell you… We want you to know…"

She stumbled to a halt and her brown eyes flooded with tears. Concerned, Sabrina started to push to her feet. The young husband stopped her with a quick explanation.

"His Excellency, he operates when no other surgeon would and saves our baby. Theresa and I… We would like to tell you he is a good doctor, a good man."

"I know," Sabrina replied softly.

When the young husband led his wife away, she swept her glance over the vast, mirrored hall until she spotted Marco. So tall, so distinguished in his white tie and tails. So damned handsome.

Yet she knew what she now felt for the man had little to do with his admittedly spectacular exterior. Sometime in the past week, she'd fallen for the whole package. Doc. Duke. Fast driver. So-so chess player. Inexhaustible, inventive, incredible lover.

With a small sigh, she turned her attention back to his friends.

Marco joined the group for the final hour before midnight. Music and laughter filled the ballroom. Tuxedoed waiters circulated with glasses with sparkling spumante. The minute hand on watches and clocks raced toward twelve.

Suddenly the lights dimmed. At a signal from the duchess, servers threw open the tall French doors leading to the wide terrace.

"Naples puts on the most spectacular fireworks display in all Italy," Marco explained. "We can watch in here, where it's warm, or out on the terrace."

Sabrina had spotted outdoor umbrella heaters during her short excursion with the admiral and didn't hesitate. "The terrace, please."

Glasses in hand, they joined the crowd outside and leaned elbows on the wide balustrade to soak in the incredible view of Naples lit up below. Strung out in a crescent of lights, the city circled the ink-black harbor guarded by the brightly illuminated Angevin fortress.

Judging by the noise that rose in waves, every Neapolitan must have spilled out in the streets. Horns honked. Spoons beat against pots. Raucous shouts and laughter competed with the reverberating bass boom of a rock band.

As if on cue, the noise died down. A hush seemed to settle over the city. Then someone on the terrace started a loud countdown.

"Dieci, nove, otto…"

Other voices joined in the chant.

"Sette, sei, cinque, quattro…"

Marco's arm tightened around Sabrina's waist. She turned a laughing face up to his.

"Tre," she sang out with him. *"Due. Uno!"*

His mouth came down on hers and *not* in a polite, celebration kiss. This was a hungry joining that kicked the New Year off with one hell of a start.

Sabrina was so lost in it, so consumed by it, she barely heard the shrill whistle of a rocket launched high into the sky. Marco ended the kiss just as the night exploded in balls of brilliant red.

He hadn't exaggerated, she decided some twenty minutes later. Naples's pyrotechnic display *had* to be the best in Italy. Synchronized to a compilation of Puccini's most famous arias, it was a joyous symphony of color and light and sound. Sabrina enjoyed every moment of the show.

She enjoyed it even more when Marco steered her to a dim corner of the terrace. Hands clasped around her waist, he lifted her to sit on the balustrade. He stood next to her, at eye level for a change.

Roman candles and starbursts continued to explode overhead. The revelry in the streets below reached fever pitch. Yet they might have been alone in the night.

His face cast in shadows, Marco reached up to tuck a wayward strand behind Sabrina's ear. "Do you remember asking me if Italians make New Year's resolutions?"

"I do. And as I recall, you said that was an all-American tradition."

"I've decided to make one tonight."

She had to smile at his solemn expression. "Want to tell me what it is?"

"It's you, Sabrina *mia*."

As if consumed by the need to touch her, Marco drew his fingertips across her cheek, brushed her lips, cupped her chin.

"I know we agreed to move one step at a time. I know you're still wrestling with the idea of opening an office in Rome. I know I'm pushing when I should be patient. But I've resolved to do whatever I can, whatever I must, to keep you in Italy. And in my heart."

Sheer surprise took her breath away.

"That's… That's some resolution," she managed finally on a shaky laugh. "They usually run more to shedding a few pounds or balancing the checkbook."

"My checkbook is balanced and I don't need to lose weight."

She couldn't argue with that. The body pressing against hers was iron hard.

"And just so you know," he murmured as he bent to brush her mouth with his, "I intend to keep this resolution."

Eleven

The ball officially ended at 2:00 a.m., after which the duchess and most of the older guests said good-night. Fifty or so of the younger set partied until dawn.

Marco played host for the champagne breakfast that greeted *Il Capodanno*—New Year's Day. The lavish spread was served on the terrace with the umbrella heaters glowing to chase away the night chill. As the first gold rays of dawn silhouetted the magnificent cathedral dominating Naples's skyline, corks popped and glasses clinked.

Marco tipped his glass to Sabrina's. "To new beginnings."

"To new beginnings," she echoed, her lungs

squeezing at the picture he made in the slowly gathering light.

He'd yanked on the ends of his tie to undo the bow and popped the top two buttons on his white shirt. The tie dangled loosely below a chin and cheeks showing a faint dark bristle. How the hell did he manage to look so sophisticated and so hot at the same time?

"Thank you for including me in these celebrations," she said with a smile. "I've had a wonderful time."

"Ah, but the best is yet to come."

"There's *more?*"

"I'm hoping there will be *less,*" he countered with a slow grin. "I've yet to see you in—or out of— those lacy red briefs you purchased at the boutique."

Sabrina's incipient weariness vaporized on the spot. "I just might be able to accommodate you there, fella. When can we ditch this crowd?"

Luckily, the party was already beginning to break up. Marco's soccer-player friend led the charge by scraping back his chair.

"Time for our traditional *Il Capodanno* swim in the bay," he announced. "Who's with me?"

He recruited ten hearty souls. Another dozen or so decided to tag along to watch. The remaining guests gathered their belongings and left, as well.

"Thank God," Marco muttered when he'd bid the last of them goodbye.

He took the time to thank the servers waiting to

clean up and pass each a generous tip before he turned to Sabrina, his eyes hot.

"I've been waiting for this all night."

The servers exchanged amused smirks as His Excellency scooped her into his arms. More than a little breathless with anticipation, she looped her arms around his neck. Her pulse leaped into high gear as he carried her up the stairs and down the long hall to his private apartments.

Marco kicked the door shut behind them, bent to flip the lock and strode into the master bedroom.

"Now, my beautiful Sabrina, we'll start the New Year in proper style."

He shifted his hold and let her slide slowly, sensuously to her feet. When he reached behind her to remove the topaz-studded comb and let her hair fall free, she felt him against every tingling inch of her. His chest flattened her breasts. His thighs cradled hers. His erection prodded urgently against her belly.

Too hungry for subtleties, Sabrina wedged her hand between their bodies and palmed his rock-hard length. The growl that ripped from the back of his throat shot thrills through her entire body.

He fumbled with the clasp of her gown and gave a frustrated oath when he couldn't figure out how to unhook the glittering leopard draped over her shoulder.

"Here." On fire with need, she brushed aside his hands. "Let me."

The gold lamé slithered over her hips and pooled around her jeweled sandals. Sabrina stepped out of the gown, kicked off her sandals and stood before him, naked except for the red lace hipsters.

"Now you. I want to see you."

He tugged off his tie, tossed it aside and shrugged out of the black tails. The tailored jacket hit the floor. The red sash came off over his head.

Sabrina held on to the sash while he shucked the rest of his clothing. With a wicked smile, she draped the wide red satin over his bare chest.

"There. Now we're a matched set."

She realized her mistake the moment he tumbled her to the bed and the jeweled decoration pin gouged into her left breast.

"Oooops! That's gotta go."

She wiggled out from under him and yanked the sash over his head again. Marco used the brief separation to tug down her panties. Kneeing her legs apart, he repositioned himself between her thighs and surged into her with an urgency that had Sabrina gasping with delight.

It must have been the long night. Maybe the champagne. Whatever the reason, it didn't occur to her that they hadn't so much as *thought* about a condom until he pulled out and thrust in again. By then, she was beyond stopping him *or* herself.

Marco dragged himself out of bed before noon but insisted Sabrina burrow in to catch up on missed sleep. She didn't argue. The long night and early morning activities had drained her.

She woke again around 3:00 p.m. and stretched languorously before padding into the bathroom. A hot, pounding shower sluiced away the lingering effects of the long night and the aftermath of their lovemaking. In the midst of soaping off the sticky residue between her thighs, she had to battle a sudden wave of worry.

Okay. All right. No need to panic. One bout of glorious, reckless sex did not a baby make. Hopefully!

Unless...

Her fingers clenched on the washcloth as Marco's New Year resolution leaped into her head. How had he phrased it? He would do whatever he could, whatever he had to, to keep her in Italy.

She dismissed the nasty suspicion almost as soon as it surfaced. No way he would stoop to that kind of dirty trick. Besides, even if one of his sperm *had* snuggled in, it would be weeks before the wiggly little tadpole made its presence known. Much too late to influence her decision to stay or not stay in Italy.

"C'mon, girl," she admonished as she rinsed off the soapy suds. "You need to get a grip *and* get your butt in gear."

Not sure of the plans for the rest of the day, she pulled on her calf-length black crinkle skirt and topped it with the fitted velvet jacket. Her ankle didn't give her so much as a twinge when slid on the black-beaded ballet shoes.

Consequently, she had a spring in her step when she exited the east wing and followed the blare of a TV to a sunny reading room overlooking the back terrace.

Marco was there, looking sexy as hell in snug jeans and a gray Italian-knit sweater that emphasized his wide shoulders. The duchess, AnnaMaria and Etienne were also present. Each of them had their eyes locked on the flat-screen TV mounted on the far wall. It was showing footage from the ball, Sabrina saw as she pitched her voice to be heard above the announcer.

"Happy New Year."

Four heads whipped in her direction. The duchess shot upright in her chair and waved an imperious hand at her son as she returned the greeting.

"Happy New Year. Marco, please turn off that annoying noise."

"You can leave it on. I'd like to see the…"

She broke off, her jaw sagging as a new image filled the screen.

There she was, in vivid high definition. Stretched out on a beach towel. Nude from the waist up. Her pubic area covered—barely!—by the minuscule triangle of her string bikini. With two small black squares blanking her nipples from the viewing audience.

She caught only a brief glimpse of the background before Marco stabbed the remote and killed the screen. It didn't matter. She knew exactly where and when that picture had been shot: Ipanema Beach—Rio—spring break of her senior year. With dozens of similarly clad coeds soaking up the sun on either side of her.

That was before MySpace and YouTube, so the photo had enjoyed only a brief shelf life in the tabloids. Not brief enough, obviously. The enterprising reporter who'd asked Marco about his new lover must have dug it out of the dustbin.

"Well, that didn't take long," she drawled, as embarrassed as she was chagrined.

"It doesn't matter," Marco replied with a shrug. "Women wear less than that on our beaches."

"True, but TV stations don't intersperse their pictures with footage from your mother's New Year's Eve gala." She blew out a ragged breath and turned to the duchess. "I'm sorry, Donna Maria. Very sorry."

"It's of no account," the older woman said with a shrug. "We have survived worse."

Sabrina couldn't quite hold back a wince.

"She means me," AnnaMaria interjected. "I almost gave birth to my son at the altar. The gossip columns, the cartoons, they ran with it for weeks. And Gia…" She pursed her lips in a moue of disgust. "That one made all our lives hell. Marco, especially, could not…"

"That's enough."

She flashed her brother an annoyed look but

yielded to his quiet command. Sabrina ignored the byplay. Her gaze had snagged on the newspapers scattered across the marble-topped coffee table. One was folded open to what was obviously the society page. A collage of the celebrities who'd attended the ball filled the top half of the page. The bottom half featured Sabrina's picture side by side with that of a vibrant Gianetta in a diamond tiara and an off-the-shoulder gown. The caption below the photos was in big, bold print.

"Sosia della moglie?" Sabrina struggled with the translation. "What does that mean?"

"It's nothing." Marco wadded the paper in his fist. "Nothing."

"Tell me."

With a muttered curse, he tossed the paper in a trash basket. "It translates loosely to 'the wife's counterpart'?"

"Oh. Of course. By counterpart, I suppose they mean double. I should have guessed it was something like that." She lifted her chin and pasted on a brittle smile. "So what are the plans for the rest of the day?"

"Sabrina, all this means nothing."

"If you say so."

He crossed the room in two strides and grasped her upper arms. "Listen to me. It means nothing. The hype, the speculation, it's only to sell papers."

"I know."

"You say that, but your eyes are flat and cold."

The eyes he'd just referred to flashed hot.

"Back off," she warned, her voice low. "This isn't something I want to discuss in front of your family."

"Very well. We'll discuss it privately."

He released her, strode across the room and bent to kiss his mother's cheeks.

"I'm taking Sabrina home, Mama. I'll speak with you soon, yes?"

"See that you do."

"*Ciao,* Etienne. AnnaMaria, kiss those brats of yours for me."

With Marco standing impatiently at the door, Sabrina had no choice but to thank the duchess for her hospitality and apologize once again for the less than flattering publicity.

"It will be old news by five o'clock," the older woman replied with a dismissive wave of her hand.

Right, Sabrina thought as she exchanged kisses with AnnaMaria and Etienne. It would.

Unless she and Marco continued their affair.

Sabrina's stomach churned throughout the drive back to Marco's villa.

Not over the substitute-wife headline. Or the seminude shot. Thank God they'd gone with that instead of the one an enterprising reporter had snapped after she'd stumbled out of party in a Los Angeles watering spot and promptly thrown up on the street.

What made her feel physically ill was the thought of putting Marco and his family through a repeat of what they'd gone through with Gianetta. Sabrina didn't know all the gritty details, but the few she *did* know cast a decided shadow over her romance with the handsome doc.

She couldn't blame anyone but herself for that shadow. She'd been so stubborn, so determined to resist the mold her father kept trying to squeeze her into, that she'd almost made a career of walking on the wild side. Now her past had come back to haunt her with a vengeance.

Miserable, she knew she had to articulate her feelings to Marco. She couldn't do it in the Ferrari, though. Not when its driver had to contend with hairpin turns and the rapidly descending dusk.

By the time they reached the villa, night had shaded the sea outside the windows to midnight blue. The restless waves crashed against the rocks below as Sabrina stood at the window, arms looped around her waist. Marco poured two snifters of brandy, handed her one and tipped his glass to hers.

"All right. We're alone. No sharp curves or oncoming headlights to distract us. Tell me why your eyes went so cold and empty when you looked at me this afternoon."

"It wasn't you. It was that newspaper—the photos—the caption." Her mouth twisted. "The wife's counterpart. God!"

"You don't believe that's why I want you, do you? As a substitute for Gianetta?" His eyes burned into her. "You can't believe it. Not for a minute."

"Of course not! But apparently that's what every-one else believes."

"Everyone, or a handful of editors and televi-sion producers who'll push garbage to build their audiences?"

"Oh, c'mon Marco. You saw the looks your friends gave me last night. The curiosity, the specu-lation they tried so hard to disguise."

"I saw them charmed out of that curiosity by an American beauty who bears only a superficial re-semblance to the woman they once knew."

"How can you be so sure it's superficial?" Sa-brina fired back. "You don't know me. You don't know my past. Trust me, there's enough juice there to give your handful of editors and television pro-ducers multiple orgasms."

"I don't care about your past. What I care about is *our* future."

"So do I!" She took a sip of the fiery brandy for courage and braced her shoulders. "That's why I think I should hop a plane to Barcelona tomorrow. I'll consult with my partner while things cool down here."

"Cool down?" His nostrils flared, as if the phrase had a bad smell. "You're leaving because of a few newspaper articles? I didn't think you were such a coward, Sabrina."

Stung, she lifted her chin. "Not a coward, a realist."

"Then we live with different realities," he snapped.

"Maybe we do!"

Okay, this wasn't how she'd intended the discussion to go. Dragging in a steadying breath, she tried for calm and rational.

"Everything happened so fast between us, Marco. A twisted ankle, a couple of games of chess and we jump into bed with each other. Next thing we know, my boobs are spotlighted on the Italian TV."

He wasn't buying calm *or* rational. Anger simmered in his terse response. "So your solution is to run away?"

"I'm not running away. I've got a bid proposal to finalize. I'll meet my partner in Barcelona, take care of business, and... And..."

"And what?"

He wasn't even *trying* to meet her halfway. Sabrina set her jaw and fought to hold on to her temper. She was doing this for his own good, dammit!

"And I'll call you."

His eyes narrowed. Above the V of his sweater, the cords of his neck stood out.

"You forget my New Year's resolution. Do you think I'll let you just pile into your rental car tomorrow and drive away from me?"

Her breath hissed out. With great care, she set her snifter aside.

"*Let?*" she echoed.

Impatience stamped across his features. "You know how I mean that."

"No, I don't. But I'm open to an interpretation."

"For God's sake, I'm not going to tie you to the

bed. Although I must admit," he added savagely, "the idea holds great appeal at the moment."

The sheer ridiculousness of that dissolved Sabrina's anger. She bit her lip, trying to hold back a grin, then gave in to her baser self.

"It sounds pretty good to me, too."

Marco's rigid shoulders relaxed. Against his will, against his every instinct, he let her tease him out of his anger. With an exasperated oath, he curled a hand around the nape of her neck and tugged her against him.

"Didn't anyone ever tell you to be careful what you wish for, Sabrina *mia?*"

She was sure he understood her intent. Absolutely convinced he knew she would leave in the morning. Otherwise Sabrina would have never spent those incredibly erotic hours with Italian silk ties knotted around her wrists.

When she emerged from the shower the next morning and told him she intended to call and change her flight yet again, Marco's brows snapped together.

"I thought we settled that."

"We did."

He rolled out of bed and dragged on his jeans in one fluid move. "You can't really want to leave."

"I don't."

Her gaze drifted to the ties still dangling from the bedposts. Everything in her ached for a repeat performance, but with Marco helpless and at *her* mercy this time. Sighing, she pleaded with him to understand.

"We need to give this some time and let the news hounds lock on to another juicy bone."

"Don't include me in that 'we.' I know what I want."

"Okay, *I* need a little time."

His jaw set. "How much time?"

"I don't know."

"A week? A month?"

"I don't know."

"And what am I supposed to do? Sit on my hands and wait until you decide the right time for us?"

The idea he might *not* wait made her feel a little sick but Sabrina didn't back down.

"I guess that's your call, Marco."

His eyes locked with hers for long, tense moments. Then his head dipped in a stiff nod.

"I'll go and make coffee. Buzz me when you're packed. I'll carry your bags upstairs."

Twelve

Sabrina hit the Autostrada and reached Rome's Ciampino Airport in time to turn in her rental car and catch a three-twelve flight to Barcelona.

She zinged Caroline an e-mail as soon as she purchased her ticket. Caro responded immediately, saying she would pick her up at the international terminal.

When she rolled her bag outside the Barcelona terminal, Sabrina was expecting to see her partner wave at her from the driver's side window of a green mini and cut over to the curb. She *wasn't* expecting the auburn-haired female who popped out of the passenger seat.

"Devon! What are you doing here?"

"Cal had to fly home for a few days," the tall, leggy redhead explained, enveloping Sabrina in a fierce hug. "I can't press ahead with the Logan Aerospace/Hauptmann Metal Works integration conference until I get his final list of attendees. So I decided to take a break from all the snow and ice in Austria and zip down to help Caro with the last of her site surveys. Here, let's toss your bag in the trunk and hit the road."

Sabrina climbed into the backseat. Devon got into the front and twisted around, her brown eyes sympathetic. "Caro filled me in on your close encounters of the ducal kind. We're dying to hear what happened."

"Not until we get to the hotel," Caroline pleaded as she struggled to nose the Mini into bumper-to-bumper airport traffic. "I don't want to miss anything. And you guys need to help me navigate."

Luckily the airport was less than ten kilometers from the resort Caro had made her home base. The pastel-hued hotel ringed a free-form pool fringed with rustling palms. Just yards from the sparkling turquoise pool, colorful sailboats and windsurfers cut through the blue-green waters of the Mediterranean.

The lobby reflected the area's rich history in its Moorish arches and bright Catalonian tiles, but the three friends barely took time to glance around before heading right for the elevators.

"I upgraded to a suite when you guys decided to fly in," Caro informed her partners. "At no cost to our client, of course."

Sabrina and Devon exchanged glances. Careful, precise Caroline Walters. They knew they could trust her to always—*always!*—play by the rules. She'd broken them once and paid a vicious price. Ever since, she'd walked the straight and narrow. Sabrina, on the other hand, was still paying for her past.

She waited to share the gory details until they all kicked off their shoes and plopped into chaise lounges on the suite's sun-drenched balcony with glasses of a local Spanish red in hand.

After admitting she'd fallen in lust at first sight, she described her time with the doc before cutting to the disastrous aftermath of the New Year's Eve ball.

"God, you should have seen the TV clip! They led off with shots of guests in long gowns and tuxes, looking so dignified as they mounted the front steps of Palazzo d'Calvetti. Then yours truly fills the screen, wearing nothing but a string bikini bottom and a stupid grin."

"They'd showed all?" Devon asked incredulously.

"All but two digital pasties blacking out my nipples."

"Whew! I can imagine how the duchess reacted. Caro tells me she's a real bitch."

"Actually, she was pretty cool about it."

Sabrina twirled the stem of her wineglass, surprised all over again Donna Maria's attempt to minimize the embarrassing incident.

"She said they'd survived worse."

Sympathy filled Caro's mist-green eyes. Devon just shook her head.

"That had to make you squirm."

"No kidding."

This is what friends were for, Sabrina thought as the tight knot in her stomach loosened a little. This is why the three of them had remained so close since that wild, wonderful year they'd roomed together at the University of Salzburg. She needed to be here with them, needed to talk through the emotions that had piled up on her in the past week.

"Marco's family has endured so much. His grandfather was gunned down on the steps of his home by Naples's version of the mafia. His father died when he was just a child. His wife was lost at sea."

She swirled her wine again, remembering the scene in the library when Marco had stared unseeing out the windows. Remembering, too, the rigid set to his shoulders as he described his wife's tragic drowning.

"He loved Gianetta—really loved her. Her death devastated him. I think he still blames himself for not getting to Naples in time to stop her from taking the boat out. I can't stand the thought of putting him through the emotional wringer again by having my picture splashed up next to his dead wife's all the time."

Devon cocked her head. Her hair spilled over her shoulder, glinting with red-gold highlights in the bright sun as she let loose with the unerring aim of an old friend.

"You don't want to put *him* through that, 'Rina? Or yourself?"

"Hey, you try standing in for a ghost sometime!"

"Do you really think that's what Marco wants? A replacement for his dead wife?"

"He said he doesn't."

"But you don't you believe him?"

"Yes, I believe him."

She did. She really did. From the first night in Marco's arms, she never doubted he was making love to her and not a memory.

"I guess... I guess it all just got to me."

"No surprise there," Caro put in with fierce loyalty. "You've had photographers snapping at your heels for most of your life."

"True," Sabrina admitted wryly. "And I did my damnedest to give them a show."

Devon brushed away the past with an impatient flick of her hand. "Let's talk about now, 'Rina. Inquiring minds want to know. What are you going to do about Marco?"

"Well..."

Her glance shifted to the waves rolling onto the beach below. They foamed on the shore, one after another, with a blessedly soporific effect.

"For the next few days, I'm not going to do anything but sit in the sun and think about his suggestion that we open a satellite office in Rome."

Devon's eyes widened. "He suggested an office in Rome?"

"He did. He also volunteered to use his contacts in the medical community to steer business our way."

Dev looked thoughtful as she turned the possibilities over in her mind. "You know, a liaison here in Europe might not be such a bad idea. It would sure cut down on travel costs."

"And provide a home base when we're working conferences or meetings over here," Caro added. "Definitely something to think about."

"That's exactly what I plan to do." Easing back, Sabrina stretched her legs out on the chaise. "Lay in the sun and think."

"Wrong," Devon countered briskly. "We have a proposal to put together, girlfriend. While Caro and I check out the last few sites, you can sit in the sun and crunch numbers."

Oddly, it was the sun that resolved Sabrina's nagging doubts early the next morning. Or rather, the lack of sun.

Caro and Devon had already left to scout the last two conference sites when thunderclouds rolled in and wind began to lash the palm trees lining the beach. Sabrina braved the elements to take her coffee mug out onto the balcony. She stood there with her hair whipping around her face and watched the sailboats and windsurfers scuttle in to shore.

Lightning arced through the darkening sky. Thunder boomed. Her heart thudded against her ribs. This was the kind of fierce Mediterranean storm that caught Gianetta. This was what killed her.

As if to punctuate her grim thoughts, another tongue of lightning speared down. The blinding flash seemed to sear right through Sabrina's doubts and confusion.

Marco's wife was dead.

Lost forever.

But *she* was alive.

Who knew how long they had? Who knew how long anyone had? Gianetta's tragic death had proved that. Yet here she was, dithering away time they might be spending together.

"Damn!" Sabrina slammed the coffee mug against the balcony rail. "I'm such a friggin' idiot."

Another ominous rumble of thunder sent her racing back into the suite. A frantic call to the airport verified there was a flight leaving for Naples in a little over two hours. A second call went to Devon's cell phone.

"It just occurred to me," she announced breathlessly. "None of us is going to live forever."

"*That* just occurred to you?"

"I could get hit by a car crossing the street. You could choke on a martini olive."

"I don't drink martinis," her bewildered partner countered.

"The point is, none of us know how much time we have left. It could be years. It could be days. Whatever time I've got, I going to spend it with Marco. Every minute. Every second. I want him. I love him."

"Then for God's sake, go get him."

"I'm on my way."

Sabrina slammed down the receiver, swore, and yanked it up again.

"I need a taxi," she informed the front desk.

It took her all of five minutes to change into a pair of jeans, a black, long-sleeved T-shirt and her faithful beaded flats. Another five to throw her things into her roller bag.

An hour and thirty minutes later, her Alitalia flight was skirting the storm that had rolled in off the sea and giving her one hell of a bumpy ride.

The front stretched all the way across the Mediterranean. Sabrina's flight landed at the Naples Airport in a torrential downpour. Soaked to the skin after a dash across the open rental car lot, she threw her bag in the trunk and set out for Marco's seaside villa.

Tackling those narrow, twisting roads in a car with windshield wipers sweeping furiously from side to side was *not* something Sabrina wanted to do again. Ever! She reached the villa a little past 1:00 p.m., dashed through the rain to the covered entry and leaned on the doorbell.

Rafaela's very surprised mama opened the door. "Signorina Russo! His Excellency does not tell me you are coming back."

"He didn't know."

"Come in, come in."

Shaking off water like a golden retriever, Sabrina stepped into the foyer. "Is Don Marco downstairs?"

"No, Signorina. He goes to Roma last night."

"Rome! But I thought... I was sure he told me he didn't have to return to the city until January fifth."

"The hospital calls," Signora Bertaldi explained. "There was an accident. A young boy, I think. His spine is crushed. They operate today."

Sabrina threw a look over her shoulder. Rain still pounded the foyer windows with unrelenting fury. Swallowing a sigh, she turned back to Signora Bertaldi.

"Do you know which hospital he went to?"

"But of course. *Bambino Gesù.* It is the finest children's hospital in Italy."

"Thanks. *Ciao,* Signora."

"Wait! You cannot drive to Roma in such a storm. Stay here until the rain stops."

She might have yielded to the older woman's urging if a thunderous boom hadn't reverberated across the sky at that moment. The storm sounded as if it would settle in the foreseeable future.

"If Don Marco calls," she said with a determined smile, "tell him I'm on my way to Rome."

Gritting her teeth, she tackled the coast roads again. A permanent knot had formed between her shoulder blades by the time she hit the Autostrada.

From that point it should have been an easy two-hour drive into Rome. Instead, the trip took a nerve-grinding four. Italians weren't as obsessed with speed as Germans, but they could lay it on when they wanted to. In a rainstorm like this one, the results often spelled disaster.

One pile-up snarled traffic for at least forty minutes. The second accident was on the other side of the divided highway but rubbernecking drivers in Sabrina's lanes dropped the pace to a near crawl.

Consequently, she hit Rome's sprawling outskirts just in time for the evening rush hour. Most of the commuters were headed out of the city, thank God, but the rain and busy city streets made even going against the bumper-to-bumper flow a nightmare.

She got lost twice trying to find the children's hospital. When she finally pulled into its parking lot, her jaw ached from grinding her teeth. Rain pelted her head and shoulders as she rushed into the lobby. Her soggy ballet shoes squishing, she zeroed in on the reception desk.

"Dr. Calvetti was supposed to operate here today," she said in her halting Italian. "Can you tell me if he's finished with the surgery?"

A few clicks of a keyboard returned the information that Dr. Calvetti was still in Operating Theater 2. Sabrina got directions to the surgical waiting room and hit the elevators.

One glimpse of the couple hunched side by side in the waiting room convinced her she shouldn't intrude. The boy's parents, she guessed. They were in their early thirties, but fear added years to their white, strained faces. Other family members clustered around them, tense and silent.

Sabrina backed away and opted to pace at the end of the hall. She was too antsy to sit after the long drive in any case…and too unsure of what Marco's reaction would be when he saw her.

Her wet, rubber-soled shoes squeaked on the tiles. With each step she breathed in the smell of antiseptic and tried not to remember the uneasy sensation in the pit of her stomach when Marco had asked what he was supposed to do while she took time to think.

She'd left him only yesterday morning. He couldn't have changed his mind about her, about what they could have together, in such a short time.

Except…

She'd changed hers.

With a little groan, Sabrina rubbed the wet sleeves of her T-shirt to disperse the goose bumps. She needed coffee, she decided—hot, steaming coffee. Better yet, the sledgehammer wallop of espresso.

The waiting room probably had a pot going but again she hesitated to intrude. Instead, she searched out a vending machine one floor down. The face that looked back at her from the machine's mirrored front drew another groan.

She looked like a hungover raccoon. Her hair straggled in wet tails. She'd chewed off any trace of lip gloss. Smudged mascara ringed her eyes. Grimacing, she grabbed her espresso and made a quick side trip to the ladies' room to attack the smears with a wet paper towel. A quick comb and a swipe of gloss later, she tossed down the thick, black coffee and headed back upstairs.

The caffeine provided exactly the jolt she needed. Sabrina was still savoring its bite when she reached the surgical waiting area. Loud, wracking sobs from the waiting room stopped her in her tracks.

Dread crashed through her in swamping waves. In her mind's eye, she saw that desperate couple hunched together. Aching for them, Sabrina peered into the waiting room.

The scene inside confirmed her worst fears. Marco was there, wearing green scrubs and antibacterial booties over his shoes. A surgical mask dangled from his neck. He had an arm around the shoulders of a woman who leaned into his chest, weeping uncontrollably.

Sabrina's heart sank like a stone.

It leaped up again a moment later, when the woman tipped her head back.

Those were tears of joy! She was smiling brilliantly through her sobs. And her husband stood beside her, pumping Marco's hand over and over.

"Thank you, Doctor. Thank you. Thank you."

Sabrina couldn't help it. She welled up, too. Big, fat tears that soon had her nose and eyes running like faucets. Edging away from the waiting room, she waited for Marco in the hall.

He emerged a good ten minutes later, smiling and rubbing the back of his neck. He looked both elated and totally exhausted.

Then he saw her.

Slowly, so slowly, he lowered his arm. She waited, her heart hammering, while his glance dropped from her still damp hair to her squishy shoes.

"Why are you wet?"

She gave a shaky laugh. She'd lined up answers to all the questions she'd thought he might ask her. That wasn't one of them.

"It's raining out. Has been all day."

He turned to the windows and lifted a brow in surprise. "So it is."

"How long have you been in surgery?"

"Since ten this morning."

"The boy? He's okay?"

"He'll need months of physical therapy, but I think he'll walk. But how did you know…?"

"I flew into Naples and drove to the villa. Signora Bertaldi told me you were here. So I jumped back in the car and drove to Rome."

"From Positano?" The beginning of a smile tugged at his mouth. "You must have ridden the brake all the way to the Autostrada."

"Pretty much."

"Why, Sabrina? Why are you here?"

At last! The question she'd been waiting for.

"I thought maybe you could help me find an office to lease."

A smile spread across his face, wiping out the lines of exhaustion. He strode over to her and cupped a hand under her chin.

"Before I drag you into the nearest exam room, tell me what brought you back."

"My New Year's resolution."

"I don't remember you making one."

"I did—that day we had dinner with your mother. We were in her Rolls driving through Naples. It hit me that we only had a few more days together. I vowed then and there to make the most of every minute."

"And now?"

"Now we have all the time in the world," she said with a misty smile, "and I intend to make the most of every minute. If you're a good boy, I might even teach you a few new chess moves."

Grinning, he wrapped an arm around her waist. All Sabrina had to do was lean against him to know she'd come home.

"You'll find me a very apt pupil. As long as the game is strip chess."

* * * * *

The Faithful Wife

DIANA
HAMILTON

Diana Hamilton is a true romantic and fell in love with her husband at first sight. They still live in England, in the fairy-tale Tudor house where they raised their three children. Now the idyll is shared with eight rescued cats and a puppy. But despite an often chaotic life-style, ever since she learned to read and write Diana has had her nose in a book—either reading or writing one—and plans to go on doing just that for a very long time to come.

PROLOGUE

CHRISTMAS morning.

Bella leaned towards the mirror and stroked bright scarlet onto her lush mouth. A flag of defiance? Or an attempt to remind herself that she was still alive?

She recapped the lipstick and dropped it into her bag, then shrugged a soft leather jacket over the misty-heather sweater that matched her worn denims. She breathed irritably through her nostrils as her hair caught beneath the collar. Grabbing the long, silky black length of it in both hands, she secured it punitively in an elastic band.

It had once been her trademark—or one of her trademarks. Her silky jet hair, her lush scarlet mouth and the startling contrast of water-clear silver eyes had earned her the envied, yet oddly unenviable position of top photographic model of the decade.

A position of make-believe, of clever camera angles, exotic backdrops and the wizardry of the make-up artist—a position she'd gladly jettisoned when she'd married Jake. Preferring reality, as she'd perceived it then. The reality of being the wife of one of the most successful financial brains to work in the City, the sexiest, most charismatic, strong-minded man she had ever met. Jake Fox.

But the reality had been his, not hers. The real world had proved a hard place to live in when his reality had been his inability to give her what she wanted.

They had met and married in a breathtakingly short space of time. For him, she now knew, it had been lust at first sight. For her something different—so different that it meant a meeting point was impossible. She pushed that thought out of her head.

It was over. She had to keep that stark reality to the forefront of her mind.

She wouldn't think about anything else—the might-have-beens or if-onlys. Not now. Not until she could begin to hope to cope with it.

Snatching up her hastily packed case, she walked from the bedroom where memories of their lost and glorious passion seemed to echo mockingly from the very walls. She dared not risk a backward glance because if she did she feared she might change her mind and stay until he decided to come home, then beg for the chance to try again, and resign herself to a life of shattered dreams.

But she had too much self-respect for that. He had proved himself incapable of giving her what was her due. She couldn't allow herself to live with that.

Her chin lifted with stoic determination as she walked through to the elegant sitting room, avoiding the state-of-the-art kitchen where last night's celebration meal was cold and congealing in delicate bone china serving dishes.

Her fingers were shaking as she took the note from her bag. She'd written it in the early hours, after he'd walked in unexpectedly on her and Guy; after that blisteringly savage word he'd thrown at her; after he'd walked out to heaven only knew where.

It was to have been their third wedding anniversary celebration, and it had turned into a wake.

When he'd phoned from the States four days ago she'd begged him to wrap up his business meetings and get home for their anniversary. A quiet celebration for two. She'd told him they had to talk and find a way through to each other. His tone had been gentler, more loving than she'd heard it in ages, when he'd assured her he'd be home in good time—as if he, too, knew they had to cement the cracks instead of blindly papering them over; as if he too needed to draw closer, reaffirm their vows.

But he hadn't come. All day she'd waited, made preparations, planning the perfect menu, choosing his favourite wine, dressing herself at last in the little black silk creation he always said made her look sexy enough to short circuit his brain. All the time listening, ears straining for the sound of him walking through the door, her eyes flicking repeatedly to her tiny gold-banded wrist-watch, her pulse rate quickening with mounting anxiety.

By ten she'd just about given up hope, given up entirely on the spoiled meal. And when she'd heard the phone ring out half an hour later she'd picked it up, almost sobbing with relief. She'd been convinced it was Jake, letting her know he'd been delayed, apologising, letting her know he was on his way.

When it had turned out to be Guy Maclaine, business associate and long-time friend, calling to wish her merry Christmas and tell her his wonderful news, she'd gone to pieces, angry tears flooding down the phone lines because Jake had obviously forgotten his promise to be here. And because her relationship with Guy went back years, was very special, he'd come straight round. And half an hour later—wouldn't you know it?—Jake had walked in.

By then, of course, it had been too late.

She propped the note against the empty wine bottle on one of the glass-topped tables where he would be sure to see it—if and when he returned. It, the bottle and the single glass were the only discordant notes in what was otherwise a perfect room. It took some doing, as much courage as she had, because that farewell letter was so final. It ended their marriage.

But she did it. She had no real choice. And took several moments to compose herself, standing by the great sweep of the windows that looked out over the Docklands development.

Everywhere, as far as the eye could see, amidst the sprawling tense unseen family gatherings, then a stiffening of her spine. This was the worst Christmas Day she had ever had to face. But she wouldn't think about it.

Bella took up her case and walked out.

CHAPTER ONE

DECEMBER 23rd. Almost a year later.

'It seems a long way to come for a few days' break,' Bella ventured, staring through the afternoon murk at the towering hillsides. Now she knew why this range went by the name of The Black Mountains!

'Nearly there, so stop grumbling!' Evie countered blithely, changing gear as they left the road for what looked like a sheer mountain track. 'It's going to be fun, I promise. Better than being cooped up in that London flat of ours for the entire holiday.'

Fun? It was a bitter reminder that the past year had been anything but. Just work and more work, taking her position as head of the agency's New Accounts section so seriously that over one of their rare, leisurely lunches Guy had warned her, 'Sweetheart—never mind everything else we've got going for us—I'm talking as your boss now, and I'm telling you to slow down.'

He'd taken her hand across the table, stroking it softly, his dark eyes concerned. 'I know life can be a bitch, and things aren't going your way right now. But working yourself to a standstill won't help either of us. You're in danger of pushing yourself into a physical breakdown.'

It was a view shared by Evie. Not that she'd ever come right out with it, but it was there in her eyes.

9

In the space of twelve months Bella had become a dedicated workaholic, using every spare minute, not allowing herself time to brood. Was that why Jake had worked so hard? To stop himself thinking about the way their marriage had been slowly unravelling, falling apart? Had he found their relationship unfulfilling right from the day he'd woken up to discover his lust had been finally slaked and there was nothing else left?

Her breath caught. She swallowed the lump in her throat with ferocity. She wouldn't let herself think about it. Or him. Ever.

It would be a long time before she would be strong enough to take out and examine just what she had lost—contemplate the disintegration of precious dreams, the slow and devastating demise of the expectations that had turned into a nightmare, without falling apart.

'It will be different,' she said. Her voice was soft as she glanced affectionately at her sister, watching the way those bright blue eyes narrowed as she concentrated on the increasingly steep and narrow track ahead, her dark curls clustering around her pretty, plump face.

This break—a week in a rented holiday cottage in the Welsh mountains—had been Evie's surprise Christmas gift. Even if Bella would have preferred to pretend Christmas wasn't happening and take enough work back to the flat she had shared with Evie since her marriage had fallen apart to keep her occupied until she could get back to the office early in the New

Year, she wouldn't have dreamed of saying so, of throwing Evie's good intentions back in her face.

'Look—' She consciously brightened her voice, making herself take an interest. 'There's already snow on the mountain tops.' Against a bright blue sky it was sparkling, festively pretty. 'I hope you've brought a shovel. If this cottage we're staying in gets buried in ten-foot drifts you're going to need it!'

'No worries!' There was a hint of banked-down excitement in Evie's voice. 'The forecast on the telly promised clear skies and frosts for the entire holiday period. The only hard graft, big sister, will be building the fire up. Promise!'

She'd have to take her sister's word for it. She rarely, if ever, watched the small screen herself. She'd tried to begin with, especially when Evie stayed in to watch something she said was unmissable. Unable to concentrate on the moving images, Bella had conjured up his face every time—Jake as she'd last seen him, the hard, handsome features stamped with bitterness and contempt.

'Keeping the fires burning can be your holiday job, kiddo.' She was doing her best to enter into the spirit of this unusual Christmas gift, to ignore the scaldingly angry pain that the mere thought of Jake sent through her. 'I'll cook the turkey—you did say everything was supplied?'

She didn't need to ask. Evie had been bombarding her with every last detail ever since she'd sprung the surprise the evening before. But it gave her something to say, something to give the impression that she was looking forward to the break, taking an appreciative interest.

Strangely, her sibling seemed at a loss for words right now, clearing her throat before she pointed out, 'According to the instructions, it should be just over the brow of this hill.'

'You're the driver.' And thank heavens for that. Bella knew she would never have found her way through this bleak landscape of winter-bare mountains and the network of rutted tracks without radar, yet Evie was driving her bright red Corsa as if she'd made the journey a thousand times before.

Sure enough, as they crested the brow the cup-shaped valley below cradled a slate-roofed stone cottage backed by a windscreen of spruce, bounded on three sides by a narrow mountain stream. In the summer it would be idyllic, a popular holiday let for people who valued solitude and simple pleasures. But in the heart of the winter?

Bella suppressed a shudder and turned on a smile. Little Evie, bless her, had done this for all the best reasons. She wasn't to know that nothing, but nothing on God's earth could stop her remembering that tomorrow would be her fourth wedding anniversary—and the day after that a whole empty, hateful year since she'd finally conceded her marriage was over.

She'd tried; heaven knew she'd tried to purge him and their ill-destined marriage from her mind, but had dismally failed. He had a way of sneaking inside her head when she was least expecting it. She hated it when that happened; it made her feel she had no control over her thoughts.

'Looks cosy,' she remarked, falsely bright, trying not to notice the sudden rush of agony to her heart. The little car bounced to a halt beside the narrow wooden footbridge that spanned the stream a few yards from the cottage. Small-paned windows were built into stout stone walls, and there was a door that looked solid enough to withstand a hurricane. Bella undid her seat belt and twisted round, reaching into the back for the two canvas bags, quickly packed last night.

'We won't need much,' Evie had stated. 'Jeans and sweaters and lots of woolly socks.'

Bella had both bags out and was shivering in the icy wind, but Evie looked glued to the drivers' seat, her voice high and thin as she smacked a fist against her forehead theatrically and wailed, 'Oh, I'm such a fool! You're not going to believe this!'

'You forgot the key,' Bella sighed, resigned to footing the bill for whatever damage they did while breaking and entering. Despite her expensive secretarial training, and her recent promotion to a high-profile job, Evie's brain sometimes took on decidedly birdlike qualities.

'Nope.' She threw the key and Bella fumbled to catch it with frozen fingers. 'The milk, eggs, fresh veggies. And the turkey, would you believe? The non-perishables are here already, but I was supposed to collect the fresh stuff from the farm we passed back there.' She restarted the engine, adding, 'I clean forgot. Go on in, there's a love. Get a fire going, huh?'

Bella shrugged, flexing her stiff body, pushing her long black hair away from her face with the back of

a gloved hand. It seemed sensible, but... 'How long
will you be?' She hadn't noticed any sign of human
habitation for what seemed like ages, and the weather
forecasters had got it wrong again. Suddenly the sky
was heavy with cloud, pressing against the mountain
flanks, the short winter day drawing to a premature
close.

'Half an hour?' Evie was releasing the handbrake.
'Get inside before you freeze.' And she was gone,
circling the car on the sweep of short winter grass,
narrowly missing the sturdy wooden picnic table that
wouldn't see any use until families came here in the
warm summer weather.

Bella smiled wryly, watching the little red car disappear over the brow of the hill. Trust Evie to forget
the perishables, drive right past the place where she
was supposed to pick them up! At twenty-five, three
years younger than Bella, and holding down a responsible job, Evie still hadn't outgrown her occasional periods of scattiness, or the impulsiveness that
was such an endearing part of her nature.

Bella shivered, glancing worriedly up at the sky.
Snow was beginning to fall, shrouding the tops of the
mountains. But if Evie had said she'd be back in half
an hour then the farm couldn't be far away. Funny—
she'd seen no sign of one herself...

Jake Fox pulled the hired Range Rover to the side of
the track and consulted Kitty's scrawled instructions.
For a schoolteacher his kid sister had appalling hand-
writing. And an unfortunate taste in men-friends if the
current cry for help was anything to go on.

His brows drew together, making a forbidding, dark line above the bridge of his thin, arrogant nose. The UK was the last place he wanted to be over the festive season. He didn't need reminders of the events of a year ago.

He was in the middle of a series of successful business meetings in Geneva and had intended to fly out to Sydney, book into a hotel and settle down to paperwork, readying himself for the raft of meetings scheduled for the New Year. No stranger to concentrated work, he now embraced it with what he himself could recognise as something amounting to obsession.

He thrust the underlying reasons for that out of his head, his frown deepening as he scanned the suddenly darkening sky, the thick, suspiciously storm-like shrouds hiding the tops of the mountains. If it hadn't been for Kitty's stricken desire for his time and attention he would have been heading for the sun...

But he'd been looking out for his sister ever since his father had brought the family to ruin, his addiction to gambling on the stockmarket losing them everything—the family-run business, the four-bedroomed house in the prosperous suburbs, the lot.

Even though Kitty was now twenty-six years old he still thought of her as the wild and troubled twelve-year-old he had held in his arms and tried to comfort when their father had taken his own life. Eight years her senior, he'd felt his responsibility keenly—especially when their mother, worn out with grief and worry, had succumbed to pneumonia six months after the shock of the death of her adored husband.

He'd never thought of himself as having a protec-

tive streak, he thought wryly. But perhaps he did, to
have agreed to cancel flights, hotel rooms and drop
everything when she'd put that call through to
Geneva, catching him at his hotel before he left for
one of his most important meetings.

'I need you, Jake. Spend Christmas with me? I've
got to have someone to talk to; there's no one else I
can turn to! And, yes, before you ask, it's Harry.'

The panic in her voice caught his attention. He said
heavily, 'I thought you and he were settled.' Of all
the men Kitty had dated—and to his knowledge they
came and went like the flowers in springtime—Harry
had become a permanent fixture.

Jake liked Harry, and had guardedly learned to trust
him. Steady, good-humoured, also a member of the
teaching profession, his influence on Jake's volatile
sister had been gratifying. They'd set up home together two months ago. Kitty's letters and phone calls
had been full of joy, and he'd planned to pay off the
mortgage on their roomy Victorian house as soon as
the banns were called.

'What went wrong?' he asked.

'I can't talk about it over the phone. But it's trouble
with a capital T.' Her normally bubbly tones were
absent; she sounded at the end of her tether. 'Look, a
couple I know offered me the use of their holiday
home in Wales. I need to get away and think, and talk
everything over with you. Please say you'll come,
Jake, just for a day or two? Please?'

He mentally jettisoned his plans for a quiet working
holiday in the sun. The thought of a cottage in the
Principality, in the dead of winter, wasn't going to

make him expire from over-excitement, but it was far enough away from London. He rarely made more than flying visits to head office now. Since he had sold the Docklands apartment.

So Wales it would be, and at least he could do his best to sort out Kitty's problems—something he seemed to remember having to do all through her teens and early twenties.

And she was saying, taking his silence for tacit consent, 'I knew you wouldn't let me down, bruv. Look, I'll post directions through to your London office. Drive up on the twenty-third. I'll try and make sure I'm there ahead of you, but, in case I'm not, there's a spare key in the woodshed at the back.'

And now, the final details of her written instructions committed to memory, he restarted the engine and drove on.

The whole package must have cost Evie a small fortune, Bella decided at the end of her tour of inspection. Two bedrooms were tucked under the eaves, small but cosy, with flowery wallpaper and high brass beds spread with top-of-the-range down duvets and patchwork covers. There was a sparklingly clean bathroom and farmhouse kitchen—pine and copper, with colourful rag rugs—complete with a real Christmas tree in a tub and a box of baubles waiting to be hung. The large living room was furnished with antique pine plus squashy chairs and a huge inglenook fireplace that promised long, cosy, relaxing evenings...

And, thinking of fires, it was time she got moving. It was the least she could do to have the place warm by the time Evie got back. And the best she could do was to forget her own unhappiness and put on a festive face, she told herself toughly as she wrapped the full-length, softly padded coat around her too-slender five feet nine inches and ran across the yard to the shed to look for fuel.

Ten minutes later she was squatting back on her heels, holding out her long-fingered hands to the dancing flames curling around the tinder-dry logs in the hearth, her ears straining for the sound of an engine that would let her know Evie was back.

She'd been gone over an hour now. A good half an hour longer than she'd predicted. Standing up, Bella switched off one of the table lamps and walked to the small-paned window, peering out into the near darkness. No need to worry. She forced her tight shoulder muscles to relax. Knowing Evie, she'd probably got into conversation with the farmer's wife, accepted a welcome cup of tea and then another, oblivious to the passing of time. But it was snowing heavily now...

It was snowing heavily now, the wipers squeaking as they cleared the windscreen. Jake gritted his teeth in a humourless grin. Kitty had said she wanted peace and quiet, time to think. Well, she'd sure as hell get it, stuck out here. And if the snow fell at this rate for a couple of hours there'd be no getting away; she'd have more time than she'd bargained for.

If it didn't stop in the next thirty minutes, he'd insist on driving her out. They could get to Abergavenny, find a hotel. He made his mind up quickly, with typical decisiveness, the deed as good as done. Then thanked his own foresight in hiring the sturdy four-wheel drive.

As the vehicle crested the brow of the hill the powerful headlights illuminated the isolated cottage. He breathed a sigh of relief. There was light shining from one of the downstairs windows. There was no sign of her car so she must have parked it at the rear. At least she'd arrived. The sense of relief told him how much he'd been worrying, wondering how she'd manage if she'd been late setting out, determined to make the rendezvous no matter what the conditions were like.

Bella saw the headlights and relaxed, smiling now. Evie.

Turning back to the fire, she fed it a couple more logs, dusted down her hands and went through to the kitchen, turning on lights and hanging up her coat on the peg behind the door.

She filled the electric kettle in readiness, taking two mugs down from the dresser. They would put the food away and discuss what to have for supper over a cup of tea. And later they'd open one of the bottles of wine that were lined up on one of the work surfaces. Really get in the festive mood—dress the tree. She owed it to Evie to do her damnedest to enjoy herself because her sister had obviously gone to a lot of trouble and expense to get this set-up organised.

She heard the clunk of the car door closing and hurried through. Evie would probably need a hand unloading. There was a smile on Bella's sultry lips as she tugged at the heavy front door. She wouldn't say 'what kept you?' or grumble about the length of time she'd been. She'd…

She froze, only her hands moving, going to cover her mouth as if to stem the cry of anguished outrage.

Jake. His tall, lithe body filled the doorframe, his broad shoulders made even hunkier by the sheepskin jacket he wore. Jake. The husband she'd parted from in a welter of anger and pain. The husband she'd never wanted to have to set eyes on ever again!

What in the name of sweet reason had brought him here? And how could she hope to forget him and all the pain and disillusionment, the shattered expectations of their marriage, when the cruellest reminder of all was standing in front of her, crucifying her with those cynical black eyes?

CHAPTER TWO

BELLA couldn't speak. The shock of seeing Jake again had paralysed her, and for a long, intense moment he too was silent. But the clenching of his hard jaw, the bitter twist of his mouth, said enough. Said it all—that she was the last person he had expected or wanted to see, that she was too contemptible to waste his breath on.

Her mouth dried and her stomach clenched sickeningly when he broke the dark, silent punishment, looked beyond her into the shadowy little hallway and called out harshly, 'Kitty!'

Clenching her hands at the sides of the soft warm leggings she'd chosen to travel in, Bella's eyes went wide. She didn't understand what was happening here, asked herself if the whole world had gone crazy, or if it was only her—or him. Then she met his accusing black stare as he switched his attention back to her.

The black glitter of his eyes was dangerous. Bella tried and signally failed to suppress a shudder. 'Where is she?' he demanded. 'If you and my sister have set this up—' He left the threat hanging on the air—heavy, implicit.

'I haven't seen your sister. Why should I?' She could answer him now, now the shock was receding, her heartbeat gradually approaching normal. 'I can't imagine why you should think Kitty might be here.'

Her water-clear grey eyes glinted coolly, but the small satisfaction of showing an aloofness she was far from feeling, evaporated like a raindrop in the heat of the sun when he remarked icily, 'Don't play games with me. I endured them when we lived together. When you walked out on our marriage I no longer had to. I don't intend to lose that freedom now.'

He strode in out of the dark, snowy evening, closing the door behind him while she flinched with pain.

She had never played games with him. Never. Not in the way he obviously meant. She had never told him lies. And it was he who had first walked out, not she. And although, as he'd stated, his freedom from their relationship was a relief, he was turning the tables, heaping all the blame for what had happened on her head. Did he actually enjoy hurting her? Couldn't he see that part of the blame was his? That he had driven her to do what she had done?

For a brief, poignantly remembered time he had given her joy. Now he only gave her pain.

Her mouth trembled and her eyes brimmed with tears, turning them to shimmering, transparent silver. Barely giving her white features a glance, Jake strode into the living room, and after a moment she reluctantly followed, only to hear his steps pounding up the narrow wooden stairs that led from the kitchen to the floor above.

She'd told him Kitty wasn't here and he didn't believe her. She crossed to the brightly burning fire and wrapped her arms around her body, shivering; the combination of the chill of the hallway and the spiralling nervous tension made her whole body shake.

She could hear him opening and closing doors. For some obscure reason he thought she and his sister had set this meeting up. But why on earth should they do that? It didn't make sense. Did he think she was angling for a reconciliation—tired of earning her own living, missing his wealth, the hedonistic, self-centred lifestyle that had been hers for the taking?

Whatever, his attitude left little room for believing that he would want any part of such an obviously untenable scenario!

She pressed her fingertips to her suddenly throbbing temples. Where the heck was Evie? What on earth could be keeping her? She should have been back ages ago. With her sister around for moral support she could tell Jake where to go, where to put his nasty suspicions. Evie would back her up. They hadn't seen Kitty and didn't expect to.

Hearing him descending the stairs, she resisted the impulse to blindly run and hide and stood straighter, pulling air deep into her lungs, the midnight-jet of her long silky hair heightening her pallor.

But he didn't seem to see her as he walked straight through and out into the night, and she thought, Thank God, he's leaving! and collapsed onto a chair and clasped her hands around her knees to stop them shaking. She let the fettered tears fall freely now because he was no longer here to see her weakness.

But he was. Within minutes he was back inside, snowflakes glittering on his thick dark hair. 'There's no sign of her car. Any car. She hasn't arrived yet.' His black brows bunched with concern. 'And how did you get here?'

'On my broomstick!' His reappearance, his wit-
nessing the hateful feebleness of her tears—the shock
of seeing him here at all—made her tongue acid. But
the level look he turned on her had her muttering defensively, 'I came with Evie. She had to go back to
the farm for provisions. We're spending Christmas
here.'

A Christmas break that was meant to take her mind
off the traumatic events of a year ago—not bring her
face to face with the man who had set those events
in train, the husband who now obviously loathed and
despised her, considered himself well rid of her!

Where are you, Evie? she agonised. She felt distraught, her sister's inexplicable lateness adding to her
distress. Her mind was painting pictures of the little
car stuck on an icy incline, or toppled over one of the
precipitous drops that seemed to cluster around each
and every one of the hairpin bends that made the
mountain tracks so picturesque.

She gritted her teeth. Picturesque she could do
without. She wished Evie had never had the bright
idea of arranging this holiday—and then her insides
churned around. What if Evie had invited Kitty along,
too? It was possible, given Jake's conviction she'd be
here.

She, Bella, had always got along well with Jake's
sister, but Kitty and Evie had struck up a firm friendship shortly after the wedding, where they'd met for
the first time.

Jake was convinced his sister was due here—had
she told him that much? Had he needed to get in touch
with her for some vital reason or other and couldn't,

not without coming in person, because there wasn't a phone?

Had he reluctantly driven up, swallowing his dislike of seeing his estranged wife again, because he had to talk to Kitty for some important reason?

If so, he would be desperately worried over her non-appearance, just as she was worrying over Evie. She took a deep breath and said, 'Was Kitty supposed to be joining us?'

She would have thought it highly unlikely, given that her own sister had booked this break in order to take Bella's mind off her broken marriage at this special and, for her at least, traumatic time of year. But, given his unshakable conviction, his very obvious concern...

Jake Fox dragged air deep into his lungs and exhaled it slowly, shudderingly, through gritted teeth.

She'd lost the small amount of weight she'd gained during their marriage, he noted bitterly—it had to be because of her return to her modelling career, he thought. But she was still the beautiful, sensuous woman who had drifted in and out of his dreams so maddeningly over the past twelve months. He could order his long waking hours with almost military precision, but he had found it impossible to regulate his dreams.

However, he was working on it.

He took a step towards where she was sitting, defensively hunched in an armchair that dwarfed her delicate frame, his body moving without direction from his brain.

Something about the hunted look in those crystal

eyes, the tremulous droop of the lush mouth that had been responsible for the birth of many a male fantasy, touched him despite himself.

That protective streak rearing its head again, he decided cynically.

'We need to get the facts out in the open.' Purposefully, he took the chair opposite hers. His heart was banging about under his ribcage but he'd sounded cool, in control, thank the Lord. He'd give up significantly more than his eye-teeth rather than let her know how she could still affect him and touch his heart.

He gave her a narrow-eyed stare. Her unbelievably long and heavy dark lashes had fallen, hiding her expression. The truth had always been there in her eyes if you looked long and hard enough to find it. As he'd found it—had had it forcibly thrust upon him—when he'd walked in on her and that creep, Guy Maclaine.

Abruptly he shifted his mind from that often-replayed scenario, watching her closely.

'You're here to spend a quiet Christmas with Evie, and you claim you had no idea Kitty was expected,' he stated levelly.

That was obviously what she meant him to believe. But he knew differently. Kitty, damn her, had used the ruse of needing to talk her problems over with him to get him here. She had needed peace and quiet, she'd said. Just the two of them. If her troubles had been as dire as she'd intimated she wouldn't have wanted his estranged wife and her sister around to add to the jollity!

Kitty wouldn't be turning up. That had never been her intention.

He watched Bella closely. Her confusion was very convincing. But to rise to the dizzy heights of top photographic model, internationally sought-after and universally fêted, she would have had to become a reasonably proficient actress. She could have set this whole thing up, drawing his own sister, and hers, into her web of deceit. Deceit had turned out to be her middle name.

She said nothing, merely nodded after considering his statement, the silky swathes of her hair falling forward, hiding her face.

'And I'm here because my sister begged me to be. She's in trouble, or so she said. She needed to talk and a friend had offered her the use of this place.'

The sardonic explanation of his presence brought her head jerking up, her silver eyes locking with his, clouded with more expertly portrayed confusion, her soft lips pouting with almost child-like perplexity. Over-acting, Jake decided, feeling his heart go hard— a not unusual occurrence these days. Her betrayal and subsequent defection had atrophied that particular organ.

'The three of you set this up.' A cold statement, spoken with concise deliberation. He could find no other explanation for the way he'd been tricked into coming here. 'If you'd wanted a meeting you could have made an appointment with my secretary. There was no need to go to such ridiculous lengths.'

He glanced impatiently at his watch. He had no intention of prolonging this farce. She deserved to be left here to stew, but his conscience wouldn't let him take that road.

He'd seen no sign of a phone when he'd investigated this place, so she couldn't contact anyone for transport out of here, and the way the weather was looking she could be marooned in the mountains for weeks. He'd drop her off at the first hotel they happened across on his way to Kitty's home in Chester. He'd rout his sister out of her cosy love-nest and give her the tongue-lashing of her lifetime for her part in this time-wasting piece of lunacy.

Bella pushed the hair off her face with the back of her hand. He was accusing her of conniving with their respective sisters to get him here. There could be only one reason why she would stoop to doing that— couldn't there just? To 'persuade' him to take her back.

'In your dreams!' She answered his accusation rawly. As if she would! His conceit was beyond belief!

She snapped to her feet, anger drenching through her. He had always treated her like a mindless doll, with no needs of her own, no thoughts that weren't his, without direction unless he pulled her strings. Simply a body to be seen on his arm, making him the envy of every red-blooded male around, and a gratifyingly willing body in his bed whenever he decided to remember to come home.

He wouldn't be able to believe she could exist and prosper without him. Even though he didn't want her anywhere near him, his conceit would make him believe she couldn't carry on without him and would go to any lengths to get him back.

He was on his feet, too, and the sheer breadth and

height of him swamped her, was in danger of sapping her will. But she wouldn't let his masculinity intimidate her. She would not! Drawing breath to tell him to get out of here, now, she held it, ears straining as she caught the distant sound of an engine.

'Evie!' she breathed, her eyes glowing with vindication. And not before time! She would back her up, tell this arrogant beast that any conspiracy was all in his twisted mind. Why should she want him to take her back when he was unable to give her the one thing she craved?

'Bravo!' Black eyes glinted with sardonic applause, even a hint of humour. 'Nice touch. But we both know your sister won't be showing her face within a hundred miles of this place, don't we?'

The story about Evie having popped down the road to pick up the groceries was thin, and that was putting it mildly. And Bella was still hamming it up, making a show of listening intently, so he, too, listened to the resounding silence, then snapped out an order.

'Get your things together while I rake out what's left of this fire. We're leaving. I'll drop you at a hotel.'

The faint sound of the engine had long since faded. A farmer making his way home along one of those tortuous mountain tracks, she decided tiredly. Disappointment hit her like a charging elephant. And then came the cruelly sharp anxiety. She stared at him, frowning, shaking her head.

'No. I'm staying here, waiting for Evie.' Didn't he care that something must have happened? Her happy-go-lucky, impulsive little sister had set out over two hours ago now, promising to be back within thirty minutes. Despite all his faults, he had never been a heartless man. So why wasn't he concerned?

Because he doesn't believe you, a weary little voice inside her head confirmed. He thinks the three of you set this up. She couldn't imagine why Kitty had been invited to share this break, or why she hadn't arrived yet. And she couldn't bother her head with it, not while she was so on edge, worrying herself silly over Evie's whereabouts, fighting to contain the pain of seeing him again.

She wrapped her arms around her body tightly. It was the only way to hold herself together. 'I'm staying. You go. Just get out of here.'

Stress made her voice tight and thin. He wasn't going to help find Evie, that was obvious. He didn't believe there was a thing to worry about, and was, as usual, too sure of himself and his opinions to be persuaded otherwise. But when he'd gone then maybe, with the trauma of actually seeing him again behind her, she could think of what to do.

He gave her a long, considering look, his jaw tight. Then shrugged the beginnings of misgivings away. They'd probably made adequate contingency plans. None of them were fools. Despite their plotting they must have allowed for the possibility of his abrupt removal from the set-up.

Without any doubt she'd have a mobile phone tucked away in her luggage, hidden amongst the filmy folds of the seductive nightwear she favoured, and as soon as he left she'd be using it to summon one or other of the girls to fetch her out of here.

Her pride wouldn't let her go with him, and he could understand that. Leaving with him would be tantamount to confessing that the star role in this farcical conspiracy was hers.

Bella watched him stride to the door, then sprang after him urgently, catching him up as he was tugging the outer door open.

'Phone the local police.' She couldn't use his name. 'The first call box or house you come across. Let them know she's missing. Promise!'

His heart missed a beat then thundered heavily on. He turned to her with warning reluctance, and for the first time he allowed himself to scan the face that had so relentlessly haunted his dreams over the past year. The lovely lines were taut with strain, the perfect skin white and transparent, terror lurking deep in those spellbinding eyes.

And for the first time very real misgivings flooded icily through him as he met his own fallibility. She'd been telling the truth—as she saw it. She wouldn't involve the police, set an area search in motion simply to save her pride. And if she had a mobile she wouldn't be asking him to do the phoning.

'Tell them I'll be here. I'll wait.' Her voice was ragged.

'OK,' he said roughly. He turned, then looked back at her. 'I'll contact them. And I'll be back.'

He saw her sag with relief, tears starting in her eyes, and resisted the violent urge to take her in his arms, hold her for a moment and comfort her. He walked quickly into the darkness, his throat tight, dragging his mind away from her.

Thank God it had at least stopped snowing. Even so, there was a good inch of the treacherous stuff underfoot. Swinging into the Range Rover, he reached for the key he'd left in the ignition then put both hands on the wheel, thinking hard.

The events of the last few minutes told him that Bella was desperately worried over her sister's non-appearance, that her story was true. She really believed that something dreadful must have happened. The shock of discovering that had driven Kitty's involvement out of his head, while anxiety over Evie's fate had never allowed it to enter Bella's.

In all probability they were both the innocent victims of a cruel conspiracy. He'd get to the nearest phone and contact Kitty before he involved the police. If his gut feeling was right, there would be no need.

There was a torch on the passenger seat and he used it to have a look at the time. A few minutes after six. Too early for Kitty and Harry to have gone out for the evening. Too late for her to be shopping. He should catch her at home.

He turned the key in the ignition and nothing happened.

Bella knew she had to pull herself together. Somehow. She moved briskly round the lamplit room, tweaking curtains, plumping up cushions that didn't need the attention, hoping the futile activities would settle her mind. A mind that was seething with all that was going on.

The shock of seeing Jake, here of all places. His cynical accusations. His cold admission that her absence from his life was a relief. Add Evie's disappearance to that little lot and you got a brain that was on the brink of blowing.

Sucking in her breath, she flew to the dying fire and carefully placed a few small logs on the embers. If Evie came back the poor love would be cold— She caught the thought, altered it savagely. Not if—when.

The police would soon be out looking for her, and that was an enormous consolation. She was scatty enough to have run out of petrol. Nothing more disastrous than that. And Jake had promised to come back and report, to wait with her.

The thought was deeply comforting. Yet she didn't want it to be! She wanted him out of her mind. It was the only way.

She turned from the replenished fire, satisfied that the fresh logs were beginning to flame, and Jake walked back in, his face black with temper.

As before, they faced each other wordlessly, until Bella found her voice and whispered, 'Did you find a phone?'

He couldn't have had time, surely? He'd only walked out a matter of minutes ago. She put a hand to her heart as if to still the suddenly violent pounding. Something was wrong. Terribly wrong.

He looked as if he wanted to shake her to within an inch of her life. His black eyes were ferocious, his jaw clenched, dark with the perpetual five o'clock shadow she had sometimes teased him about in former, happier, long-gone times, knowing he had to shave twice a day if he wasn't to look like a hooligan with piratical tendencies.

'Hardly.' His voice was dry. Coming further into the room, he removed his coat, tossed it over the back of one chair and sprawled down in the other. The hard line of his mouth told her he was controlling his temper, but only just; her head was beginning to ache, and there was an insistent thrumming noise inside her ears.

Both hands flew up to either side of her head, as if to hold it on her shoulders, as she rasped out thinly, 'What are you doing?'

Sprawled out in a chair while Evie was missing somewhere on the bleak, cold mountainside! Oh, how could he? Long legs in soft dark cords stretched out endlessly, only the tense, hard line of the hunky shoulders beneath the Aran sweater testifying that his pose wasn't as relaxed as he was trying to pretend it was.

'You tell me,' he came back, talking through his teeth. 'I'm in your hands. You win, for the moment.' He gave her a thin, completely humourless smile. 'Remove the distributor cap, take the rotor arm and no one's going anywhere. Evie's final chore before she high-tailed it back to civilisation? Neat. But not neat enough. I'm walking out of here at first light. You can do what you damn well like!'

CHAPTER THREE

'I'LL go with you,' Bella said in a tight, emphatic voice. She would begin the long walk right now; her need to get away from here, and him, was enormous. But she knew it would be madness. Better and far less hazardous to make the trek in daylight.

A strange calmness filled her. A kind of numbness. Everything began to slot into place, like the pieces of a hitherto exasperating jigsaw puzzle. She didn't feel any pride in the achievement. On the contrary, she felt used, betrayed. A fool.

'We've both been set up.' Was he feeling the same way? she wondered with a stab of sympathy. But she would need to develop a far more inventive mind to imagine him feeling foolish. Or used. He was always very much in control. Of everything.

She glanced up at him, but his features told her nothing. Blank. So what was new? Hadn't he always closed her out, guarding his emotions, keeping them to himself? Except when they'd been making love, she recalled unwillingly, feeling the colour come and go on her face. 'I'm sorry,' she whispered, her voice thick.

She didn't know why she was apologising. His sister was just as much to blame as hers. She heaved another log onto the fire, for something to do with her hands. She didn't know where to put herself; the sud-

35

den, swamping embarrassment at having been forced into this situation was intense.

He said nothing. Just stared at her. Bella verbalised her thoughts, putting everything in order, hoping that that would help her cope.

'They've been friends ever since we married. But you know that, of course. They obviously hatched the idea of getting us back together.' She smiled thinly, an acknowledgement of the vain futility of that forlorn hope. 'Kitty was to get you here, on some pretext or other, while my devious sister drove me down and dumped me. It would have been Evie who hung around until she knew you'd arrived, then spiked your car.'

She saw one dark brow slowly rise at that, but didn't grasp the significance—not then. She moved, heading for the kitchen. 'I'll make tea. But I warn you, there won't be any milk.' She was trying to be adult about this—this dreadful situation. They were in it together whether they liked it or not, until the morning anyway, and there was no point in behaving like a pair of squabbling children, sulking and not speaking to each other.

'Try the fridge,' he offered drily. He'd followed her through. She wished he hadn't. It was easier to act normally if there was space between them.

Bella plugged in the kettle she'd filled earlier. It felt more like a hundred years than a couple of hours ago since she'd heard the car arrive and had confidently expected Evie to come in out of the cold, needing a hot cup of tea.

She shook her head slightly at his suggestion, even

managing a small, condescending smile. There would
be no fresh provisions; she already knew that. But she
crossed to the fridge and opened it, simply to humour
him.

No one could have crammed another item in, even
with a shoehorn. Her wretched sister's doing! She'd
been nothing if not thorough! She'd been out all day
yesterday—Christmas shopping, she'd said. When in
reality she must have come up here, stocked the
fridge, made sure everything was ready.

'I can't believe it,' she said thinly.

Jake standing beside her now, murmured, 'No?'

Bella closed her eyes. Her head spun as the warm,
intimate male scent of him overpowered her, forcing
her to remember how it had once been for them: the
deep, endlessly intense need, the hopes, the dreams,
the loving—oh, the loving...

'Aren't you going to read it?'

The laid-back taunt made her eyes flip open, erotic
memories thankfully slipping away, extinguished by
his obvious and habitual disbelief in her which released her to enquire breathlessly, 'Read what?'

'Oh, come on, honey!' He reached for the stainless
steel handle and reopened the door.

Bella bit her lip. Why dredge up that old endearment? Why employ that tone—half-amused, half-
exasperated? The tone he'd used when he'd continually brushed aside every last argument she'd ever
produced whenever she'd tried to make him see things
her way.

'This is the next step in the game, I imagine.' He
indicated a rolled up piece of paper tied to a leg of

the fresh turkey with a festive bow of scarlet ribbon. He removed it, closed the door with his foot and handed her the paper, his eyes coldly mocking. 'Your cue to straighten things out, I guess. Exonerate yourself and put me in the picture—just in case I've lost the wits I was born with and am still staring into space, wondering why you're here and Kitty isn't.'

She dropped the paper as if it were contaminated. She was going to scream, have hysterics—she knew she was; she could feel the pressure building up inside her!

Turkey legs tied up with red ribbon! Cryptic notes he seemed to know all about! His attitude—oh, his attitude! Pitying yet contemptuous...

The paper was back in her hand almost before she knew it, his steely fingers closing over her own. 'Read it,' he demanded, his voice hard, intolerant of argument.

Hand on hand, fingers on fingers. The slight contact immediately became the core of her very existence. Every atom of her body, every beat of her pulse, was centred on his touch, the abrasive warmth of his skin, the underlying steel of sinew and bone.

A whole year, and nothing had changed—not for her. She only had to look at him to need him, and his touch—ah, his touch...

Her breath quivered in her lungs, fighting against the sudden, biting constriction of throat muscles, and his hand moved abruptly away, leaving her cold with a creeping coldness that invaded every part of her.

'Well?' he prompted cuttingly. 'Don't you want to

know what it says? Or perhaps you already know? Dictated it, did you?'

Her eyes moved to his, locking with the black, glittering depths until she could no longer stand the pain. A deep shudder raked through her, and her fingers were shaking as she unfurled the note.

Despite everything, he still believed she was the prime mover, that she'd set this thing up. Well, he would, wouldn't he? When had he ever believed a word she said?

It was the final straw, she thought, her eyes blurring as Evie's distinctive scrawl danced around on the paper. Her hands flew to her face, hiding the scalding outpouring of silent, unstoppable tears, the paper fluttering to the floor again. And through the storm of her emotions she heard Jake move, heard him drawl, reading aloud, every word a bitter punishment.

'You'll forgive us eventually, I promise! But it's all your own faults. Yes, really! You won't see each other, talk to each other, even though you're still crazy about each other. Yes, you are! So marooning you together was the only answer. We were driven to it! So work things out, for pity's sake. Happy Christmas! E.'

And then silence. A long, hateful silence while the sobs built up inside her, threatening to pull her to shreds. How could Evie have done this to her? Dumped her in this hatefully embarrassing, hurtful situation?

They'd always been so close, looked out for each

other since they were children—and now this, this shattering betrayal. Oh, how could she?

She'd accepted that something like this must have happened, but she hadn't taken it in—not properly. Not until now.

The sheer awfulness of the situation hit her—Jake plainly believing she'd masterminded the entire thing, the gut-wrenching pain of seeing him, feeling his contempt, the deep anxiety she'd gone through when her sister hadn't returned, her imagination working overtime, dreaming up worst-case scenarios!

Reaction set in, releasing a crescendo of weeping, her whole body shaking with the force of it. Then the shock of feeling his hands on her shoulders, turning her gently to face him, made it worse. So much worse.

She would die if he offered her the comfort of his arms, and she'd die if he didn't!

He didn't.

He wanted to hold her, but he didn't. Hell, if he took her in his arms he'd be a lost man! Common sense, the self-discipline of a rational human being, the primary human urge towards self-protection—all down the drain.

His hands dropped to his sides. 'Calm down. You'll make yourself ill.'

His shoulders rigid, he turned to make that forgotten pot of tea. Her sobs were a little less frenzied now, he noted. The Bella he had known had never cried. She'd had, in his experience, a pragmatic approach to problems. Yet she was clearly distressed now—deeply distressed—and all he could do was offer her tea?

She was distressed because he'd seen through the charade, because he'd realised she had to be the instigator, he reminded himself cynically. Had she really imagined he wouldn't. The whole thing smacked of complicity.

Pouring tea, he recalled how she'd drawn his attention to the distant sound of an engine. He hadn't caught it himself, but she'd obviously been waiting, ears straining, for the sound that would tell her the job had been done, and that Evie was triumphantly driving out of this winter wilderness with the rotor arm in her pocket.

She hadn't been able to hide her pleasure so she'd dressed it up as relief at the return of her so-called missing sister. And then, and only then, had she thrown herself into the anxiety act, begging him to contact the police, safe in the knowledge that he wouldn't be going anywhere.

Not tonight, at least. Tomorrow he'd be out of here, even if he walked the soles clean off his shoes! Although she'd said she'd go with him, he recognised that as sheer bravado. She could stay here and play the reconciliation scene to an empty house!

He turned, put two cups of tea on the central table. She was standing where he'd left her. Not weeping now, not doing anything. Her ashen face and the anguished twist of her mouth wrenched at his guts.

His mouth went dry, his throat muscles clenching. Had she wanted a reconciliation that badly? Badly enough to make her dream up this last-ditch farce?

Not allowing himself to even think of that, he said tersely, 'Drink this; you look as if you need it.' He went to the work surface where the bottles were lined up like an invitation to a week-long bacchanalia. He selected a brandy, noting the expense she had been prepared to go to, and poured two generous measures into glasses that he unearthed from one of the cupboards.

Bella watched him from heavy eyes. The hard, lean body was full of grace, despite all that sharply honed power. She knew that body as well as she knew her own. Better. She had never tired of watching him, of drowning in the effect he had on her—an effect that was threatening to swamp her all over again with its full and shattering force.

Her stomach twisted with unwanted excitement, her pulses going into overdrive, blood throbbing thickly through her veins. She whimpered, angry with herself, with the wretched body that couldn't accept that their marriage, their love—everything—was over.

She wanted to walk out of this room but couldn't move. There was potent chemistry here, keeping her immobile, a subtle kind of magic holding her against her will. She watched him turn. He was holding what looked like two huge doses of brandy in his elegant, capable hands.

'Sit,' he commanded tersely. 'Tea and then a shot of brandy could help.'

'I don't want it.' She dragged her eyes from the heart-stopping wonder of him, fixing them on the floor, not caring if she looked and sounded like a sulky child.

She was no longer his wife, not in any real sense,

so she didn't have to let him pull her strings, tell her what to do and when to do it. Not any more.

Besottedly in love with him, she'd never made a fuss when things hadn't worked out the way she wanted them to. She'd taken it for granted that, because he loved her, the decisions he made regarding the present and the future were the best for them. She'd believed he had some grand plan, the details of which had been a mystery to her.

Love had made her turn herself into a doormat. She now knew he had never loved her—couldn't have done—so was it any wonder he'd thought nothing at all of walking all over her?

Thrusting the disturbing revelation aside, she lifted her head and gave him a defiant look. 'I'm going to bed. I've had as much of today as I can stomach.' She was doing the dictating now, and in some perverse way was almost enjoying it. 'You said you'd be making tracks in the morning. Don't go without me.' She stared at him from glass-clear, challenging eyes. 'My sense of direction is nil, as you might remember. So take it as self-preservation on my part, not a warped desire for your company.'

Let him chew that over! Engineered this unlikely set-up, had she? Conceited brute!

She was at the foot of the wooden staircase when his terse voice stopped her in her tracks.

'Have you eaten today? You won't get far on what will probably turn out to be a ten-mile hike to get to anything remotely approaching civilisation on a diet of vinegary spleen.' His tone wasn't remotely humorous, nor even a touch compassionate. It was totally judgemental. 'Was losing weight part of your job requirements? Stick insects still high fashion, are they?'

She ignored the lash of anger in his voice. What did he care, anyway? She could get thin enough to disappear with the bathwater and he wouldn't blink an eye. It would save him the trouble of divorcing her.

But he was right about one thing—she should at least try to eat something. The walk out of here tomorrow would be exhausting, and the single slice of toast she'd had at breakfast was nothing more than a distant memory.

Much as she now hated to do anything he suggested—a backlash from the days when she'd practically turned herself inside out to please him—she turned back, and would have rooted around for the bread and some cheese and taken it through to eat by the probably dying fire, but he got in before her.

'I'll fix something. There appears to be enough food laid on to provision a garrison so it shouldn't be difficult. Why don't you drink that tea?'

No anger now, merely a smooth, impersonal politeness. It reminded her of her former attempts to be adult about the situation. So she'd play it his way— forget being bolshie, drink her tea like the man said.

It was tepid, but she got through half of it and ignored the brandy. He was sipping his as he moved around. Her eyes narrowed as she watched him. He was good in a kitchen, and she'd never known it.

She'd always been there, waiting for him to fit in a visit home between his tight work schedules. So pleased to see him, so eager for the time he could spare her—had condescended to spare her!—that she'd practically fallen over herself to make their time together as smoothly memorable as possible. After all, she'd had little else to do until she'd taken the initiative and gone back to work. He'd hated that!

The helping of grilled Cumberland sausages and tomato halves he quickly and efficiently produced was enormous enough to make her groan inwardly, and the mug of milky cocoa made her eyes go wide.

Had he secretly yearned for nursery food while she'd dished up sophisticated delicacies—potted shrimps, *navarin* of lamb, home-made sorbets so delicious they brought tears to the eye? All exquisitely served on the finest bone china—accompanied by superb wines, of course.

All the effort and dedicated planning that had gone into every meal she had ever produced for him, when all the time he might well have preferred a plate of sausages and a mug of cocoa!

Now she would never know. She most certainly wouldn't ask.

The forced intimacy of the situation frayed her nerve-endings, while the heart-clenching nearness of him on the opposite side of the small table brought the sensations she'd been battling to forget for a whole year burgeoning back to life. Which didn't help her appetite.

And she couldn't make an attempt at light, relaxing conversation. Relaxation didn't get a look in while he was around. And they didn't have a single thing to say to each other that didn't reek of contention.

Even the small sound of cutlery on earthenware

platters became too much to bear. She stood up, pushing back her chair more sharply and clumsily than she'd intended.

'Thank you.' She meant for the food she had barely touched, the cocoa she hadn't touched at all. 'But I think I'll turn in. One way or another, it's been an extremely unpleasant day.'

She made it to the stairs before he had time to respond. She truly hadn't meant to snap, but hadn't been able to keep the acid out of her voice.

Her hair prickling on the back of her neck, she bounded up the staircase. She felt like a rabbit with a fox on its heels. Jacob Charles Fox by name, and foxy by nature, she thought half-hysterically as she breathlessly gained the room she'd earmarked for herself long hours ago when she'd innocently believed she'd be sharing the isolated cottage with Evie.

But he didn't follow her, as she feared he might, to drag her down and force her to eat the food he'd cooked. Of course he didn't.

Why the heck should he want to bother? she reminded herself tiredly as she sagged back against the door, one hand at her breast as if to still the wild beating of her heart. Secure in her room, with no sound of following footsteps or angry commands from below, she couldn't imagine why she'd panicked.

He had done what he would have considered to be his duty. Reminded her that she had to eat, produced the food. It was up to her whether she ate it or not. He couldn't care either way. So the absence of a lock on the door was no problem either, was it? He wouldn't try to claim his conjugal rights.

He didn't want his rights. He couldn't care less.

Jake heard her thumping up the stairs, his mouth quirking with a reluctant smile. Her languid grace had always been part of her fabled mystique, and now she was clumping around like an ill-disciplined hoyden in hobnailed boots. She who had always been so poised, so amiably cooperative, had developed a will of her own—if his hijacking was anything to go on—not to mention a sharp little tongue.

She must have been desperate to try and work things out between them to have pulled a stunt like this.

He still didn't want to think about the ramifications, but knew he had to. And, let's face it, he hadn't made it easy for her to approach him in a more conventional manner—out of the country far more than he was in it, deliberately avoiding her and anyone who knew her.

He finished the remains of his brandy and leaned back in the chair, long fingers toying with the stem of the glass, his mind absorbed.

Over the past year he'd avoided all contact and allowed her none. His solicitor had paid her allowance into her bank account each month, and those of his staff who knew his movements had been instructed to be politely noncommittal if his estranged wife had ever shown any desire to know his whereabouts.

As far as he knew, she never had. It had appeared that she, too, had written their three years of marriage off as experience—one, in his case, never to be repeated—and was getting on with her life, with the resumption both of her modelling career and her steamy, hole-and-corner affair with the much-married Maclaine.

His mouth tightened. He could never forgive that ugly betrayal, her cold-blooded deceit. Never!

He pushed the empty glass across the table, picked up her untouched one, swallowed the contents in one long draught and snapped to his feet.

However long and loudly she protested he couldn't believe she was an innocent victim of sibling mischief. For one thing, his sister knew better than to take it into her head to meddle with his life. She knew he refused to have Bella's name mentioned in his presence.

He was sure Bella had set the whole thing up, somehow convincing Kitty that deceiving him into coming here was in his best interests. Not too difficult a task to accomplish, given the way she'd pulled the wool over his eyes through three years of marriage!

Well, she'd wanted him here and now she'd got him here, so they might as well have things out in the open. And whatever her reasons, and however desperate those reasons were, he had one answer only.

There was no going back. It was over. If she had any doubts at all it was time they were knocked on the head. And there was no time like the present...

He squared his shoulders and strode to the stairs.

CHAPTER FOUR

BELLA was too strung up to sleep. In any case, it was hours before her normal bedtime. The paperback she'd brought along to read wasn't making any sense. The words slid past her eyes. She was taking nothing in. She closed the book and shivered.

The room was cold, and to make matters worse she'd discovered that Evie—rot her socks!—had performed yet another major interfering act. Her devious little sister must have sneaked into her room at home while Bella had been in the shower and replaced the old, cosy pyjamas she'd packed herself with slivers of sheer silk and lace—the sort of seductive nonsense she hadn't worn since she and Jake had been living together.

Her first defiant thought had been to go to bed in the leggings and woolly sweater she was wearing. Every last thing she'd bundled into the canvas bag the previous evening had been replaced.

No serviceable jeans and cosy sweaters to be found, just fabulous designer gear, almost forgotten leftovers from her time as Jake's wife. They had been languishing, unworn, at the back of a cupboard at the flat she shared with that devious, double-dealing sister of hers!

She couldn't trek out of here, heading for

Aberwhatever-it-was, wearing a long slinky shirt or flowing silk trousers!

Nearly spitting with rage she'd stripped off the comfy leggings and sweater, reserving them for the morning, and hugged into a clinging dream of white satin-sheen silk, the tantalisingly revealing lace top supported by the narrowest, flimsiest of shoestring threads.

What had those two she-devils had in mind? A flaunting, a seduction, a reconciliation followed by Happy-Ever-After? What did they have between their ears? Fluff, or rocks?

Her eyes savage with bottled-up temper, she dug her head into the pillow and dragged the duvet up over her ears to shut out the sound of the howling wind. And heard instead the squeak of the door hinges, followed one second later by Jake's incisive voice.

'It's time we talked.'

'Get out of here!'

Bella shot up against the pillows, regardless of the next-to-nothing she was wearing, her eyes narrowed with temper. She had never been this angry in the whole of her life, and now she had someone to vent it on!

Her formative years had been spent in a restless round of moving from one place to another, the family being dragged by her feckless father to wherever the grass was supposedly greener but never was. She'd become adept at keeping her head down, quiet as a mouse, in case she got noticed and hauled into her parents' blistering, roof-raising rows.

Then there had been marriage to the man who could have given her everything but hadn't. And the only legacy she had from their marriage was bitterness.

She had tried to be everything he wanted her to be: glamorous, cool, acquiescent, the perfect wife, anxious—too anxious—to hold onto a will-o'-the-wisp, workaholic husband who was here today and gone tomorrow.

Here today and gone for at least a month! she amended in her head. Well, the black-eyed devil had finally walked out for good, and now she didn't have to subordinate herself to him or anyone else!

'I said, get out,' she repeated when he made no move.

He was seemingly rooted to the spot in the open doorway, his straddle-legged stance familiarly dominant, thumbs hooked into the back pockets of his jeans, dark hair falling over one eye, the unintentional designer stubble adding to the aura of rakish danger that was coming off him in waves, filling the room...

Tantrums suited her, he thought, hooded eyes appraising the wild black tumble of hair falling over naked creamy shoulders, the hectic flares of colour on those perfect cheekbones, the silver fire of her eyes, the tempting glimpse of pert, palm-sized breasts glimmering beneath the lace of that piece of seductive night wear he remembered so well. One out of many such pieces of sorcery, designed to send a man out of his mind...

He hauled his unwise thought processes back on line. Sure, she could still fire him up, but it was only

common or garden lust, not the rare and precious
bloom of love. That had died when he'd moved
heaven and earth to get back to her for what had been
left of their third wedding anniversary—and found her
wrapped around Maclaine.

Bleak anger settled in his heart, turning it to stone.
Had Maclaine dumped her? Was that what this was
all about? Had she set this thing up—wasting his time,
trying his patience to the limit—because she was conceited enough or stupid enough to believe that she
only had to bat those fabulous lashes at him to get
him to take her back, live with her and miraculously
forget she was an adulterous bitch?

Sure, she'd told him in no uncertain manner to get
out of her room. But that was only for openers; the
end game would be something else entirely.

She'd made no attempt to cover herself—and what
sensible woman packed such man-trap bait for a holiday in the winter wilds of Wales with her kid sister?

Her protestations of innocence regarding her part in
this wearisome farce would have held a darn sight
more water if she'd been muffled in flannelette right
up to her pretty pink ears!

'Right.' He cleared his throat. He tried to pull his
eyes from her but couldn't; they were stubbornly intent on drinking in all that sensual loveliness, and
there didn't seem to be a damn thing he could do
about it. 'Let's get things sorted out.'

His voice had husky undertones, Bella noted. Oh, he'd
tried to make it crisp, but he'd dismally failed. She
knew that tone, recognised the sultry gleam in those

hooded eyes. He wanted her. He couldn't disguise it. Not from her.

Two years into their marriage, around the time she'd gone back to work with Guy, he'd stopped wanting her. He'd barely been at home at all, and had been exhausted when he was. The lust that had led him to marry her had finally been slaked. But it hadn't completely died...

The shock of it made her stomach twist, ignite with curling flames of fever that rampaged through her body. She sucked in a sharp breath and dragged the duvet up to her chin. The passion of her rage with Evie and Kitty for landing her in this mess had encompassed him, making her oblivious to what she was wearing.

'Go away.' She knew she sounded feeble now, hated herself for it. And, far from doing as she'd said, he took a few more paces into the room. Any closer and she'd weakly give in to the temptation to beg him to take her in his arms, hold her and make love to her again. Beg him to take them both back to the beginning, when she'd believed everything to be perfect and that he could give her everything she wanted.

'I'll go when you've explained why you were so desperate to get me here.'

The delayed modesty, the wide, troubled eyes, didn't fool him. It was all a cynical act. It took one to know one, he thought tiredly, wanting to get this sorted out, packed away and put behind him as he had assumed—wrongly, it would seem—it had been for the whole of the past twelve months.

'You don't believe a word I say,' she accused, her

voice shaky. He thought she was a scheming liar. It hurt. It shouldn't, because she ought to be used to it, but it did. Unbearably.

Her eyes filled with tears. If he didn't leave this room, right now, she'd go to pieces, and her pride wouldn't let that happen twice in one day. Just as her pride hadn't let her try to make contact of any kind with him after he'd ended their marriage by walking out.

'Just tell me what it's all about,' he suggested tiredly. Suddenly he felt drained. He didn't want to argue with her, to have to play it her way and coax and cajole her into explaining herself. He wanted out.

Bella saw bored indifference, heard it in his voice, and anger stirred again, deep, deep inside her. 'How can I, when I don't know?' she said through gritted teeth. She saw him shrug, turn away, and knew she wanted to feel relief because he was on his way out but, perversely, didn't.

She wanted to beg him to stay, to stop accusing her of something she hadn't done, talk to her, just talk to her, treat her like an intelligent human being for once.

'Well, don't say I didn't give you the opportunity,' he said tonelessly. 'I can't force you to tell me why you set this up, and quite frankly I don't want to put myself to that kind of trouble. If you've blown the opportunity to tell me your reasons you've only yourself to blame.

'I'll be leaving at first light, and you won't be going with me. Even getting to the nearest farmhouse and a telephone won't be a picnic, and I'll make better headway on my own. Let me know if you want me to arrange transport to get you out of here.'

Closing the door behind him, he clattered down the staircase. No way could he spend the night tossing and turning in a bed only a few feet away from hers, with only a partition wall separating them.

Seeing her again had brought needs he'd subjugated for twelve arid months bludgeoning back to life. He was only flesh and blood!

Hell! Here he was, Jake Fox, subject of enough articles in the financial press to fill a ten-ton container, having made his first paper million on the money markets before he was twenty-two and now, at thirty-four years of age, the head of his own worldwide insurance company—yet he was totally unable to handle this woman and what she did to him, take her dubious machinations in his stride.

But hadn't she always made a sucker out of him?

Tossing an armload of dry logs on the embers, he sank into a chair, almost welcoming the hypnotic howl of the wind, the insistent memories that now could not be denied...

The very first time he'd set eyes on her...

The first time he set eyes on her she was wearing a gold satin beaded shift that shimmered when she moved. And how she moved!

Clutching an unwanted, untouched glass of white wine in his hand, he couldn't find words to describe what he was seeing—the sinuous grace, the endless legs, the softly seductive curves of hip and breast. The sheer poetry as her head turned slowly on the perfection of the long and fragile stem of her neck. The strange, fabulous eyes meeting his briefly across the room, holding for a moment—almost as if the contact puzzled her—before she turned back to her companion.

He was holding his breath, he discovered. He hadn't wanted to come to this party. But he hadn't not wanted to, either—just killing time until his dinner date.

'Eyes off, buddy!' Alex muttered at his side. 'The lady's taken.'

'Sorry?' Jake's brows met. He'd bumped into Alex Griffith in the City, just as he'd emerged from his Lombard Street head office, his mind still on his recent successful Far Eastern acquisition trip.

Friends since schooldays, they kept in touch more—as now—by luck than arrangement.

'Have dinner?' Alex had suggested.

Jake had shaken his head in regret, they had a lot of catching up to do. 'Sorry. I promised to feed Kitty at The Dorchester. She's thinking of applying for a teaching post in Chester. Wants my advice.'

'Not boyfriend trouble this time?' Alex's tawny eyes had crinkled at the corners and Jake had grinned.

'Happily not, it would seem. Though I'm not counting my chickens. Something like that could be behind the sudden need to move to the sticks.'

His kid sister brought as much dedication to her social life as she did to her chosen profession. And more often than not Jake was landed with the job of picking up the pieces. Looking out for Kitty was something he'd got used to. What else were brothers for—especially as there were no parents around to sort out the crises she seemed to thrive on?

'Tomorrow? Lunch?'

'Flying out to Dubai.'

'Tell you what,' Alex had shot a glance at his watch. 'I'm due at this cocktail thrash around now. Duty thing—know how it is? Daren't miss it, or I'd suggest a quiet drink. Why not keep me company?'

So here he was, almost wishing he'd not tagged along, until his attention had been riveted by the raven-haired beauty in the shimmering dress. He couldn't take his eyes away.

'Who is she?'

'The face of La Donna.' Alex hadn't had to ask who Jake was talking about. 'Shock to the system, what? I've met her once or twice. Got myself introduced during an interval at Covent Garden. But no dice. If I thought I stood a chance I'd be in there, trying my luck—along with the rest of the male population!'

Jake ignored that, dismissed it as an irrelevance, although it was to come back and haunt him time after time. 'The face of what?' The question was spiked with urgency, a tinge of irritation.

'Where've you been the last couple of years, buddy? No, don't tell me—too busy plotting how to make your company's next billion to read the glossies or watch the hoardings!'

Then as if he sensed the brooding intensity in the dark eyes that suddenly flicked his way, Alex cut the banter and volunteered, 'Appropriately, her name's

Bella. Bella Harcourt, supermodel. She was picked to be the face of La Donna—cosmetics and stuff. Since then her career's taken off in a big way. And the guy she's with is head of the agency which handles the La Donna account. Guy Maclaine—a big name in advertising circles. He took her under his wing from the outset.'

'And?'

'And into his bed. Rumour has it he's going for his second divorce, and that the answer to every man's sexual fantasies will be Mrs Guy Maclaine the third.'

Over Jake's dead body!

His eyes narrowed, intent, Jake watched the way she smiled at Maclaine, never moving from his side, her sinuous body curving into the shelter of his like a delicate vine seeking support.

Maclaine was a big brute, with the kind of near-ugly looks some women might find attractive. She obviously did. But if he could do it, he'd take her away from him.

He had never felt like this before. The assault on his emotions, the upheaval going on in his normally rational mind, would have rocked him on his heels had he not surrendered himself to the inevitability of what was happening here.

Without false modesty he knew he was what his mother would have called 'eligible'. Neither repellent nor in his dotage, and going places in the dangerously unstable world of high finance, beautiful women came with the territory. They came and they went; he didn't have time for a committed relationship and was always careful to point that out. But this—this was something very different...

He picked his moment, shouldering his way through the knots of brightly partying people just as Maclaine was politely allowing himself to be cornered by a red-haired, red-taloned woman of questionable sobriety.

'Jake Fox,' he introduced himself, catching a flicker of uncertainty in those strangely fabulous eyes, an automatic withdrawal. 'Single, solvent, law-abiding.'

He could have added 'besotted', but didn't. And wouldn't—not until he'd come to terms with it himself, with this new and terrifyingly exciting experience. But he wasn't going to waste time on preliminaries either.

'I'm giving my sister dinner tonight; I would very much like you to join us. The Dorchester. If you need reassurance that I am neither a seducer or a white-slaver, then Alex Griffith—whom I believe you've met—can vouch for my integrity.'

He angled his shoulders, effectively screening her from the rest of the party-goers, consciously staking his claim to her undivided attention. And watched as a million glittering lights danced in her eyes, her lush mouth quirking as she tilted her head back on her long, long neck.

His heart thumped violently. If she told him to get lost he'd have to try another tack, pursue her until she gave in out of sheer exhaustion!

The smile she had been trying to swallow defeated her, and she laughed. It was a ripple of perfection amongst the babble and shriek going on around them.

'You have an intriguingly novel approach, Mr Fox! Direct, but not explicitly offensive. Tell me, does it always work?'

'I don't know. I've never tried it before.' He grinned—probably fatuously, he thought. Her voice was as beautiful as she was. 'And it's Jake. And you're gorgeous. And dinner—you will join us?'

She gave no direct answer. 'You've been watching me. Since you arrived with Alex you've been watching me.'

A simple statement of fact. Yet it made his heart lilt. Apart from that brief moment when their eyes had locked she had, to all appearances, concentrated all her attention on Maclaine. But appearances were deceptive, because she'd been aware of him, aware of the way he'd been watching her, mesmerised. Aware. Of him. Maclaine might be her lover, but that didn't mean he couldn't cut him out!

'Guilty. But, looking the way you do, you must take the blame.'

Suddenly her poise fell away. Her head drooped forward and soft tendrils of the artfully piled lustrous, midnight-dark hair gently moved against the pale, fragile neck, awakening in him a deep, atavistic desire to protect.

It was then he knew. Knew without a shadow of doubt that he wanted to possess this woman in every way there was. Take her, hold her, care for her. Make her his, and only his.

Marry her.

If marriage had ever crossed his mind it had been as something to be thought about some time in the distant future. When the future was safe, secure. When he was sure—sure that what he had to offer was solid and firm, couldn't be blown away by the cruel winds of chance that destroyed home and family in their backlash. As he had seen his home and family virtually destroyed by his father's obsessive and disastrously unsuccessful gambling on the world money markets.

But she had driven all that caution out of his head.

'You will join us.' He made it a statement, as if there could be no question about the way their relationship would begin and develop. He didn't know he'd been holding his breath until she suddenly raised her head, the brilliance of her eyes, her smile, stunning him.

'You've made me an offer I can't refuse.' Mischief silvered her eyes with dancing starlight. 'I'm dying to meet your sister!'

Then, just as quickly, her smile faded and her eyes became thoughtful, as if she was wondering what it was that had made her accept his invitation. With a minimal shrug of exquisite shoulders she turned to murmur her excuses to Maclaine, and Jake knew then—precisely then—that she was his...

Bella and Kitty had got along famously; dinner had been an unqualified success. Even if Bella had given her attention almost exclusively to the younger girl he had been content to watch and wait, knowing by the heightened colour that had glowed along her perfect cheekbones, the way she'd immediately veiled her eyes if they encountered his, that she'd been just as aware of the sizzling sexual tension as he was.

Leaving her at the mews apartment she'd shared with her younger sister, he had taken her acceptance of his offer to give her lunch the next day for granted. He'd rescheduled his Dubai meetings and had set out to win what he'd already considered his.

They'd been married eight weeks later. He had claimed the woman he'd been born to love, promising to keep her unto him until death did them part...

So much for promises, for dreams. Pain pushed at him. He pushed it away. He'd already spent too long on the rack of jealousy, so why prolong the agony? His face set, he raked out the dying embers and went slowly upstairs. Tomorrow couldn't come soon enough.

Still sleepless, Bella heard his feet on the uncarpeted stairs and stared into the darkness, wide-eyed, holding her breath.

But the footsteps passed her door, and she curled herself on her side and cried herself to sleep. Because she had wanted him to come to her, to make love to her for one last time, to give her a final memory she could live with.

The memory she did have, of the single, blistering word he'd used before turning on his heels and walking out on her and Guy, was too demeaning to live with.

CHAPTER FIVE

BELLA came awake to the distinctive aroma of freshly brewing coffee wafting up from the kitchen directly beneath her bedroom.

The window was heavily curtained, so she had no way of knowing if the late winter dawn had broken, but one thing she did know: Jake was getting ready to leave. Without her.

She wasn't going to stay here on her own!

Jumping out of bed, shivering in the chilly air, she scrambled into the warm leggings and sweater she'd worn the day before and pushed her feet into her sturdy walking shoes, panic making her heartbeat very fast.

There was no time for refinements, even the most basic ones such as bathing, or brushing her hair. She wouldn't put it past him to be walking out of here right now, creeping out, because he wouldn't want her to wake and come racing after him! He had certainly made it perfectly clear that he didn't want her tagging along, under any circumstances. He didn't want her anywhere near him.

Well, he couldn't force her to stay. So she'd dog his footsteps every inch of the way, and if he didn't like it he could lump it!

Already breathless from her haste, she flew down the stairs and arrived in the kitchen with a clatter. The room was filled with clear bright light and the enticing fragrance of coffee. Jake, wearing the bulky sweater and warm dark cords he'd had on yesterday, was staring out of the window.

'No need to break your neck. Nobody's going anywhere,' he said drily.

He turned from the window, his mouth curling. But it wasn't a smile, Bella saw. That tight-lipped grimace could easily have developed into a full-blown snarl if he'd let it; she didn't have to be an expert in facial expressions to recognise that. But it didn't stop her wretched body responding to him as if the reaction had been programmed in, right from the day of her birth.

He hadn't shaved, and the darkness of his tough jawline was more than the mere affectation of designer stubble. It made him look more dangerous, more forbiddingly exciting than ever before. And what was he talking about? Why had he altered his plans?

Answering her unspoken questions, he narrowed his eyes and drawled softly, 'You even have the weather on your side. So how did you manage that? Magic?'

He turned abruptly away, bunching his hands in the pockets of his trousers, staring bleakly through the window at the winter wasteland.

Pushing past the hurtful contempt of his words, Bella made sudden sense of what he was implying and went to stand beside him at the window, careful not to brush against him—because touching him would be her undoing, she knew darn well it would.

Stealthy snow had fallen silently in the night, blown into drifts by the howling wind. Drifts of the glittering, pure white stuff were piled up against the sturdy cottage to the height of the window-frame. Imprisoning them here together. Evie and Kitty couldn't have hoped for a better result!

'There's coffee in the pot.' He stepped back quickly, away from her. She could sense the tension in his hard body, hear it in his dark, gravelly voice.

She was right; he couldn't bear her to be anywhere near him. Finding her with Guy on that fateful night had made her physically repulsive to him. Yet there had been moments when she'd hoped...

'We're going to have to try to live with this impossible situation.'

She could hear him moving about, and she could detect resignation in his voice now. A toneless monotone that told her quite plainly that being forced to endure her undiluted company was not something he was wildly excited about.

She could have done without his earlier sarcastic implication that she'd magicked up a snowstorm to keep him here. Very much against his will. She didn't know which hurt the most, bitter sarcasm or bleak resignation, but she wasn't going to give him a clue to the way he was tearing her to pieces.

Turning reluctantly to face him, her eyes went wide. He was shrugging into his sheepskin coat, already turning up the collar against the bitter weather outside.

He was going to try his level best to get out of here, preferring to take his chances in the arctic wilderness out there rather than spend another moment with her. He was leaving her stranded, walking out on her, dismissing her from his life all over again!

She knew he didn't love her, or trust her. But she hadn't realised just how much he hated her.

'Where are you going?' Her voice sounded tinny, frantic even, and her face had gone red. She could feel heat creeping all over her skin. She had sounded like a nagging wife, but she couldn't help it. She didn't want him walking out on her. Not again.

'Don't worry. You and the weather have me neatly trapped.' His voice sounded as cold as the snow on the mountain tops. 'Though what you hope to achieve is beyond me, particularly since you refuse to be honest enough to tell me.'

Bella narrowed her eyes into slits and glared right back at him, her temper rising rapidly now. How could you hate a person yet want him with a force that was pretty near overwhelming? Were love and hate really the different sides of the same coin, as people said?

He went to the outer door and drew back the bolts. 'I'm going to dig a way through to the fuel store. I'd appreciate it if you did your part and fixed breakfast.'

He sounded weary, Bella noted crossly. Weary of the situation he found himself in. Weary of her. She watched him force the door open against the weight of snow, her chin jutting mutinously.

Anger was her only defence. She dredged up every last bit she could find. Do as you're told; she mimicked his voice inside her head. And vowed she wouldn't. Not ever again.

Besides, would it hurt him to offer her a kind word? Or, if he really couldn't manage that, simply a civil one would do! Didn't the insensitive brute remember what day it was? Christmas Eve—their fourth wedding anniversary! Did the date mean so little to him that he'd blanked it out of his mind?

Tears welled in her eyes and she blinked them furiously away, despising herself for the weakness of wanting things he could never give her—his love, his trust, the way things had been for them at the very beginning, when it had been as if he had known she was his woman, and had reached out and taken her.

And she'd gone willingly because, almost from the time they'd met, she'd known she was his—for always.

But it hadn't turned out that way. The veneer of perfection had been very thin. Scratch it, and something ugly was staring you in the face.

As soon as he was out of sight she reached for her padded coat. She hadn't wanted him to walk out on her, but she was going to walk out on him. She couldn't and wouldn't endure the situation a moment longer!

Bella knew she was acting irrationally, but how could she think straight when he was around, looking at her with those black, contemptuous eyes, making it plain he believed she had instigated this unholy mess?

Walking out of here would show him just how wrong he was about that! And remove her from the disastrously growing temptation to try to make him believe she still needed him, that she only had to see him, hear his voice, to crave the touch of his lips, his hands—because for her the wanting had never stopped.

And even if he did believe her—which was highly unlikely—his vaguely contemptuous pity would be the best she could hope to achieve. He would tell her to control her libido until she could get back to Guy. And that she could do without!

Because of the wind direction there was less snow piled up in front of the cottage than there was at the rear. The sun shone brightly from a clear blue sky, and that was a heartening omen. She'd go carefully, she promised herself, sucking in lungfuls of the cold, cold air, pick her way until she came to the nearest habitation.

She'd show him she hadn't planned this sick farce! By taking this initiative, she'd damn well prove it!

By the time he'd split enough dry logs to last for twenty-four hours, Jake's temper was high. And rising. He'd long since discarded his sheepskin coat, the heavy exercise keeping him warm, but his trousers were wet through to well above his knees—the unpleasant result of wading through the drifts to get to the shed to look for a shovel to clear the damn stuff!

He replaced the axe and shovel in the shed, flung his coat over his shoulder, gathered up an armful of logs and set off along the track he'd cleared from the shed to the cottage. He'd hoped for a rapid thaw, but it looked as if he wasn't going to get one. Great snow clouds were gathering ominously now, blocking out the sky.

He had never threatened physical harm to a woman in his life, but right now he felt like shaking Bella until her teeth fell out!

Why wouldn't the woman come clean and tell him exactly what she'd wanted to achieve when she'd ganged up with the sisters from hell and tricked him into coming here? The frustration of not knowing was almost worse than the deed itself.

There was no sign of breakfast, and the coffee-pot was cold. He told himself he wasn't surprised, and went through to dump the logs on the hearth, eyeing the cold ashes grimly.

She was probably holed up in her room, painting her nails and doing her face, expecting him to do all the donkey work!

He took the stairs two at a time, his black frown deepening as the wet fabric of his trousers clung clammily to his legs. If they were going to survive this damned incarceration without coming to blows there was going to have to be some give and take around here!

It took him less than five minutes to discover she was nowhere in the cottage, and mere seconds more to check out the front and verify what he'd sinkingly begun to suspect.

Footprints heading out of there, imprinted in the deep snow. Had the woman gone completely mad?

He collected his coat, glowered at the sky and slammed the cottage door behind him. Attention seeking, that was what this latest crazy stunt was all about!

He'd made his irritation with the situation pretty clear, refusing to play along with her game—whatever it was. So she'd trudged out into the snow, knowing full well he would feel obliged to fetch her back, thereby forcing him to give her his undivided attention.

When picking out this cottage for their 'unexpected' reunion, she'd have made good and sure it was remote, far enough from any other habitation to make getting out on foot anything but easy—and totally impossible in these conditions.

And if he didn't have a conscience he'd sit back and let her get on with it, leave her to come crawling back when she realised that playing the injured heroine wasn't getting results!

By his reckoning, he'd spent around half an hour clearing the path and splitting wood. Even if she'd shot out of the front door the moment he'd exited the back, she couldn't have gone far in that small amount of time. And when he caught up with her he'd haul her back and lay down a few firm ground rules. By hell, he would!

Half an hour later he'd followed her trail to the rim of the valley and over, zig-zagging to avoid obvious drifts and on across the flanks of the now trackless mountains. Trouble was, it had started snowing again almost as soon as he'd set out, and it was rapidly becoming a blizzard.

The powdery snow was being blown around in ever-thickening flurries, filling in the marks of her passage. If he gave the storm another ten minutes, he wouldn't have a clue how to track her down. If he didn't find her soon, he never would.

Anxiety quickened his heart rate and he forced himself to move faster, cursing the elements. Despite her height, she was too fragile to last long in these desperate conditions.

He thought of the slenderness of her bones, the delicate grace of that ultra-feminine body, and groaned, pushing himself harder. His breathing was ragged now, more from the persistently clawing anxiety than from the very real exertion.

If anything happened to her he would never forgive himself.

When a rent in the swirling clouds of snow revealed a figure up ahead, gallantly trying to get up off her knees and pathetically failing, the sense of relief he felt forced him to face what he'd tried so hard to hide—he still cared deeply for the little witch. If he'd lost her out here his life wouldn't have been worth living; his future wouldn't have been worth having.

It took him two desperate minutes to reach her, to scoop her up from her knees and hold her as tightly as he could without crushing her slender bones.

'Oh, Jake—'

Her voice was a whispery thread of sound against the wail of the wind, but he heard it, and it reached deep inside him and touched him where it hurt. It hurt like hell.

'Don't talk,' he commanded gruffly, his heart twisting inside him as his hands went to steady her shoulders to allow him to search her face.

White skin was transparent with fatigue; lips were tinged blue with cold. But her eyes were clear bright pools, pools he could drown in, and the barriers went crashing down, each and all of them, as she spoke to him.

'I'm so sorry, so sorry. Criminally…stupid…' The words were strung out, as if she hadn't the strength to say them but would, even if it was the last thing she ever did. 'Stupid thing…to do.'

'I said, don't talk,' he reiterated thickly, his throat tight. He rubbed the balls of his thumbs gently over the parchment-thin skin stretched over her cheek-bones, then cradled her head between his hands and bent to touch his lips to hers, moving them slowly, softly, transmitting what he could of his warmth to her.

He felt the sweet movement of her cold lips beneath his—opening, receptive, stroking, growing warmer, much warmer now. His heart rate quickened, sending the blood pounding thickly through his veins, until the smothered whimper of pleasure that seemed to come from the depths of her being—sapping what little energy she had left—had him reluctantly moving his mouth from hers.

This wasn't the time, and it most decidedly wasn't the place.

'Let's get you home,' he muttered, sweeping her into his arms. 'Trust me, you'll soon be warm and dry.'

'Jake—I can walk!'

'Shut up,' he ordered smoothly, briefly touching his lips to her eyelids, closing the fatigue-bruised skin over those perfect, precious eyes. Then he lengthened his stride. The elements would have to do a damn sight better than this if they wanted to stop him taking her to safety!

He barely noticed the weather as he fought through the blizzard, and her slight weight was nothing. Immeasurable relief overrode everything else; aching muscles didn't get a look in.

At one point she seemed to fall asleep, nestled in his arms, her head tucked in beneath his chin. But she woke when he shouldered open the cottage door, momentarily cuddling closer into his body before murmuring, 'Put me down, Jake. You must be exhausted.' She was deeply reluctant to leave the haven of his arms, to relinquish the closeness of the last hour when he'd found her, held her and kissed her and carried her back every step of the way. But his effort had been monumental and, strong though he was, every muscle had to be aching.

If only they could stay this close, scrub out the past and build on the future...

'I've managed this far; a few more steps won't hurt me.'

There was no condemnation in his voice, just a gruff thread of something she couldn't put a name to, and she wound her arms around his neck as he carried her up to the bathroom with no apparent effort at all.

He slid her down his body to put her on her feet, and she did her best not to sway or wobble. Out there, when the storm had worsened, she'd been truly frightened. But her hero had come and brought her home.

He had always been her hero. Even when she couldn't understand him, had believed he'd never really loved her and had married her because he lusted after her, she'd never been able to topple him off the pedestal she'd created for him in her mind. Which was strange, considering everything.

Her throat tightened. There were things that had to be said. Now, in this softer, more receptive mood, surely he would listen?

He released his hold on her slowly, as if reassuring himself that she wouldn't fall in a wet and soggy heap, and bent to turn the bath taps on.

She reached out and touched his arm, and he straightened immediately at the slight contact, his breath bunching painfully in his lungs. Turning to her, his eyes narrowed with concern as he saw the glitter of unshed tears in her eyes.

'I'm sorry, Jake—'

'You're back now, no damage done,' he said quickly, his eyes sweeping her tense features. 'Don't waste your breath apologising.'

'I want to! Not just for taking off like that, but for everything else!' she cried, needing him to know how much she regretted what she'd done, needing him to understand why she'd done it. There had been too many thoughts left unspoken in the past, culminating in a total lack of communication. She should have tried harder to make him listen, make him understand. She could see that now.

'Shh.' He placed two fingers against her lips, silencing her, clamping his jaw tightly as he felt her mouth tremble beneath the gentle pressure, and stamping on the near-desperate urge to kiss her senseless as her lids fluttered closed, colour stealing into her flawless skin.

He couldn't listen to her raking over the past, hear her apologising for the act of adultery, promising it would never happen again. 'No post mortems,' he said thickly, taking his fingers from her mouth because touching her hadn't been one of his better ideas.

He tested the temperature of the water and turned off the taps. 'What you need is a warm bath and a hot drink.' He unbuttoned her soggy coat and removed it, his hands brisk, impersonal, his movements economical. Then he bent to tackle the laces of her walking shoes.

Looking down at his dark head, his wet hair plastered to his skull, Bella bit back a groan as the breath snagged in her lungs, making her heart race. Willing her fingers not to reach out and touch—not yet—she curved them sharply into her palms.

Maybe in a moment she could make her move...ask him to share the bath with her...? If the signs were right... If she had the courage...

Out of those three years of their marriage they'd spent a total of one hundred and thirty-one days together. She knew the tally exactly. She'd kept a record.

But she'd done her best, for the first couple of years at least, to make the most of their time together. And they'd shared a bath on many memorable occasions. Highly memorable occasions...

Her heart felt as if it were about to explode in her chest, her body too narrow to contain such tumultuous emotions. They'd been so good together—sexually at least—their need, their physical generosity, dovetailing perfectly, their passion carrying each other ever higher, reaching unbelievable realms of rapture.

Surely that spectacular closeness couldn't all be lost? There had to be something left they could build on. There had to be!

She stood like a rag doll as he undressed her. She could manage for herself perfectly well, but wasn't about to tell him so. Her damp sweater disposed of, he hooked impersonal fingers beneath the waistband of her leggings and dragged them down over her slender hips.

Bella shuddered as molten fire pooled deep down inside her. She wanted him so; her entire body was on fire for him, transformed into a silent, desperate cry of need, a plea for his lovemaking—a cry he surely must hear deep inside him, an inner cry of such longing she could almost hear it throbbing on the air.

His eyes slid over her body, lingering, dark colour slashing his hard, prominent cheekbones. And she knew, even before she heard the harsh rasp of his breath, that her body's silent cry of need had reached him, touched him....

Instinctively her hands went out, small palms sliding against the darkly stubbled, hewn contours of his face, long and elegant fingers resting on his temples, feeling the violence of the pulse there.

Jake moved sharply back, as if stung by a horde of angry hornets, his eyes bleak and mouth compressed as he delivered tersely, 'Shout if you need anything. I'll leave the door open.'

And he walked out on her, chilling indifference clearly stamped on the rigid lines of his broad back.

CHAPTER SIX

BACK in his room, Jake leaned against the closed door, teeth gritted, his head thrown back.

It had been a close call. Damn it, his body was still shaking. For several minutes his concern for her had been his salvation, helping him to strip her down as if he were a professional carer.

Only when she'd stood before him wearing nothing but those wicked wisps of lace that so lovingly cupped inviting, rosy-tipped breasts, and yet another scrap of lace-trimmed silk that covered...

He groaned, levering himself forward and shrugging out of his soaked jacket. He'd been doing fine until then. Just fine. But looking at her, remembering the passion and glory of their lovemaking, the meeting of their souls that had made them seem indivisible, had brought him to the point of reaching out for her, holding her, making her his again, and only his, for the rest of time.

But the smouldering, drowning invitation in her eyes when she'd slowly reached out and touched his face had brought him right back to his senses. Back with a hard, resounding crack.

Sex had been something she'd always been good at. Very good. As insatiable as he'd been himself where she was concerned.

So insatiable, indeed, she'd been hopping into bed

with that wife-stealing, wife-cheating bastard Maclaine whenever he'd been away. While he'd been working his guts out for them both, determined to secure their future, she'd been playing around with the man who'd been her lover all those years ago.

He'd keep that firmly to the forefront of his mind. It was a cast-iron, rock-solid defence against whatever acts of sorcery she dreamed up next!

It would be masochistic madness to weave the fabric of his life with hers again, naively hoping she would stay faithful. He couldn't take the heartbreak and disillusionment a second time around.

He'd been short on trust ever since his father—the man he'd loved, respected and, above all, trusted—had committed that ultimate betrayal, taking his own life and leaving his family to make what they could of the financial mess he'd left behind.

When Bella walked down the stairs, reluctantly dressed in flowing black silk trousers topped by a sleekly narrow white linen jacket worn over a black body, she was perfectly in control.

Watching as he'd walked out of that bathroom, she'd been devastated, hardly able to believe he'd been turning his back on the possibility of a mutual admission that they still cared for each other.

Because for a little while they'd been close, she knew they had, both physically and mentally. Closer than they'd been for a long time before their marriage had finally broken up. She'd felt it in her bones, felt the blossoming of hope in the quiet certainty of her heart.

The briefly wonderful hope had been cruelly shattered when he'd walked out of the door. He'd fought the growing closeness because he didn't want it. So be it. She could handle it, couldn't she? What was that old saying? You could take a horse to water but you couldn't make it drink...

Getting through to him when his mind was made up was impossible. She remembered now exactly when that fact of life had finally hit home...

Bella let herself into the Docklands apartment and thanked heaven for the central heating. The late-January evening was bitterly cold.

She removed her suit jacket and kicked off her shoes. And smiled. She'd been doing a lot of that just lately—smiling. Ever since Guy had made that proposition, given her existence a meaning that had been strangely absent during the two years and one month of her largely solitary marriage, she'd been feeling euphoric.

Dear, darling Guy!

They'd been heavily involved all day, and she felt pleasantly tired and thankful that she wasn't hungry because she had nothing in. Life had been too hectic since Guy had put forward his tempting offer to spare time for boring things like food shopping!

Deciding to listen to music, open a bottle of wine and come down from the high she now seemed permanently on, before getting an early night, she frowned as the phone in the living room shrilled out.

But it could be Guy. She lifted the receiver expectantly and Jake said, 'I'm at Heathrow. Can you fetch me, or shall I hire a car?'

He sounded desperately tired. 'I'm on my way,' she said quickly, her brows drawing together. He never flew in unexpectedly; he always let her know when he'd be home. She hoped there was nothing wrong.

'You work too hard,' she chided when she eventually drove them from the airport car park. He looked exhausted. 'Is there anything wrong?'

'Nothing that a few days of your home cooking and tender ministrations won't cure!' For a moment the teasing, sultry note was back in his voice, the slow smile he turned on her wiping the exhaustion from his face for a fleeting fraction of time.

Bella bit down on her lower lip, and concentrated fiercely on her driving. Now wasn't the right time to tell him she wouldn't be around. She could hardly let Guy down at this early stage of their renewed relationship.

Questions about his latest business trip elicited perfunctory answers, but the gist was that it had been highly satisfactory so she stopped asking and told herself he had obviously worked himself to a near standstill. She enquired instead, 'Are you hungry?'

'Ravenous.'

'Then we'll find a restaurant; I'm low on provisions. OK?'

'Fine. Somewhere low-key. Food, then bed. With you. Those are my priorities.'

Something in his voice told her that food came a very definite second on his list of two. Her whole body quivered. Their lovemaking was always spectacular, but his first night home after an absence that often stretched to weeks was sublime.

Without thinking—although later she was to wonder if it had been an unconscious wish to push the truth under his nose—she chose the small Italian restaurant in Canning Town where Guy had given her lunch and put his proposition to her. He often ate there, mostly in the evenings. His wife was again on a protracted visit to her parents, and as head of a thriving advertising agency he worked his socks off and couldn't face having to make himself a meal.

Not smart, the tiny restaurant was warm and friendly, the aroma of cooking appetising. They chose simply—pasta with spicy vegetables and a carafe of gutsy red wine.

Jake ate as if he were starving, as if he needed the wholesome, hot food, and the light was back in his eyes as he took her hand across the table and told her, 'I've missed you, Bel. Know something? You get more beautiful every time I see you. And know something else? I think I've made a decision—'

'Ah—the lovely Bella!' Whatever Jake had been about to tell her was cut short by the theatrical emergence of the proprietor from the kitchen. Carlo, Guy had introduced him over lunch that day. He had shiny black hair and a very big smile, and a tea-towel tied around his ample waist, tucked into his trousers at the back.

'You come again! My good friend Guy brings often new customers—people who want no frills, just good Italian food, home cooked. I tell him he has good taste—especially in his choice of so beautiful a companion!'

Bella felt something happen to her spine. Something like an army of ants scurrying up and down wearing needles of ice on their feet! Big on friendliness Carlo might be, but he was lamentably short on tact. He was seemingly oblivious to the black hostility in Jake's eyes as he beamingly asked, 'Is everything OK? *Dolce*, maybe?'

'Nothing.' Jake's reply was terse, his eyes hard as when they were alone again, he turned them on Bella's suddenly white face, raking them over her features as if he was trying to read what was going on in her mind. 'You come here often? You and Maclaine?'

'No, of course not.' The Italian had made it sound that way, but she'd only been here that one time. She twisted her napkin in her fingers. She was going to have to tell him now, and he wouldn't be pleased! In the past, whenever she'd mentioned Guy's name, Jake had changed the subject. He must have guessed, or heard, something about their former relationship. He was very possessive. 'I had lunch here with him. Once.'

It was then, precisely then, that he withdrew from her—quite possibly from their marriage. It was the beginning of the end, although she didn't know that then. She saw suspicion in his eyes, and did her best to counter it.

'I need to do something with my life, Jake. Can't you see that? Guy's offered me work; I've taken it.'

'Is that what you call it?'

Was he referring to her former modelling career? She knew he'd been happy when she'd given it up. As he'd said at the time, only half-jokingly, she suspected, he didn't like every Tom, Dick and Harry lusting after his much photographed wife.

Or did he mean something much darker?

'Jake, listen—' Her voice shook with the intensity of her need to make him hear her out, understand. 'This job, it's—'

'Leave it.' He was slapping banknotes down to cover the bill. 'If you want to work, go ahead. I wouldn't dream of asking you not to. If being my wife isn't "doing something with your life" then who am I to argue?'

He sounded indifferent.

He slept in the spare room that night, exhaustion his thin excuse. And over the following months he spent even more time away, and, when home with her, carefully avoided any mention of her job. And she, in turn, closed in on herself. Lack of communication became almost an art form...

Now the aroma of fresh coffee teased her nostrils as she walked through the kitchen. She ignored it, just as she made herself ignore the weakening effects of the past traumatic hours.

She'd used every last bit of her former expertise when she'd made herself up to match the clothes Evie's skulduggery had forced her to wear, carefully hiding her pallor and the lines of strain around her eyes. She needed confidence, control; she couldn't emerge from this nightmare with her self-respect intact without both held firmly in her hands.

She could hear him moving around in the living room. She took a deep breath, forced a serene expression and walked through.

Her eyes immediately went to him, lingering, drinking him in, as if her brain had no say in the matter. Changed into loose black denims topped by a rib-hugging black cashmere sweater, he should have looked menacing, intimidating. But he didn't. He looked heart-twistingly sexy.

She only had to look at him to experience the scorching, ravaging flames of desire, feel them wreaking their fiery onslaught through every tingling cell in her body. She dragged in a shuddery breath and prayed her inner turmoil didn't show.

He returned her riveted gaze with a slow, brooding appraisal, black eyes indolently skimming every line of her tautly held body as if he were stripping away the unlikely, elegant garments to the warm, suddenly trembling flesh beneath. And the air in the cosy little room became wildly over-heated, sizzling with churning sexual awareness.

Until he spoke, his cool, sardonic tone cutting through the atmosphere, one dark brow lifting upwards. 'I see you brought your designer labels along. Perfect choice for a winter break in the wilds of Wales.'

His sarcasm chilled her. 'Evie made a furtive last-minute substitution.' He wouldn't believe her. He wouldn't believe her if she said roses had thorns. And the twist of his long mouth told her she was correct in that assumption.

'You're slipping, Bella.' Glittering black eyes taunted her cruelly. 'You used to be such a good liar. Through three years of marriage you had me believing you were a faithful wife.'

Now, surely, was the time to put that right, to tell him that the fault was his, that she would never have left him if he had given her what she most needed, to explain exactly what that was.

'We need to discuss this,' she told him, her black-lashed, water-clear eyes huge with entreaty.

But he shook his head, frowning sharply. 'There's nothing to discuss—except how we're going to get through the next few days. It is Christmas, remember?'

He bent to tend the fledgling fire, and Bella swallowed the lump in her throat. Nothing to discuss. Their past, present and future relationship was too unimportant to waste breath on.

And of course she knew it was Christmas; she didn't need reminding.

It had become such a very special time of year for her, more than ordinarily so. Their whirlwind romance, followed by a Christmas Eve wedding. The first few days of their rapturous honeymoon spent in a quiet, rambling sixteenth-century inn tucked away in the Cotswolds. All the festive trimmings—roaring log fires, red-berried holly, even a light flurry of snow. Carol-singers, young voices crystal-clear in the frosty air, sparkly days and long nights filled with love and laughter. And talking.

Oh, how she'd talked, spilling out hopes she had never shared with anyone before. Hopes that had never been fulfilled.

'Yes, I remember,' she answered him, her voice flat. Over the past year anguish had been a constant companion. She'd thought she had learned to live with it, learned to cope. Clearly, she hadn't. 'I'll go and pour us some of that coffee.'

It was suddenly an effort to speak. The pain of disappointment hit her. She had so hoped, expected— yes, actually and foolishly expected...

'I'll do it. Stay here, get warm.' He was out of the room before she could argue. Not that she had the energy to argue about anything.

Slowly she moved to the fire and held her hands out to the warmth of the flames.

Reaction to this morning's hare-brained escapade was setting in. That was why she had been air-headed enough to imagine, for one single moment, that somehow they could work things out, that he did still care for her a little.

She didn't realise she'd been swaying on her feet until Jake thrust the tray he'd carried through down on a side table, put long-fingered hands on her shoulders and pressured her down onto the fireside chair.

Not that he needed to exert much pressure. Her legs felt as if they were made of water. He reached for the tray and placed it on her knees.

'Eat. Drink. I don't want you collapsing on me. I've no way of summoning medical aid, don't forget.'

Barely focusing, her eyes registered a china beaker of steaming coffee and a plate of lavishly buttered hot toast. His cool command made sense. Always the practical one, always able to find reasons why he couldn't give her what she craved.

She drank the coffee and forced down some of the toast, and managed a dull little, 'Thank you. I needed that.'

Jake removed the tray and said tersely, 'Too right, you did. You've actually got some colour back in your face that hasn't come out of a pot.'

Her cheeks, smooth as a rose petal, had a touch of pink beneath the translucent surface, and her lips had lost that worrying bluish tinge—formerly apparent in the whiteness around the coral lipstick she had so carefully painted on. He took up an unknowingly dominant stance in front of the hearth, breathed deeply and tried to make himself relax.

They were stuck out here, and there was no way he was going to spend Christmas in an ill-tempered, explosive atmosphere.

'I've a suggestion to make.' A stab of something fierce and hot knifed through him as her eyes winged up and locked with his. She had piled the silky mass of her black hair elegantly on the top of her head. The purity of the line from the crown of her head to the angle of her jaw, to the slender length of her neck, was sheer poetry. It made him ache.

He clenched his hands in the pockets of his jeans. And tried again. 'I suggest we try to make the best of the situation.' Suddenly it was vitally important to him that she agree to a truce. He cleared his throat and continued with a careful lack of inflection. 'We're stuck here. Whether we like it or not. In my opinion, it wouldn't make a whole heap of sense to spend Christmas glowering at each other from opposite ends of the room.'

The clear luminosity of her eyes cut to his soul. She looked as though she was hanging on every word, like a child who was waiting to hear the details of a long-awaited treat. Despite the veneer of elegant sophistication those expressive eyes made her look so trusting, so innocent.

Yet she was light years away from innocence, he reminded himself with a brutality he suddenly felt was very necessary.

'So why don't we forget the past for a couple of days, call a truce and behave like rational adults?'

He knew he'd sounded harsher than he'd meant to, and instantly regretted it as he watched her head droop, those eyes not intent on him now, but on the long-fingered hands that lay clasped in her lap.

He held his breath, expecting the retaliation of total non-compliance or, at best, the silent withdrawal that had tainted the last year of their marriage. Though he, too, had been guilty in that respect, he recognised now.

'Sounds like sense to me, too.' Bella did her best to sound like the rational adult he'd suggested she try to be. The spiky lump in her throat was her own fault. Stupid of her to have thought, at first, that he was trying to tell her that they should use this time to try to resurrect their marriage, work on their shattered relationship, talk things out.

But his harshly impatient suggestion that they forget the past, just for a day or so, had knocked that fantasy on the head.

He wanted to forget that they'd ever meant anything to each other. She had no option but to play it his way, and she knew that if she were to survive the next few days without making a shameful fool of herself she would have to convince her stupid heart that their separation was the first step in rectifying a bad mistake. Perhaps even steel herself to mention divorce.

She got to her feet, and challenged him. 'I won't glower, if you won't. And, to make it easier, shall we dress the tree? There's one in the kitchen, in case you hadn't noticed.'

'I could hardly have failed, since I almost poked my eye out on the darned thing a couple of times.'

She hadn't left out a single thing when she'd made her minute arrangements for the 'surprise' reunion! Jake stamped on the thought. No past, no recriminations, simply a polite coexistence—on the surface, anyway. He was working on it. He had to. It had been his idea, hadn't it? He'd do anything to make the next few days as amicable as they could be. Polite formality was definitely the only safe atmosphere to aim for.

He would do anything to avoid any attempts on her part to affect a reconciliation. That had to be why she'd set this up. And she had enough witchery at her command to make him follow his heart, ignore the sullied past and resume their marriage.

He would fight to the last breath to avoid putting himself through that kind of hell again.

'I'll carry it through; you decide where you think it would look best.'

In the end they both agreed the tree would look perfect in the alcove at the side of the inglenook.

'Out of the way of any flying sparks,' Jake approved. 'Shall you hang the bits and bobs, or shall I?'

'Why don't we do it together?' Immediately the question was out she regretted it. It sounded pushy. Togetherness was something that had been missing from their relationship for a long time now. No chance of finding it again either. He didn't want to find it so they wouldn't. What Jake wanted, Jake got.

'One of us has to fix lunch,' he told her, smoothly glossing over her mistake. 'Breakfast, for me, was a non-event, and yours—two bites of toast just now— doesn't count. I'll forage in the kitchen while you deck the tree.'

It wasn't cowardice, he told himself grimly as he jerked the fridge door open and glared at the brimming contents. He needed to keep things cool, polite—if only superficially. It was the only way he could get through this without his emotions ending up in chaos.

He pulled a slab of cold roasted beef from the well-stocked shelves and began to slice at it for sandwiches. He had nothing to fear, he reminded himself. Not a damn thing. He had the protection of her past infidelities, hadn't he? Not to mention the reinforcement of her latest devious behaviour—the setting up of this farce.

Jake eyed the mound of meat he'd hacked with grim hostility. The slices were distinctly uneven, ragged, as if someone had set about the cold roast with an axe. And he wondered why he had to keep reminding himself of the reasons for keeping her at arm's length.

After what she'd done to him, to their marriage, he would have thought his heart would have grown a protective shell a mile thick, the reasons for keeping her at a firm distance permanently engraved on his brain.

He shouldn't have to work on it.

It shouldn't have to be so hard!

If he allowed her back into his life he would deserve all he got. Heartbreak. Forever wondering if she was sneaking off to be with Maclaine whenever his back was turned. He couldn't face the pain of that again.

CHAPTER SEVEN

AT FIRST Bella had been all fumbling thumbs and deep and nervy embarrassment at having left herself wide open to that rebuff. Play the game—for a game it surely was—as if they were mere acquaintances, politely resigned to spending time together; that was the way Jake wanted it. So that was the way he'd get it, she'd told herself firmly. She would demonstrate that she could play the game as well as he. Better, even!

But soon the glittering festive baubles had entranced her: gold, silver and scarlet, glimmering and twinkling amongst the dark evergreen branches, swags of shiny red beads roping in and out of the pine-fragrant foliage. It all made her forget, for a few precious minutes, the hurting hatefulness of her situation.

She was standing back, her head tipped to one side, wondering if the effect she'd achieved looked as good as she thought it did, when Jake walked back in from the kitchen, carrying a loaded tray.

'How does it look? OK?' She didn't turn after that initial over-the-shoulder glance. Still caught up in almost child-like excitement, she took Jake's long moment of intense silence for consideration of her artistic efforts. The result had to be a bit odd or he wouldn't be taking so long to offer an opinion. 'Did I put too much on? Is it over the top? I've never dressed a tree before.'

Jake put the tray down on the table, his mouth curving cynically. For a few moments back there she'd had him entranced. Standing there, a great and glittering gold star clutched in her hands, her lovely face radiating pleasure, there'd been no sign of the sleek 'top model' sophistication he'd always associated with Bella. The breathy, whispery excitement in her voice had almost fooled him, too.

He clattered plates. 'Never dressed a tree? Pull the other one! Then come and eat.'

So she wasn't even to be allowed the fleeting distraction of doing something pleasurable for the very first time. And why did he have to believe that every time she opened her mouth a lie came out?

She swung round on her heels. It was time he got a few things straight. She didn't lie, for one.

Tossing the glittery star on the tabletop, she told him levelly, 'It happens to be the truth. If you can't believe it, then that's your tough luck. Not mine.'

Still unloading the tray, he gave her a penetrating look. Maybe he was taking distrust too far. Distrust had been stamped on his soul when his father had taken his life. Of his parents, his father had been his rock, a larger than life figure he had respected as well as loved. The loss of financial security and the huge debts his father had left behind had been as nothing compared with that final betrayal.

To begin with, he'd believed he had learned to trust again with Bella. But infidelity made a mockery of marriage vows, turned them into lies. Infidelity was a sure-fire way of killing trust.

He pulled out a chair for her and took one for himself on the opposite side of the table. 'So tell me about it. Didn't your parents let you help dress the tree when you were a kid?'

She took her chair, shrugged very slightly. 'It's not important.'

'Probably not.' He pushed a plate of sandwiches towards her. 'But it would help pass the time. And, now I come to think of it, you've told me very little about your past.'

Pass the time. It stretched endlessly before her, arid, awkward and painful. She blinked rapidly. She would not cry. She took a sandwich of doorstep proportions, refused the soggy-looking salad garnish he'd prepared.

'I thought, for the purposes of Christmas peace and goodwill, we had to ignore the past.' She threw his cool stricture back in his face. The little rebellion helped to smother the feeling of hurt. She calmly eyed the thing on her plate and wondered if she could open her mouth wide enough to take a bite.

'The distant past doesn't count.' He found himself approving this new spark of defiance. And, watching her, he had to fight to stop himself from grinning like a clown. If he'd been asked to describe the marital meals she'd used to go to such endearingly endless trouble to prepare for him, he would have said elegant. And beautiful to look at. Ten out of ten for presentation, and two out of ten for hunger-quelling content.

Right now she was having difficulty hiding her dismay. He hadn't gone out of his way to produce such massive, untidy offerings. He couldn't have been concentrating on what he was doing.

'OK.' She capitulated, and reached for a knife to cut the sandwich into smaller, more manageable pieces. 'I suppose it wouldn't help the festive spirit much if we both sat here in gloomy silence. I'll go along with you, and try to avoid contentious subjects. But I warn you, I'm not going to pussy-foot around, double-checking everything before it trips off my tongue, like a reformed trollop at a vicar's tea party.'

He did grin then, but hid it behind the rim of his wineglass. An excellent vintage claret, he'd noted back in the kitchen, twisting the corkscrew with cynical ferocity. She'd spared no expense to get the party moving, to find the right mood!

He caught the thought, examined it. Was he being unfair? Was she in some kind of trouble? Had she engineered this time together because she needed his help? It was something to think about. Maybe if she relaxed enough she would tell him the truth.

'So?' he prompted gently, watching her long, narrow hands as she cut into the thick, crusty bread and the filling of hacked meat. He wondered why she didn't push it fastidiously aside and float out to prepare a medallion of tenderloin on a bed of unidentifiable leaves. She was obviously trying hard to please.

'So Dad thought Christmas was a waste of money, right? But Mum always did her best to make sure Evie and I had a package to open on Christmas morning.

Granted, money was in short supply—but he didn't even make an effort, and wouldn't let us try, either.'

She chewed reflectively on a piece of her sandwich; the meat was wonderfully tender, spiced up with just the right amount of mustard. His sandwiches were no way as inedible as they looked.

'I like to think he wasn't a Scrooge by nature, but acted like one because it upset him to think he couldn't give his family everything they wanted.'

She looked so earnest, Jake thought, watching her closely. Somehow he couldn't bring himself to say what was on his mind—that any father who didn't make the effort to find some way of making Christmas special for his kids didn't deserve to have any. Let her keep her manufactured delusions if they helped her.

'Dad was mostly out of work, and we were always on the move,' she was telling him, long fingers idly stroking the stem of her wineglass now. 'He always thought the grass would be greener in the next county or town. It never was, though. Things just seemed to go from bad to worse. Smaller flats in seedier areas. And moving meant Mum had to keep finding new jobs to make ends meet. Sometimes she couldn't. Things got really tough then.'

Her mother had never complained. Bella wondered if she'd inherited those doormat genes, making her willing to let Jake call all the shots during the time they'd lived together.

Unconsciously she shook her head. Now wasn't the time to delve into cause and effect.

Jake said, his voice surprisingly gentle, 'I remember you telling me your parents were separated, and your mother settled in New Zealand with her widowed sister.'

'Yes, but Mum going out to live with Auntie May came much later. She wouldn't have dreamed of leaving us until Evie and I were both on our feet. But Dad walked out on the lot of us when I was fourteen. We stayed put, then, and for a couple of years the three of us had our first settled home. A two-bedroom flat above a greengrocer's in a backstreet in Newcastle. Downmarket, but home.'

She was twisting the glass now. Jake expected the contents to spill out at any moment. There was a lot of tension there, waiting to be released.

'It must have been about that time I knew what I wanted out of life.'

She wasn't looking at him; her expression told him she was in another world. But at least she was trying to share it with him. Funny how they'd never really talked, either of them, never delved deeply enough to find out what made each other tick.

Too busy making love, discovering each other physically to begin with. And then, after the initial honeymoon stage, he'd been too busy. Full-stop.

Not sure that he should want to, but feeling driven to know, Jake asked, 'And what was that?'

Christmas every day of the year? Everything her deprived childhood had seemingly put out of reach? Designer clothes, jewels, fast cars and slow, sybaritic holidays in far-flung places?

Heaven knew, she'd earned enough in her own right to indulge every whim, and the Docklands home he'd provided on their marriage had been glamorous enough to negate the memories of any number of back-street flats.

Yet it hadn't been enough. His love hadn't been enough. Being his wife, in spite of all the financial advantages—like not having to work for her extremely comfortable living—had become a bore. So much so that she had sought forbidden excitement with her former lover.

Bella, glancing across at him between dark and tangled lashes, saw the ferocity darkening his face and made up her mind. Conscious, suddenly, that she was in danger of snapping the stem of her glass, she made herself loosen up, unknotting her fingers and lifting the brimming glass to her mouth.

They'd agreed not to raise any contentious spectres from the past—but it might dent his huge ego, and certainly wouldn't hurt him, to know that one of the things she had most wanted—not the most important, but important nevertheless—was something else he'd resolutely refused to give her. She had nothing to lose because she'd already lost everything that mattered to her.

'I did tell you once, but I guess you didn't listen. You never listened to what I said if it wasn't what you wanted to hear. Eventually I stopped saying anything important.' She looked him straight in the eye and knew a moment's vindication when she watched his dark brows pull down as her shot hit home.

She gave a small shrug, slender shoulders lifting elegantly beneath the beautifully styled white jacket.

'I wanted a proper home and a loving family to share it with,' she said with a touch of cool defiance.

She looked at her empty glass with a glimmer of surprise and put it down. Swallowing wine as if it were water wouldn't help. She sat rigidly upright in her chair, her hands knotted in her lap, and added, 'Nothing grand, just a homey place with a garden, and fields and woods around for the children to play in.' And a husband who was home, sharing the ups and downs of family life, the two of them growing closer as the years went by, not further and further apart until they were like strangers.

She frowned unconsciously, and tacked on tartly, 'No grimy backstreets, litter and graffiti everywhere— some place where it was safe to walk, with fresh air to breathe. A modest enough dream, but one I valued.'

She'd said enough. Perhaps too much. The silence from him was like a shock. But, oddly, she felt unburdened, lighter. She wasn't so self-centred that his refusal to even think about the occasional suggestions she'd made regarding a future move out of the City would have made her decide their marriage wasn't worth keeping.

But she wouldn't think about that; she couldn't afford to. Dwelling on what had gone so badly wrong wouldn't help her to get through the next few days, or keep up the pretence that they were mere acquaintances.

She swept to her feet and began to gather the lunch things together, and told him politely, very politely, 'I'll clear away. Would you mind fixing the star to the top of the tree? I couldn't reach.'

With the kitchen door closed firmly behind her, Bella released a long, shuddery sigh. She wanted to kill Evie for putting her in this situation! Kitty, too, for her part in it! The only thing that gave her any consolation whatsoever was knowing that this place, fully and lavishly provisioned, would have cost them at least an arm and a couple of legs apiece!

Their intentions had been good, though; she had to give them that. But they were living in cloud-cuckoo-land if they thought that this enforced and probably prolonged contact would have the desired results.

Jake didn't even like her any more. He didn't trust her. He would sooner handcuff himself to a baboon for the rest of his life than take her back!

Tears rushed to her eyes. She blinked them away and sniffed ferociously, took the tray to the sink and did the dishes, then collected the clothes they'd worn earlier in the blizzard and pushed them into the washer-drier. Anything to keep busy, keep out of the way of the man she had loved and lost.

From behind the closed door Jake could hear the clink of china. At odds with his chaotic emotions, Bella was prosaically washing the dishes. The sheer unexpectedness of what she'd said had robbed him of speech.

Of course he'd listened when she'd dreamily told him of what she envisaged for their future. Late-night lover-talk, he'd thought it, with her hair splayed against the pillows like a black silk shawl.

He could remember it now, too vividly for comfort—cocooned together in the secret love-cave of the four-poster bed in that quaint old Cotswolds inn where they'd spent the first Christmas of their honey-moon. Her eyes dreamy, romantic, her voice soft and sweet with talk of country cottages, roses round the door, children—their children—fantasy children she'd created for him.

His fingers stroking her hair, her face, the trembling starting up inside him again, his hand sliding down to the sensual swell of her breasts, his mouth covering hers, silencing her. His love for her, his need to drown himself yet again in the perfection of her overwhelming him...

The groan that was torn from him was driven. Oh, God, if only he could wipe his mind clean of all memories! He gritted his teeth, making himself back-track to what she had actually said, recalling the defiance, the tension in the way she'd said it.

True, in the first couple of years of their marriage she had sometimes mentioned the possibility of moving to the country and starting a family. But she hadn't made a song and dance about it, and had quietly accepted it when he had decided they should stay where they were.

He'd assumed she meant some place tamed and tidy, chocolate-box rural. And he'd had damn good reasons for not wanting to alter his *modus operandi* at that time. He'd explained that a move, putting down roots and starting a family, was out of the question. For the time being anyway. He hadn't known how much—and why—she'd wanted what she called a proper home.

Why hadn't she told him? In view of her deprived childhood—and that was something else she hadn't told him about—he would have understood. And, understanding, he would have set about doing something about it.

He had loved her more than life, and would have done anything to make her happy.

Were there other things he didn't know about her? Things she'd kept back, kept hidden? His jaw tightened. Damn it, he'd been her husband; he'd had a right to know!

And yet he hadn't made his motives clear, had he? At least, not the underlying motives. The sudden thought washed his mind with icy clarity. Had he been too arrogant, too driven by his own needs, too intent on doing things his way to share the essence of himself with her?

He didn't feel comfortable with himself about that. His face darkened, tightened, and self-disgust turned into a hard, sharp lump inside him. He had watched her become more withdrawn, more closed in on herself, and had done nothing about it, preferring to assume that it was nothing important. After all, so he had told himself, he'd given her every material advantage any woman could possibly want, and their lovemaking had still been as explosively rapturous as ever.

But that hadn't been enough. She'd been seeing Maclaine when he was away and had agreed to work with him again. She had been sleeping with him again. All the signs had pointed to it.

He could hear her moving about in the next room. He'd go in there and fetch her. Tell her he'd been wrong about forgetting the past while they were trapped here together. It wouldn't let itself be forgotten!

So they'd talk, go into this thing, thrash it all out until there was nothing left to know. And maybe, along the way, he'd discover whether he'd been responsible for driving her back into Maclaine's arms.

He was on his way to do just that when he heard the sound of a tractor. He turned quickly on the balls of his feet and strode to the window.

The machine had already crested the brow of the hill, the snow-plough attachment steadily but surely clearing the track towards the cottage.

This was his way out. Out of here, back to civilisation, where he could arrange for transport out for Bella. And then he could get on with his life, let her get on with hers. They would go their separate ways again.

His way out. If he wanted to take it.

He grabbed his sheepskin from the hook on the back of the kitchen door and walked out into the cold winter afternoon.

CHAPTER EIGHT

BELLA remembered noticing storage heaters upstairs, and went up and switched them on. At least the bedrooms would be less arctic tonight.

Tonight. Her heart filled with a painful mixture of yearning and bleak despair. Another endless, restless night, knowing Jake was in the next room, a few yards away, yet so distant from her he might as well be on the far side of the moon.

There had been moments when she'd really thought he still cared, but that had been nothing more than self-delusion, wishful thinking. She put it down to his determination to get through the next few days with as little friction as possible. He wouldn't want a rerun of this morning's crazy escape attempt, or hysterics or sulks.

Steeling herself, she started down the stairs to join him again, deeply envying his ability to cut his losses, write the three years of their marriage off as an unfortunate mistake and get on with his life. She wished she cared so little about him that she could do the same.

Part of the way down she heard the laboured sound of a tractor. She froze, unable to believe it at first, then ran back up to the tiny window at the head of the staircase and peered out.

Jake, still shrugging into his coat, was pushing

through the snow towards the tractor. It had already cleared most of the track. Numb, clutching onto the window-sill, Bella watched as Jake reached the vehicle.

She could imagine the conversation going on between him and the driver. He would be asking for a lift out of here, explaining that his car wasn't functioning. And as Jake reached into an inside pocket she turned away, trudging down the stairs on leaden legs.

They'd be out of here before nightfall—or he would, at least. Jake would fix that. He always managed to get his own way.

She wanted to put back her head and howl, and the urge to weep her heart out was almost irresistible. But she wouldn't do either of those things. She wouldn't let herself be such a fool.

'The cavalry's arrived!' Five minutes later he walked back in, bringing a wave of crisp frosty air with him.

That was why she was shivering all over, Bella decided, and forced herself to sound interested. 'So I saw. We can't be as isolated as we thought we were.'

The snow plough was back in operation again. The noise was growing louder as the driver approached the cottage.

'How on earth did he know we were snowed-up here?' She felt too dead inside to really care, but it was something to say, a way of masking her foolish inner dread at the coming parting.

But perhaps the ending of their enforced stay was a blessing, she decided dully, doing her best to convince herself. Being with him only brought back all the pain of wanting him, the mental and physical agony of knowing he could hardly bear to be anywhere around her.

The only real question was, would Jake go back in the cab with the driver alone, or would he take her with him? He was looking mightily pleased with himself, and was making no effort to remove his coat.

Which meant he was intending to leave any time now. She thought about the clothes still in the drier, the packing she'd have to do, the brightly burning fire which would have to burn down to ashes before it was safe to be left, and knew Jake wouldn't hang around until everything was sorted. Neither, in all probability, would the tractor driver.

Jake was going to leave her behind, and was looking insultingly happy about it. Grinning!

'The owners of the cottage got in touch with him. He farms in the locality and the council uses him to clear some of the lanes. They—the owners—didn't want their holiday tenants to feel snowed in and abandoned.'

She watched him walk to the fire, hold his hands to the flames. Even though his back was firmly turned to her she knew he was still looking pleased with himself. He couldn't wait to wash his hands of her!

As the tractor reached the cottage, did an ungainly three-point turn then stopped, Jake swung round and walked to the door, obviously leaving without even saying goodbye, and Bella said rawly, 'I take it you're going back with the driver. Would you ask him to wait while I get ready to leave, too?'

She simply couldn't bear the thought of being here

alone, with these new and hurtful memories to add to all the rest. It was too much heavy baggage to have to carry through the long, lonely years that stretched ahead.

Jake turned, scanning her features with narrowed eyes. If the arrival of the snow plough had surprised him, it had obviously shocked her. Ruined all her carefully laid plans. He could read the dredging disappointment in her beautiful eyes.

Well, he was going to let her get her own way. He hadn't known why he'd done it, not at first. But now he did. They were going to talk the whole thing through, and for that they needed time and space.

He needed to learn her secrets—if she had any more to divulge—discover exactly how and why their marriage had failed.

Because then, and only then, would he be able to put it all behind him and attain the freedom he needed to get on with the rest of his life, unfettered by memories and regrets.

Knowing that the prospect of freedom from the spell she'd cast on him the very first time he'd seen her had to be responsible for his present adrenalin-high, he made no attempt to keep the underlying hint of laughter from his voice as he told her, 'We're not going anywhere for a couple of days. Put the kettle on; we have a guest.'

The driver of the tractor was a wiry little man, swamped by a thick waxed jacket and a big red knitted hat. His name was Evan Evans, and he insisted on removing his boots.

His knitted socks were red, too, Bella noted, hurrying to make the hot drink Jake had offered, her heart winging with a great surge of happiness she desperately tried to suppress.

Jake could have left; there'd been nothing to stop him. Except the desire to stay?

But she mustn't think like a naive teenager, she chided herself as she moved round the kitchen, the murmur of masculine voices coming from the other room a backdrop to her thoughts.

He had no desire to be with her—hadn't he made that crystal-clear? For the past twelve months their marriage hadn't been either one thing or another. He probably wanted to get everything sorted out, discuss divorce, tidy everything up.

The cold almost certainty of that left her feeling physically and mentally drained. Yet hope lingered, a feeble but stubbornly burning flame at the back of her mind. She didn't want hope, not when it would surely turn out to be false.

Telling herself to keep her chaotic emotions in check, she made hot chocolate for the men and found a tin of biscuits. She opened it and put it beside the mugs on the kitchen table, then called them through.

'There's lovely, isn't it?' Evan picked up his mug and cradled it in mittened hands. 'Just what I needed.' He refused to sit, blowing on his drink to cool it, and Bella handed Jake his mug, careful not to look at his face. He might see those futile hopes warring with the bleak certainties in her eyes.

'So I'll phone the recovery service and give them your details, and ask them to bring the part out on Boxing Day. Is it set on spending Christmas you are?

Snow or no snow?' Evan finished his drink. 'It's a tidy enough place.' He glanced around him, his eyes twinkling with open appreciation as they rested on Bella. 'Don't blame you, mind. Do the same in your shoes! Though who'd go vandalising your car is beyond me.'

He scratched the side of his head and the knitted cap rose higher, looking, Bella decided half-hysterically, like a melting church steeple.

'Don't worry about it,' Jake said smoothly. 'We're very grateful for your help.'

Bella tried to analyse his tone. Satisfaction, or amusement? She couldn't decide which. And Evan was getting ready to leave.

'Missus'll be wondering where I've got to. We've got all the family back with us for Christmas, as usual. Five grandchildren in all. Little imps! Mind you—' bright brown eyes twinkled beneath the scarlet of the rearing hat '—Christmas wouldn't be the same without their racket, would it? *And*—' he stressed the word heavily, smiling broadly '—I'm doing Santa duty again. Each year I tell myself it's the last time I'm dressing up in all that stuff. Seems I never learn!'

Bella watched him go, accompanied by Jake, to find his boots, and envied him. She closed her eyes and desperately envied all the families happily getting ready to celebrate this special season. And when Jake joined her there were tears in her eyes.

'Why didn't you go with him?' she demanded thickly. Attack was the best form of defence—defence against the reckless need to hurl herself into his arms and beg him to fall in love with her again, to want her with the almost obsessive need that had driven them both ever since the very first time they'd met.

To beg him to take the hurt away.

'Because I've finally reached the conclusion that we need to talk. We've spent a whole year avoiding each other and it doesn't make any kind of sense. We've got to find a way to put the past behind us. We both need to be free to get on with our lives.'

'Yes, I see.' She turned away, trying to conceal the hurt. She'd guessed his motives for staying on here, but that didn't make it any easier to bear. He was going to suggest divorce.

'But not right now. There's plenty of time. A couple of days,' he said, his voice softening. There were tough questions to be asked, tough decisions to be made. It wouldn't be easy on either of them. And right now she looked so vulnerable, almost utterly defeated, and that wasn't like the Bella he knew.

The range and depth of the sweeping wave of compassion he felt for her came as a shock. For a moment it took his breath away.

Suddenly restless he suggested, 'So why don't we try to relax, get a breath of air before it gets dark?' He watched the graceful tilt of her head as she turned huge, questioning eyes to him. 'I don't mean a repeat of this morning's marathon!' he assured her, reliving the long minutes of frantic concern when he'd been afraid he'd never find her, wondering what that reckless journey of hers out into the blizzard had been meant to prove.

He pushed a log further onto the glowing embers with a booted foot, needing action of some kind, no matter how small, and then added more harshly than he'd intended, 'It was a suggestion, that's all. You don't have to come. But I need air.'

'I'll be two minutes.' Relief washed through her, washed away the tension, making her body feel light as air as she went to the kitchen. The terrible conversation that would lead to the legal ending of their marriage was to be postponed. Maybe, later, she'd find the strength from somewhere to handle it with dignity.

She fished the clothes from the drier and sped up the stairs, casting aside all that out-of-place elegance. She dressed hurriedly in the leggings and sweater, clean and still warm from the dryer, and pulled his bulky Aran jumper on over the top because her own coat was still damp.

Her hair had come adrift. She gave it an impatient look in the mirror, and sped out of the room and down the stairs. She didn't have time to fiddle.

'Just ten minutes. Right?' Jake asked as she joined him.

'Right.' The smile she gave him was unpremeditated. But the look of approval in his eyes as he swept them over her altered, casual appearance had warmed away all her cool defences.

And his suggestion had been a good one. The air was stingingly cold, but it made her feel suddenly alive. Vitally, joyously alive—something she hadn't experienced since they'd separated. The misty orange sun was low in the washed-out blue of the sky, casting long, dark shadows on the glittering snow.

Bella quickened her pace, revelling in the way her

blood seemed to positively bounce through her veins, until Jake gently hauled her back, the strength of his hand tight and protective on her arm.

'Hey! Cool it. The track's slippery as hell now. A broken leg we can do without!'

Eyes wary, her heart beating skittishly, she fell in step beside him, expecting him to release her arm as soon as he'd successfully reined her in. He didn't. He held her more tightly, gathering her towards him, tucking her closely to the side of his body.

Every nerve-end stood to attention, and her stomach lurched. Didn't he know what his touch did to her? Had he forgotten that she only had to be near him to go up in flames? Were his memories of all they had been to each other so easily, so callously erased?

Her eyes fixed on the now-glassy surface of the compacted snow on the track ahead, she battled to find something to say, something to defuse the sharply coiling sexual tension that seemed to be eating her alive.

She came up with, 'So you didn't tell Mr Evans who had vandalised your car.' Her voice was shaky. She tried to turn the wobble into a laugh. 'The poor guy will spend months wondering if he's going to wake up in the morning and find no wheels on his tractor. He'll be looking at perfectly innocent local lads—wondering which of them has developed the urge to sneak around putting other people's vehicles out of commission!'

Jake stopped, his black eyes glittering down at her. 'What would you have had me say?' he wanted to know. 'That my wife arranged a little sabotage?' He turned back towards the cottage, his grip on her arm tightening cruelly.

Bella dug her heels into the compacted snow, dragged her arm from his grasp and flung at him, 'I had nothing to do with it—nothing!' Her eyes narrowed, anger whipping colour into her cheeks, she planted her hands on her hips and shouted, 'I don't know which makes me madder—what Evie did or you refusing to believe she did it!'

Jake quirked an eyebrow and had difficulty keeping his mouth straight. She looked incredibly fragile, and endearingly feisty. A kitten spitting tacks at a tiger! And he knew that nothing, short of kissing her until she was breathless, would stop the tirade.

Something deep inside him shuddered. Kissing her would be a bad mistake, the worst he could make.

'If she was here right now I'd throttle her!' Her mouth compressed against her teeth as she spat out tightly, 'What gives her the right to interfere? She's done it before, in a big way. It turned out OK that time—but this time it's an unmitigated disaster!'

She pushed the hair out of her eyes with an angry swipe. 'I'm going in. I'm cold! And I'm sick of the company I'm being forced to keep!'

She stamped along the track. She wasn't cold, she was burning with rage. At him. At Evie. At every mortal thing! And she was sick of him thinking she didn't know the meaning of truth!

She felt her feet go from under her at the very same time she heard Jake's warning shout, felt him reach out for her—but too late. She was floundering in the huge pile of snow shifted by the snow plough, all the breath knocked out of her lungs, with Jake's big body sprawled on top of her because he'd lost his footing trying to prevent her from falling.

He saw her eyes go wide, diamond lights glittering in those water-clear depths, and knew she hadn't hurt herself. There was nothing wrong with her except for a bad case of temper.

Her silky black hair was spread against the soft white snow, her kissable lips parted, her breasts straining against him as she tried to recapture her breath. Sudden desire for her—the desire that had never died no matter how hard he'd tried to kill it—hit him like a hammer-blow. Blood pounded through his veins, throbbing at his temples.

She was magic, and, as ever, he was under her spell. Whatever she was, whatever she had done, he wanted her, needed her...

Bella glared up at him, at his face just inches from hers. The utter humiliation of taking a header into the snow added to her rage. She wanted to tell him to let her up, get off her, but hadn't got her breath back. She did the only thing she could—grabbed a handful of snow and pushed it in his face.

Jake brushed the snow away with what to Bella seemed like contempt; the suddenly hard line of his mouth was a fearful thing.

He was fighting for control. Her puny attack invited retaliation—and he knew how to subdue her, what it would take. A long, slow mastery, first of her senses and then of her body—a slow and very deliberate and highly satisfactory easing of the tension, an assuaging of the long, aching emptiness that was hunger—taking her with him to where they could both find the sweet solace of physical release.

But that wasn't the way, he knew that, and as his mind won over his physical needs he pushed his hands beneath the bulk of the sweater she wore, his own sweater, and began to tickle her remorselessly. His strong features relaxed into a grin as the anger went out of her lovely face and she giggled and writhed and hiccuped beneath his relentless fingers.

'Right, madam!' He let his hands slide away, giving in at last to her squeals for mercy, pulling himself up onto his knees. 'Punishment over. Don't push snow in my face again or you'll know what to expect!' The impossibly inviting yet potentially damaging situation was defused, or so he thought.

Until her eyes met his. Sparkling with the laughter-tears that spangled and tangled her long dark lashes, they drew him closer, ever closer, inviting, promising... An irresistible promise fatally reinforced by the curved, parted lips...

Jake groaned silently, trying to force his body's response out of existence—the incredible hardening, tightening, the pooling of scalding heat in his loins, the thudding beat of his heart, the desperate need for her and only her.

If he took what was being offered he knew he would be doomed—binding himself to her again, with the knowledge of her previous unfaithfulness, the mental agony of wondering if she was sneaking off to be with Maclaine whenever his back was turned eating into him like acid.

The mental reminder of her lover got him to his feet. He brushed the powdery snow from his clothes, his eyes glinting narrowly as she made no move to get to her own feet. She simply held out her hands to him, her eyes still dancing with laughter. Or wicked, wilful, wanton promise?

He took her hands and hauled her unceremoniously out of the bank of snow, the familiar sensation as her slender fingers curled around his slamming into his body. To smother it he said, with what he hoped would come over as bland indifference, 'I never knew you were so ticklish. You live and learn.'

'Well, we never did play games, did we?' Still slightly breathless, her voice emerged huskily and she gave him an unknowingly provocative glance from beneath tangled lashes.

'As I recall, we did.' His face went hard. 'The games we played in bed were mind-blowing.' He turned from her, covering the last few yards to the cottage quickly.

Bella scurried after him. 'I didn't mean that!'

Why dredge up all that had been so wonderful, so right between them, and throw it in her face? To her intense aggravation she felt herself blushing as he turned those narrowed black eyes on her.

She looked so flustered, so innocent. With a harsh inner voice he reminded himself that she wasn't. 'No? You could have won an Olympic gold, the games you played. You must have had an excellent coach. Just Maclaine? Or were there others?'

For a moment his words didn't sink in. And when they did she didn't believe it—and then she did. Oh, she believed it, all right. He would hold her relation-ship with Guy against her for the rest of his life, not understanding it, twisting it, making it ugly and un-recognisable with his total lack of trust—the way he could think the very worst of her. No room for doubts, questions. No fair hearing. Simply a blind and dev-astatingly insulting acceptance of her non-existent in-fidelity!

She stared at him, her face drained of colour, her eyes wide and dark with pain. 'Guy has never been my lover.' Her eyes dropped from his, her soft mouth trembling. The purity of her profile tugged at his heart, making it ache. 'Though there seems little point in telling you. You won't believe me.'

Too right, he wouldn't.

Before he'd met her, her relationship with Maclaine had been common knowledge. The two of them—with the bastard's wife of the moment making an un-easy third—had been the subject of endless behind-the-hand gossip, according to Alex Griffith, the long-time friend who had persuaded him to go to that fateful party. He had no reason to doubt his friend's word. He would have had no reason whatsoever for inventing such a story.

Neither of them had ever discussed her long-running affair. She, naturally enough, had never brought the subject up, and he had done his best to forget it. She'd been his—his alone—and he hadn't been able to bear to think of her sharing such inti-macies with another man. It had made him sick with jealousy. So he'd pushed it to the back of his mind, the present and the future all that mattered.

But the present and the future had been irreversibly soured when he'd walked in and found them in each others arms. Though the rot had set in long before that, when he'd discovered she'd been seeing the other man and had gone back to work for his agency.

He took his bunched hands from his pockets and pushed on the door, and she said, her voice shaky but challenging, 'There was only one man before you. And that was a short-lived disaster.'

He turned to look at her. It was a mistake. The huge eyes were pleading, begging for his trust, and she was trying to blink back tears, biting down on her lip to still the trembling. The desire to stop the trembling with his own mouth was strong enough to make him shake.

He pulled in a ragged breath, forcibly reminding himself of her acting abilities, of the manipulative, devious side of her nature which had hatched the complex plan to get him here.

'And why was that? Wasn't he wealthy enough?'

The deliberate insult was sheer, instinctive self-defence. The moment the words were said he regretted them deeply. His own wealth had never interested her during their marriage, and afterwards she'd returned every one of the generous monthly allowance cheques he'd had his solicitor send on his behalf.

To his eternal shame, he saw her slim shoulders shake with sobs, her pale hands covering her face. He abandoned his hard-won caution and pulled her into his arms. What he felt for this woman was far stronger than wisdom.

He loved her, moral warts and all. He had tried, God knew he'd tried, but he couldn't stop loving her.

'Don't cry. Please don't cry!' His voice was raw with emotion. He couldn't bear her to be hurt. He'd accused her of being something she never could be— a gold-digger, someone with her eye on the main chance. He knew that whatever else she was, she wasn't that. She had always been extraordinarily naive about financial matters. 'What I said was unforgivable,' he declared against her hair, gathering her closer.

Bella lifted her head from his shoulder to search his face, and the emotion coming from him bound them together in something sweeter than mere forgiveness. The anguish in his eyes was unmistakable. He rarely showed his emotions—she knew that—but when he did they were the genuine article.

The way he'd lashed out at her had torn her apart, but his remorse was cementing the pieces back together. She opened her mouth to accept his apology and heard him groan, his head dipping as his lips stopped the words in her throat.

His kiss was raw passion. Bella returned it—because this was what she'd been born for. To be his love, and only his. She had always loved him, always would. Like it or not, this man was her destiny.

The wild race of blood through her veins matched the burning fever of his as, bodies clinging, lips plundering and willingly plundered, they moved, dreamlike, into the tiny hall and Jake closed the door behind them with his foot.

'Bella—' he murmured, but she made a guttural

sound of protest and pulled his head down to hers again. She moved her mouth slowly, erotically, over his, tasting, stroking, melting under the onslaught of his wild response, her sweet seduction bringing his answering driven passion.

She curled her arms more tightly around his shoulders, wanting to stay where she belonged. In his arms. Under his skin.

In his life?

CHAPTER NINE

IT WAS the sweet breath of sanity at last, drawing them back to where they belonged. Together. As they were meant to be, as they'd been born to be—no longer apart, lost souls in an empty, cold, black void. Together.

Her bedroom. Bella didn't exactly know how they'd got there. It wasn't important. Only the hot hunger of Jake's mouth as he branded every inch of her body with his raw possession mattered.

Her flesh trembled, ached, burned for him. And her hands were making a clear, silent statement of fevered repossession as her fingers dug deeply, stroked and stroked again, exploring every millimetre of that strong, demanding male body. The body she knew so intimately—every muscle, every bone, every last pore of his sweat-slicked skin marked on her brain, never to be forgotten, not even if their parting had lasted through eternity. That was what was important, too. Nothing else.

Clothing scattered everywhere. Heated bodies close together, twisting, writhing in the immensity of their need to be closer still, so close that each was absorbed into the other. Fever and passion and the inescapable, beautiful simplicity of home-coming.

Bella arched her hips expressively, demandingly towards him, her whole body quivering. Her mouth was

urgently seeking his, tasting him, opening to the renewed savage plunder of his lips, responding fever-
ishly, drawing him into her, the invitation accepted by
him with a ragged groan as he slid deeply between
her parted thighs.

One moment of sheer, exquisite ecstasy. A still, un-
moving savouring of the rapturous, breathtaking moment of joining. Her body tightly enclosed his until
he gave a ferocious cry and plunged deeper, taking
them higher and higher into the wild storm of passion
until it took them both and shook them into a million
brilliant shards of pulsating light.

And then the slow descent to peace. Soft murmurs,
slow touching, the gentle glow of the aftermath—slick
bodies close, but softly now, her hair splayed out
across his firm, wide chest, her head fitting naturally
into the angle of his rangy shoulder and her lips moving softly against his hot skin. One of his hands idly
stroking the gentle flare of her hip, the other resting
heavily on the damp tangle of curls between her
thighs.

Bella sighed, a tiny fluttering exhalation, as peace
and tranquillity, both strangers for so long, took her
gently down to sleep.

The sky was black against the windowpanes but the
bedside light was on when she woke to the sound of
the door opening—Jake, naked, soft dark hair rumpled, carrying a tray.

'What time is it?' She raised herself up on one elbow, pushing her hair out of her drowsy eyes—
drowsy eyes drowning in love for him.

'Almost eleven. One more hour and it will be Christmas morning.' His lazy grin was heart-stopping. Bella actually felt her heart stop then start again, racing on out of control as he instructed gruffly, 'Move over, woman. I'm freezing. Warm me.'

She lifted the edge of the soft down duvet, her heart clenching with unadulterated joy as he slid his big body in beside her. Everything was right again; she knew it was. It just had to be!

Nothing had been said. Talk hadn't been necessary, after all. Their bodies had said everything that needed to be said.

Wrapping her arms around him, she cuddled her warm body against his icy skin, totally forgetting the loaded tray until Jake growled, 'Watch it! You want to share a bed with a mountain of toast and a lake of tea?'

The temptation to heave the tray off the bed and take her in his arms was enormous. They had made love in the very truest sense of the time-honoured phrase, and it had been all he had dreamed of during the last barren year. And more. So much more.

Yet there were questions he had to ask. Everything had seemed so cut and dried a year ago, almost to the hour, when he'd discovered her in her former lover's arms. The end. The love of a lifetime over and done with, shattered by what his eyes had told him.

But the events of the last couple of days, and the explosive need of the last hours, had shown him differently. It was far from over. Whatever happened it could never be completely over, not for him. Or for her?

He had to find out how much blame he carried for the way she'd taken up her old career, her old lover.

She was sitting up amongst the pillows, the pert, rosy tips of her breasts just visible above the edge of the duvet, her black hair a silken cloak around her slender white shoulders.

Jake said round the sudden constriction in his throat, 'Eat up. I woke starving, and didn't think either of us would want to cook at this time of night. My earlier efforts with sandwiches were enterprising, but scarcely edifying, so I played safe and made toast.'

'Looks scrummy.' Bella took a thick slice of hot buttered toast from the plate and bit into it enthusiastically, telling him round a mouthful, 'Your sandwiches were delicious, once I managed to get my mouth around them! Don't put yourself down. And I ate my share, or didn't you notice?'

He watched the tip of her tongue peep out, licking buttery fingers, and his heart clenched inside his chest. Of course he'd noticed. He noticed everything about her. Always had.

He took his mug of tea, cradling it in his hands, his voice carefully level as he asked, 'You mentioned that dream you had—about having a home in the country, a family. Did it mean so very much to you?'

She gave him a smiling, sideways look and helped herself to another slice of toast. She hadn't realised just how hungry she was. All the frantic, physical activity of a few hours ago, she thought, her cheeks going pink.

'It was what I'd always wanted,' she agreed. But it

didn't seem so important now. Jake's love, his trust, was all she craved. 'I suppose,' she added thoughtfully, 'the whole thing—a settled home, a loving family life—something I'd never had—took more room in my head than it should have done. Basically, I was lonely. You were away so much. Out of the three years of our marriage we spent one hundred and thirty-one days together. I kept a record. Does that make me paranoid?'

She supposed she must have been. She had counted days and hours, yearned for what she couldn't have, losing sight of what was truly important—that she loved him, no matter what.

'I had to be away, you knew that—or I thought you did,' he reminded her gently, his eyes soft as he watched how hungrily she devoured the toast.

He'd always known he had to stay ahead of the pack, not let anyone or anything pull him down. He had to be where the action was, use his brain, not rely on capricious luck as his father had done—losing everything in one fell swoop, plunging his loved ones into penury.

'You could have travelled with me,' he pointed out without rancour. If he'd known about her family background he would have understood the needs she'd had. It was important now for her to open up. And she seemed very relaxed right now, even smiling that wonderful, lazy smile of hers, the one that melted his bones right through to the core.

'I tried that, remember? Brussels, Rome, New York.' She took a gulp of tea. 'There was only so much window-shopping I could stomach, and the museums all began to look the same. I usually found myself having dinner alone in our suite because you were held up in meetings. And when you did get back you were toting loads of paperwork. So that kept you occupied until the small hours, and— Oh!'

Her hand hovered over the last slice of toast, withdrew. She picked up the plate and offered it to him guiltily. 'I've eaten the lot. I just wasn't thinking. Take this slice. I'm a greedy pig!'

'You want it, you eat it. I ate mine while I was making yours,' he fabricated. He would willingly starve rather than see her want for a single thing. Watching her eat with such unselfconscious enjoyment filled him with tenderness.

'So I gave up and decided I might as well stay home,' she completed. 'Not that it matters. Not now. Not at all.'

But it did. Jake knew it did. He knew now that he had his own burden of blame to carry. What had happened hadn't been all down to her. If they got this right—and he prayed to God that against all the odds they would—things would have to change. He was willing, if she was.

'And because you were bored you took up your modelling career again.' He could understand that now, though it had made him possessively jealous at the time. It had been her career, and one she had handled well.

He hadn't put any pressure on her, but had been deeply thankful when she'd abandoned it on their marriage. He had never been able to quell the unreasonable jealousy, the desire to make her his exclusive

property, the overweening distaste at the thought of
millions of nameless males lusting after her much-
photographed face and body.

That, too, would have to change. If she wanted to
pursue her career then that was what he wanted, too.

She twisted round in the cosy bed, and Jake moved
imperceptibly away. He was aroused enough already.
If she touched him there would be no more talk...

'You got it wrong,' she assured him, her lovely
eyes shadowed. 'I've finished with modelling. You
know that. When we married I told you I'd never
stand in front of the cameras again. I meant it. Guy
offered me the job of assistant manager in his agency's New Accounts department. So I took it. And I
know we didn't need the money. My modelling career
called on reserves of physical stamina, not the intel-
lect, but I'm not a fool, Jake. I knew the healthy state
of your bank balance, your investment portfolio.

'I knew all that.' She smiled into his eyes, not
wanting to denigrate everything he'd given her, but
knowing it was important to explain the way she'd
felt. 'And, honestly, I knew our apartment was the
last word in luxury—but you couldn't grow roses
round the door or walk out barefooted onto dewy
grass on a June morning. And there was a limit to the
number of times I could change the decor, buy cushions and rugs and flowers.

'I guess—' her eyes mirrored her regret '—that by
the time I decided to take that job as a way of occupying my time, we weren't heavily into communication. I told you I'd decided to accept Guy's job offer.

You assumed I'd be prancing in front of the cameras again.'

Not heavily into communication was an understatement, Jake accepted ruefully. During that last year of their marriage there'd been a total lack of anything remotely like togetherness.

He'd been increasingly aware of it at the time, putting it down to the large amounts of time he spent away from home. He had made up his mind to do something about it, had been on the point of telling her he'd delegate more, stay home, work from the London office. But it had been too late. He'd learned she'd been seeing Maclaine, had taken up her former career—or so he'd apparently wrongly assumed. He hadn't been able to handle that.

He removed the tray from where it lay on the bed between them and told himself it wasn't too late. He wouldn't let it be.

Already he had accepted the lion's share of the blame for what had happened. Bella had wanted, with more reason than most, the ordinary everyday things other people took for granted. A home that was a real home—not a sterile apartment that could have earned an award for being avant-garde—a husband who was around, babies. All the things he'd refused to give her.

The worst part would be coming to terms with her affair with Maclaine. The sudden insight hit him hard.

He didn't know whether he could handle it, learn to trust her again.

Bella watched as a shadow crossed his impressive features and took the light from his eyes. Her heart jerked. Had she complained too much when putting her point of view? But the air needed to be cleared if they were to go on. Were they to go on? And where to?

Had Jake made love to her simply because she was there? The sexual chemistry between them was as strong as ever; that was a fact of life and it wouldn't go away. Had her viewpoint of their marriage reinforced his conviction that they were poles apart in what they wanted, that all they had going for them was sex? Had he simply used her?

No, she thought decisively. Jake had far more integrity than that. And she was going to have to find a way to convince him that her dreams didn't matter. She'd woken up at last. The reality of loving him was the most important thing in her life.

'I'm going to take a shower.' She slid her long legs out of the bed, needing to lighten the atmosphere that had for some reason suddenly become brittle.

Perhaps her assumptions had been wrong, because the slow smile he gave her was warm enough to be reassuring. But he didn't follow her to share the shower, as she had more than half expected him to. When she emerged at last, clean and scented and unwrapping herself from a bath sheet, she thought he was asleep.

Eyes half-closed, she watched him. His male perfection made her breath stop in her throat. For all his muscular strength, his body was lean and elegant. He had fallen asleep on his back, his arms crossed behind his head, and Bella, suddenly, had never felt less like sleep in her life.

But she wouldn't wake him. She'd creep beneath

the duvet, cuddle up and stay awake all night, savouring every moment of this reconciliation.

Because it was a reconciliation, wasn't it?

Refusing to entertain negative thoughts, she selected a slinky, bias-cut satin nightie and wriggled
into it. For the first time she thanked Evie for her
meddling. Brushed cotton pyjamas wouldn't have had
the same allure.

When he woke, Bella knew from delicious experience, Jake would make a slow, erotic game out of
removing it. And it wouldn't be easy. A soft smile
curved her mouth as she glanced down at herself. The
oyster-coloured fabric clung to her breasts and
tummy, then flared softly from just below her hips.
Not a comfy garment to sleep in, but it made her feel
good, supremely conscious of her femininity, her sen-
suality. She hadn't felt like that since she and Jake
had broken up.

Her movements unconsciously sinuous, she walked
towards the bed, her hand going out to snick off the
bedside lamp, and Jake said, 'If you've finished, I'll
use the bathroom.'

He sounded much too alert to have just this second
woken. Why hadn't he spoken to her? Why had he
kept his eyes so firmly closed? In the past, he had
loved to watch her getting ready for bed, lazily teasing
her, suggesting which of her huge selection of nightwear she should choose, then wickedly speculating on
how long it would take him to remove it.

She almost switched the light back on so she could
read his expression when she asked him. But she

didn't do either. At this early stage of their reconciliation it might be too soon.

'Get some sleep, Bella.' His voice, she noted sinkingly, was distinctly abrasive. He vacated the bed as
soon as she slid beneath the duvet. 'Watch the stars.'
He sounded softer now, the suggestion light. 'It's a
beautiful night, and if you listen hard enough you
might just get to hear sleigh-bells!'

And then he was gone. Bella wanted to jump out
of bed and run after him, but common sense stopped
her. They'd been apart for a year, the break-up full
of acrimony and distrust, their coming together again
volcanic. He would need a little space to get things
straight in his head, come to terms with the resumption of their marriage, let it sink in.

Just because she had no doubts at all it didn't mean
he didn't have a few lingering around somewhere. So
she'd give him that space and time. For as long as it
took him to shower and come back to bed, anyway.

Then she'd wrap her arms around him and hold him
close and tell him how much she loved him. How very
much. Assure him that things would be different, that
she wouldn't ask for what he couldn't give her. His
love was all she needed.

Whenever he had to be away on business she'd go
with him. Take a crash secretarial course, perhaps, kill
two birds with one stone—feel useful and be useful.

Guy wouldn't be pleased when she quit on him.
But he'd soon find someone to fill her post and, valued friend though Guy was, being with Jake was far
more important.

Jake stood under the punishingly cold needles of the shower, his teeth gritted, his emotions in chaos. He'd never know how he'd kept his hands off her.

When she'd dropped the bath towel her skin, in the dim light, had gleamed like magnolia petals, the gentle, sensuous curves and planes of her body a voluptuary's dream.

He'd closed his eyes and kept them closed, fighting to quell the need—the need to make love to her until there was no space in his head for thought. But that would be morally wrong.

He loved her, and always would; that wasn't in doubt. And earlier their lovemaking had been spontaneous, inevitable. He grimaced, turning off the shower and reaching for a towel. He wouldn't touch her again until he knew he could take her back into his life without bitterness.

Until he came to terms with her affair, put it out of his head and learned to trust her again, there was no real way they could make a future together.

He was going to have to discover if that was possible.

He hoped to hell it was.

CHAPTER TEN

'YOU'RE up early,' Jake said.

Christmas morning, not yet quite light. And, yes, Bella was up early. She'd been up for ages. She was moving around the kitchen doing housewifey things to keep her mind from brooding over everything else.

'There's fresh coffee in the pot, and orange juice in the fridge. Help yourself while I cook breakfast.'

She sounded bright enough and normal, didn't she? She looked OK, clad in the faithful leggings and sweater, her hair neatly scooped back and fastened at the nape of her neck, the skilful application of make-up hiding the tell-tale signs of a miserable, wakeful night.

Just an ordinary woman doing ordinary things. Disguising the utter misery inside her, the hateful feeling of being used and discarded.

She laid bacon slices and tomato halves on the grill pan, then reached for the eggs, and Jake said, 'The full works, is it?'

He was leaning against the worktop sipping his juice, and her head came up as she caught the thread of tension in his voice. Dark sweater, dark jeans, shadowed black eyes. He had shaved, but he still looked as if he had a five o'clock shadow, the harsh lines of his face telling the story of his own restless night.

'As we're leaving tomorrow I thought we should use as much as we can from the fridge. Such a waste, otherwise.' She slid the bacon under the grill and drizzled some oil into the frying pan. Did she sound laid back and in charge of her life, all that inner despair and hopelessness nowhere in sight?

And what right did he have to look as if he'd spent last night tossing and turning, agonising, when she knew differently?

Waiting for him, all done up in slinky oyster satin, she'd snuggled into the blissful warmth of the duvet, watching the stars just as he'd suggested, rehearsing exactly how she'd tell him how much she loved him, how she'd changed her plans for the future so they'd fit happily with his. That he mustn't think she was making sacrifices because, when it came down to it, all she wanted was him.

She'd sort of mesmerised herself into falling asleep, waking in the early hours and not finding him beside her. Bewildered, disorientated and alone, she'd switched on the light and checked the time. Two o'clock. He couldn't have been in the shower for two whole hours!

Anxiety had taken over then. Had he slipped on the soap and knocked himself out? Leaping from the bed, she'd scurried to check. That vividly imagined disaster hadn't happened. But another one had. She'd discovered him sound asleep in his own bed.

He hadn't been lying awake, pretending, had he? She hadn't taken time to check. Just flicked the light on, viewed the rigid mound under the duvet that was similar to her own, and flicked it back off again. She'd

crept back to her own room on leaden legs, saturated
with that hateful, hurtful feeling of having been used.

He'd had no reason to pretend to be asleep. The
facts punched holes in her brain. He hadn't wanted to
be here, that was for sure. He'd even said their separation was a relief. He was a very physical man and
she'd been around, and willing—more than—and was
still his wife, of sorts. So he'd done what any man
with rampaging male hormones would have done—
taken advantage.

Used her and discarded her.

If he'd seen a future for them and their marriage
he sure as hell wouldn't have gone back to his own
bed! He would have come back to her, if only to talk,
maybe suggest they try again, make a go of their marriage this time.

Suddenly aware that she was rapidly losing her precious control, rattling cutlery like castanets, practically hurling the china onto the table, and that Jake
was watching her with narrowed eyes, she did her best
to calm down.

She dragged in a deep and wobbly breath, and Jake
took the knives and forks from her shaky hands.

'I'll see to the table; you keep an eye on the food.'

She turned away jerkily. She couldn't meet his
eyes, not wanting to see cynical understanding or,
even worse, lurking amusement.

Bacon was sizzling; eggs were popping and almost
jumping around in the pan. She turned the heat down
under them and rescued the bacon, making her movements smooth and contained now, forcing herself to
keep calm because he was more than astute enough

to read her mind, to laugh at her inside his head for being dumb enough to think that a couple of hours of mind-bending sex could alter anything.

He'd made the toast, and was dropping it into the rack when she slid the loaded plates down on the linen place-mats.

He held her chair out for her and she arranged herself in her seat, praying she looked relaxed enough to put him off the scent.

'Happy Christmas, Bella.' It sounded more like a question than a salutation. He joined her at the table. 'I don't have a gift for you, but you'll understand why, given the circumstances.'

Last year he'd chosen diamonds in New York. The only stones he knew that could come anywhere near the brilliance of her eyes.

The velvet-lined box had been in his breast pocket when he'd walked in the door and found her wrapped around Guy Maclaine.

He'd handed the gems over to charity.

'I could give you the perfume I'd brought along as a gift for Evie, only I don't quite see you ever using it,' she offered, the lightness of her tone achieved with enormous difficulty.

It was a silly, pointless conversation to be having, when the air they breathed was full of tension. Well, for her, at least. But she supposed the show had to go on—and all that stiff upper lip stuff. She picked up her cutlery and unconsciously emulated Jake, cutting her bacon into very small pieces and pushing them around her plate, unaware of his suddenly narrowed eyes focusing on her.

'You said Evie had meddled in your life before?' He gave up all pretence of eating and poured coffee for them both. Hot and strong and black, the way they both liked it. Could she have been telling the truth? Had she had nothing to do with this set-up at all?

Whoever had arranged it had done him a huge favour; he accepted that now. His hurt, the sense of bitter betrayal, had been too great to let him seek her out. Being forced into her company had allowed him to accept that he still loved her.

At first he'd disbelieved everything she'd said, colouring every word that came out of her mouth with the dark shades of that final betrayal. But he'd come to see that a lot of the blame for what had happened had been his, and he didn't want to believe that most of what she'd said to him was lies.

If he could get to the bottom of what had happened here it would be a start. She hadn't answered, was staring into space, apparently, cradling her cup in her long white hands. 'So what happened? What did she do?' He gave her a gentle verbal prod.

What did it matter? Bella gave an involuntary shrug and replaced her cup on its saucer. Still, she supposed the subject was unimportant enough—it certainly didn't have any bearing on what had happened between them last night—a subject he wouldn't want to have to discuss—and it would beat sitting around in silence.

And if last night hadn't meant a damn thing to him, had been simply a way of assuaging lust, then she could pretend it had been the same for her. Couldn't she?

'She entered a photograph of me for a nationwide competition to find what they called "the face of La Donna"—to launch the then-new exclusive range of cosmetics and fragrances. I didn't know a thing about it until I heard I'd won.'

She gave him a level look, hoping she was boring his socks off. The rags to riches storyline wouldn't mean a thing to him. As far as she knew he took the privilege of wealth for granted. All he'd ever wanted, in her experience, was more of it.

'At first I was embarrassed,' she remembered, 'then furious with her. A modelling career had never entered my head. But she was little more than a kid—only thirteen at the time—and we'd always been close, so I couldn't stay mad with her for long.'

'It must have changed your life.' He had always assumed she'd gone out for fame and fortune herself, capitalising on her fantastic looks. A slight frown indented his brow as he replenished their cups from the pot.

Had he assumed too much? If he'd been wrong about one thing, could he be wrong about others? Why hadn't he asked her more than the most basic questions about her earlier life? Because, to him, the past hadn't mattered. Only the present. He had won the only woman he'd ever truly wanted, and the time he'd spent with her had been filled with the wonder of the achievement, the wonder of her.

And the rest of the time—the majority of it, as she'd reminded him—he'd been bent on achieving success on success in the world of high finance. So what did that make him?

An over-achiever with no room in his head for the little things, the things that mattered. His self-esteem reached rock bottom.

'Dramatically,' she agreed, oblivious to his mental turmoil, gone away from him into the past. 'I was still in shock when I went for that first meeting with Guy. He was, and still is, of course, head of the agency which was running the launch campaign. I was painfully awkward, stiff and shy and terrified. He took me right under his wing,' she recalled, her mouth softening fondly. 'Guy made me see there was nothing to be frightened of and everything to go for. I honestly don't think I could have gone through with it without him.'

'Well, bully for him!' Everything inside him froze at her repeated and doting mention of that hated name. His reaction was instinctive, the bitterness of a man for his enemy.

Bella gave him a look of shock which quickly turned to angry, defensive castigation.

'He was the only person I could trust in those early days. He was my friend!' A true friend.

She gathered up the breakfast dishes with an angry clatter and dumped them on the drainer, her back to him as she snapped out, 'Without his monumental kindness I'd have backed out of the whole thing. Without his patience and expertise I would have frozen rigid the first time the cameras pointed in my direction!'

She turned the hot water on with a savage twist of her wrist. 'And I'd have missed out on the opportunity to give Mum an easier life, provide her with the things she'd never been able to afford to have.' She swiped their uneaten food into the wastebin. 'And because when Dad was with us we were always moving around Evie's education had been as patchy as mine. So we could then afford a private tutor for her, right? And first-rate secretarial training later. So I owe all that to Guy. Right?'

She was angry enough to do him physical damage. She skittered round on her heels and faced him. There had been no need for him to use that sarcastic tone. What had Guy Maclaine ever done to him? She had already countered his wretched suspicion of an affair between them. Or didn't he believe her?

The absence of trust had ended their marriage, but it hadn't ruined their reconciliation because there hadn't really been one. Just a cruel slaking of lust on his part and the obliteration of a stupid dream she'd had no right to indulge in on hers.

Or didn't trust really come into it as far as he was concerned? When he'd found her with Guy on that dreadful night, might it have been the escape route he'd been looking for? Had he grown tired of her? Bored?

She spat the new and hateful suspicions at him, her hurt at the way he'd used her love for him last night not letting her hold anything back. 'You want to believe I had an affair with Guy! It gave you the excuse you'd been looking for, didn't it? You never questioned what he was doing at our apartment that night, did you? You just called me a vile name and walked out!'

'If I'd stayed I wouldn't have trusted myself not to

wring both your necks!' He was on his feet now,
black eyes slits, tormented by the memories of the
thing he was trying so hard to come to terms with. 'I
came back when I'd cooled down. You'd gone. Not
to him, of course; he was still married. The note you
left told me our marriage was over. I had to accept
that—it made sense, after all.'

Bella stared at him, the pent-up emotions inside her
making her shake. So little faith, and no trust at all.

She could have told him exactly why she'd been
wrapped up in Guy's arms, but she wouldn't demean
herself by offering explanations he wouldn't believe.
Possibly because he wouldn't want to believe them.

'Believe what the hell you like—I'm beyond caring!' she ground out untruthfully, and, snatching her
coat from the peg on the door, she walked out into
the bright dawn of Christmas morning.

Jake forced back his instinct to go after her. She
needed time to calm down. There was no doubt about
it, he had a tigress on his hands.

There was a hidden emotional depth that he had
never taken the time to plumb—that was going to
change. If she'd agree to start over, he'd spend the
rest of his life getting to know her. The real Bella,
not just the fantastic face and body that had bewitched
him from the moment he'd first seen her.

Keeping a watchful eye on her ferociously stamping progress up and down the cleared track, he me-
thodically cleared up in the kitchen and lit a roaring
fire. She'd come back inside when she'd got rid of all
that fury.

And he'd treat her like spun glass, so gently, win her back to him.

The sensation of being at peace with himself at last flooded through him. He believed now that Evie had meddled with Bella's life in a big way for the second time, with the help of his own sister this time. But that didn't matter—or only inasmuch as he was back on course, trusting her not to lie to him.

What really mattered was the way he'd finally and suddenly come to terms with her infidelity.

He could easily understand how the affair had begun. Maclaine was attractive to women, and she'd been very young when he'd met her. And she'd been grateful to him for helping her to achieve the financial security she and her family had never known.

And later his own long absences, his dedication to his work, his thoughtless prevarication when she'd mentioned babies, telling her they'd discuss all that some time in the vague future, had eventually driven her back to her former lover—the man who, or so it now seemed, had given her one hundred per cent of his attention.

His shoulders were broad enough to carry all of the blame, and in the future—if she'd give them a future—he would provide her with everything she craved for. He'd sort that out as soon as they got away from here.

But until he could show her that his good intentions were more than the hot air and vague promises he'd carelessly tossed at her in the past, and could offer her the solid physical proof that everything had changed, he'd walk as if he were treading on eggs.

He wouldn't use their physical need for each other to blackmail her into being part of his life again.

The release from the canker of bitterness and anger was exhilarating. It had been nudged out of sight by the one great constant in his life—his love for her.

He crossed again to the window. Halfway down the track her slender body was dwarfed by the icy immensity of the snow-clad mountains. His heart surged with the determination to make their future as perfect as it could possibly be, keep her close to him, as much a part of his life as she was a part of his heart.

He prayed to God she'd give him a second chance.

When Bella walked back in, the scene was festive. Leaping firelight, sherry and two small tulip glasses side by side on the coffee-table, Jake fixing a strand of multicoloured fairy lights on the tree.

She felt as if she were on the outside looking in, a kid with her nose pressed to the window pane watching yearningly something it could never be part of.

'You forgot to use the lights.' Carefully Jake gave her the most casual glance, the smallest smile. He wouldn't give her so much as a nudge towards the decision he was determined she would make when he'd put his own life in order.

'I didn't know how to fix them.'

If he wanted innocuous conversation she'd give it to him. Right now she felt too weary to fight him. She'd walked the rage out of her system and, although it would probably come back—trailing hurt and the feeling of being used and discarded—she was too drained at the moment to cope with anything other than the superficial.

Jake crawled round the base of the tree and pushed the plug into the socket. 'There.' He stood up, veiled eyes on her face, watching the way her eyes widened as the brilliant little lights came on, all the colours of the rainbow strung along the forest-green branches of the tree.

Something caught at his heart and tipped it over. Until her success she'd probably never had her own Christmas tree. Her father wouldn't have wasted money on such a thing, and after he'd run out on them all her family had probably had a struggle even to afford to eat.

Their first Christmas together had been spent at that rambling, Elizabethan inn, the two subsequent ones in the sophisticated elegance of a Bahamian hotel. The third—the third had been an unmitigated disaster.

But from here on in things were going to change. A sudden mental picture of the two of them dressing an enormous tree, stacking brightly wrapped gifts around it, flashed into his mind. It was followed by the moving image of a bunch of children—their children—galloping down the stairs at first light to investigate what Santa had brought them.

The future as she had always wanted it to be was what he wanted, too. And it was what they were going to have.

'What should we do about that turkey?' he asked lightly. He wanted to take her in his arms and paint a picture of the future they would have together. But it was too soon. He had to tread gently, give her proof positive of his good intentions first.

'Oh.' Bella blinked, and the dancing lights stopped mesmerising her. 'Cook it and eat it, I suppose.' Could she pretend they were a normal couple spending a normal Christmas together?

It was, she supposed, the only civilised thing to do.

'Then we'll do it together.'

Bella flinched. His smile was so warm it hurt her. She nodded, walking into the kitchen ahead of him, taking off her coat as she went. He was an enigma.

Two hours ago they'd been almost at each others throats, the pain of the last year spilling out. And now he was behaving as if it hadn't happened. As if last night hadn't happened.

What had happened between them last night was something he'd already put behind him. He didn't want to talk about it, or think about it, and he certainly didn't want to repeat it. As far as he was concerned it had been a one-night stand.

She would have to dig deep to find the strength to cope.

CHAPTER ELEVEN

IT WAS almost a relief to be heading away from the cottage at last. She wouldn't let herself dwell on all the painful regrets.

Bella sneaked a look at Jake's strong profile, and then wished she hadn't. There was an aura of excitement about him that was positively tangible. If she touched him she'd probably get an electric shock.

The prospect of getting away and dumping her safely back at her flat, out of the way, getting on with his own highly successful life must have mega-appeal if it made him look like that. It was as if he simply couldn't wait!

'The mechanic they sent out was on the ball,' he commented as they left the valley behind them and turned carefully onto the mountain road, the surface of which was compacted with frozen snow, just as the valley track had been. 'With us at nine, on the dot. That's what I call service.'

Bella said nothing. What was there to say? His heart-felt, appreciative comment had only reinforced what she'd just been thinking about his eagerness to put her out of his life again.

He'd been ready and waiting when she'd come downstairs that morning at a few minutes before nine, champing at the bit, as she'd described his mood to herself. He must have been up for hours. Everywhere was clean and tidy—the hearth swept clear of ashes, the baubles and lights taken down from the tree and stowed neatly away in their box. And that, more than anything else, had made her feel as if her world had stopped.

It was as if the time they'd spent together hadn't happened. And when the rescue vehicle had come into sight, advancing slowly down the track, he'd been out of the door as if someone had sprung a trap.

She'd built up a foolish dream, founded on nothing more substantial than hope, and he'd stamped on it. And this morning's breathtaking eagerness to get back to his life was grinding her silly dream into the ground.

And it hurt!

'I must remember to arrange to have flowers sent to Evans' wife,' he murmured, concentrating minutely on his driving because the conditions were on the side of downright dangerous.

Because the driver of the tractor had been instrumental in arranging his escape, Bella deduced acidly. She wished he didn't feel he had to make idle conversation, as if she were a stranger he felt he had to entertain.

'I suppose,' she answered dully, too miserable to care, and Jake took his eyes from the road for a second, sweeping them over her tight features.

'Headache still bothering you?' he asked softly.

As if he cared! 'Not at all,' she disclaimed stiffly, and looked pointedly out of the window at her side. The headache was fictional. She'd made it up because

she hadn't been able to stand another second of the
false spirit of Christmas.

Yesterday, while the turkey had been roasting,
they'd lunched on nuts and sherry, picked at a salad
and a bowl of fresh fruit. And he'd followed her
everywhere. Wherever she'd been he was there, at her
shoulder. Helping. They'd prepared the vegetables together and he'd laid the table in the living room, un-
earthing candles from somewhere, so they'd dined by
candlelight and firelight and the glitter from the tree.

Oh, she'd tried to be adult and civilised about it,
but the tension had wound her up to the point of almost saying something she'd regret, coming out with
something decidedly personal, like telling him she
loved him so much she thought she was dying from
it, and begging him to take her back!

She wouldn't have been able to bear his pity, contempt or plain disbelief when he thanked her for the
offer but said he wouldn't take it up, if it was all the
same with her. Because that was what would have
happened; she knew it in her bones. Otherwise why
had he brought the shutters down so effectively?

So she'd invented a headache, blamed it on too
much wine, and gone to bed. Where she'd known
she'd be safe. And so she had been. He hadn't so
much as poked his head round the door to say good-
night.

She spent most of the seemingly interminable journey wishing it was over so she could crawl into her
own space, be alone and lick her wounds. But when
at last they drew up in front of the mews flat she
shared with Evie, Bella panicked. He was her hus-

band, and she'd probably never see him again. If the past year was anything to go on he'd avoid her like the plague.

She simply couldn't go on like this.

He cut the engine and turned to her, and she got in first, before he could say anything—anything at all. 'We never did get around to discussing the divorce.' And she watched his face go tight.

'Divorce isn't in the frame,' he ground out through his teeth.

Was that anger in his black, black eyes? Or shock? Bella didn't know, or care. It was enough to have brought it home to him that she did exist, as his wife, albeit estranged. That she wasn't a passing stranger he had decided to be polite to, to the extent of making general, idle conversation to while away the time.

If he didn't like to be reminded that they were still legally tied, then tough! She would force the situation down his throat if she had to.

Ever since they'd made love he'd brought the shutters down. He treated her with politeness, with impersonal consideration, like a stranger. It was far harder to bear than when he'd been openly scathing, angry with her and at the situation they'd been put in.

'Why not?' she countered, her voice splintering with anger. She'd get a real response from him if it killed her! 'Our marriage is over, despite the mutually satisfying romp we had on the night of our fourth wedding anniversary.'

She'd stress that, oh, she would! He'd hurt her too much. The need to retaliate in kind was despicable, she knew that, but she hadn't been able to stop the raging words from falling off her tongue.

'You don't know what you're saying,' he told her. His face was white beneath the olive tones of his skin.

So she had forced a reaction, even if it was merely anger at her temerity in daring to mention something he had probably already conveniently forgotten.

'Oh, but I do,' she answered him back. 'Despite the sex, which I have to admit was well up to standard, our marriage was over the moment I knew you didn't trust me. I knew you didn't love me because, the way I see it, trust has to be the biggest part of loving. You immediately thought the worst, and went on thinking it. And believing it. I knew then that there wasn't any point.'

He wasn't answering. He looked as if she had just exploded a bomb under him. 'If you don't want to discuss divorce, we'll forget it,' she conceded finally, flatly, the fight draining from her, leaving her feeling weak and hopeless.

Divorce wasn't in any way important to her. It wasn't as if she would ever want to remarry. Jake was the only man she had ever loved, could ever love. She'd only mentioned it to get a real response.

She could see his point of view, too. Despite her having returned every one of the allowance cheques that had come through his solicitor, he might be understandably wary of the final break.

A divorce settlement could cost him heavily. The acquisition of wealth seemed the only thing that mattered to him. He wasn't to know she would never accept a penny from him, and he might suspect she would take him for all she could get, simply out of spite, if the break was made final.

'Bella—' He shifted in his seat, facing her now. He took one of her hands in both of his, and she let it stay there. It was beyond her power to snatch it away, and she self-destructively impressed this final touch on her memory banks. 'We do need to talk. Make arrangements for the future. At the cottage—' impressive shoulders lifted heavily '—the time wasn't right. You said trust was important.'

His eyes seemed to be probing her soul. 'I'm working on it, believe me. And I'm asking you to trust me now. We'll meet soon, have dinner, sort everything out.' The look in his eyes told her he wanted that very much.

Stupid hope soared again, filling her heart until she felt it might burst, and try as she might she couldn't stop it.

'When?' she asked, her voice low and husky, hoping he'd suggest the very next day.

'Soon,' he promised vaguely, his eyes hooded now as he rubbed his thumbs over her knuckles lightly before releasing her hand. 'I'll be in touch. I can't say when. I've a fair amount of business to attend to.'

So what else was new?

She released her seat belt, the momentary insanity of hope draining away. Business would always take precedence. Didn't she already know that? She scrambled out onto the slushy pavement. He would have far more important things to do than wine and dine his estranged wife, to talk her into accepting the status quo.

Because that was what it was all about. She was sure of that now—keep everything the same, a wife, but no wife, tucked away, never seen, making no demands. Avoid having to swallow a divorce settlement that would make a dent in all that money!

'I'll see you when I see you, then.' Echoes of the past! Of the times when she'd watched him walk out of the apartment, immaculately suited, briefcase in hand, his thoughts already gone from her, on another plane entirely. And had that been her voice, all high and hard?

She slammed the passenger door, lifted her bags and walked away, knowing she wouldn't see him again—because when he did get round to finding the time to make that date she'd tell him to get his solicitor to put whatever was on his mind in writing!

No way would she put herself through the hell of seeing him again.

For the rest of that day and the whole of the next Bella was alone. No sign of Evie. She felt more isolated than she'd been at the cottage. At least she'd had Jake for company.

But she wouldn't think about Jake, she vowed. Not ever again. Yet when the phone rang, startling in the silence, her stomach churned over sickeningly. Jake? Making that dinner date? Making time for her in his busy, busy life?

It was her mother, phoning long distance.

'I tried to get you on Christmas Day. Both out enjoying yourselves, were you?' She didn't wait for a reply. 'Your auntie sends her love. She's thinking of coming back with me when I visit again in the summer. You won't mind? Is Evie in? Is she still seeing that Mitchell boy? He's something in computers, isn't he?'

A sudden change of tone told Bella that she was about to come out with what had been uppermost in her mind. 'Have you and Jake got together yet and tried to sort things out?'

Bella ignored that for the moment. She'd answer briefly and in context. 'Evie's not here. She found out Bob Mitchell was already married and dropped him. At the moment I think she's got a crush on her new boss, so she's bounced back, as usual. And Jake and I have nothing to sort out. Our marriage is over. And my job's keeping me—'

Her mother wasn't interested in her job. 'Both you and Jake need a spanking!' she cut in. 'You're two lovely people, you had a lovely marriage. So you had a tiff, a difference of opinion—that's not the end of the world. All couples have them—'

Bella switched off. 'A difference of opinion' was putting it too mildly. They had both wanted vastly different things. But she had been willing to change, to want what he wanted, because she'd wanted to be back in his life. She'd been sure she could learn to live with his lack of trust; surely she could if she really tried? It was a flaw in his character she could do nothing about.

She would have told him, tried to pull their marriage back together, but he'd withdrawn the intimacy that would have made it possible. And now she was thankful she hadn't set herself up for the unbearable

humiliation of having him tell her he wasn't interested.

'So it isn't any wonder, is it? Bella?'

'Sorry, Mum, I didn't quite catch that.'

'That I worry about you.'

'Then don't. I'm fine, really I am. Getting on with
my life, making friends.' She gently steered the conversation away from the subject. Her mother had had
a dreadful marriage and, understandably, she wanted
her daughters to fare better. Bella couldn't blame her
for nagging, but when the call ended she knew she
had to do what she'd said—get on with her life.

She had her job and she enjoyed it. And she had
the new friends she'd made at the agency. In the past,
when she'd been invited to socialise, she'd always
politely refused. Not any more. She would start to do
some inviting of her own.

She picked up the phone. She'd call Guy and Ruth
first, find out if the New Year party they were throwing at their home, with agency staff welcome, was still
on. If it was she'd invite herself.

She heard the key in the lock as she ended the call.
Evie. Anger at what her sister had done came back
with a blistering whoosh.

Wearing a blue silk shift that matched the colour
of her eyes and clung to her curvily plump figure as
if it had been grafted on, Evie swayed on her very
high heels and croaked, 'What are you doing here?'

'Waiting for you. Wondering which floorboard to
bury your body under!'

'Oh, don't!' Evie looked as if she was about to
burst into tears. 'Don't shout. I'm dead on my feet! I

went to a party on Christmas night and it went on and on. I'm *still* recovering from it—I've got this splitting head!'

'Good.'

'And I'm freezing cold. I lost my coat—or someone stole it. I swear I'll never go to another of Lizanne's parties again as long as I live!'

'For an adult woman with a new boss and responsible job you certainly know how to act like a cretin!' Bella snapped. The Christmas conspiracy involving her and Jake and the type of irresponsible adolescent party that went on for forty-eight hours coalesced into one huge, unforgivable whole.

Then, seeing the tears trickle down the pale, pretty face, Bella relented. The mention of her job, the new boss Evie rarely stopped talking about, was probably responsible for the overflow.

Sisterly feeling prompted her to offer, 'Take those ridiculous shoes off and go and sit down. I'll make a pot of black coffee.'

All her life, or so it seemed, she'd been caring for Evie. She could vividly recall the two of them snuggling down in bed, the blankets pulled up over their heads to muffle out the sound of their parents shouting at each other, and Bella telling stories to take her little sister's mind off what was going on.

And later, after their father had gone, she'd had to take full responsibility for the bouncy, irrepressible Evie because their mother had had to be out at work to keep them.

So she'd learned responsibility early; it was only a pity some of it hadn't rubbed off on her sibling!

'What you and Kitty did was inexcusable,' she stated now, her clear eyes condemning. Strong black coffee and the warmth of the central heating had worked wonders; Evie looked almost like her old, bouncy self. 'You had no right to interfere in my life—or Jake's, for that matter!'

Evie curled herself more closely into the back of the armchair, pulling the cushion from behind her and wrapping her arms around it as if for protection against sisterly wrath.

'It was the only thing we could think of,' she defended. 'You're both obviously still crazy about each other, but refused to get together and thrash things out. Too much pride,' she tacked on scornfully. 'So Kitty and I worked out the scam last October—to force you to meet and stay together for at least a couple of days. We thought it was time enough for you to get your act together, anyway.'

Bella, pacing the room, swivelled round and glared. 'My only consolation is that the ''scam'', as you call it, will have cost you both a mini fortune!'

'I guess you're telling me it didn't work,' Evie said mournfully. 'We only did it for the best. Cos we love you, even if you are both stupid! Think about the mess our parents made of their marriage and compare it with what you and Jake had.' Her voice wobbled. 'What you had was beautiful. It used to be a joy to see you together.'

Bella stopped mid-pace, her justifiable annoyance over Evie's meddling washed away by a flood of tears that brimmed her eyes and clogged her throat. The two younger sisters had been desperate to help. But all the beauty had gone out of the marriage that had started so perfectly. Nothing could make it come back.

She swallowed hard and made herself go and perch on the arm of Evie's chair. 'You're going to have to accept that it's over,' she said quietly. 'I have. And no amount of good-intentioned meddling will alter that.'

Evie lifted a troubled face. 'Did you explain about that Maclaine chap? Tell Jake it wasn't what he thought it was?'

'Yes. I told him Guy had never been my lover.'

'And?'

Bella shrugged expressively. She'd told him the truth, but she didn't know now whether he'd believed her. How could trust be so easily shattered?

'After he'd got over his anger at the way we'd been tricked he behaved reasonably and considerately.' She wouldn't confess to the way they'd made love. She couldn't. It had happened because she still loved him and he still lusted after her. The sexual chemistry between them was still as explosive as ever. But it wasn't enough for either of them.

'Then, when he dropped me off here on Boxing Day, he would have driven away with nothing more than a polite goodbye. But I mentioned divorce, to remind him we were still married. But he doesn't want one. Too costly, I would imagine.'

Her voice hardened. 'He wouldn't want a dent in his precious fortune.' She pushed herself on, knowing she had to forestall any questions before she could draw a line beneath the traumatic episode. 'He then

decided he'd better give me dinner some time—fit it
in when he had a convenient space in his work schedule—to persuade me that this separation should continue as it is, in his own best interests.'

'Oh, Bel, don't be so cynical! It's not like you.'

'Just looking at life through untinted specs.' Bella
pushed herself to her feet. She couldn't talk about it
any more, relive the pain in words that skimmed the
surface of the truth and left out the emotions that
wouldn't go away. 'I'll forget what you did on the
condition it's never mentioned again. And now I think
it's time we both turned in.'

Bella had dug deep in the back of her wardrobe and
found the perfect dress for the party. Shimmering gold
tissue, scoop-necked and clingy—displaying too
much leg maybe, but why the heck not? If you've got
it, flaunt it, as her model friends would have said!

Anyway, it was New Year's Eve, and she was going to have fun. Yes, she was, she told the annoyingly
sad eyes that stared back at her from her bedroom
mirror.

Ruth, Guy's wife, had said, 'Oh, yes, do come,
Bella. The more the merrier, truly! Most of the agency
staff are going to be putting in an appearance at some
stage, not to mention a load of mine and Guy's
friends. I just hope the noise won't disturb the
twins. But Mother-in-law came up from Sussex for
Christmas, and she's still here. So she'll be on hand
if they do wake. She's an old battleaxe, but she's really good with the babies.'

So she would socialise for a change. Besides, Jake

hadn't contacted her. She hadn't really expected him to, had she? Giving her dinner, talking over the arrangements for their separate future would come very low down on his list of priorities.

Everyone else would be taking a break over the festive season, but he would be jetting to wherever the next killing could be made, poring over balance sheets and financial projections.

She caught her thoughts and slapped them down brutally. She'd made an early New Year resolution never to think of him again. She was going to stick to it!

Starting the fiddly business of piling her hair on top of her head, she thought about Guy and Ruth instead. They had moved to a big family house in Hampstead before the birth of the twins. She was truly happy for them, and wasn't going to fall into the trap of envy.

They'd had a rough ride. A year into the La Donna campaign Guy—her dear friend by then, and professional support—had confided that he and Ruth were having a trial separation. They were finding it difficult to be around each other, he had told her.

'Ruth's desperate to have kids, but nothing happens. We've had every test known to medical science and we're both OK. So she blames me for not caring either way, and herself for caring too much. She can't leave it alone. She's getting paranoid and I'm getting irritable. Next thing, she'll be blaming the government, or the weather! We thought we'd be better apart for a while, before we start throwing things at each other.'

But things had worked out for them in the end.

When Guy had phoned on Christmas Eve, over a year ago—

No. No. No! She must not, *would* not think of any of that!

'Your taxi's here.' Evie poked her dark curly head round the bedroom door. 'Are you ready, or shall I ask him to wait?'

'Ready.' Bella pushed the final pin into her hair and stood up, reaching for her wrap and the gold kid evening purse that went with the dress. 'Are you sure you don't mind being on your own? You could come with me. One more won't make any difference.'

Evie shook her head decisively. 'After Lizanne's thrash I'm off parties.' Her blue eyes went dreamy. 'I thought I'd check through my wardrobe to find something suitable but less stuffy to wear for work. Maybe try out a new hairstyle.'

The new boss, Bella thought, turning away quickly and descending the stairs as rapidly as she could in high, spindly heels.

She could hardly bear to see the glow in the younger girl's eyes.

She could remember exactly what it felt like to fall in love.

CHAPTER TWELVE

HE WOULD be gatecrashing, but Jake didn't give a damn!

When he'd phoned from his hotel near Regent's Park he'd got Evie. He'd missed Bella by about half an hour.

Evie had started to apologise for tricking him, and putting his hired car out of commission, but he'd cut her short. After that getting information on Bella's whereabouts had been like pulling hen's teeth.

The information had come reluctantly. She didn't know when her sister would be back. Late, probably. It was New Year's Eve.

She had gone to a party.

A party in Hampstead.

And—this came most reluctantly of all—a party at the home of Guy and Ruth Maclaine.

The address had had to be forced out of her, and then she'd gone on to say something else, something rushed and breathless which he had cut short, telling her thanks and goodbye.

When he'd put down the receiver his heart had been pounding, the hatefully familiar shaft of jealousy which he'd believed he had conquered twisting his gut.

But he wouldn't let all that concentrated hard work go to waste. Not without a bloody hard fight.

He'd spent the last five days on the phone, setting up meetings and dragging people from family celebrations, pulling rank and generally making himself unpopular, fitting in a flight to Brussels, where he'd worked into the small hours consolidating deals, and then back to London to appoint key personnel.

He hadn't borrowed precious time from other people's family Christmases and worked himself to the point where exhaustion felt like a distinct possibility to get stymied at this last moment—particularly not by his own possessive streak where Bella alone was concerned.

He pushed any unwelcome doubts roughly aside and strode through the foyer, past the elaborately uniformed doorman, into the flurries of sleet that came on the back of a biting wind.

He didn't notice the cold or the damp flakes of wet snow that settled on the shoulders of his dark-grey suit jacket and drifted amongst the soft strands of his black hair, or the glittering Christmas decorations strung overhead as he flagged down a cruising taxi and gave the Hampstead address in a hard, tight voice.

Back at the cottage, when she'd told him Maclaine had never been her lover, he hadn't believed her. He had believed what his old friend Alex had said all those years ago because he had no reason not to. But, more importantly, he had believed the evidence of his own eyes.

Mercifully, he'd come to terms with it. He'd made too many wrong assumptions in the past—about Bella's resumption of her modelling career, the set-up back at the holiday cottage. Had he been wrong to assume she'd been unfaithful? Could what he had seen that dreadful night have a perfectly innocent explanation?

He didn't know, not for sure. How could he?

He pushed that thought roughly aside. He had to build on the future and not brood negatively on the past.

When she'd talked to him of trust, and his lack of it within their marriage, sincerity had been exhaled with every breath, had shone steadfastly in those fantastic eyes.

Against all the evidence he had instinctively accepted her innocence. What he had seen could be explained away. He had to believe that. He only had to ask.

He remembered his decision not to ask her there and then to resume their marriage, not to plead with her. And wondered for the first time if it had been the right one to make. Self-doubt was a stranger to him, though, and he knew what he wanted. Knew that what he wanted would be the right thing to do.

When he gave her the gift of the rest of his life, his entire future, his complete and infinitely loving attention, he wanted it to be whole, accomplished, not vague promises which—and with hindsight he couldn't blame her—she very probably wouldn't take seriously.

That was what he had now—the gift of his total commitment. He prayed to God it wasn't too late.

When she'd mentioned divorce, spoken so tonelessly of that mutual eruption of need—the wild desire, the fulfilment they'd both ached for twelve long months—the temptation to take her in his arms, kiss her until she was unable to think of anything but him, had been almost unbearable.

But he'd stuck to his original decision, and all he had been able to do was promise to contact her as soon as he was able, ask her to give him what he'd been unable to give her. Trust.

But what if he'd been wrong? Had she decided that an affair with Maclaine was the better option?

If rumour was correct, the Maclaine marriage had been on the rocks. But they were obviously together now. Was that a so-called civilised arrangement? Was Maclaine presenting a façade of a contented marriage but unable to let go of his creation—the exquisitely beautiful face and body of La Donna?

And was Bella clinging to him because he was a constant in her life? Her father sure as hell hadn't been, and he, although he hadn't realised it at the time, hadn't been much better.

He closed his eyes, his teeth clamped together. He would not let himself think like that. He would not doubt her. Not again. He would not!

The taxi pulled up outside the large Edwardian house. Lights blazed from the lower-floor windows, and security spotlights illuminated a sweeping drive-way packed with parked cars.

Asking the driver to wait, Jake strode towards the house, unaware that the sleet had turned to heavy rain, soaking him, plastering his hair to his skull.

Bella wished she hadn't come, and tried to hide it. Her first attempt at socialising wasn't bringing her any pleasure—far from it.

Maybe it was simply down to the time of year. The Christmas season was for sharing with loved ones. Everyone here was part of a couple, and the crunch had come when she'd overheard one woman saying to another, 'Getting babysitters at this time of year is almost impossible. And New Year's Eve—we had to pay an absolute fortune!'

And her companion had confided, rubbing her slightly bulging tummy, 'My dear, John and I will be in the same boat this time next year. Oh, lovely thought! We're both ecstatic at the prospect of starting a family.'

Bella had wished herself a million miles away, because everything reminded her of what she wanted and couldn't have.

Jake. Jake's love. Jake's babies.

Bella's fingers tightened round her wineglass. She'd drunk half of it, but it hadn't helped get her in the party mood, and Ruth said concernedly, 'Are you all right? You went quite pale just then.'

'I'm fine.' Bella managed a creditable smile. 'A bit tired, that's all.'

'Hectic Christmas?'

'You could say!' Traumatic, devastating, ecstatic and truly, truly painful. Did that add up to 'hectic'? She wondered how she could still be smiling. The smile was stuck to her face, she supposed.

Ruth said, raising her voice because the noise level was continually increasing, 'I'm going to slip away and check on the twins and Ma-in-law. Would you like to see them?'

'I—' Bella didn't see a way to get out of this. But gazing at four-month-old baby boys didn't seem a good idea right now, not when she was feeling so vulnerable.

Then Guy came to her rescue, catching the tail-end of the conversation, throwing an affectionate arm around Ruth's shoulders.

'Bella can gaze in wonder at my handsome twin heirs later. Right now I've a business proposition to put to the lady.'

'Oh— You!' Ruth twisted in his arms and reached up to brush her knuckles playfully over his rock-solid chin. 'Business, business! Give the girl a break—she's come to a party, not a strategy meeting, or whatever!' Nevertheless, she went, wagging her fingers at Bella. 'See you later. If you want to party, tell him to get lost!'

But Bella heaved a sigh of relief at the timely interruption. She had never felt less like partying in her life, and, though normally she would have loved to slope away and peek at the little boys, she knew it would be her undoing. Tears and abject misery for all she had lost and could never now have would have made her the party-pooper from hell!

'Listen...' Guy took her arm and drew her to a marginally quieter corner of the big room, away from the lavish buffet. 'I've been thinking of you. We had a big—and I mean big—commission confirmed just before Christmas. In New Accounts you'll know all about it—the new top-of-the-range sports car, aimed primarily at top-of-the-range females?'

Bella nodded; she knew all about the prestigious account. Her immediate superior had worked his socks off to clinch it. A smile tugged at the corners of her mouth as Guy's bushy eyebrows met over the bridge of his crooked nose—broken on the rugby field, so Ruth had told her—his head tipped to one side as he peered down into her face.

He was her boss, and if he wanted to talk shop she was more than game. Her job was all she had now.

'I want you on it—not on the account; I can replace you in that department without too much trouble. But on film. As you know, the company want a series of six commercials running through spring and summer. I can't think of anyone who'd be as perfect as you. Will you do it? For me?'

His smile took her acceptance for granted, and it lit up his near-ugly face, making it wickedly attractive. Bella couldn't help responding in kind, but she knew she'd never go back to her former career. She had grown to hate all those greedy eyes, the endless speculation, the cruel, gossiping tongues.

She shook her head, reminding him, 'I've been out of it for too long. Four years, remember.'

'Nonsense.' He took her chin between his thumb and forefinger, eyes intently assessing every detail of her face. 'You're as beautiful as when you started out. More. You've acquired the gloss, the sophistication our clients want. You're one classy lady, Bella, and there's not a sag, wrinkle or line in sight!'

Her chin still captured in his hand, she gave him a

wistful smile. She would do a lot for Guy, but not this. Right through her earlier career he had been her rock, her very good friend. He had always been there for her when it had mattered, and, although only around fifteen years her senior, she had come to look on him as a father-figure.

'I'm sorry,' she whispered regretfully. 'But I'm happy as a pen-pusher. I couldn't go back to all that hype and frenzy—flashbulbs exploding wherever I go, spiteful gossip in the press, endless speculation.' She gave him an impish grin. 'I only did it because we were flat broke, and the money meant Mum could take it easy and Evie could realise her full potential and not end up as another unemployment statistic. You know that!'

She saw the light go out of his eyes, and knew he'd had the campaign sorted in his head, with her in the starring role. She felt a tug of compassion. Lifting a hand, she laid it softly on the side of his craggy face. 'With your talent for picking winners, you'll find the perfect girl, I promise. There are literally hundreds of young and beautiful models out there, waiting for the opportunity you can offer. Go out and find that special one, Guy, and leave me pushing my pen.'

Standing in the open doorway, Jake felt his eyes home in on her immediately. He didn't see the crowd, the groups of chattering, laughing people. Only Bella and Maclaine.

The sensation of *déjà vu* was intense, jealousy, pain and the feeling of betrayal taking him by the throat, shaking him. Just as it had done on the night of Christmas Eve over a year ago.

As when he'd first seen her, at the party Alex had dragged him to she was the focus of all his attention, all his needs and desires. A raven-haired beauty in a shimmering dress. Maclaine was cupping her delicate face in his big paw, and she was, as before, curving her slender body into the support of his.

She was listening to what he was saying intently, her fascinating eyes locked with his, smiling a little now. And as Jake, in this crowded, over-heated room, saw only the two of them, so they, obviously, saw only each other.

His eyes closed as a pain so savage he thought it might rip him apart rocked him back on his heels. And when he forced them open again he saw her reach out a pale, slender hand and place it lovingly on the side of his goddamn ugly face.

And he knew he had lost her. For one moment, as his head bowed and his body sagged against the door-frame, he accepted his loss, and his world became a dark, empty, bleak place, a place he didn't want to be.

But only for a moment. He wouldn't jump to con-clusions. And he knew with a wild lifting of his heart that he trusted her. The scars had healed. Where he loved, he could trust.

Unaware of the curious eyes now turned to him, the gradual silencing of party-time chatter, he lifted his head, straightened his shoulders and pushed his way through the crowded room, his face, though grey with fatigue, scored with the arrogance of his determination.

The changing, charged atmosphere must have penetrated even their mutual absorption, he noted grimly as she turned and met the savage single-mindedness of his narrowed black eyes.

What colour she did have drained from her lovely face and then quickly returned, concentrated in two hectic splashes lying against the high perfection of her cheekbones.

He reached out, his fingers curling around her arm, just above her elbow, keeping himself under tight control because he couldn't bear to bruise that tender flesh. He would never do her even the slightest harm.

'What the hell do you think you're doing?'

Maclaine didn't recognise him at first; Jake could see it in his eyes. Then why should he? He hadn't gone out of the way to seek his former enemy's company. And he guessed the violence of his emotions must be stamped all over his face. Little wonder the man looked as if he was squaring up to throw him out of his house!

Jake left him in no doubt as to his identity, telling him smoothly, 'I've come to collect my wife. Lovely party, but I'm afraid we can't stay.'

Bella went with him without a murmur. She was shaking inside, but wouldn't let it show. Aware of the intense silence in the room, the murmurs that were beginning to break out in their wake, the politely muffled hum of excitement, she stared steadily ahead, every nerve in her body stinging in sharp response to the determined man at her side.

She didn't bother to find her wrap, didn't even think of it, wasn't aware of the lack of it until the cold wind, the deluge of rain, made her gasp.

Silently, he swept her into his arms and strode rapidly between the parked cars. His body was as taut as steel. Anger? Her shocked mind hopelessly grappled for reasons.

There was a black cab waiting at the kerb, the meter ticking over. Jake put Bella in the back and went to give the driver instructions, giving her the opportunity to get her head together.

His behaviour could only mean one thing—he still believed she and Guy were having an affair.

Could all that inner tension stem from the fact that she was still nominally his wife, his property, albeit unwanted property?

She couldn't believe that. He was the most urbane, controlled man she had ever known. It had to be something more, and yet she couldn't allow herself to hope. If he still loved her, needed her in his life, he would have told her so.

Wouldn't he?

'There was no need to act like a caveman,' she said in a rough little voice she didn't recognise as her own as he joined her and the cab drew away from the kerb. 'I would have left if you'd asked me in the normal manner. And you could have stayed, had a drink, joined in our conversation.'

She was plucking nervously at the hem of her dress. The fabric was sodden, even though he'd whisked her through the deluge as quickly as possible. And his clothes were worse, his hair plastered to his head.

In the dim interior light she could see the harsh black glitter of his eyes. He was having trouble hanging onto his precarious control; she knew that. The way his voice shook told her that. And one more push could do the trick, make him lose the last, tenuous hold and tell her exactly what this was all about.

She thought she knew—she hoped she'd got it right—but she needed to hear it from him.

Taking her courage in both hands, reminding herself that it was probably now or never, she said tartly, 'You still think I'm capable of having an affair with Guy, right under Ruth's nose! Is that what you think of me? And now you'll never know—were we whispering sweet nothings, counting the minutes until we could be properly alone? Or were we having a nice, friendly, innocent conversation? Tough, isn't it?'

She got a response. Not the one she'd expected. But the way he gave a smothered groan and dragged her into his arms told her all she wanted to know.

Jake felt her body tremble in fevered response, her arms going out to him, fingers tangled in his hair, holding his head to deepen the already fathomless kiss.

His mouth moved slowly over hers, tasting the sweet moistness of her lips. His hands stroked over her body, needing to touch all of her, feel the heady warmth of her flesh beneath the clinging damp cloth.

She still wanted him physically; he knew that. Nothing she could ever say or do could hide that from him. Not when he touched her. And that was all he ever had to do. She couldn't hide the fire and the fury, the sheer meltdown of her response.

It was something to build on, something no other man could ever take from him. All he had to do was convince her that his scars had healed, that he could trust her, could be there for her always if she still wanted him to be. All she had to do was say yes.

Becoming aware that the taxi was at a standstill, Jake lifted his head and almost drowned in the shine of her luminous, bewitching eyes.

'Where are we?' she murmured dizzily, hating the necessary withdrawal. In his arms there were no doubts, no fears. Together, close, they were one being, elemental.

'My hotel.' He helped her out. His voice was ragged. The doorman hurried down, holding a huge striped umbrella over them both. Bella felt certainty, the joy of coming home, swell up in her heart, spilling over in a smile that would not go away, and was still there, hovering on her mouth, when they reached his suite.

But his eyes were serious, his mouth tight. 'Get out of those wet things. Shower. I'll ring room service and get into dry clothes. After that, I've something to say to you.'

She shook her head and felt her hair finally tumble down, cloaking her shoulders. She pushed it back from her face impatiently. She wanted to get the talking over now. Stop him hurting. Tell him what she should have told him over a year ago.

If he didn't trust her as far as he could throw her, did it really matter? What right had she to expect him to be perfect? And would she have trusted him, in a similar situation?

A year ago she'd been rigid with pride. Now she had none where he was concerned. She stretched out her hands to him. 'Say it now. Please.'

'Later.' He ignored the offer to take her hands in his. His face could have been carved from stone. 'You're wet and cold. Do as I asked.' He tipped his head. 'The bathroom's through there.'

Dictatorial devil! she thought, but did as she was told because it seemed the quickest way to hear what he wanted to say to her. That he had decided to end the marriage, whatever the cost, seemed a distinct possibility. And yet the way he had claimed her, frog-marched her away from Guy and the party, the way he'd kissed her, his earthy moans of triumph when she had kissed him back...

Quivering with the tension of not knowing, she stripped off her sodden clothes and left them in a heap on the marble tiled floor. She felt as if she'd been wired up to an electric charge and any moment now would explode in a million fizzing sparks.

Her time under the shower was the absolute minimum, and she wrapped herself in the towelling robe supplied by the hotel management. All that done in record time, she suddenly quailed at the thought of going out there and hearing what he had to say.

She felt like a prisoner in the dock, waiting for the jury's verdict!

Grabbing a towel, roughly drying her hair, she felt armoured enough to face him. An attitude of casual insouciance would surely help her cope, hide the state of her nerves.

But the room was empty. And there was nothing in

the room to offer her any comfort. Luxurious, but impersonal. No sign of his occupation. She wondered how long he'd been staying here. Did he base himself here when he was working from London? She knew he'd off-loaded the Docklands apartment.

Didn't he ever feel the need for a home? A real, lived-in family home, where he could relax, let the rest of the world go hang, secure in his own personalised space?

Or didn't his surroundings matter to him? Was the acquisition of wealth and power the only truly important thing in his life?

And did surroundings matter to her? The answer, she knew, was yes. But he mattered more. She would live in a shoe-box with him, if he'd let her.

Room service had already delivered a tray of coffee. She wondered whether to pour herself a cup, but was afraid she wouldn't manage it. Her hands were shaking too much.

She let the towel slide from her edgy fingers, and stuffed her hands into the deep pockets of the robe. He walked through from what she presumed was the bedroom, and her heart stood still.

She loved him so much it was a physical pain. He'd changed into a pair of scuffed dark denims, and a black, soft cashmere sweater. He looked sexy as hell, but remote, grimly determined.

Her eyes met the dark enigma of his. She tried to read what was on his mind, but only when he spoke to her did she know. And when she did her heart twisted over and seemed to die, because surely this had to be the end.

'In spite of what I'd heard—that before we met you were more in Maclaine's bed than out of it—and in spite of what I'd actually seen, I tried to believe you spoke the truth when you told me you'd never had an affair with him,' Jake said bluntly, releasing her gaze as he walked over to the tray and poured from the elegant coffee-pot. 'I even managed it for a time. To believe you, that is.'

He passed her a cup, one brow lifting as she took it, the cup rattling on the saucer in her jittery hands.

Bella put it quickly down on a glass-topped table, and put herself on the cream hide-covered sofa. It was a case of sitting down before she fell down. Her legs had turned to water.

'But when I saw the two of you together tonight, I had to accept you could have lied. No—' he shook his head impatiently as she would have spoken in self-defence '—don't say a word. Hear me out.'

He was pacing the floor now, endlessly, the muscles of his body taut. 'And in that moment the whole world went black. But only for a moment. Trust came like a lightning bolt. I'd carried possessiveness too far, made too many false assumptions. Not waiting for answers, not believing them when they were given—as they were given when you told me you had nothing to do with the set-up in that mountain cottage. I knew I could trust you with my life.'

The pacing stopped. He faced her. There was a self-denigrating twist to his mouth she had never seen before. It astounded her.

'Can you ever forgive me for that lack?' he asked rawly. 'I failed you in every way that was important to you. I want us to start again. If you agree, things will be different, I promise.' He spread his hands, palms upwards, as if he held his life in them, offering all that he was to her.

'I've spent the last five days reorganising my working life. Delegating. Someone else can do the legwork. It's done. Sorted. My time will be spent with you and our family. If you still want my children.'

For the very first time she saw him unsure of himself, and she hated it. He shouldn't have to beg for what she freely wanted to give him. That he should subjugate his own needs, relinquish the cut and thrust of business, was a measure of his love for her.

She had only ever wanted his love, his trust. Everything else was irrelevant.

Happiness gushed through her like a wave breaking on rocks, and pure energy ran through her veins as she shot to her feet and covered the distance between them in jaunty strides.

'Now you listen.' She sounded breathless. 'It's my turn to come out with a few home truths.' She saw him flinch, every muscle tightening as if to prepare himself for a body blow, and couldn't bear it. Her hands went up to cup his beloved face, and she saw the vital spark of hope light up his eyes as she said throatily, 'Jake, I love you. Only you.'

She recognised the glow of intent deep in his eyes, and knew that in a moment she'd be held in his arms and there wouldn't be time for words, or any coherent thought left in her head. So she said with simple sincerity, 'I'm glad you sorted things out in your head and learned to trust me. I can't tell you how much that means to me. But, to put the record straight, whatever you've heard about my relationship with Guy isn't true. Just sly gossip, spread by people with nothing better to do.

'I've already explained how he looked out for me, and he was and is my friend. And, yes, his marriage did go through a rough patch, largely to do with Ruth's apparent inability to conceive. But he desperately wanted it to work because he'd been married before and it broke up. I don't know why; he didn't tell me.

'And, yes, we were seen around together. In my job there were a lot of functions and parties and stuff I had to attend. I had no one to escort me. I'd only had one man-friend, and that relationship turned out to be a disaster.'

He had taken her hands in his, his dark head bent as he pressed tiny, lingering kisses into her palms. She dragged in a helpful breath and gabbled on, not sure how much time she had left to get everything said before her mind blanked out beneath this sensual onslaught.

'He was a photographer who, I found out, thought bedding his female subjects one of the perks of his trade. If I thought very hard I might be able to remember his name! So Guy escorted me, and we ignored the gossip, and Ruth knew it wasn't true. And, tonight, he was trying to persuade me to take it up again—modelling. I told him no.'

He surely wasn't hearing a thing she said! His mouth had found the pulse points of the tender insides of her wrists. She didn't know how long she could hang onto her shaky control.

She dragged her hands away. 'Listen to me!' She backed away, putting the tenuous safety of a small distance between them. 'You walked in that night and found me in Guy's arms. And, yes, I guess it did look suspicious,' she agreed, seeing his body go tense again, his eyes take on that watchful, assessing look that told her he was weighing every word.

'He was comforting me. Being a friend. I'd been crying my eyes out over you, and he was telling me you'd have a good reason for being delayed.'

The watchful look had intensified. It made her bones shiver. But she'd allowed his lack of trust to ruin what had been left of their marriage before; she wouldn't let it happen again. Besides, hadn't he said he trusted her now?

To escape his eyes she turned and picked up her coffee, drained her cup. Her hands were completely steady now. She was, she decided, inhabiting the calm eye at the centre of the storm.

'You were to be home that Christmas Eve. I'd planned to make it special. You'd promised to be there, and, talking to you on the phone, I had the feeling that you wanted to get everything right again as much as I did. We both knew something was going wrong. But you didn't come. The meal had been prepared for hours. I'd put my glad rags on. My ears were sticking out on stalks listening for the sound of your key in the door. The phone rang—I thought it had to be you, telling me you'd been delayed, were on your way.'

She shivered, the memory of what had happened fraying her. 'It was Guy, phoning to wish us happy Christmas and spread his good news. Ruth had had her pregnancy confirmed. They were expecting twins. I wasn't listening,' she confessed tightly. 'I was bursting into sobs of disappointment because it wasn't you. And Guy and Ruth, like the good friends they are, came straight on round. Ruth was in the kitchen making fresh coffee and Guy was still trying to comfort me when you walked in, called me a vile name and walked out again. And didn't come back.

'I should have told you all this, waited around until you did decide to show up,' she whispered miserably. 'Got Guy and Ruth in to confirm it, if you couldn't believe me. But pride got in the way. You didn't trust me, and at the time I couldn't live with that. I didn't know then that you'd heard the old gossip about me and Guy, let alone believed it.'

She felt his arms go around her waist, and leant back against the strength of his body. Her voice was shaky as she told him, 'I want you to believe me now—not for my sake, but for yours. I don't want you to be hurt by doubt.'

'Sweetheart!' His voice was rough with emotion. He turned her in his arms. 'I hate myself for ever doubting you, for taking a later flight than I'd originally intended. But mistakes don't matter if we both learn from them. And I have learned, I promise.' His mouth claimed hers as he breathed, 'Oh, God, how I love you!'

She would treasure those words for the rest of her life, do her utmost to deserve them.

For the second time that evening he scooped her into his arms, but this time those black eyes were glittering with another emotion entirely, his intended destination far removed from the back of a cab. He dropped her on the big double bed and joined her, their limbs tangling instinctively, inevitably, no parting conceivable, not in their lifetime.

Bella awoke to a gentle rapping on the bedroom door. She yawned drowsily, delicately, like a cat, her body sated from passion.

She peered up at Jake through a tangle of black lashes. Sitting upright, propped against the pillows, his naked body gleamed like dull satin in the half-light of a winter's morning. His wide mouth was soft, tender, his eyes loving as he stroked the tumbled hair from her eyes then called 'Come.' His eyes held hers as he told her, 'Breakfast. Something special to mark a new beginning.' He got up and took the loaded tray from the room service waiter.

Scrambled eggs and smoked salmon. Bella forked up delicious mouthfuls as Jake poured champagne. He rejoined her amongst the wickedly rumpled sheets, holding his glass to hers, holding her eyes with his.

'Happy New Year, sweetheart.' His eyes glittered with sinful intent. 'Shall we start it as we mean to go on?'

Her heart quickened with immediate response. But there was something she really had to say. 'About your giving up work—you made it sound as if you were taking a very early retirement.' She couldn't ask that of him, let alone expect it. It was too much for him to sacrifice.

'I did some thinking,' she explained, idly running a fingertip across the rangy breadth of his chest. 'I could take a secretarial course and help you out on trips abroad. That way we'd be doing things together. I know how much work means to you. I can't see you staying put and twiddling your thumbs.'

'I have no intention of twiddling anything—well, certainly not my thumbs.' He grinned, planting a light kiss on the end of her nose. 'I grew up with an obsession about security. When I was a kid we seemed to have it all—a good home, everything any of us wanted, within reason. Dad owned a successful high-street hardware store, but he lost it, lost the house—everything. He found gambling on the stock market more exciting than selling screws and buckets.

'He killed himself soon after he'd been made bankrupt, and we were forced to live on the State, try to make sense of what had happened. I would have trusted that man to the ends of the earth. After what happened, the way he just left us to cope without him, mistrust came easily.

'I inherited Dad's fascination with the money markets,' he told her soberly. 'But, fortunately, not his capacity to make mistakes. But it was always there, at the back of my mind—the fear that I could come unstuck in a big way. It drove me to work harder and harder, determined that any family of mine would never have to suffer the way my father's did. It became an obsession. I didn't stay still long enough to register the fact that I'd got enough financial security to last several lifetimes.'

He rubbed his thumb over her lower lip. 'I've at last woken up to the fact that I want to make a life with you. A real life. Now, if you're still of the same mind, shall we see if we can begin to make that family of ours?'

The sinuous, seductive twist of her body against his was all the answer he needed.

EPILOGUE

'IT'S going to be a white Christmas,' Jake said, drawing the heavy brocade curtains, closing out the wintry landscape.

'Perfect!' Bella fixed the diaphanous fairy on the top of the tree and shuffled round on the stool she was standing on, holding out her arms to her beloved husband.

He helped her down, holding her close. In spite of her condition, in spite of his objections, she'd insisted on dressing the tree herself, as she did every year. She rested her head against his chest, twisting sideways a little because of her bulk. He felt the new life they were expecting in a few weeks' time kick against his body, and his hand went to hold her glossy dark head exactly where it was for a few more moments.

She was the most precious thing in his life, and her happiness spilled over and made his whole life bright.

A crash, a delighted squeal and a definite chortle alerted him to the fact that the second most precious thing in his life was up to mischief.

Incorrigible mischief—which was why they'd put him in his walker while the tree was being dressed, out of harm's way—or so they had thought.

'Bedtime, I think,' Jake stated, marching to the rescue, and Bella waddled after him, giggling as she retrieved the scattered brightly wrapped packages she'd stacked in a corner waiting to go under the tree after Jamie had gone to bed.

Starfish hands had found them. Jake gently ungripped the tiny fingers and lifted his son into his arms, where the grip was immediately transferred to his hair. 'I'll bath him,' he said. 'Put your feet up.'

'I'll make supper.'

'You'll put your feet up.'

Bossy, she thought, kissing her squirming son a fond goodnight and watching with love-drenched eyes as her husband walked from the room. She turned then, allowing the mellow homeliness of the room— one of over a dozen in this converted farmhouse—to soak into her.

Sometimes the perfection of her life overwhelmed her, filled her heart until she thought it would burst.

The perfect home, found only days after that ecstatic reconciliation. Deep in rolling countryside yet only an hour's drive from London.

The perfect child, and another to come.

The perfect husband. Oh, he still kept a finger decidedly on the pulse of his business affairs, but he worked from his study at the side of the house. It was a book-lined room, bristling with the technological monsters that allowed him to use his talents as an independent international financier, the head of a huge insurance company and a highly successful backer in the industrial and technological arenas of the world.

He still made time to share her life, care for her, taking a hands-on interest in helping her make a garden, manage the strip of woodland that bordered their very own lake.

The perfect husband, except for that bossy streak. Bella threw another log on the fire and went to make the supper, wondering if he'd like the gift she'd selected for him.

After a great deal of thought she'd decided on a chainsaw.

'Keep still, young Jamie. Kicking's fine when I'm teaching you the rudiments of football. Right now I'm trying to get you into this sleeping suit.'

Jamie talked back at him in baby talk, very fast and rather loud, and, mission accomplished, Jake squatted back on his heels and eyed his son. His son eyed him back then yawned, his dark eyes drooping.

Jake grinned and scooped him up, holding him close to his heart as he carried him out of a bathroom that looked as if a hurricane had struck. Somehow, when he took over Jamie's bathtime, it always ended up that way. And he got soaked.

As soon as he'd got him bedded down in the nursery he'd change and then make supper. He hoped Bella was doing as he'd told her—resting.

He was creeping carefully from the dimly lit nursery when Bella joined him.

'Asleep?'

He nodded. Their son had needed a whole bunch of stories, plus several not-very-tuneful renditions of lullabies—recalled out of desperation—before he'd consented to settle down.

Jake reached out and pulled her into the circle of his arms and Bella whispered, without a hint of contrition, 'Supper's almost ready. You'll just have time to change out of your wet things.'

'I thought I told you to rest,' he muttered gruffly as he helped her down the stairs, making sure she didn't trip. She had a mind of her own, and he loved her all the more for it. And he knew darn well he was only being allowed to help her down the staircase she used unaided twenty times a day because she liked him to touch her!

He wasn't what he'd call averse to it himself. As they successfully reached the foot of the stairs, just before he kissed her, he wondered if buying her a ride-on lawnmower had been the right choice of a gift for Christmas.

Constantino's Pregnant Bride

CATHERINE
SPENCER

Catherine Spencer, once an English teacher, fell into writing through eavesdropping on a conversation about romances. Within two months she changed careers and sold her first book to Mills & Boon in 1984. She moved to Canada from England thirty years ago and lives in Vancouver. She is married to a Canadian and has four grown children—two daughters and two sons—plus three dogs and a cat. In her spare time she plays the piano, collects antiques, and grows tropical shrubs.

CHAPTER ONE

CASSANDRA WILDE stepped out of the elevator of the office complex where her company was located, and pushed open the heavy plate-glass doors of Ariel Enterprises. Immediately, the discreet hum of success surrounded her, from the restrained and melodic chime of the phone, to the quiet conversation of clients in the open lounge to the left of the reception area.

Normally, she'd have stopped to acknowledge familiar faces, and make sure people visiting for the first time were being well looked after. But not today. There was nothing "normal" about today.

"Oh, Cassie!" Meghan called out as she passed her personal assistant's desk. "There's a visitor—"

But Cassie merely shook her head and kept on going until she was safely inside the sanctuary of her own office. Then, and only then, did her tight, professional smile slip into obscurity, washed away by yet another fit of soundless, hopeless weeping.

Leaning against the closed door, she stared through her tears at the blurred image before her. Sunlight bounced in rainbow prisms through the floor-to-ceiling windows and fell across the pale gray carpet in a swath of gold. It turned her rich mahogany desk into a cube of iridescent ruby, and studded the silver frame holding a photograph of her late mother with shimmering ersatz diamonds.

One end of the sliding windows stood open a foot or two. Outside, on the small balcony, a planter of freesias dispersed their delicate scent on the warm March breeze wafting into the room. From fourteen floors below, the muted din of street traffic merged with the raucous shriek of seagulls soaring under the blue bowl of the sky.

It was a perfect spring day in San Francisco. And one of the bleakest Cassie had known in all her twenty-seven years. But crying about it would do no one any good, nor would it change her situation, so making a real effort to control herself, she stepped away from the door.

She needed to calm down. Confront matters head-on. Adjust her plans for the future which, all at once, had changed shape dramatically. She needed to *focus!*

But her thoughts kept harking back to a chance meeting with a man who lingered in her thoughts, as sharply defined as if she'd last seen him just yesterday; as if it had been only last night that he'd taken her in his arms and taught her how pale and insignificant her previous sexual encounters with men had been.

How slender the coincidence which had brought them together. And yet, how fatally life-altering!

It had begun innocently enough, early the previous summer. She and Patricia Farrell, her best friend since Grade Two and, for the last four years, her business partner, had driven up to the Napa Valley to confer with Nuncio Zanetti, a valued client and owner of one of California's most acclaimed wineries. Twice a year, he rewarded his employees with a dinner cruise on *The Ariel,* the ninety-six-foot motor yacht which she and Trish had bought at the beginning of their working relationship.

Nuncio was a generous man who enjoyed spending money and whose tastes ran to the extravagant. But he was also demanding, and expected of others the same

attention to detail he brought to his own endeavors.
Choreographing one of his social events entailed months
of meticulous organization, an iron-clad guarantee that
every clause in his contract would be honored, and a
willingness, particularly on Cassie's part, to take the
time to consult with him in person, whenever he re-
quested, even if it was only to confirm that plans were
moving ahead smoothly and according to the blueprint
they'd drawn up together.

That particular sun-filled day, when she and Trish had
arrived to finalize arrangements for his Midsummer
Night's cruise, he introduced them to Benedict
Constantino. A childhood friend of Nuncio's, Benedict
told them he now lived mostly in New York from where
he oversaw international distribution of his family's citrus products.

"Most especially the bergamot," he told them, when
they asked. "It grows only in a very small area of southern Italy, which makes it a rare commodity worldwide.
You're probably familiar with its use in fine perfumes,
but what you might not be aware of is that, among its
other applications, it's of great value to the pharmaceutical industry."

Later, when the discussion turned to living in New
York, he'd smiled at Cassie with particular warmth, and
said, "I find the energy of the city exciting, but I can
see many advantages to dividing my time between there
and the west coast. California, I suddenly discover, holds
unsuspected attractions, also."

Thoroughly captivated by his European charm and sophistication, Cassie and Trish had been easily persuaded
to join both men for lunch in the winery's beautiful private garden, once the business of the day was concluded.
They'd spent a delightful three hours, lingering over

scallop ceviche and the sparkling red wine for which the Zanetti vineyard was famous, and if Cassie had thought her imagination was working overtime in believing the handsome stranger had shown more than a passing interest in her, she certainly learned differently, the next time they happened to meet.

An imperious rap at her office door brought a swift end to her reminiscing. A second later, Trish stepped into the room, her brow furrowed with concern. "Cassie? I saw you come in just now and you didn't look...quite right. Is everything okay?"

For a few brief moments, Cassie had managed if not to forget the predicament facing her, then at least to relegate it to the sidelines. But at her friend's question, it came roaring back to the forefront of her mind, and the waterworks started up all over again, gushing forth with renewed vigor.

Trish let out a horrified gasp, promptly shut the door before the ragged sobs reached the ears of the people in the outer office, and whispered, "Cass, you're scaring me! The last time I saw you this upset was at your mom's funeral, and the time before that was when we were six and went to see the movie *Bambi*."

"Well, crying's the last thing in the world I planned to do right now," Cassie wailed, lurching behind the desk and flopping down in her chair. But the irony implicit in the word "planned" sent her already raging hormones into overdrive and produced another round of humiliating tears.

Trish perched on the arm of the chair, stroked Cassie's hair away from her forehead, and begged, "Talk to me! Whatever the problem is, we'll handle it together, the way we always do."

"Not this time," Cassie sniffed, so awash in self-pity,

regret and morning sickness that she didn't care if she lived or died. "This is a mess entirely of my own making."

"It can't be that bad."

"It's worse than bad. It's...inexcusable. Shameful."

"Shameful?" Trish rolled the word around her palate as if it were a morsel of unfamiliar food, and when she spoke again, there was a note of amusement in her voice. "Hey, I know you had an outside appointment this morning and that you were perfectly fine before that, so what happened between the time you left here and the time you came back again, that you now have reason to feel ashamed? Did you lose one our biggest accounts? Make such a colossal miscalculation on a quote that we're headed for bankruptcy?"

"No. The company's never been more solidly in the black. It's my personal life that's falling apart." Aware of the thread of anxiety underlying Trish's attempt to treat the situation lightly, Cassie plucked a tissue from the box at her elbow and made a heroic effort to pull herself together.

She blew her nose and deciding she might just as well come straight to the point since dancing around the subject would do nothing to lessen its impact, said bluntly, "My appointment this morning had nothing to do with business. I went to see a doctor. An obstetrician." She waited a second to let the significance of that sink in, then finished off with the obvious. "I'm pregnant."

"Pregnant? No, you're not!" Trish scoffed. "You never find time for a steady relationship with anyone, and you're definitely not the one-night stand type."

Cassie didn't answer. Couldn't, if truth be told, because she was too embarrassed even to look her friend in the eye. But her silence spoke revealing volumes and Trish was too astute to miss their meaning.

Her mouth fell open. "Good grief, you did! *Cassandra!* You had a one-night stand!"

"Uh-huh." Cassie swallowed. "And that's not the worst of it. There's more."

But the rest—the part which hadn't struck Cassie as too terrible while she was in the doctor's office, but which had grown more foreboding with every passing minute since—went ignored. Trish was still reeling, too shell-shocked from what she'd already learned, to cope with "more." "Are you absolutely sure—that you're pregnant, I mean?"

"I'm sure."

You're a good ten weeks along, the obstetrician had confirmed. *With proper care and if you're very lucky, you'll be hanging an extra stocking from the mantel next Christmas.*

If you're very lucky...

"But—" Trish paused, clearly trying to step as delicately as possible through the minefield suddenly confronting her "—who's the father?"

Cassie opened her mouth to reply, but fear closed her throat. *What if the pregnancy didn't go well? If the complication the doctor suspected did, in fact, occur?*

"Cass?" As the silence lengthened, Trish draped her arm around Cassie's shoulders. "You *do* know who he is, don't you?"

Outraged, Cassie spluttered, "Well, of course I do! I might be all kinds of a fool, but I'm not a slut!"

"Honey, I never meant to suggest you were! But if you were coerced..." Trish's voice sank to a near whisper, as if loath to put into words the ugly suspicion suddenly tainting her thoughts. "If you didn't know the man...if he forced you....

"I wasn't raped, if that's what you're afraid of," Cassie said hurriedly. "I knew the man, and I was...more than willing."

Embarrassingly enthusiastic, in fact! Depressingly eager!

"So he has a name." Less a statement than a question, the remark hung in the air, stubbornly waiting to be acknowledged.

On a sigh of defeat, Cassie wiped a hand over her face. "Yes, he has a name. It's...Benedict Constantino."

She muttered the name furtively, as if she were afraid the walls had ears. Trish, though, exercised no such discretion. "Benedict Constantino?" she squealed, loudly enough to send the seagull perched on the balcony railing fluttering away in alarm. *"Benedict Constantino?"*

"Broadcast it to the whole world while you're at it, why don't you?" Cassie said peevishly, too nauseated to care that she was making a rare exhibition of herself.

Immediately contrite, Trish said, "I'm sorry, I really am. But if you'd asked me to guess who in the world might have lured you into his bed, for a one-night stand of all things, Benedict Constantino's is the last name I'd have chosen. He's so aloofly correct. So...gorgeously unattainable."

Hardly words to describe him the last time she'd seen him, Cassie thought, turning hot inside even all these months later, at the fresh onslaught of memory. *That* night, the man she'd previously known only as the charming friend of a business acquaintance had shown himself capable of blistering passion, and all without benefit of anything as mundane as a bed!

Trish was regarding her as if she'd suddenly sprouted two heads. "How did it...happen?"

"Well, how do you think?" Cassie snapped. "He might be rich, powerful and beautiful, but he still puts his pants on one leg at a time, just like any other man."

"And takes them off the same way, it would seem, but I wasn't asking about *that*," Trish said. "We might have been friends for a lifetime, but that hardly entitles me to poke my nose into every last intimate detail affecting your life. What I meant was, how did you happen to run into him again? It's not as if he lives down the street, after all. New York's not exactly next door to San Francisco."

"He flew out for Nuncio Zanetti's New Year's Eve party."

"New Year's...?" Trish's eyes grew big as saucers, as awareness dawned. "Oh! *Oh! That* night!"

"Yes, that night," Cassie echoed glumly.

"So it really was a spur of the moment fling. If it hadn't been that one of our staff got sick and couldn't work the New Year's Eve cruise, you'd probably have spent the night watching TV at home. Instead, you stepped in to cover her absence, ran into Benedict again, and—"

"And while the rest of the guests on board welcomed the New Year in traditional style, Benedict and I celebrated less conventionally, and I was left with a gift that'll keep on giving for the rest of my life!" The tears began again, swamping her voice. "I feel like such an idiot!"

Trish pushed the box of tissues closer. "Come on, Cassie, this isn't like you!" she said bracingly. "You've never been the type to fold under pressure. You don't weep and wail, you cope."

"Not this time, I don't!"

"Of course you do! You're not the first woman to find herself facing an unplanned pregnancy, and you won't be the last. If you absolutely feel a baby's more than you can handle, you do have other options. There's adoption and...abortion."

"As if I'd even consider either one!" Cassie wailed, pressing protective hands over her womb and wondering if she was destined to weep her way through the next six and a half months.

"Then why the emotional meltdown? Is it Benedict? Has he refused to acknowledge that the baby's his?"

Hearing the mixture of confusion and exasperation in her friend's voice, Cassie made a monumental effort to bring her runaway emotions to heel. "No, it's not about Benedict!" she said, which wasn't true, because of course it was partly about him. But she'd had ten weeks to adjust to the fact that while she hadn't been able to forget him or the circumstances which had led to their making love, he'd clearly had no trouble wiping all memory of the event, and her, clean out of his mind. "It's...my mother."

"Oh, honey!" Trish's voice softened. "I know how much you miss her, and you must find it especially painful at a time like this, but you're not alone. You have me and Ian, and while I know we'll never fill Nancy's shoes, you really can count on us to be there for you."

"It's not that, either. It's..." Another flood of tears welled up, threatening to drown her. Swallowing, she forced them down again. "It's that the baby's due on...October the eighth."

Trish sucked in a sympathetic breath. "Your mom's birthday?"

"Mmm-hmm. I don't know why it should upset me

so much. If anything, it ought to make me feel better—
as if Mom's somehow watching over me. As if she's
giving me the gift of another life, to make up for losing
her.'' Cassie mopped her eyes one last time, and managed a smile at the expression on her friend's face.
''Stop looking at me as if I've lost my mind! Pregnant
women are allowed to be fanciful. It goes with the territory.''

''Maybe. But you've been under a lot of stress lately,
what with business heating up as the summer approaches, and now this.'' Trish regarded her doubtfully.
''Maybe you should forget work, and take a few days
off. Maybe arrange to meet Benedict somewhere, and
both of you come to terms with this new development.
How do you think he'll take the news?''

''He won't. I don't plan to tell him.''

''Not tell him? But he has a right to know, Cassie!
It's his child, as well, and two parents are almost always
better than just one.''

''It didn't hurt me, growing up without a father.''

''Oh, yes, it did. You just learned at an early age not
to let it show. But there's no reason to saddle this baby
with more of the same. Although I don't pretend to know
him well, Benedict Constantino strikes me as the hon-
orable type—the kind of man who'd face up to his mistakes and do the right thing.''

''He wasn't too concerned with doing the right thing
when he had sex with me on New Year's Eve.''

''At risk of stating the obvious, it takes two, Cass, and
let me remind you that, by your admission, you didn't
exactly rebuff him.''

''No, I didn't,'' Cassie admitted, not so far gone in
self-pity that she'd delude herself on that score. ''But it

was his fault. He was just too…seductive for me to say 'no.'"

Trish grinned. "I can see how that might happen. He gives new depth and meaning to the term, *tall, dark and handsome,* and all I can say is that between his genes and yours, you'll have made a beautiful baby."

Beautiful, yes. Provided…

"And one he'd want to acknowledge, even if it turned out to be homely as a board fence. You really do have to let him know, Cass."

So they were back to that again, were they! "I'm not telling him," Cassie said flatly, "and neither are you. Let me be very clear on this, Patricia! What I've just told you remains in this room."

"Well, I'm not about to take out a full page ad in *The San Francisco Chronicle,* if that's what you're afraid of, but I surely don't have to point out that this isn't the kind of secret you can keep indefinitely."

"This is my first baby. I probably won't show that much."

"Possibly not. But the next time Benedict shows up in town, which likely will be for Nuncio's Midsummer Night's party this June, you'll be a good six months along, my dear, and sticking out in front enough that there'll be no hiding the fact that you are, as they say in polite society, with child. So how do you plan to handle that?"

"I'll take a vacation and leave you to deal with Nuncio."

"I'm in charge of catering, not marketing and PR. That's your department, Cassie."

"Then I'll take care of things over the phone or by e-mail."

"You're dreaming! Nuncio will be expecting the personal, hands-on approach he's always received from you, and given the size of his account with us, you can't afford to disappoint him. This isn't just about you anymore, you know. You have a child's future to think of, and babies don't come cheap these days.''

"For heaven's sake, Trish, I'm not exactly short of money!''

"You're not exactly worth millions, either,'' Trish said, ''so if you're determined to go the parenting route alone, you'd better be willing to cater to the likes of Signor Zanetti, because I'm here to tell you, you're going to be glad of accounts like his when it comes time to think about medical expenses, private schools, orthodontics, riding lessons, and all the other extras you'll want to lavish on this child.''

"Fine,'' Cassie said, too overwhelmed by the possible problems facing her in the next few months to worry about what might happen years from now. ''Then I'll have all the arrangements nailed down by the beginning of May which is only six weeks away. I won't be showing then, nor will I be in any danger of accidentally running into Benedict.''

"And how long do you think you can keep this secret?''

"Until enough time has passed that no one's going to question when or by whom I became pregnant.''

Trish glanced at her watch and rolled her eyes. "You're dreaming!'' she said again. ''If it weren't that I'm running late for a meeting with a supplier, I'd stay and point out the folly of such thinking, but don't for a moment think I'm leaving it at that. The subject is by no means closed.''

"Oh, yes, it is,'' Cassie said, leaning back in her chair and pressing the heels of her hands against her eyes as the door swung shut behind her friend. "I've made up my mind. Everything's settled."

Scarcely had she spoken though, when she sensed, rather than saw or heard, that she was not alone, after all. A trembling heartbeat later, she knew it for certain as a voice seasoned with dark, rich mocha, flavored with hints of sunny Italy, and laced with a forbidding undercurrent of steel, announced softly, "Everything is indeed settled, Cassandra."

Dismayed, she dropped her hands and gaped in stunned amazement as Benedict Constantino stepped into the room through the partially open glass door leading from the balcony.

"But not," he continued, his long legs carrying him across the carpet with frighteningly stealthy speed, "quite the way you suppose. Far from it, in fact."

Clearly, he'd listened in on every word of her conversation with Trish. Clearly, he'd understood the exact context of what he'd heard and didn't like it one little bit. A complete stranger lacking the usual complement of brain cells could have taken one look at his face, and recognized immediately that he was furious and in no mood to play games.

But Cassie, sitting there as if she'd been poleaxed, paid no heed to the evidence staring her in the face, and instead climbed on her woefully inappropriate high horse and said haughtily, "I don't know what you're talking about, but I *would* like to know how you managed to break into my office. You have exactly one minute to explain yourself, and then I'm calling Security."

"Be silent!" he commanded, oozing contempt. "You will call no one!"

She'd been intimate with him. He'd seen her with her

breasts exposed. With her skirt drawn up around her waist, and her legs spread wide to accommodate him.

He'd touched her most private flesh. He'd known how hungry for him she'd been. How willing. She'd gazed in awe at the power of his arousal. Cradled its pulsing weight in her hand. In her body.

She had trusted him that much.

Looking at him now, though, she was afraid of him. Because that fierce, burning passion he'd shown before was still there. And once again, it was directed at her. But this time, it had taken a deadly turn.

CHAPTER TWO

CASSIE'S glance wavered. Strayed from his face to the closed door across the room; to the telephone mere inches away. If she moved quickly, she could scoot past him and be in the safety of the outer office before he realized her intent. If she leaned forward a fraction, she could punch the speaker button on the phone console, and call for help.

Either was preferable to her current predicament. Neither, though, proved to be an option.

"No, Cassandra," he said, interpreting her thoughts all too accurately. "You will neither leave this room, nor call for reinforcements—unless, of course, you'd prefer we discuss our situation in front of an audience?" He bent over her desk and lifted the telephone receiver. Dangled it in front of her nose. "If that's the case, then by all means go ahead. Alert every occupant in the building, if it pleases you. Or shall I do it for you?"

"Put that thing down!" she implored, furious at how feeble she sounded. Furious that, even when she felt threatened by him, she still found him fascinating—the moth drawn to a devastating flame.

"Certainly, *cara*. The last thing in the world I intend is to distress you anymore than I already have." Gently, he returned the phone to its cradle, then dropped into one of the chairs on the other side of the desk, stretched out his long legs, and said conversationally, "So, there is a baby on the way. How do you propose we deal with this unexpected turn of events?"

Somewhat reassured by his more reasonable tone, she said, "*We* don't. This isn't your problem, Benedict."

"A child is never a problem. But if I am the father, then it most assuredly becomes my concern." His dark brown gaze scrutinized her features, searching for indecision, for deceit. "*Is* this baby mine, Cassandra?"

If she'd thought she could get away with it, she'd have lied and said "no." But he'd already heard her admit the truth to Trish, and even if he hadn't, it was a simple enough matter these days to obtain irrefutable clinical proof of paternity. "It's yours."

"Then our next move is clear enough. We shall be married."

"*Married?*" she choked, laughter bubbling hysterically in her throat. "You must be joking!"

"About taking a wife? Hardly!"

"Then you're insane. Marriage between us...it's simply not possible."

"Do you have a husband you neglected to mention before now?"

"Of course I don't!"

"There you are then." He lifted his hand. "Since I have no wife, marriage between us is entirely possible."

"For heaven's sake, Benedict, we were together once, and that was nearly three months ago. Since then, I've heard not a word from you."

"I've been out of the country."

"Well, I haven't! I've been here every day. The telephone works around the world, and so does e-mail. But you elected not to use either one, which leads me to believe that, as far I was concerned, 'out of sight' meant 'out of mind' to you. That being the case, you'll understand, I'm sure, why I find the idea of your wanting to marry me completely ludicrous."

He examined his short, immaculate fingernails, seemed to find them satisfactory, and favored her with another glance. "It isn't a question of wanting. I consider it to be my obligation."

It wasn't *what* he said, so much as the calm resignation with which he said it, that started her crying again. Not outwardly—pride wouldn't allow that—but inside, it was as if he'd stabbed a sharp needle into her heart. She'd known clients negotiate business contracts with more warmth and emotion!

"I don't want a husband who sees me as an obligation," she said, when she trusted herself to speak again.

"What do you want in a husband, Cassandra?"

"Love, friendship, commitment, passion—none of which I'm likely to find with you."

"None?" he echoed lazily. "Do you not remember how it was for us, last New Year's Eve?"

Not remember? She'd have laughed at such a preposterous question if she hadn't suddenly found herself floundering in a wash of déjà vu so intense that her face burned. Whatever other elements might have been missing that night, passion hadn't been among them. "Yes. And as I said a moment ago, it was one time only."

"Yet even today, the mention of it stirs you. I think I can promise you more of the same. I'm a normal, red-blooded man—as you so succinctly pointed out to your friend, Patricia. And you, *cara,* although technically no longer a virgin, remain in many ways such an innocent that you can't begin to know the power of sex—of how it can tame even the most reluctant heart, or weld the most unlikely union." From the table beside him, he picked up the art deco figure of a woman, and traced his finger over her eyelids and down her cheek to her throat. "It will be my very great privilege to instruct you."

He might as well have touched Cassie. Her flush deepened, spread. Raced the length of her body until it found its mark, and bathed her panties in dew.

Sometimes, the obstetrician had informed her, as he detailed what she could expect over the next six and a half months if everything went according to plan, *women lose all interest in sex during their pregnancies. Others can't seem to get enough of it.*

Was she, she wondered mournfully, destined to belong to the latter group? Was there no end to the day's humiliation? Hadn't she enough to contend with already?

Embarrassed, she squirmed in the chair, despising the tiny electric charge pulsing between her legs. And Benedict…he *smiled.* He *knew!*

"I don't want to have this discussion with you, especially not now, and definitely not here," she said.

"I can see that." Replacing the statuette, he eased himself out of the chair. "We'll continue it this evening then. I can arrange for a private dinner in my hotel suite, if you like, or shall I come to your home?"

Neither, if she had a choice. But the hard, determined set of his jaw told her that if she refused to see him, he'd simply waylay her the next time she set foot in the office. And he might not be quite so discreet, the next time!

She grabbed a pen. Scribbled on a notepad, tore off the page, and thrust it at him. "To my home," she said from between clenched teeth. "Here's the address."

At least she'd be in control there. Could show him the door when she'd had enough.

"At what time?"

"Seven o'clock. But don't expect anything elaborate

in the way of food. Mealtimes are a bit of a trial for me, at the moment.''

''I understand.'' He nodded, and assuming that was his way of taking his leave, she thought he'd make straight for the door. Instead, he came around the desk toward her.

As hastily as her queasy stomach would allow, she sprang up from the chair. She felt at enough of a disadvantage as it was, without having him loom over her even more than his eight-inch height advantage already allowed.

''Goodbye,'' she said, and thrust out her right hand. It might be a ridiculous gesture, considering she was carrying his baby and he'd just proposed, but it was safer to keep things formal.

Unfortunately, he had other ideas, though she didn't at first realize it. Instead of shaking her hand, as she'd intended he should, he turned it over and, dipping his head, kissed the inside of her wrist, right on the pulse point.

Her blood leaped wildly, and she let out a muffled squeak of surprise, at which he smoothed open her tightly clenched fingers and planted another, slower kiss on the palm of her hand. Then he lifted his head a fraction, blinked so that his lashes brushed over the skin of her arm, murmured, ''*Arrivederci,* Cassandra,'' and a moment later, the door clicked shut behind him.

With sunset, the air turned cool enough to warrant putting a match to the kindling in the hearth. Once the flames took hold, Cassie threw on two small logs, then stood back and spared one last glance around the living room.

The silk-shaded lamp on the desk cast gentle shadows

over the curved ceiling, and painted an overlay of gold on the glass doors of the built-in bookcases on each side of the river rock fireplace. An arrangement of fresh arum lilies stood in the bay window, the blooms creamy white against the navy background of sky outside.

A small epergne of pink roses, tall candles, and her grandmother's china graced the table in the dining alcove. In the kitchen, Veal Prince Orloff simmered in the oven. A bottle of white burgundy chilled in the refrigerator.

Had she gone to too much trouble? Made it look as if she cared what Benedict Constantino thought of her style and taste? Should she have made the occasion more casual, and served pizza in the den, with the TV turned to the evening news, instead of playing Claude Debussy's Piano Preludes playing softly on the stereo? Should she have chosen to wear jeans and a sweater, rather than a long silk caftan and pearls?

Uncertain, excited, nervous, she was on the point of returning to the bedroom to change, when the downstairs buzzer sounded. Peering from the living-room window, she saw Benedict standing under the awning on the street below, perusing the list of other residents in the building. He had on what appeared to be the same dark suit he'd worn earlier. Probably the same shirt and tie, too. He might be willing to marry her, but clearly didn't give a rap about impressing her!

"Something smells wonderful," he said, when he arrived at her door on the second floor. Then, to put paid to any notion she might entertain that he was referring to her perfume, added, "I thought Patricia was the expert chef in your partnership."

"She is. I shopped at a gourmet deli on the way home. The only thing I've contributed to the meal is the salad."

It wasn't the same suit, after all, but another superbly tailored effort in dark gray, with a shirt the color of mist, and a silk tie midway between the two shades. He looked altogether too divine for her to handle with equanimity, and to stop herself from staring, she buried her nose in the flowers he'd brought. "Mmm, freesias! How did you know they're one of my favorites?"

"Why else would you have them growing outside your office window?"

"You noticed? Well, thank you. They're lovely."

"*Prego!*" He smiled—something else she found disturbingly attractive.

Indicating the living room, she said, "Make yourself comfortable while I find a vase for them."

"I would have brought wine," he remarked, ignoring her direction and following her into the kitchen, "but I assume you're avoiding alcohol these days."

"You assume correctly. But that doesn't mean you can't enjoy a predinner drink. You have the choice of scotch, sherry, campari or wine."

"Perhaps a glass of wine later, with the meal. For now, I'm content to watch you."

Another of those annoying flushes stole up her neck. "I wish you wouldn't say things like that."

"Why not? I enjoy looking at you, which is a good thing, since you're about to become my wife and we'll be seeing rather a lot of each other."

"That hasn't been decided, Benedict," she said firmly. "I've yet to be convinced there's any merit to your proposal."

"But certainly there is," he said, his Italian accent suddenly more pronounced. "In my country, a man marries the mother of his child. It's as simple as that."

"But this is the United States. Things are done differently here."

"Differently, perhaps, but that doesn't make them better, or right." He touched her cheek. "You're troubled that we're not in love, but where I was born, it used to be that other factors carried more weight when it came to marriage, such as building respect for one's spouse, and working together to create a good home for one's children. If love of the kind you're referring to entered the picture, it was by coincidence and deemed a secondary consideration."

"In other words, you're talking about arranged marriages." She tossed her head contemptuously. "Maybe there are some women who don't mind being treated like chattels, but I'm not one of them."

"Arranged, yes, but also lasting. Divorce was unheard of in my parents' day, Cassandra. Family came first, and all the rest—the fondness between a man and his wife, the devotion—fell into place after that. Even now, seldom does a widow of my mother's generation choose to remarry—surely a powerful endorsement of the durability of a union based on reason rather than romance?"

"That's one way of looking at it, I suppose. But it could just as well be that, having at last gotten out from under one man's thumb, she's in no hurry to repeat the experience with another."

He laughed, a low husky sound that sent his breath rippling warmly against her neck. "Are you afraid I'll hold *you* under my thumb, *cara?*"

"Not in the least."

"That's good. Because I can think of many more pleasurable ways to keep my bride close."

"Well, I hope she enjoys them, whoever she is." Cassie picked up the vase and carried it through to the living room, leaving him to accompany her or not, as he pleased. ''But you might as well accept that it won't be me, Benedict. I have no intention of settling for a marriage based on *fondness.*''

He followed her down the hall, his footsteps slow and measured on the planked oak floor. ''You *will* marry me,'' he said, with unshakable confidence. ''The only thing yet to be decided is how long it will take for me to convince you of it.''

She looked past where he'd stationed himself near the fire, to the carriage clock on the mantel behind him. ''Think in terms of two hours, Benedict. I plan to be in bed, *alone,* no later than half past nine.''

''You're not feeling well?''

''Apart from a little queasiness now and then, I'm perfectly fine,'' she lied, unwilling to give him another reason to pressure her. ''My doctor said everything's proceeding swimmingly.''

Actually, what he'd said was, *I don't want to alarm you unnecessarily, but your cervix is a little softer than it should be in a woman at this stage of her first pregnancy, so I'm sending you for a sonogram sooner than usual. If the results warrant it, we need to take preventative measures to minimize the risk of a premature birth, or miscarriage.*

When she'd first suspected she might be pregnant, she'd been ambivalent about the idea. But the specter of possible miscarriage terrified her. Only then had she realized how much, during those early weeks, she'd connected with the tiny life growing inside her.

What sort of measures? she'd asked.

The medical term for the procedure is a Circlage. It involves a local anesthetic and the placing of sutures through and around the cervix, thereby drawing the opening firmly closed. In layman's language, it's sometimes referred to as "the purse string" operation, which actually describes it rather well. The sutures are removed around the thirty-sixth week of pregnancy, to allow for normal dilation of the cervix as birth becomes imminent.

Is there any risk to the baby?

Some slight risk, yes, but the earlier the procedure is performed, the safer it is for both mother and child, which is why I'm bringing it to your attention now.

"If everything's going swimmingly," Benedict said, interrupting her thoughts so suddenly that she almost dropped the vase, "why are you looking so apprehensive? What aren't you telling me, Cassandra?"

"Nothing. I'm wondering if I'm overcooking the Veal Prince Orloff, that's all."

"I can't imagine that gazing pensively at a container of freesias is going to give you the answer."

"You're right," she said, placing the flower arrangement on the corner table between the sofas. "Excuse me while I check the oven."

This time, he didn't follow her and when she returned to the living room, she found him examining the framed antique floral prints on the wall. "You have some very fine things in your home, *cara.*"

"Much of what you see I inherited."

He strolled about the room, stopping to admire the voluptuous shape and contrasting wood of her prized bombé chest, and ended up in the arched entrance to the dining alcove. "And the rest?"

"I bought. Haunting antique auctions is one of my hobbies."

"You have excellent taste."

"Thank you." The reception rooms were large, but he made them seem cramped and airless. If he wasn't standing close enough to ruffle her hair with his breath, his shadow was reaching out to touch her.

She found it unsettling. The sooner he was gone, the better. "We should start on our first course. The veal is almost done."

He pulled out her chair at the head of the long, oval table, took his own place opposite and, while she served the asparagus soup, poured himself a glass of the wine chilling in a silver wine cooler at his elbow.

"I very much appreciate this," he commented, breaking apart a fluffy dinner roll still hot from the oven. "Hotel food serves well enough when it must, but it doesn't approach the pleasure found in a home-prepared meal."

She could hardly take exception to that and for the next fifteen minutes or so, they exchanged the kind of pleasant small talk any couple might enjoy. Relaxing despite her previous reservations, Cassie was able to manage her soup and a small helping of the salad which followed.

It was a different story with the main course. The rich combination of veal layered with mushrooms and onion, and covered with cheese sauce, was more than she could stomach. And of course, Benedict noticed.

"You're not eating, Cassandra," he remarked, eyeing the way she was pushing the food around her plate with very little of it making its way to her mouth.

"I'm suddenly not very hungry."

"Isn't it a bit late in the day for morning sickness?"

"My body doesn't seem able to tell the time."

"You've discussed this with a doctor?"

"Yes."

"And?"

"And nothing." She sipped her ice water and prayed she wouldn't have to make an undignified dash for the bathroom. "My digestive problems don't exactly make for sparkling dinner conversation. Can we please talk about something else?"

"If you wish. But I'd like the name of this doctor."

"Why?" Her stomach rumbled a warning.

"To satisfy myself that he's competent."

"He's more than just a run-of-the-mill doctor. He's an obstetrician. He specializes in pregnancies."

"So you say."

"Don't you believe me?"

He regarded her silently a moment, then said, "Yes, but I'm not sure I believe you've told me everything there is to know. I'm anxious about you."

This time, it was more than a warning. This time, her stomach heaved a protest. "Well, don't be. I'm in very good hands."

"I intend to make sure that you are. I intend to speak with this doctor, with or without your cooperation."

She took another cautious sip of ice water and, as calmly as she could, said, "No. It's none of your concern."

"It's very much my concern, Cassandra. Make no mistake about that."

"Perhaps you haven't heard about doctor-patient confidentiality. You don't have the *right* to information about me."

"*Not have the right?* As the father of your child, I have *every* right, and I assure you I intend to exercise it."

The edge in his voice unnerved her. Rumor had it that he was wealthy, a tycoon with international connections;

that he represented his family's North American business interests, and acted as its transaction agent and import specialist. He was undoubtedly accustomed to negotiating with other powerful magnates and coming out on top.

And she? At her best, she'd be hard-pressed to beat him at his own game. In her present condition, she was in no shape to go toe-to-toe with him on the weather, let alone his paternal rights.

Right on cue, Prince Orloff's veal swirled unpleasantly in her stomach. She clamped her napkin to her mouth and pushed away from the table.

"Excuse me," she muttered, and fled.

When she came back some fifteen minutes later to discover the dining room dark and only the lamp on the desk burning, she thought he'd left. Dispirited at finding her relief mixed with regret—did she want his attention, or not?—she sank onto the couch and folded her legs under her. But no sooner was she settled than footsteps approaching from the kitchen told her he hadn't abandoned her, after all.

A second later he came into the living room.

"I brought you some tea and dry toast," he said, placing a tray on the coffee table, and the genuine concern in his voice brought tears trembling to her lashes. "Sorry it took me so long. I had to find my way around your kitchen. Hope you don't mind."

"No," she said. "How did you know to do this—serve me dry toast, that is?"

"I have two nephews, and well remember the misery they caused my sister before they were born. This was her remedy and she swore by it."

Cassie sipped from the cup he passed to her, aware

that he watched the entire time, that he missed not a flicker of expression on her face.

Eventually he said, "What is it, *cara?* Do I make such dreadful tea, that you look so unhappy?"

Again, the compassion in his voice undid her. Helplessly, she shook her head and pressed her lips together, struggling to hang on to her composure. Even when she felt able to speak again, her voice remained thick with tears. "The tea's fine. It's everything else...."

"I'm sorry about the baby. Not that I wish it harm, but that it was conceived so carelessly." He took her hand and covered it with both of his. "I blame myself, Cassandra. I'm past the age where such impulses are forgivable in a man which is why I beg you to let me atone in the best way I know how."

His hand slid up her arm, caressed her shoulder, slipped inside the loose cowl collar of her caftan and cupped the back of her neck.

She flinched at his touch—so gentle, so subtly erotic. How was she supposed to remain immune to it? To cling to her resolve not to weaken under his persuasion?

"Are you afraid of me?" he asked.

"Yes," she said, looking him straight in the eye.

"Will you tell me why?"

She fell silent then because she daren't admit how insidious her attraction to him was.

He continued to watch her, to stroke her nape. After a while, he said, "What happened, that you grew up without a father, Cassandra?"

"I was conceived before my parents married. My father stayed around long enough to know he had a daughter, then left my mother and me for another woman when I was seventeen months old. We never heard from him again."

"That won't happen to us. I give you my word that I'll honor my wedding vows. I will take care of you and our child."

"I don't need taking care of," she told him, even though a part of her yearned to accept what he offered. Just once, it would be nice to know how it felt to have a strong male shoulder to lean on, a big warm masculine body to curl up against at night. "If my mother could take care of herself and a child, I can."

"Don't you see that you shouldn't have to? That this is a shared responsibility?"

"I'm not saying I won't let you be part of this baby's life. That wouldn't be fair to either of you."

"That's not what you told Patricia this morning. I distinctly heard you say it hadn't hurt you growing up without a father. You also said you weren't going to tell me you're pregnant."

"Well, I feel differently now, since you found out anyway and it turns out that, unlike my father, you don't mind being saddled with a child."

His long, strong fingers massaged the tension knotting the base of her neck. In the warm, drugging sense of relief that followed, it was all she could not to groan with pleasure. "Or with that child's mother," he whispered against her ear.

Like the first warning tremor of an approaching earthquake, she felt her resistance waver and begin to topple frighteningly close to acquiescence. Sidestepping the danger just in time, she pulled away from him and said, "Stop pressuring me, Benedict. I've had enough for one day."

"Then we'll leave it for now, and talk again when you're feeling more rested. Thank you for allowing me to come here, and for the wonderful dinner."

"Hardly wonderful! I never got around to offering you dessert or coffee," she said, on a small laugh.

He rose and shot his cuffs into place. "You offered a glimpse inside your head and your heart, *cara.* There isn't a dessert in the world to compare with that."

"How long will you be in town?" she asked, following him to the foyer and opening the front door.

He paused on the threshold and looked down at her. His remarkable eyes, so dark a brown they were almost black, caressed her face, feature by feature. His silky lashes drooped lazily at half-mast, as though concealing a joke he wasn't ready to share. "As long as it takes for you to learn to trust me," he said, and pressed his lips to her cheek.

They stayed there too long, took vaguely erotic liberties against her skin, and she opened her mouth to tell him so. He promptly took advantage of her error. So swiftly and smoothly she was caught completely off guard, his lips covered hers, and there was nothing the least bit vague about their message this time.

They spoke of raw passion barely held in check. Of wicked, delicious midnight-dark delight hers to enjoy if only she'd let herself. They stole the very things she most needed to cling to: her sense of purpose, her conviction—and a little bit more of her heart.

And the reprimand she'd been about to hurl at him? Poor thing, it simply withered in the heat of his kiss. Died without a murmur or even a whimper.

"As long as it takes, *mi amore,*" he said again, and leaving her clinging limply to the door frame, he ran swiftly down the stairs and out to the street.

She shut her door, rammed home the dead bolt, and tottered back to the living room where the snack he'd prepared remained virtually untouched. Suddenly starving, she devoured the toast, drank the tea and, appetite still not satisfied, swept up the tray and went to the kitchen.

She saw at once that he'd made himself useful while she was busy throwing up. The leftovers from dinner were stored in the refrigerator, the china and silver rinsed and loaded in the dishwasher.

It's difficult to nurture immunity toward a man as thoughtful as this, she decided, boiling water to make a poached egg, and popping another slice of bread in the toaster. *Maybe I'm being too rash in rejecting his proposal out of hand. Maybe New Year's Eve wasn't an end in itself, but the beginning of something incredible. Maybe, against all odds, I've found the man destiny created me for.*

If she could be sure he was right in saying that a marriage was stronger for being founded on trust, respect and family values, with a soupcon of chemistry thrown in for good measure, she might be willing to take the plunge. If, as well, there was some hope, however slender, that the potential for consuming love might also be in the cards, she'd definitely consider it worth the risk.

She broke an egg into a cup, swirled the boiling water vigorously, and dropped the egg in the eye of the vortex she'd created. While it cooked, she buttered the toast lightly, and poured herself a glass of milk.

He had been kind and thoughtful. He wanted to be a physical presence in his child's life. He'd shown concern for her physical well-being, her mental state. They weren't bad qualities in a father, a husband. She could do a lot worse.

How long will you be in town?

As long as it takes for you to learn to trust me...as long as it takes, mi amore....

How long was that?

The egg was done. She scooped it onto a slotted spoon, let it drain a moment, then slid it, all fluffy white around the edges with a hint of yellow at its center, onto the toast. Drizzled on a little salt, a speck of pepper. For the first time in days, the smell of the food—melting butter, hot, fresh egg—made her mouth water.

She stacked everything on the tray he'd used earlier, and carried it to the window nook overlooking the terrace. Her daytime planner lay face down in the middle of the little wrought-iron table where she normally ate breakfast. When she turned the book over, she found it open at that day's page. It showed her obstetrician's name and telephone number, as well as the time of her appointment that morning. And on the floor, where it must have fallen without his noticing, was a business card with Benedict Constantino's name on it.

She didn't have to be a mental giant to figure out what had taken place while she'd been losing her dinner.

I had to find my way around your kitchen. Hope you don't mind....

How about, *I snooped through your private possessions?* she thought furiously. How about, *I made a note of your doctor's name and phone number on one of my business cards and didn't notice that I'd pulled out two by mistake and left the second behind as evidence of my deception?*

All at once, the egg smelled like sulfur. Looked as slippery as he was. So much for his professed concern! He must have gloated all the way back to his hotel at how easily he'd hoodwinked her!

"How long before I learn to trust you, Benedict?" she muttered bitterly, shoveling the toast and egg into the sink and flushing it down the waste disposer. "When hell freezes over, that's when, and not a minute sooner!"

CHAPTER THREE

"WELL, at least he's got good taste." Trish brushed a gentle finger over the mist of baby's breath interspersed among the six dozen long-stemmed pink roses over-shadowing everything else on the board-room table. "If you won't have them in your office, I'll take them in mine."

"Take them, and Benedict Constantino as well!" Cassie fumed.

"I don't think it's me he wants, dearie. I think he's prepared to do whatever it takes to make sure he winds up with you."

"Then all I can say is, he's got some strange ideas of how to go about it, if he thinks rifling through my personal records is the way to win me over."

"He looked at your daybook, for heaven's sake, not stole your inheritance out from under you! And from what you've told me, you pretty much drove him to it."

"I might have known you'd take his side. You've never been able to resist tall, black-haired men."

"I'm not taking anyone's side," Trish said, in the sort of reasonable tone an adult might adopt when dealing with a fractious child. "I'm trying to make you see reason. The man obviously cares about you. Since when is that a crime?"

"Since he resorted to conniving tactics, that's when! It shows an underhanded side to his character that I don't care for. And it goes beyond what he did last night, Trish. Don't forget he also eavesdropped on a conversation between you and me, and made not the slightest attempt to announce himself.''

"He probably didn't feel you left him any other choice. If it had been up to you, he'd still be in the dark about the pregnancy. How's he supposed to know what else you might be keeping from him?'' She cast a last envious glance at the arrangement of roses. "And regardless of his sins, imagined or otherwise, there's no denying he's earned a few Brownie points with these. Even the container is gorgeous.''

"It's ostentatious.'' Cassie glared at the huge crystal bowl, easily the size of a medicine ball with the top cut off. "Talk about overkill! Your problem is that you're a pushover for appearances.''

"Well, what else do you expect? I'm a chef. Quality and presentation are everything. And whether or not you admit it, that's one beautiful vase, Cassie.''

"Vase?'' Cassie sniffed disparagingly, and tried not to be swayed by the alluring scent of roses she managed to inhale along with a healthy dose of indignation. "I could practically take a bath in it!''

"Not for much longer. Pretty soon, you won't fit through the opening.''

"You're not helping matters, Patricia!''

"Yes, I am,'' her friend said. "I'm doing my level best to make you face the facts without blowing everything out of proportion. Benedict didn't have to offer to marry you. He didn't even have to take your word for it that he's the baby's father. That he did both without hesitation says a lot more about the kind of man he is, than the fact that he took an uninvited look at your day book or listened in on a conversation some people might argue he had a right to hear. He's a rare specimen in this day and age, and you'd be a fool not to at least consider his proposal.''

"But we're not in love!''

Expression somber, Trish looked away. "Maybe not, but you were in lust enough to get pregnant by him, and that ought to take precedence over all else. It would, if I were in your place.''

"I know it would,'' Cassie said contritely. Trish and her husband Ian had been trying for a baby for over three years, without success. "I'm sorry, Trish. You're the last person I should be confiding in about this.''

"That's what friends are all about—to lend an ear when it's needed, and dole out advice whether it's needed or not. Besides, who else can you trust but me to set you straight?''

Not a soul! She had no siblings, no aunts or uncles or cousins—at least, none that she knew about. Trish was more than just her dearest friend; she was like a sister and, since Cassie's mother's death the previous October, the closest thing to family Cassie had. She had other friends, of course, but none as loyal or trustworthy. None who knew her so well, nor any whose opinion she valued more.

"You really think I'm judging him too harshly?''

"I think you're being hasty. It would be different if you couldn't stand to be around him. But Cassie, you should see your face when you talk about him! You might wish you could hate him, but the simple fact of the matter is, you can't. You're *very* attracted to him. And it's pretty clear he's just as taken with you.''

"He's interested in our baby. I just happen to be the womb in which it's planted.''

"Oh, give me a break! If that's the case, what was he

doing here yesterday, before he even knew you were pregnant?''

Cassie shrugged. ''I neither know nor care.''

''Well, sooner or later, you're going to have to come to grips with it, because he's not going to conveniently disappear. He came back to see you for some unknown reason, and found another, more compelling reason to stick around. So far, he's made all the concessions, and these…'' Trish touched the tip of her finger to one perfect pink rose and sighed. ''These are a blatant message that he's willing to make a few more.''

''They're just flowers, for heaven's sake! A 'thank you for the dinner' gesture.''

''No. If that's all he was trying to say, a potted plant would have done the job.''

''So what are you suggesting—that I just cave in to his demands because he bought out a florist's entire supply of roses?''

''I'm suggesting that you make the next move and show yourself to be amenable to discussion and compromise.'' Trish picked up the phone. ''And I'm suggesting you do it now. Because although he might be tall in stature, I suspect our gorgeous Italian is pretty short on tolerance when it comes to being pushed around. If you insist on playing hardball with Benedict Constantino, you'll be taking on a lot more than you can handle.''

She was going to throw up again! And the manner in which Trish was waving the phone around in such a way that it looked like a cobra about to strike didn't help any! ''I don't know where he's staying.''

''You know his cell phone number. It's printed right there on his card.''

''But he won't appreciate being disturbed during business hours. I'm not the primary reason he's in town. He's here to work, or visit his good friend Nuncio.''

"He'll have voice mail.'' The coiled phone cord writhed, the handset bobbed menacingly. "You can leave a message.''

"Saying what?''

"Oh, I don't know. Something complicated and obtuse, such as 'Hello, Benedict, this is Cassandra. Please give me a call when you have a moment free.'

"If I do that, will you then leave me to wallow in my own misery?''

"Absolutely.'' Trish thrust the phone at her.

Wearily, Cassie punched in his number and prepared to deliver her message to some impersonal answering service.

He picked up on the first ring. Thoroughly unhinged, as much by the deep, scxy timbre of his voice as the fact that she was left suddenly tongue-tied, Cassie held the phone away and stared at it in horror. She'd have hung up on him, if Trish hadn't muttered in a stage whisper people in the next room probably heard, "Say something, Cass!''

"Cassandra?'' Her name flowed from the ear piece like music, a melodic cascade of sound about two octaves below middle C.

"Hell...o....'' she croaked.

"Ah,'' he said. Just that, followed by a pause as pregnant as she was.

Desperate to fill it, she babbled, "Thank you for the roses. They're lovely. Pink is my favorite. You shouldn't have. It wasn't necessary.''

Trish snickered, covered her mouth with her hand, and turned away.

"It was entirely necessary, Cassandra,'' he said smoothly, dark, quiet laughter lacing his answer. "It was also my pleasure." When she didn't reply, he let the silence spin out a second or two more, then asked, "Is that the only reason you called?"

"Um…no."

Another, longer pause ensued, teeming with tension. At last, he said gently, "And the other?"

"I don't—can't…I don't like doing it on the phone."

Good grief, that sounded indecent! Obscene! And from the way Trisha turned purple, grabbed a tissue, and choked into it, she obviously thought so, too!

Drawing in a calming breath, Cassie started over. "What I'm trying to say is, I'd just as soon discuss the matter with you in person. Face-to-face."

"*Senz'altro*—of course! But this time, you won't cook for me. Instead, I'll take you to dinner at a favorite *ristorante* of mine, a quiet, tranquil—"

"No!" she said hastily, wishing his lilting accent didn't turn even the simplest remark into a caress. "Not dinner."

"Lunch, then."

"Yes."

"Today."

"Yes."

"*Eccellente!* I'll pick you up—"

"No," she said again, not about to find herself confined in a car with him, or hustled into some dark and intimate restaurant. "There's a sandwich shop in the lobby of my office building. I'll see you there at noon."

"If you insist," he said, sounding as if she'd suggested they meet at the city dump.

"I insist."

"You look somewhat discomposed," Trish tittered, when the call ended.

"More like *de*composed!" Cassie grabbed a binder and used it as a fan to cool her face. "I don't know what it is about that man that sets me off like this."

"Beyond finding him fatally attractive, you mean?"

"Is that really what it is? I'm drawn to dangerous men?"

"He's hardly dangerous, Cass!"

"Yes, he is," Cassie said. "There's something…iron hard underneath that charmingly compliant front he puts on."

"That shouldn't come as any surprise. How else do you suppose he climbed to the top of the tycoon heap? In any case, you'd never have let yourself be seduced by a pantywaist." Trish's eyes glimmered with further amusement. "Or did you seduce him, you little devil?"

"I most certainly did not!"

"No invitational glances in the moonlight? No locked gazes across a crowded deck?"

Cassie opened her mouth to refute those suggestions, too, then snapped it shut again, swamped in sudden, guilty memories….

"Will you dance with me, *signorina?*"

"I shouldn't. I'm here to work."

But she'd gone into his arms anyway. Let him hold her close enough to be vibrantly conscious of the lean strength of his torso, his long, powerful legs. Across San Francisco Bay, a premature burst of fireworks littered the sky with sprays of silver and gold, and a little of their sparkle inexplicably landed on her and left her glowing from the inside out.

"I hadn't expected you'd be here alone," he said, smiling down at her.

"I hadn't expected to be here at all," she said, "but

our social convener came down with the flu, and finding someone able to take over her job at short notice, especially on the busiest night of the year, was impossible.''

He tightened his hold, gave her hand a meaningful squeeze. "How unfortunate that your employee fell ill— and what a stroke of good luck for me.''

Aware of his jaw grazing the crown of her head, of his fingers warmly enfolding hers, and most of all, of the current of untoward excitement coursing through her blood, she said, "I'm very glad that you're enjoying your evening, Mr. Constantino, but you'll have to excuse me now. I really must get back to work and make sure Mr. Zanetti's guests have everything they need.''

"You're already working," he replied. "You're making sure I have everything *I* need.''

A simmering heat had begun to consume her, and with every word, every nuance of meaning, he stoked the flames a little higher. Breathless, she'd tried to extricate herself from a situation she felt powerless to control.

As if he sensed she was on the brink of flight, he pulled her closer, not enough that anyone else would have noticed and made comment, but close enough for her to understand the specific nature of his "need.''

But did she rebuff him? Stalk off in a snit? Fell him with a haughty glare?

Not a bit! She melted against him and when the music stopped, she withdrew from his hold with marked reluctance, an inch at a time, until only the tips of her fingers touched his. Apart from the fire in his dark eyes, he looked entirely collected. Of all the people on the covered, candlelit afterdeck, only she knew how provocatively other, more distant parts of his body had stirred against her. But *she* was burning all over, from her cheeks to her knees, and half expected to find the silk of her ivory cocktail dress singed everywhere he'd touched it.

"Thank you for the dance," she stammered, desperately trying to project a semblance of poise, and failing miserably.

But he, with his signature elegance of manner, murmured, "*Grazie,* Cassandra? *Per favore,* the honor was mine! That it's been so short-lived is my only regret."

Afraid that if she didn't turn away, she'd fly back into his arms, she'd sped—as much as her high heels would allow—back to her station in the main saloon where Trish's senior assistant was supervising the final preparations for the buffet supper. For the next hour, she lent a hand where one was needed, but although her fingers were kept otherwise engaged, her thoughts continued to dwell on Benedict Constantino.

Given his parting remark, perhaps she ought to have been suspicious when, half an hour before midnight, a crew member came to inform her she was urgently needed below deck. But fearing someone had been taken ill, she put Benedict out of her mind and followed the crewman down to the private quarters located in the stern of the boat.

The entrance to the suite had been unlocked, and although the lamp gleaming softly on the polished mahogany walls of the little foyer no sign of anyone waiting there, a swath of light fell dimly from the sitting room where she sometimes worked. Well, that made sense, she supposed.

She turned to tell the crewman that she'd take matters from there and he could return to his duties on the bridge, only to find he'd already left and closed the door behind him. More puzzled by the second, she crossed to the sitting room, peeped inside, and gasped audibly.

A dozen or more candles flickered about the cabin. On a table covered with a snowy linen cloth stood a silver wine cooler containing a bottle of champagne. Two crystal glasses, clouded with frost, and a single red rose in a bud vase completed the setting. And lounging against the bulkhead beside the window, with his jacket unbuttoned and his hands in his pockets, was Benedict Constantino.

Caught between vexation and amusement, Cassie said, "I hope you have a good explanation for this. I was led to believe there was some sort of emergency down here."

"But indeed there is, Cassandra," he replied, unfazed. "I most urgently need to be alone with you."

Repressing the little melting burst of delight brought on by his words, she said, "Very flattering, I'm sure, *Signor* Constantino, but it's hardly appropriate for me to single out one guest and neglect the rest."

He came to her and caught her hands in his. "Listen!" he commanded, drawing her to him and indicating with a nod of his handsome head the sounds of revelry taking place on the deck above them. "Does that sound to you like a crowd of people suffering from neglect?"

"That's hardly the point," she protested faintly.

"Indeed not," he murmured against her mouth. "But this most certainly is."

And he kissed her. Very thoroughly.

And she…she couldn't help herself. She kissed him back. The instant his lips touched hers, she was consumed with hunger. His to do with as he wished.

Fortunately, he wasn't quite as lacking in self-control. "That," he said hoarsely, putting her from him with hands which shook a little, "was premature, and by no means my primary reason for luring you down here."

"Oh," she whimpered, past caring that she sounded woefully disappointed. "What *was* the reason, then?"

"To welcome the new year in seclusion, with you."

"But that's not possible! They'll be expecting me on deck."

"Not for another twenty minutes, *cara*," he said, leaving her weak-kneed with all sorts of vague and prohibited longing, while he attended to the business of uncorking the wine. "Admittedly not an ideal length of time, but certainly long enough for us to toast one another in private."

The champagne foamed exuberantly in the glasses, in much the same way that her blood sang through her veins as he offered her one of the flutes.

"I really shouldn't," she protested weakly, knowing perfectly well that she really would.

"It's but a little sin," he said, his voice wrapping her in velvet. "Nothing at all to lose sleep over." He raised his own glass, clinked it lightly against hers. "*Buona fortuna,* Cassandra! May the coming year see the fulfillment of all your dreams."

"Thank you." She couldn't look at him. *Dare* not. She was too afraid of what he might see in her eyes, and even more terrified of what she might detect in his. "Is this how you always celebrate New Year's Eve?"

"Not quite," he said. "I make it a rule to avoid parties such as the one taking place on deck. I don't care to be obliged to kiss every woman present, simply as a matter of custom. In this instance, however, a different set of rules apply. I am only too happy to kiss you."

And he did. Again. More thoroughly than ever, in a lovely, hot, damp, searching exploration of her mouth that left her yearning against him. That had her parting her lips and letting him taste the champagne she'd sipped.

Exactly when matters progressed beyond a kiss she couldn't have said, because she was incapable of rational thought, let alone speech. All she knew was that, for the first time in her life, a man was holding her as if she were the most precious creature on earth, and she never wanted him to let go.

She didn't care that she knew next to nothing about him. That was the brain's department and her brain most definitely was not in charge at that moment. Reason had no place in what was happening, nor had caution or propriety.

What mattered was that he inspired in her the kind of wild sexual longing and quivering expectation she'd read about but never really believed in. Her skin vibrated with awareness of him, the very pores seeming to reach out to absorb the texture of him. When he slid his hand down her throat and dipped a finger into the valley between her breasts, a reckless greed took hold of her, making itself heard in tiny, inarticulate moans buried somewhere deep in her throat.

With shocking audacity, she covered his hand with hers. Guided it to her breast. Pressed herself against his palm in brazen offering.

He responded in kind, pinning her against his hips in such a way that awareness jolted through her. He was hard as a rock. Hot as a fire. Strong and pulsing with contained passion.

He found the zipper holding closed her dress and lowered it far enough that the wide shawl neck of her dress slid away from her shoulders. She wore cream satin underneath, trimmed with French lace. It whispered audacious permission for him to push it aside. And then—at last, praise heaven!—he was cupping her bare breast, and lowering his head to tug gently at her nipple as if he were seeking to rob her of her soul.

She very nearly cried out loud. Desire skittered over her, puckering her skin and puddling between her thighs. She ached inside, a heavy, crescendo of sensation, part pain, and part ecstasy.

When his hand slipped over the curve of her bottom and began inching up her skirt, anticipation became craving; hunger turned to greed. She wanted him touching her bare skin; wanted him to find that throbbing, hidden place and answer its silent, tormented pleas.

She wanted to touch him. To feel the silken weight of him against her palm; to make him groan and shudder uncontrollably, just as he made her.

Perhaps she said as much. Perhaps, because of the fever consuming her, the words came tumbling out involuntarily, raw and shockingly frank. *I want to see your penis, stroke it...help me...give me permission...!*

Yes, she must have said exactly that because, in the next instant, *he* was the one holding *her* hand captive, right *there,* where the fine black wool of his dress pants stretched taut and expectant over the swell of his erection. She fumbled with his zipper, too eager, too clumsy, and so he helped her, showing himself to her without shame.

He was beautiful beyond anything she'd ever known. At once primitive and elegant. Strong and smooth and vital.

Awestruck, she gazed at him. Touched him tentatively and, encouraged by his smothered exclamation, closed both her hands around him and reveled in the convulsive jerk of his flesh. "Am I doing this right?" she whispered. "Do you like it?"

He rolled his eyes, growled something explosive in Italian, and the next instant, she was lying flat on her back on the carpet, with the full skirt of her dress spread around her like a collapsed parachute. When he discovered her sheer silk stockings left the top of her legs bare, he brushed his lips along her inner thigh, and murmured, *"Tua pelle…perfetta."*

"I'm not sure what that means," she quavered, teetering on the fine edge of a dazzling unknown, "but it sounds wonderful."

He lifted his head and let his gaze drift over her, warm and caressing as a lazy tropical breeze. "Your skin, Cassandra, it is perfect. *You* are perfect."

Then he touched her, in the exact spot where her body cried out for him with thick, heavy tears. Swept his finger and his tongue over her, and finally, when she was weeping all over, and begging him to end the torture, he entered her. Filled her completely.

For a few divine minutes, the outside world ceased to exist. He *was* her world; her universe. And when she shattered in his arms mere seconds before he relinquished control of his own body, she felt as if she were stardust free-falling from heaven.

Up on the afterdeck, cheers and whistles broke out. Ships' horns echoed across the Bay. Fireworks exploded, filling the sky with fountains of color. But she, still caught up in the euphoria of spent passion, did not at first recognize their significance. Then, as reality seeped back, she stared up at him, horrified. "We missed midnight!"

He shrugged. "I doubt anyone noticed."

They weren't the words she wanted to hear. Too dispassionate by far, they brought her back to earth with a bang. Squirming with embarrassment, she turned her face away and he, taking the hint, rolled off her and sprang lithely to his feet. By the time she'd done the same, albeit less vigorously, he'd restored his clothing to order and merely looked slightly disheveled.

She, however, was a complete mess. Her panties hung from one ankle, and maintaining her dignity while she put them back where they belonged proved an exercise in futility. She'd lost one shoe; it sprawled upside down under the table, looking every bit as wanton as she now felt. Her dress was as crumpled as if she'd slept in it—which, to phrase it delicately, was pretty much what she'd done. In retrospect, though, and as the afterglow faded, a much uglier term assigned itself to her behavior.

Benedict cleared his throat. "Cassandra," he began.

"Don't!" she said sharply, refusing to meet his glance. "Don't say another word. Just please go and spare us both the embarrassment of trying to behave as if what just happened amounted to anything other than animal lust."

"And leave you in complete disarray? That would not be gentlemanly of me."

"*Gentlemanly?*" If she hadn't been so utterly mortified, she'd have laughed at the notion that he understood the meaning of the word. "It's a bit late to be thinking along those lines, Mr. Constantino."

"And more than a little late for such formality, *cara*. My name, as you very well know, is Benedict."

"Fine. Go back on deck, Benedict, before your good friend Nuncio comes looking for you. I'm not exactly dressed for company."

Not bothering to wait for his response, she marched to the bathroom and locked herself in. When she came out again fifteen minutes later, the only reminders that he'd ever set foot in the suite were the champagne flutes and half-empty bottle of 1992 Bollinger *Vieilles Vignes Francaises*....

Trish's face was a study in curiosity. "You appear to be having difficulty processing my question, Cass," she remarked snidely, "so let me rephrase it. Did you lead Benedict on?"

"If I did," Cassie said uncomfortably, "it was unintentional. I certainly didn't expect we'd end up having sex, and to be fair, I don't think he did, either."

"Obviously not, or one of you would have had the foresight to use protection, and you wouldn't now be facing your present dilemma." Trish eyed her sympathetically. "Do you think you could learn to love him in time?"

"It's possible."

"So you're not against the idea?"

"No," Cassie said. "I'm just afraid of it."

"Why is that?"

"For a start, he's such a control freak—one of those drag-you-off-by-the-hair, Me Master, You Slave types!"

"Fifty-one per cent wonderful, forty-nine per cent impossible, in other words." Trish lifted one shoulder in a nonchalant shrug. "Well, nobody's perfect, Cass, and I can't see you ever submitting to being molded to the underside of any man's heel, so I'm not worried on that score."

"Well, I am, because I don't want to wind up falling in love with a man who might never love me back. I'm not putting myself or my baby through the misery my mother went through when my father decided he'd had enough of the family scene."

"It's not fair to label Benedict with your father's sins of omission. He deserves to be judged on his own merit."

"I know—which is why I agreed to meet him again and take another look at our options."

"Then don't let me keep you. It's almost noon, and you need to apply a bit more blusher and some lip gloss. Nausea might make some women look pale and interesting, but it doesn't become you at all."

CHAPTER FOUR

SHE did not look well. Unaware that he was watching her from the other side of the lobby, she stepped out of the elevator, and hovered near a smoked-glass wall mirror to check her appearance. Apparently dissatisfied with what she saw, she fluffed a hand through her short blond hair, pinched her cheeks to give them added color, and retied the crimson scarf at her throat.

As if any of that was enough to disguise the mauve shadows beneath her eyes, or the general pallor underlying the carefully applied cosmetics!

"Oh, there you are!" she said, on a nervous breath, when he intercepted her as she mingled with the stream of people headed for the sandwich shop she'd mentioned. "Have you been waiting long?"

"Long enough to see that you need a change of pace from what this place has to offer." He took her elbow and steered her through the building's massive main entrance, and out into the street. "We'll eat in the park. I'm told there's one not five minutes walk from here."

"They don't serve lunch in the park," she objected, dragging her feet.

"There's a delicatessen two doors away. We'll get them to fix us a picnic."

"I don't have time for that. Half an hour is all I can spare."

"Make the time, Cassandra," he said flatly. "Half an hour isn't enough."

She wrenched her elbow free and flung him a resentful

glare. "I don't have much taste for petty dictators, either."

"And I seldom find it necessary to issue orders, but when the need arises, when a woman doesn't show the good sense she was born with, as is the case now, then I'm more than equal to the task." He took her arm again, and marched her into deli. "So, here we are, *cara mia*. What do you feel like ordering—besides my head on a plate?"

"Nothing," she snapped, pinching her lips into a tight line and stubbornly refusing to look at the selection of prepared foods arranged in the glass-fronted display case. "I'm not hungry."

"Then I'll decide for both of us."

"Why am I not surprised to hear that, I wonder?"

"Someone has to make sure you take proper care of yourself," he pointed out, "and who has a more vested interest in your health than I?"

She sighed and rolled her eyes. "Just get a move on, will you? I don't have all day, and we have more important issues waiting to be resolved than whether you want pastrami on rye for lunch, or smoked beef in a bun."

Then, as if the mention of food was enough to turn her stomach, she grew paler than ever, and hurried outside to sit in the shade of an umbrella at one of the sidewalk tables.

Keeping an eye on her to make sure she didn't bolt, he bought slices of cold roasted chicken breast, Melba toast squares, a small wedge of mild cheese, some pale green grapes, and two bottles of mineral water. "We can eat out here, if you wish," he said, joining her at the table.

But she shook her head. "No. I'd rather sit in the

park.'' She swallowed, mopped her glistening upper lip with a dainty handkerchief, and gestured weakly at the open door of the deli. ''The smell in there…anything like that…it's overpowering these days.''

''I understand. Do you feel up to the walk, or shall I call for a taxi?''

''Oh let's walk, and the sooner, the better!'' She pointed across the street to a pedestrian lane winding between two apartment complexes. ''We can take that short cut. It'll get us there in no time.''

He put his hand in the small of her back while they waited for a break in the traffic, and couldn't help noticing not only that she looked unwell, but that she felt much more fragile than she had just over two months ago. Not that she'd ever been a big woman, but there'd been a sweet roundness to her arms and legs before, a gentle flare to her hips, a softer curve to her cheek.

Now, she was all skin and bone; fragile to the point of brittle. Still beautiful, of course—she had the kind of skeletal structure which would make her beautiful even when she was old and gray. But there was no bloom to her; no evidence of the radiance he'd witnessed in his sister when she'd been pregnant. Simply put, Cassandra looked ill.

''Still queasy?'' he asked, as they left the buildings behind and followed a path over a grassy slope in the park to a sunlit glade where a little waterfall splashed into a pond.

''No,'' she said irritably. ''Stop fussing! And stop looking at me as if you're afraid I'm going to drop dead at your feet.''

But he wasn't deceived by her flimsy bravado. She was wilting visibly, and he regretted that he'd not gone along with her wish to remain in her office building.

Alas, where she was concerned, he regretted many things!

"Sit," he said, spreading his jacket on the grass.

This time, she didn't object to being told what to do. With obvious relief, she sank down with her legs tucked beneath her, and accepted the bottle of water he handed to her from the picnic box. "Thank you. You're very kind."

"I'm very concerned, Cassandra. You are too pale, too thin. What does your doctor have to say about this?"

"You mean to say, you didn't show up at his office first thing this morning, to ask him yourself?"

"How could I? You refused to tell me his name."

Two spots of angry color stained her cheeks, emphasizing the pallor of the rest of her face. "I'm in no mood for your lies, Benedict."

"What lies?" he asked, suppressing the surge of anger her accusation inspired. Had she been a man...! "I do not lie."

"How can you stand there looking so offended, when we both know you made it your business to find out who my doctor is, and we both know how you went about it?"

"I haven't the faintest idea what you're talking about," he told her stiffly. "Nor do I care for your tone."

"Oh, please!" She cast him an evil glance from under her lashes. "Drop the act! You're too sophisticated and about twenty years too late to carry off the role of injured innocent."

"I'm thirty-four, Cassandra, and yes, I'm a man of the world. But I've yet to master the art of mind reading. So, I repeat, I don't know what it is that you think I've done. Enlighten me, please, before I lose all patience."

"You made yourself at home in my kitchen last night."

"Indeed yes. And I explained why. I was trying to spare you having to clean up after the meal. Did I not meet your standards of housekeeping excellence?"

"*Indeed, yes!*" she exclaimed with heavy sarcasm. "You'll make some woman a fine wife, one day—either that, or an international spy!"

He'd never thought he'd find himself so livid with her when she looked so frail, but her last insult was something he would not overlook. "Are you so mired in middle-class mores that my turning my hand to domestic chores when you're ill makes me less of a man in your eyes? Because if so, Cassandra, then we have both made a grave error in judgment, I for believing you to be a woman of intelligence, and you for having taken me to be a fool."

To her credit, she had the grace to look ashamed. "I'm sorry. I shouldn't have said that about being someone's wife. But I'm sticking with your making a good spy."

"And why is that?"

"You found my day-planner."

"Yes," he said. "And the crime attached to having done so?"

"You looked in it. You deliberately sought out information which was none of your business."

"Take care," he warned her, and knew from the sudden wary look in her eyes that she felt the chill in his tone. "Because you're carrying my child, I'm willing to make allowances, but even you step on dangerous ground when you question my integrity and continue to fling unfounded accusations in my face. Don't push me too far, *mia bella gestante*. You might not like the outcome.''

Her eyes, a deep, enchanting blue, turned dark with suspicion. ''What's a *gestante?*''

''An expectant mother. What did you think?''

''That if I'm tossing insults at you, you might be inclined to toss a few back at me.''

''No, Cassandra. I have other ways of getting even.''

''I'm sure you have,'' she said, ''but we're straying from the subject. If you weren't snooping for information last night, what was one of your business cards doing on the floor next to the table where I'd left my dayplanner?''

''I planned to leave without saying goodbye. You were so long in your room, I thought perhaps you'd gone to bed because the sickness did not pass. So I took out one of my cards, to write a note telling you I'd be in touch later today, but found I'd left my pen in the briefcase in my car. I saw there was a pencil on the table and was about to use it when I heard you return to the *salone*. I forgot about the note then, and made you toast and tea instead. The card must have fallen to the floor without my noticing, perhaps because I thought it more important to attend to you in person. What was so terrible about that?''

She plucked at the blades of grass edging his jacket, and looked so abject that his irritation melted into compassion. ''Nothing,'' she said finally. ''Except that I've made an idiot of myself over nothing. I seem to be doing that rather often, these days.''

''It's a trying time for you,'' he said, wishing she didn't stir him so deeply. She was confident and successful, a woman of many talents and a great deal of charm. She didn't need his protection. And yet, he felt the need to look after her. Or was it the baby she carried that moved him so profoundly?

He couldn't say. Mother and child were inextricably bound together. They always would be.

Briefly, she met his gaze. "For you, too. A week ago, I'm sure you had no intention of asking me to marry you."

"That is true," he said. "A week ago, many things occupied my mind, but taking a wife was not among them."

"You see? That's why marriage is all wrong for us. We were never lovers in the real sense of the word, nor even friends. We're merely acquaintances."

"We are also adults, and therefore accountable for our actions. Our child is not to blame for having been conceived. This is a situation entirely of our own creating, and we have to make the best of it."

"You make it sound as simple as one and one adding up to two. But it's not."

He smiled. "Indeed no. In this case, one and one adds up to three—unless you happen to be carrying twins."

"Perish the thought! This is no joke, Benedict!"

"It doesn't have to be a tragedy, either." Drawing her to her feet, he grazed her chin with his knuckles, a fleeting caress only, and tried not to notice how, set in mutinous lines though it might be, her mouth remained temptingly delicious. It was obsessing about just such trifles that had landed him in so much trouble with her to begin with. "Look at me, Cassandra. Am I so hideous that you can't bring yourself to like me just a little? Do I repel you? Does the thought of my kissing you, touching you, leave you sick to your stomach?"

He saw the conflict in her eyes, the faint blush staining her cheeks, the erratic leap of her pulse at the corner of her jaw. "No," she admitted reluctantly. "If it did, I'd never have made love with you."

"Then let us build on that. The spark exists, *cara*. With luck and perseverance, we can fan it into a flame."

"But it's not that easy! It takes a lot more than one night of sex to build the solid foundation for marriage."

"You underestimate my determination," he told her. "When I set my sights on a goal, nothing stops me until I achieve it."

"Which I might find flattering if your goal was to win me. But we both know it isn't. If I weren't pregnant, you'd never have proposed."

"Are you so sure of that?"

"Well, *yes!* Let's not pretend otherwise."

"Very well, we won't pretend. Instead, we'll be brutally honest with one another. So here is the way I see things." He caught her hands in his. "I find you interesting and beautiful, both in mind and body. I admire your spirit and drive, the confidence and grace with which you approach life. We are sexually compatible. All good things for two people considering a lifelong union, yes?"

"I suppose so, but—"

He squeezed her fingers, drew her a fraction closer. "There is more. I believe in the sanctity of marriage, and of the family, and hold both sacred. I will allow nothing to harm either one. Although becoming a husband and father has happened sooner than I anticipated, I hold an aversion for neither. I shall honor you as my wife, and be proud to acknowledge you as the mother of my child. You will never want for material comfort or emotional support." He took a step backward, searched her face to learn something of what she was thinking, of what she might be feeling. "There, I am done. Now it's your turn."

"Oh," she said, a trifle breathlessly. "After all that, I hardly know what to say."

"You could tell me you don't believe me."

"But I do," she said ruefully. "That's half the trouble."

"It's half the battle, Cassandra. If you trust me enough to take my word on matters as important as these, how can marriage fail to bind us ever closer to one another?"

"You sound so sure."

"Because I am convinced this is the case."

"But there's so much we don't know about one another."

"We have the rest of our lives to learn, which is as it should be. A good marriage isn't static, *cara*. It continues to grow and become richer."

"I have to agree with you on that, but what about the logistics? My business is here on the West Coast, and you're based in New York."

"Only because it is closer to Europe and slightly more convenient. But with a wife and baby to think of, my priorities change and the world, after all, is a very small place. East Coast, West Coast, it makes little difference to me."

"You'd move here, just to be with me?"

"Yes, because it is important to you. And I hope, if the situation were reversed, that I could say the same of you. Otherwise, what use would we be to one another or our child?"

"Oh, Benedict," she sighed, leaning against him. "You make it very hard for me to turn you down."

"Then we'll be married? Is that what you're telling me?"

A trembling shudder ran over her, reminding him of a butterfly trapped in a net. "Oh, why not?" she whispered on an exhausted breath. "What have we got to lose?"

It was hardly the enthusiastic response he'd hoped for. He was not a man who did things by halves. He had little tolerance for people unable or unwilling to take a stand on issues of consequence, and in his view, marriage fell under that heading. But at least she was no longer flatly refusing to consider his proposal and so, conscious of the need not to pressure her into giving more than she felt able to afford just then, he said with matching nonchalance, "Not a thing, Cassandra, but we stand to gain a great deal. Shall we eat?"

"We might as well."

She knelt beside him and laid out the food. "How soon do you think we should do it—get married, I mean?"

"Will a week give you enough time to find a gown and order flowers and send out invitations?"

For the first time since he'd learned of her pregnancy, she actually laughed. "How like a man to ask such a question! Things like that take months to arrange, Benedict. But in our case, it's irrelevant, because I don't want a wedding dress or flowers, or a crowd of well-wishers. A private marriage ceremony before a justice of the peace, with two witnesses, is enough."

"So it is to be a bare-bones formality, with none of the romantic trimmings usually so dear to a woman's heart?"

"Under the circumstances, yes."

"Then how about a honeymoon in Italy, to make up for it?"

"I don't need a honeymoon, either."

Irritation mounting, he was on the point of telling her that if she planned to bring to their marriage the same lack of enthusiasm she showed for her wedding, it was bound to fail miserably. But sensing she needed little encouragement to call the whole thing off, he tempered his annoyance and said as pleasantly as he knew how, "Nevertheless, I would like to give you one. I believe, from the looks of you, that a holiday will do you good. And it so happens that, for reasons to do with my family's business undertakings, I must return shortly to my home in Calabria."

Helping herself to a sliver of chicken breast, she said, "Where's that? You'll have to forgive my ignorance, but I've never visited Italy, so my knowledge of its geography is a bit sketchy. Show me a map, and I can point to major cities like Rome and Milan, but Calabria—"

"Is right down in the toe of the country, across the Strait of Messina from Sicily."

She looked startled. "Isn't Sicily the home of the Mafia?"

"You watch too much television, Cassandra," he said lightly. "I have a beautiful vacation home in Sicily, and it's never once been under attack from the Mafia."

Thoughtfully, she nibbled at a square of melba toast. "Well, I'm sure I'd enjoy seeing it some day, but I'm not convinced this is the time. If you've got family business to attend to, you don't need me traipsing along for the ride. Why don't we put marriage on hold until you come back to the States?"

"And leave you to cope alone with this pregnancy?

Not a chance! I assure you I can deal with my family and still find plenty of time to pay attention to my wife.''

She looked suddenly apprehensive. ''But I'm not sure I *should* be traveling right now. My doctor might not approve.''

''In that case, we'll discuss it with him. If he advises against it, I'll postpone the visit until you feel well enough to make the journey.'' But she continued to look uncertain and, remembering her earlier remark about not having visited Italy, he said, ''What are you really afraid of, *cara?* Is it the idea of flying?''

She shook her head. ''Not at all. It's just that these early weeks of pregnancy have taken such a toll on my energy.''

''All the more reason to take you away from the rigors of work. Calabria is beautiful, Cassandra, a paradise of pristine beaches and clear warm seas. You'll be required to do nothing but relax and let my mother and sisters pamper you.''

''What about your father? What's he going to say about your mixing a honeymoon with business?''

''My father died four years ago.''

''I'm sorry.''

''Don't be,'' he said. ''You had no way of knowing.''

''That's what scares me.'' A frown creased the perfection of her brow. ''One way or another, you've learned quite a bit about me, but I know little about you, and absolutely nothing about the members of your family beyond the fact that they grow a special kind of citrus fruit—bergamot, isn't it?''

''That is it exactly. So you are not as uninformed as you like to pretend.''

''Oh, yes, I am! I wouldn't know a bergamot, if it jumped up and bit me.''

"The bergamot orange is very distinctive. You'll soon learn to recognize it."

"Bergamot...." She lay flat on her back, and ran the word over her tongue, imitating the way he rolled the R. Her hair fanned around her head, a bright halo against the dark green of the grass. "You make it sound so exotic."

"It is a remarkable fruit."

She propped herself up on one elbow to sip at her water, then lay down again and gazed at the canopy of trees overhead. "I remember your telling me, the first time we met, that it's used in the most expensive perfumes, and as a pharmaceutical agent. Is it edible, too?"

"Not in its natural state, but you'll find essence of bergamot used as a flavoring in liquors, tea, and preserved sweets."

"So your family's involved in very big business."

"We make a living."

She slewed a glance at him. The sunlight piercing the branches lent her skin an opalescent gleam and filmed her blue eyes with brilliance, reminding him of the jewelry studded with precious gems created by Calabrian goldsmiths. At another time and in a more private setting, he would have shown her with few words how alluring he found her.

"I'm not asking you how much you're worth, Benedict, if that's what you're thinking," she said soberly. "Just the opposite, in fact. *The Ariel* is a very successful enterprise, and I can well afford to bring up this baby alone. So if you're thinking perhaps I'm marrying you for your money—"

"It never occurred to me that you are, nor is that the reason I proposed. We are marrying because we both wish to do what is best for our child."

She sat up again and helped herself to the grapes. "Just as long as we're both clear on that."

"*Assolutamente!* Would you care for a little cheese with the fruit?"

"You know, I think I would," she said, sounding surprised, and patted her waist lightly. "The fresh air seems to have settled my stomach."

"Or else knowing that the future is more settled has done the trick."

She sampled the cheese thoughtfully a moment, before replying, "Well, I don't mind admitting, the idea of belonging to a large family is rather appealing. I've felt very alone since my mother passed away." She shuffled over to make room for him next to her on his jacket. "Tell me more about your sisters. Are they older or younger than you?"

"Bianca is my age—not surprising, since we're twins!—and is married with two children, a boy, Stefano who's seven, and a girl, Pia, who's three. My brother-in-law Enrico is a lawyer and looks after the legal side of the business, as well as managing our Milano operation—did I mention that we have a few vineyards in Lombardy?"

"No," she said, enchanting him with the lilt of amusement in her voice. "That little detail somehow slipped your mind. But do go on."

"Francesca is twenty-five and still single. She works closely with our mother, running the Calabrian end of things—administration, book-keeping, that kind of thing. We have nearly seventy employees in Calabria, and another thirty in Milano."

"Are you sure there's room for me in such a busy family?"

"They will be overjoyed to welcome you, *cara*," he

said, hoping it was true. "Every Italian mother wants to see her son produce *un bambino* or two."

"Right now, it's all I can do to manage one and keep track of my appointments." She made a face, a quaint, endearing wrinkling of her elegant nose, and checked the gold fob watch pinned to the lapel of her jacket. "Speaking of which, I have a client meeting in twenty minutes."

"I'll walk you back to the office."

Instead of arguing the point, as she might have done earlier, she merely packed up the remains of their lunch, then brushed the loose grass from his jacket and passed it to him. "I'm glad I wasn't able to talk you out of coming here," she said. "It's a lovely spot, and there's something very soothing in the sound of the waterfall splashing into the pond."

"At my summer home in Sicily," he said, coming up behind her and sliding his arms around her waist, "the sound of the sea lapping on the shore is a night-long lullaby. You will fall asleep with the moon casting stark shadows over the land, and awaken the next morning to golden sunlight and the scent of verbena and rosemary and jasmine."

She leaned against him; let him rest his chin on the crown of her head. "You make it sound idyllic. Can you guarantee that's how our marriage will be?"

"No, *cara*," he murmured, turning her slowly to face him. "The most I can promise is that I will make it the best that it can be. Inevitably, there will be storms, but there will be the calm that follows, and many, many times in between heated by a different passion."

"What kind?" she said, flirting with him from beneath lowered lashes.

"The kind better demonstrated than described in words."

He kissed her then, something he'd been wanting to do ever since she'd stepped out of the elevator almost an hour before. Kissed her long and deeply, and as her mouth softened beneath his, the blood rushed to his loins.

He ached to touch her more intimately; to lay his hand on her belly, where the life within her flourished. His seed, his child...and soon, his wife.

She must have know that he was aroused, yet still she didn't pull away, but instead slipped her hands around his neck, pressed herself closer to him, and whispered unsteadily, "Oh, *that* kind!"

"That," he told her, "is but a token, a promise, if you will, of better things to come."

She drew in a broken sigh. "Suddenly, I wish I didn't have a client waiting for me at the office."

"It's as well that you do," he said, reluctantly putting her from him. "When next we make love, it will be behind closed doors, not in a public park with the ever-present chance of unwelcome visitors intruding on the moment."

She nodded and, with the casual intimacy of a wife or lover, reached up to wipe a fleck of something from the corner of his mouth. "Lipstick," she said, mischief dancing in her eyes. "And it's not your shade at all."

They strolled back along the busy street, the silence between them now easy. "I don't suppose there's any point in my asking you not to work too hard?" he said, as they slowed to a stop next to where a street vendor had set up his flower stall outside her office building.

"Not really. But I promise not to overdo it." She favored him with a brief and lovely smile.

Behind her on the stall, tiny bunches of small, purple flowers echoed the color of her eyes and gave emphasis to the porcelain perfection of her skin. On a whim, he bought one of the sprigs and slipped it behind the pin holding her watch in place.

She gave a muted exclamation of pleasure and dipped her head to sniff the fragrance. "Violets! How did you know I love them?"

"Lucky guess," he said, his attention captured by the slender curve of her neck. "They're small and delicate, like you. *Bella,* like you."

"Sometimes, you say the nicest things." A faint blush accompanied her smile and she touched her fingertips to his hand. "Forgive me having leapt to all the wrong conclusions about last night."

"Consider it forgotten. Focus on the future, instead."

"Yes." She lingered a moment longer, as though reluctant to leave, then wrinkled her nose again in that habit which he found so charming. "I really must go. My client will be waiting."

"We'll talk again," he said. "Very soon."

"Yes." She hesitated, turned away, then at the last moment swung back and kissed his cheek. "Thank you again for lunch," she whispered at his ear, "and...for everything else."

And then she was gone, sweeping gracefully up the marble steps and through the revolving glass door. He stood watching as the dove gray of her suit merged with the colors other people milling about the lobby were wearing. Until her slight figure and blond head were hidden behind larger, anonymous bodies.

He remained there long after the crowd was swallowed up in the elevator, his thoughts troubled. There were serious problems awaiting him in Calabria. Was he being fair to Cassandra in taking her with him, knowing what he did? Yet she was carrying his child so how, in good conscience, could he leave her behind?

He could not. Would not. Which begged another question. How best to break the news to his family that, at a time when so much else was uncertain, he was bringing to the mix a bride who was a stranger to them and to the culture and customs which bound their lives?

CHAPTER FIVE

DINNER was over, the movie finished, the lights dimmed. Cushioned in luxurious leather beside a window in the *Magnifica* section of the Alitalia 767 jet, Cassandra raised her footrest and adjusted her seat to a reclining position. Next to her, her brand-new husband lifted his glance from the report he was studying just long enough to ask, "Comfortable?"

"Mmm-hmm." She tucked the fleecy airline blanket more securely around her legs.

"Think you'll be able to get some rest?"

She nodded and closed her eyes. But sleep, the one thing she never seemed able to get enough of since she'd become pregnant, eluded her. Instead, the events of the last six days raced in living color through her mind like a movie reel come unspooled....

"What did he do to get you to change your mind?" Trish had wondered, when Cassandra returned from her lunch with Benedict and said she'd accepted his proposal.

"Bowled me over with sweet reason, mostly."

"How about dazzled you with his smile? Seduced you with his long-lashed, bedroom eyes?"

"That, too." She'd lifted her lapel, buried her nose again in the damp, sweet-smelling violets. "He can be very convincing when he puts his mind to it."

And very efficient. Leaving her with no time for second thoughts, he'd swung into action. Within seventy-two hours, they'd purchased their marriage license, booked a time for the ceremony to take place at the County Clerk's office, reserved their flight to Italy, and consulted by phone with her obstetrician who, upon hearing of their travel plans, immediately ordered a sonogram, "just to be on the safe side."

"A week or two of rest and relaxation is just what she needs," the doctor affirmed, when they met with him the next afternoon. "However, although the findings of the ultrasound are inconclusive at this stage, the cervix remains a matter of slight concern. We'll reassess the situation when you return but, for the time being, I recommend you refrain from marital relations. Not the kind of news a couple wants to take away with them on a honeymoon, I know, but when a high-risk pregnancy is at stake...."

"This is the first I've heard about there being any kind of risk attached to the pregnancy," Benedict had said, shooting an accusatory look Cassandra's way. "Explain, if you will, Doctor, the possible difficulties my wife will be facing."

Later, over dinner at Pier 39, she'd again suggested they postpone the wedding until such time as they could enjoy a normal honeymoon.

"Absolutely not," Benedict ruled. "Marriage is about more than just sex, Cassandra, and in our case, about a lot more than just you and me. The safety of our baby takes precedence over all else."

His stoic acceptance of the doctor's ruling, added to the brisk, almost businesslike manner with which he treated her thereafter, rendered Trish's parting gift of a diaphanous negligee somewhat pointless, Cassie thought, conscious of the unfamiliar weight of the heavy gold ring on her finger. That it signified marriage was as foreign a concept as the fact that the man sitting next to her was her husband. No matter how many times she told herself, *I am now, for better or worse, Mrs. Benedict Constantino,* the reality didn't sink in. Even yesterday's wedding possessed the elements of a dream fraught with a touch of nightmare.

"I don't even know his birthday!" she'd wailed to Trish. "I don't know his middle name, or what size shirt he wears. I don't know if he likes pajamas or sleeps naked, drives a Mercedes or a pickup truck!"

Trish, ever practical, had said, "Check out the marriage license for his birth date and middle name. As for what he drives, you've only got to look at the man to know it's a Ferrari or a Porsche, and you'll find out soon enough what he wears in bed. Quit fretting about minor details, Cass, and put your shoes on. Ian's bringing the car round, and we don't want to keep the groom or City Hall waiting."

"I can't leave yet," she'd protested, swamped in a rush of panic at what she was about to do. "I think I'm going to be sick again."

"It'll have to wait until after the ceremony," Trish had decreed unsympathetically. "You'll smear your lip gloss and make your mascara run if you throw up now."

But the nausea had persisted. Was with her still, caused not by the pregnancy, or the sudden swooping dip of the aircraft as it hit a patch of turbulence, but by the nervous shock of realizing she'd thrown in her lot with a virtual stranger.

How long before the panic subsided, before being addressed as Signora Constantino stopped taking her by surprise? And how long before Benedict became the man who'd wooed her so persuasively that, within twenty-four hours of his learning she was carrying his child, she'd agreed to marry him?

Beside her, she heard the rustle of papers, the snap of his briefcase closing, the sibilant whisper of the soft leather seat as his body made itself comfortable for the night. His elbow nudged hers, remained there, warm and solid. She felt, rather than heard his breathing become slow and relaxed.

Alert for a sign that he'd fallen asleep, she waited five minutes...ten. The man in the row behind snored loudly enough to be heard over the drone of the jet engines, but not Benedict. If he slept, and she thought from the utter stillness of his body that he must, it was with the same unruffled competence that he did everything else.

At last, cautiously, she turned her head, and opened her eyes. Yes, he was sleeping, sprawled elegantly in his seat with his hands clasped loosely in his lap, which left her free to examine at leisure the strong, clean lines of his profile.

He looked just as he had the previous morning, when they exchanged their wedding vows: a study in charcoal and bronze, iron-jawed and unsmiling. Thoroughly masculine, thoroughly composed. No untoward dreams would disturb his rest. They wouldn't dare!

His lashes, thick and luxuriant enough to make a woman weep with envy, smudged dark against his high cheekbones. His hair, usually tamed to within an inch of its life, lay slightly rumpled across his brow. And his mouth...?

She studied the patrician curve of his lips and her throat went dry. But a flush of heat settled between her legs as if *that* part of her body had stolen all her moisture to ease its sudden ache.

No question about it! She knew more about his mouth—how it tasted and felt, and what it could do to drive her crazy with desire—than she did about any other part of him.

What sort of a basis did *that* make for a solid marriage?

She was still pondering the thought when, without a flicker of warning, his lashes swept up and she found herself trapped in the unblinking enigma of his dark eyes.

"Well?" he said, his voice low and commanding. "Will I do?"

Taking refuge in the absurdly obvious, she said, "I thought you were sleeping."

The corner of his mouth lifted in the ghost of a smile. "Your kind of intense, unswerving scrutiny could raise the dead, Cassandra, let alone awaken a sleeping man. But you haven't answered my question. *Will* I do, or are you already regretting having married me?"

"You're very handsome," she allowed. "Very aristocratic-looking, and very...decent. A woman would have to be crazy to regret being your wife."

"And at this moment, you're having serious doubts about your sanity, yes?"

She wanted to wrench her gaze away, but found she couldn't. Found herself compelled by the candor in his eyes to respond in kind. "I admit, at the moment, I'm feeling somewhat overwhelmed."

"I wish I could reassure you," he said, "but that's something only time can achieve. The best I can do is tell you that I am exactly as I've presented myself to you: a man bound by honor and tradition to abide by his marriage vows and provide well for his wife and baby. Furthermore, I consider myself fortunate in the extreme to have found a woman of such beauty and intelligence to be the mother of my child."

He reached across the console dividing their seats and touched the sleeve of her wedding outfit, a deep aquamarine silk knit dress with a knee-length skirt and matching jacket, which she and Trish had shopped for during their lunch hour, earlier in the week. She'd worn it again today because it was both comfortable and stylish, and she wanted to look her best when she met his family. "We didn't have an elaborate wedding," he said, "but you made a beautiful bride, nevertheless."

"I hope your family thinks so. You never did tell me how they received the news, when you phoned to tell them you were bringing back a wife. Were they pleased?"

"They responded much as I expected they would."

The ambiguity of his reply was not lost on her. Uneasily, she said, "That doesn't sound very promising."

He gave her hand a perfunctory pat, as if she were a child incapable of understanding the complexities of the grown-up world he occupied. "Leave me to worry about my family, Cassandra, and concentrate only of giving birth to a healthy, full-term baby."

"Don't brush me off like that, Benedict," she said sharply. "If this marriage of ours is to stand any sort of chance at all, the very least you can do is address my concerns, just as you expect me to address yours."

He expelled a sigh, though whether of annoyance or fatigue she couldn't tell. "Very well. It's fair to say my family was surprised."

"And happy for you?"

"I didn't ask them."

More disquieted by the second, she said, "Why not?"

"Because the call was brief, and the connection poor. We will be in Italy only a matter of a week or two. That being the case, my family's happiness, or lack thereof, is scarcely relevant."

Although he answered straightforwardly enough, she knew there was more to it than he was telling her. It showed in the sudden tightening of his mouth, the way he shifted impatiently in his seat.

"They don't approve, do they?" she said. "They don't want you bringing home a bride."

"What does it matter, Cassandra? *I* wanted it, which leaves them with little choice but to accept you." The almost clinical detachment with which he spoke turned his meager crumbs of comfort to poison. "You and I are, as our French friends would say, a *fait accompli,* and there's not a damned thing anyone can do or say to change that."

Crushed, she turned her head and gazed bleakly out at the star-spattered sky beyond the porthole. Any other husband en route to introducing his new wife to his family would have said, *They'll adore you, just as I do.* But unlike most bridegrooms, Benedict was not besotted with his new wife,

Nor did he pretend to be. "I wanted *it,*" he'd said, meaning "the marriage." Not, "I wanted *you.*" And the reason, as she'd known from the outset, was that she was pregnant with his child. So why the sudden stinging hurt, the acute sense that she'd been robbed?

"Will the whole family be meeting us in Milan?" she asked, praying they would not. Nine hours of jet travel, no matter how comfortable the accommodation on board or forgiving the outfit she was wearing, did not leave any woman looking her best, and it seemed she already had her work cut out to make a favorable impression.

"No. Only Bianca and Enrico will be there. As I already explained, there's no direct flight from New York to my family home, and Milan lies almost a thousand kilometers north of Calabria. It makes no sense for my mother and Francesca to cover such a distance when they'll meet you anyway the following day.'' He yawned and closed his eyes. ''Get some sleep, Cassandra. You've had a hectic couple of days, what with flying from San Francisco to New York yesterday, and now this. You must be exhausted.''

Exhausted, Benedict? she thought, turning her face away from him and refusing to allow another hormonally induced rash of tears to take hold. *How about discouraged, offended, and resentful? Just who do these relatives of yours think they are, to judge me unfavorably before they've even laid eyes on me?*

''Does Cassandra not speak any Italian?'' Bianca asked.

''A word or two—*ciao, grazie, arrivederci.* Common, everyday words only. Enough to be polite but not enough to carry on a conversation.''

''Benedict, are you mad to have brought her here at this time? You know how she'll be received by our mother.''

He shrugged and kept on walking. The evening was mild for late March, the parklike grounds of his sister's country home, an hour's drive from the city, a feast for the eyes with its tree-shaded paths and long sweeps of lawn rimmed with flower beds just beginning to bloom. ''Leave me to enjoy tonight, Bianca. Tomorrow is soon enough to worry about our mother. Regardless of how she might react to my marriage, you know I'll deal with her.''

''Not easily, for something this momentous, and especially not at this time.'' She slipped an affectionate arm through his. ''I didn't want to burden you with bad news when you phoned to tell us you were getting married, but she's becoming more irrational by the day, and I'm afraid the situation's even worse now than it was when last you were here.''

''I don't see how that's possible. There were only a handful of people left working the land then, and I paid them handsomely to stay on the job, with the promise of a further bonus when I returned.''

''And as far as I know, only a very few have remained loyal. The rest are gone. Even worse, the dissatisfaction has spread to the kitchen and household staff. Sergio walked out at the weekend, which meant his wife and daughter went with him. Then, two days ago, Guido left. The only one still there is Speranza, and how much abuse she's taking as a result isn't something I like to dwell on.''

''That's completely unacceptable!'' Speranza was past seventy, had been with his family since well before Benedict was born, and would, he knew, die on the job before she'd abandon the family she loved as if it were her own. For her to be attending to her own work and taking on that of four others, all considerably younger, was not to be tolerated.

''Of course it is!'' Bianca gave a troubled sigh. ''How did this happen so fast, Benedict? A year ago, everything was running smoothly, everyone was happy. Now, we have a full-scale disaster on our hands, and I dread to think how we'll manage when harvesting the bergamot begins again in October. Unless you can turn things around quickly, we'll default on some of our most important client contracts. Should that happen, not only will we stand to lose money but, far worse, our reputation, too.''

"It won't happen," he promised. "I'll handle everything."

"On your honeymoon? I don't see the two mixing well!"

"It's a working holiday. Cassandra understands that."

"But she looks frail and anxious, this little wife of yours, and sad, too. And you...you're not glowing with happiness, either. Shouldn't you be concentrating on each other, and not business?"

"We're both tired, that's all. The last week's been hectic, what with making travel arrangements and then the wedding."

"Is there a reason that it took place so suddenly?"

He blew out a long, uneven breath. "Oh, yes! She's pregnant."

"Dio!" Her face a study in shocked exasperation, Bianca pulled her arm free and planted herself in his path. "Benedict, how could you have allowed—?"

"I know, I know! You expected better of me. I expected better of myself. But things are what they are, and I have to make the best of them."

"You're not in love with Cassandra?"

"I am drawn to her. She wouldn't be carrying my child otherwise."

"Does our mother know?"

"About the baby, no. Nor do I plan to tell her until I see how things go. But I'm confiding in you, Bianca, because we've always been close and I know you'll accept Cassandra without censure."

"Of course! She's a sweet and lovely woman. I can see why you'd be attracted to her, and I welcome her as my sister. But Benedict..." She looked away and he knew from the way that she lapsed into silence that she was deeply concerned.

"But I've disappointed you." His smile was part amusement, part regret. "I've fallen off my pedestal and shown myself to be as human as the next man,"

"Oh, it's not that! You're my brother and I'd never judge you." She let out another sigh. "But the difficulties I spoke of at home in the south…well, they don't end with our mother."

"You mean, there's more, and it's worse? I don't see how that's possible!"

"I'm afraid it is. Apparently, those few retainers who've remained loyal to the family are being bullied by defectors with blood contacts in the Aspromonte." She cast him a worried look. "We both know the kind of danger that presents, Benedict. We're dealing with *la 'ndrangheta,* something which never would have happened in our father's day because he would never have hired such ruffians in the first place."

Benedict was no coward, but this latest revelation gave rise to a thread of uneasiness which ran too close to fear for his peace of mind. The threat from *la 'ndrangheta*—the local Mafia, whose chief source of income was kidnapping members of wealthy families and extorting huge ransoms for their safe return—was not something to be taken lightly. Lawless and without conscience, they lived in the wild mountainous region of the interior of the province and were answerable to no one but themselves.

"If that's the case, we have a critical situation on our hands," he said, again questioning how wise he'd been to insist on having Cassandra accompany him on this trip. "To expect that they'll feel themselves bound by the moral dictates which govern the rest of our lives is unrealistic. If vengeance is an issue, they'll deal with it in ways we can't begin to imagine."

"Exactly. We grew up hearing the stories—about the people who disappear and are never heard from again, the vendettas carried out—and nothing's changed. I'm afraid for Francesca, as well as for our mother." She tucked her hand more firmly under his arm. "And I'm afraid for you, as well, Benedict."

"Don't be," he said. "I can take care of myself, and Francesca and our mother, too. But Cassandra is another matter. If the situation at the palazzo strikes me as too risky, I'd like to know I can send her to you for refuge."

"Of course! As often, and for as long as you need."

"Thank you." He stopped and squeezed her hand. "I've always been able to rely on you."

"We've relied on each other, *caro,* and that doesn't change just because we're both now married. We're family. We always will be."

They resumed walking. Dusk had fallen, and lamplight shone behind many of the windows fronting the house. But looking up, Benedict located the room where Cassandra waited in the wide guest bed, and saw that it lay in darkness. Did that mean she was asleep?

He hoped so. He wasn't sure he could face her again tonight and not have his concern show.

Hidden by a fold in the filmy drapes, Cassie looked down on the gardens. Earlier, peacocks had strutted across the lawn and the children playing hide-and-seek. But now, with the moon rising in the east, the garden was deserted except for the figures of her husband and his twin strolling back along the night-shadowed path to the balustraded forecourt below her window. They were enviably at ease in each other's company—and so oblivious of her that she might as well not exist.

Not that she hadn't been well received by his sister

and her husband. When they'd met at Malpensa airport, Bianca Constantino Manzini had folded Cassie in a hug, kissed her on both cheeks, and said in charmingly accented but otherwise perfect English, "I am so happy to meet you, Cassandra, and so thrilled that my brother has found someone with whom to share his life. Welcome to Milano and our family!"

Equally warm, Enrico had echoed his wife's sentiments, which ought to have reassured Cassandra. And perhaps it would have, had Benedict not grown correspondingly more remote, more preoccupied. But immediately upon arrival at the Manzini residence, he'd disappeared without a word into Enrico's home office, and left his wife to fend for herself.

"Family business," Bianca had explained apologetically, noticing Cassie's dismay at being so soon abandoned among strangers. "Always with this family, the business must be attended to first, and then we play. So, *cara,* while our men pore over legal documents and international import regulations, come and meet my children. They're so eager to greet their new aunt, and you're here for such a short spell this time, that I kept my son home from school today so that he could make the most of your visit."

As she spoke, she'd led the way to a large sunny room at the rear of the house, where a boy worked on a model aircraft at a table, and a girl played on the floor with a doll house. Both of them dark and beautiful like their mother, they stopped what they were doing and stood politely during the formal introductions.

"Hello," the boy had murmured shyly, shaking Cassie's hand. "You are welcoming to *Italia.*"

"Stefano's been practicing saying that in English ever since Benedict phoned to let us know he was bringing you to meet us," Bianca told her in an amused aside. "I'm afraid, though, that he still doesn't have it quite right."

"Never mind," Cassie had replied, completely won over by the boy's smile. "His English is a whole lot better than my Italian. He puts me to shame."

The girl, Pia, unwilling to remain in her brother's shade, rattled off a stream of Italian of which only *Ciao!* meant anything to Cassie. But she understood what was expected of her when the child tugged at her hand and pulled her over to admire the doll's house which, with its elaborate facade and rooms full of exquisite furniture, was truly a work of art.

"A gift from Benedict," Bianca said. "He's a very indulgent uncle and will be, I'm sure, an equally indulgent husband."

Perhaps not, if his recent attitude was anything to go by, Cassie thought now, letting the drapes fall back into place as Benedict and Bianca disappeared from view, although his apparent devotion to his niece and nephew boded well for his own child. But then, she already knew that because, as he was so fond of saying, "The baby comes first."

Down below, a door thudded closed and voices, one deeply resonant as only a man's could be, the other feminine and full of laughter, drifted up from the entrance hall in a vivacious burst of rapid-fire Italian. Opening the bedroom door a crack, Cassie caught the occasional word—*domani...bambini,* and her own name, Cassandra.

Beyond that, she hadn't the first clue what her husband and sister-in-law were talking about, and promised herself that, tomorrow, she'd buy an Italian phrase book at the airport, and study it during the short flight to

Calabria. Hopefully, if she memorized a few common expressions—*I'm very pleased to meet you. How are you? You have a lovely home*—it might persuade her new mother-in-law to look upon her more favorably.

And Benedict? Would her effort to absorb something of his culture and background move him to treat her with the kind of warmth he'd initially shown when he sought her out again in San Francisco? Or was his present courteous reserve all she had to look forward to, now that he'd achieved his ambition and made her his wife?

Oh, he was kind enough, in an abstract sort of way, but somewhere between his asking her to marry him, and her saying "I do," the sexual electricity which had charged their every encounter had flickered and died. Beyond a sedate kiss on the cheek, an impersonal hand at her elbow to help her cross the street or climb out of a car, he made no attempt to touch her anymore.

At first, she'd put down the change in him to his having too many other matters occupying his attention, too many demands on his time. She'd told herself that, once they'd left all the rush behind, and it was just the two of them in Italy, he'd be his former self again and the old attraction would resurface.

But it hadn't happened. If anything, with each passing hour, he became more...*absentmindedly paternalistic.* And she hated it!

The moon, now fully risen above the trees, cast a pale and melancholy light over the room, and reduced the warm wood of the elegant furniture to a chill, tomblike gray. And she, on her supposed honeymoon, sat propped up by pillows, alone in the wide, wrought-iron bed.

Too drained to flick on the reading lamp and lose herself in the paperback novel lying in her lap, too homesick for the familiar comfort of her own house and friends, and too at odds with her tangled emotions to take refuge in sleep, she stared into the semi-darkness.

How long she remained like that, utterly motionless, utterly miserable, she neither knew nor cared. At some level, she was aware of the house gradually sinking into peaceful silence, but it could have been hours or only minutes before she heard the well-oiled *snick* of the door opening, and saw Benedict's tall figure on the threshold, silhouetted by the soft glow of a night-light in the upper hall.

Quietly, he closed the door, and picked his way across the floor, clearly intending to shut himself in the adjoining dressing room so as not to disturb her. But she, anticipating just such a move, announced coldly, "It's quite all right to turn on the light, Benedict. Contrary to your express command, I am not sleeping."

Startled into dropping the shoes he'd been carrying, he let out a smothered exclamation, and groped for the switch on the bedside lamp. "Then why the devil are you sitting here in the dark?"

She blinked in the sudden bright glare. "What does it look like?" she said. "I'm waiting for my husband to come to bed, the way all brides do on their honeymoon. Or isn't that the custom in Italy?"

CHAPTER SIX

HE MADE a big production of removing his jacket and tie, and hanging them in the wardrobe. "If I'd known you were still wide-awake—"

"You'd have done what?" she snapped, glaring at his back. "Stayed here to keep me company, instead of going for an evening stroll with your sister?"

He spun back to face her, a frown creasing his brow. "I wasn't aware you knew we'd gone out. Were you watching us?"

"I *saw* you, which isn't quite the same thing. And I wondered if there was a reason you sent me off to bed, instead of asking me to join you."

"Cassandra," he said, standing at the foot of the bed, and adopting that reasonable I-know-what's-best-for-you tone she was beginning to loathe, "you were fading so noticeably over dinner that it simply didn't occur to me to ask you to come with us."

"I'm pregnant, Benedict, not terminally ill. And I'm old enough to decide for myself when I need to retire for the night."

"Fine!" He shrugged, removed his cuff links, and took his time rolling his shirtsleeves midway up his forearms. "Forgive me for caring enough about your welfare to give a damn! In future, do as you please."

"I intend to," she informed him. "And right now, it pleases me to discover why you're more interested in acting like my guardian than my husband. A week ago, you couldn't get enough of my company. Now, you're so busy keeping your distance, I'm beginning to feel like Typhoid Mary.''

His mouth fell open and for a long, silent moment, he simply stared at her. Then he leaned against the dresser and let fly with a great, rich burst of merriment unlike anything she'd heard from him before. "I don't recall ever having met such a person," he finally managed to splutter. "Do I take it she's not particularly nice to be near?''

"Stop being trying to be cute, Benedict! It doesn't suit you. And while you're at it, you can stop guffawing, as well, and just give me a straight answer.''

He stroked his chin and made a pitiful effort to keep a straight face, but when he spoke, his voice still quivered with suppressed laughter. "I'm trying, but if only you could see yourself, *cara,* perched there among your mountain of pillows, looking for all the world like a queen reprimanding a wayward subject.''

To her horror and chagrin, tears overflowed her eyes and leaked down her face. "I'm glad one of us finds this amusing.''

"Ah, Cassandra...!'' In one swift stride, he came to her and perched on the edge of the mattress. "Where is all this nonsense coming from? If you wanted to come with Bianca and me this evening, all you had to do was say so.''

"I didn't, not really,'' she sniffed, knowing she was being absurd and hating the fact that she had so little control of her emotions these days. "I'd probably have been in the way.''

"Not so. Bianca was telling me how much she likes you.'' He cupped her jaw, his touch warm and tender. "Has someone else made you feel unwelcome here?''

"No. Bianca and Enrico couldn't be kinder, their children are a delight, and their house staff very helpful. But let's face it, Benedict, for all that they're trying not to let it show, your sister and brother-in-law are reeling with shock at your showing up with a wife, and hardly know what to make of our marriage. And frankly, in light of your growing indifference toward me, nor do I."

He reared back, shock evident in every feature. "You believe I'm indifferent to you?"

"Maybe not," she said, on a miserable sigh. "Maybe it's just me, overreacting again. All I know is that I'm a stranger in a strange land, miles away from anyone who really cares about me."

"*I* care, Cassandra."

"Only because I'm pregnant."

"Not only because of that," he said, leaning forward to capture her hands. "And if you think the reason I'm keeping my distance is that I don't want to be near you, then you're not just pregnant, you're hopelessly naive as well."

"In that case, come to bed," she begged, hanging on to him for dear life. "Don't let this be a repeat of two nights ago."

He grew very still. "I'm not sure I understand you."

"I might be naive, Benedict, but I'm not delusional. I went to bed alone on our wedding night, awoke after midnight to find myself still alone, and had the same thing happen again, the next morning."

"I didn't want to disturb you," he said. "You'd had a very long day, and before that, a very busy week. When I came to the bedroom, you were sleeping so deeply that I thought it best if I stayed on the sofa in my study."

"Well, I'm not sleeping now."

"But you should be. Your doctor wouldn't be pleased to know you're defying his instructions."

"He wouldn't be pleased to know I'm stressed out because my husband's ignoring me, either!"

His gaze burned into hers. He was not a man given to indecision, yet at that moment she saw torment in his eyes and she quaked inside at what it might signify. Did he find her repugnant, with her heavy breasts and subtle thickening at the waist, and endless bouts of nausea? Or had the rashness of their decision to marry finally hit home, and he was horrified at the commitment he'd made?

Whatever the cause, eventually he lifted his shoulders in mute surrender and disappeared into the dressing room. Shortly after, she heard the door to the en suite bathroom close, and the sound of water running in the shower. When he returned to the bedroom some fifteen minutes later, she'd turned off the reading lamp and lay beneath the lightweight duvet, taut with a mixture of anticipation and dread.

The moon, peeping through the window, illuminated his path to the bed. Without a word, he climbed in beside her and lay on his back, motionless, with his hands clasped behind his head. On the nightstand, a small gilt clock marked the passing time...*tick...tick...tick...*

Only a few inches of mattress separated his body from hers, yet it might as well have been an abyss, and she couldn't bear it. Whispering his name, she turned to him and laid her hand on his bare chest. His skin was cool and smooth beneath a dusting of hair. Dark against the ghostly white of the bed linen. Sculpted by underlying muscle.

But except for the steady beat of his heart and the

slow rise and fall of his breathing, he might as well have been dead, so unmoved was her by her touch.

Her voice awash with tearful pleading, she said again, "Benedict, I feel so alone!"

"You're not alone, Cassandra. I'm here."

"Then hold me. Let me feel your warmth."

He unclasped his hands and slipped a wary, avuncular arm around her shoulders. Starving for his touch, she burrowed against him and pressed her mouth to the side of his neck, savoring the scent of soap and man.

Immediately, he pulled away. "Stop that!" he muttered, his voice strangled.

"Why?" she said. "Don't you want me?"

"So badly I can taste it," he replied. "But I can't have you. Not now. Not yet. You can do your worst to tempt me, Cassandra, but I will do nothing to endanger your pregnancy."

"But we can touch, can't we?" She splayed her fingers over his chest again, circled the raised point of his nipples. "We can caress. We can kiss."

"I kiss you," he said. "I kissed you good night before you came upstairs."

"Not the way you did before. Not as if you can't get enough of me." She raised herself up on one elbow and leaned over him. "Not like this," she said, lowering her mouth to his and sweeping her tongue over his lower lip.

Roughly, he turned his head aside and swore—at least, she supposed he did, given the stifled violence in his tone, even though she didn't understand the words he used. "You go too far, Cassandra!" he said hoarsely. "Let it be enough that we're married!"

"I can't," she said, encouraged by the betraying, savage rasp of his breathing. "What if you grow tired of being a husband in name only?"

"Do you think me an animal, that I can't control my carnal appetite?"

She stroked her hand over his stomach, pushed down the briefs he wore, and with the tip of her finger traced the curve of skin where the top of his thigh met his hip. "No," she said, smiling a little at his dignified usage of English because it bore no relation whatsoever to the highly indecorous response of his body. "I think you are a man who deserves better than to be lying in bed with a wife who can't pleasure you."

"Cassandra, I'm begging you...!"

He was big and hard and heavy. Pulsing and alive. *Alive for her...!*

"Be quiet, Benedict," she said gently, and lowering her head, closed her lips around his penis.

He tasted divine, and she wanted all of him—everything he had to give. And so she took, repeatedly drawing him deep into her mouth.

He knotted his fingers in her hair.

Groaned and shuddered.

Arched up to meet her.

Cursed her. Forbade her. Threatened her.

Fought as only a man of iron will could fight—until his soul lay shredded within him, and his strength gave out.

Only then, when nothing he invoked deterred her, did he concede defeat and, with a wrenching involuntary spasm that shook his entire body, spilled into her mouth.

"So much for taking a long, cold, unpleasant shower before joining you in bed," he said grimly, when his heart rate diminished enough that he could speak again. "I hope you're satisfied with what you accomplished."

She raised her head and looked at him. His eyes glittered in the moonlight and sweat gleamed on his skin. "Oh, yes, Benedict," she said, dutifully, the way a compliant wife should. "Are you?"

He swore again, the same thing he'd said before, but uttered mellifluously this time. Like music; like a love song.

He stretched out his hand. "Come here," he said, and drew her up to lie close beside him. "And listen to me. This is not how it should be between a man and a woman, that the pleasure is all his while she receives nothing."

"Whoever made up that rule didn't know what he was talking about."

"Nevertheless, it is the Italian way."

A warm and lovely lassitude crept over her, leaving her limbs heavy and her spirit more peaceful than it had felt in days. "Then stop being so Italian," she purred. "Just say 'thank you' and accept the fact that, sometimes, giving pleasure to her man is all the reward a woman needs."

She sensed his smile. Heard it in his murmured, *"Mi scusi, cara. Grazie, e buona notte!"*

Cassie thought herself well-prepared to meet her mother-in-law. Throughout the one and a half hour flight from Milan to Calabria, she'd memorized *Buono giorno, Signora Constantino. Lieto di conoscerla*—which, according to her phrase book, amounted pretty much to, "Hello, Mrs. Constantino. Lovely to meet you."

By the time the plane touched down at Lamezia Terme, she was confident that, when the moment presented itself, she could recite her greeting with reasonable fluency.

She might as well have studied Swahili, for all the good it did her!

First of all, the forty kilometer drive from the airport to Benedict's family home, though passing through exquisite countryside, meant taking a narrow, twisting coastal road which at times seemed to hang by a thread from the steep cliffs hugging the shore. As if that alone wasn't enough to sweep her mind clear of everything but white-knuckled terror, his car was no conservative family sedan but a low-slung red Lamborghini Diablo designed for speed. And that, she quickly surmised, clinging to the edge of her seat and praying they'd arrive alive, was clearly the chief reason he'd chosen it, because he drove with the death-defying disregard of a man competing in the Indy 500.

However, apart from a short stop to buy bottled water in one of the villages they passed through, they completed the journey without incident, and with little in the way of conversation. Although his manner toward Cassie was warmer, he appeared preoccupied and when they arrived at his family home, Cassie could well see why.

Unlike Bianca's light and airy residence, the Palazzo Constantino was a great gothic heap of a place, with high walls and narrow windows. Accessed by an electronic gate, it sat within a vast, rather unkempt garden overlooking the sea, its facade so forbidding that Cassie's first thought was that it looked more like a medieval prison than a home.

Not a soul came out to welcome them as the car passed beneath a stone arch and snarled to a stop in an inner courtyard bound on all four sides by the palazzo walls, nor did Benedict seem to find this strange. "I'll bring in the luggage later," he said, ushering her into a vast stone-paved entrance hall. "Let's get you settled first."

Outside, the sun shone from a cloudless sky, but nothing of its warmth penetrated that cold interior. Nor did it touch the throaty contralto of the woman who suddenly appeared from the shadow of the massive central staircase dominating the area. Although she spoke in her native tongue, her displeasure was unmistakable and sent a chill of foreboding up Cassie's spine.

It had no such effect on Benedict. Leading Cassie forward, he said in English, "I have brought my wife to meet you, Mother, and she does not speak Italian. And so, in her presence, neither will we. Cassandra, may I present to you my mother, Elvira."

Before Cassie could pull herself together enough to recite her little speech, Elvira Constantino stepped closer, skimmed her in a disparaging head-to-toe gaze, and turned to Benedict. "So, *le mio figlio,*" she drawled, her tone insultingly close to a sneer, "this is the woman of whom you spoke on the telephone."

Not about to show her dismay at such a reception, Cassie boldly stared back. When they'd stopped to buy their water, she'd noticed black-clad women, with shawls covering their heads, sitting in house doorways, knitting or weaving, and chattering animatedly among themselves. Many had stopped what they were doing long enough to smile broadly, and wave a greeting.

In common with them, Elvira also wore black, but there the similarity ended. Not for her the villagers' simple cotton or friendly greeting, but attitude to spare, all dressed up in Italian haute couture at its most elegant. Her tailored suit of finely corded silk was exquisite, her shoes fashioned from leather so soft they appeared to caress her feet, rather than encase them.

Her nails were lacquered and she wore gem-studded rings on the fingers of both hands. Gold hoops swung from her ears and her hair, a magnificent shining ebony mass with not a hint of silver, was swept up in a classic chignon to showcase her smooth olive complexion and aristocratic features.

Although her dark eyes snapped with hostility and her mouth curved in scorn for the pale, pathetic specimen her son had landed on her doorstep, she had been a great beauty in her youth and remained an indisputably handsome woman.

"This is my *wife* and her name is *Cassandra*," Benedict repeated in a tone that, had he addressed Cassie in such a way, would have left her withering on the spot. "And I expect you to make her feel at home here, Elvira."

"I am no miracle worker," the woman returned disdainfully. "Calabria is for Calabrians and it's well-known that foreigners do not adapt easily to our way of life. But..." She lifted her elegant shoulders as though importuning the gods to reward her well for her charity. "I will do my best."

Her immediate "best" was to lean forward and touch her cheek to her daughter-in-law's, and it was all Cassie could do not to shrink from the contact. A corpse possessed more warmth!

"So..." She stepped away again and subjected Cassie to another sweeping survey. "You would like to repair yourself before we share a little refreshment, yes?"

Cassie had taken great pains with her appearance that morning, choosing fine wool slacks and a tunic top in hyacinth-blue, with ivory low-heeled shoes which were every bit as elegant in their way as Elvira's black pumps. Nevertheless, she quailed under that contemptuous stare and, feeling suddenly as dusty and travel-stained as a stray picked up off the side of the road, muttered lamely, "Thank you. That would be very nice."

Dismissing her with a languid blink of her magnificent dark eyes, Elvira stepped to the wall and pulled on a chain which resulted in a bell sounding distantly, somewhere in the bowels of the building. "I have arranged for you and your wife to stay in the blue suite on the third floor, Benedict. It offers more space than your usual room," she said. "Speranza will show her the way."

"Oh, that's not necessary," Cassie began. The idea of being shipped off with a stranger, to some remote part of this mausoleum, had all the makings of a horror movie she'd just as soon not be taking part in. "I can wait until Benedict's ready to go up, as well."

But her words fell on deaf ears. "That will not be for quite some time. There are matters I must discuss with my son which hold no interest for you," Elvira informed her bluntly, and proceeded to match action to her words by interspersing herself between Cassie and Benedict, and making her way toward a room opening to the right of the staircase. "The problems we spoke of last week, Benedict," she said, tossing the words over her shoulder, "have intensified. We must take immediate action to prevent any further disruption to our operations."

"Bianca mentioned as much," he replied, following his mother, and Cassie knew from his distracted expression that he'd already relegated his wife to the back of his mind.

Well, what else did she expect? Hadn't Bianca warned her, *Always with this family, the business must be attended to first?*

But recognizing the truth of the statement did little to

mitigate the sense of abandonment sweeping over her as she stood alone in that chill, unfriendly place. Never before in her life had she felt so utterly and completely irrelevant.

The blue suite turned out to be a dim and cavernous pair of overfurnished rooms, with cold marble floors, heavy, dark draperies at the windows, and a vaguely damp smell permeating the air. It lay at the end of a long corridor on the third floor, and Cassie feared for the poor soul commandeered to show her the way.

Speranza was an ancient little lady, doubled over with age, arthritis, or a combination of both, and how she managed the stairs so nimbly was nothing short of extraordinary. She spoke not a word of English, but her eyes, though sharply observant, were kind, and her smile genuine as she pointed out *il balcone* off the sitting area, the massive iron four-poster in the bedroom, and finished off the grand tour with the en suite bathroom.

"Il bagno," she declared proudly, flinging open the door with a flourish. *"Moderno, si?"*

"Si," Cassie agreed, although there was no shower stall and the deep, claw-foot tub and washbasin, with their large brass faucets, bore the stamp of an earlier era. But the toilet and bidet were of more recent vintage, and the towels, folded neatly on a glass shelf, thick and luxurious. *"Grazie."*

"Prego!" Nodding and smiling encouragingly, the old woman poked herself in the chest. *"Sono Speranza,"* she declared.

"You're Speranza?"

"Si, si!" Eyebrows raised inquiringly, she pointed at Cassie. *"Come si chiama?"*

"Cassie," she replied, guessing she'd been asked her name.

"Cass-ee. *Eccellente!*" Grinning approval, Speranza patted her arm, then shuffled back to her duties below stairs, leaving a vast and lonely silence in her wake.

Were the other rooms on this floor occupied, or were she and Benedict to live up here in splendid isolation, Cassie wondered, drawing back the draperies in the bedroom, and gazing down at the courtyard.

To her surprise, she saw Benedict there, hauling their luggage out of the car, with Elvira standing close by. Gesticulating wildly, she spoke to him in rapid, staccato bursts, and although her words were indistinguishable, her voice, hoarse with urgency—or anger—floated clearly up the chimneylike enclosure formed by the surrounding walls.

Eventually, Benedict answered with something short and imperative which stopped her in midstream. She took a step back from him, held a hand to each side of her perfectly coiffed head, and rocked it back and forth as if in great pain. After observing her in silence a moment, he spoke again, less harshly this time, but the genuine affection Cassie had witnessed between him and his sister the evening before was markedly absent.

Elvira spat a reply and turned to stare across the courtyard which lay cast in shadow already, even though the sky remained a clear and tranquil blue. A still, black figure in a gray and somber setting, she'd have resembled the evil witch in a fairy tale had she been bent and gnarled with age. Instead, she stood tall and regally proud, every line in her body proclaiming her a woman who'd make a formidable enemy for anyone who, in any way, thwarted her ambitions.

Suddenly, as if sensing she was being observed, she

tilted her gaze up to the window three floors above. Even though she stood some forty or more feet away, the rage in her eyes was so apparent that Cassie recoiled. Not normally given to superstition, she experienced such a chilling prescience of tragedy that her skin puckered with dread.

Her movement did not go unnoticed. Elvira's joyless mouth widened in a smile as purely malevolent as anything Cassie ever hoped to encounter.

CHAPTER SEVEN

ALTHOUGH the face was the same, the virago who'd alternately railed and sniped at Benedict for the last hour bore no resemblance to the mother he'd known as a child. Nor, for that matter, was she anything like the woman she'd been a year ago.

There was a malice in her now which soured everything she touched, including her relationship with him. He might have attributed the change to grief at losing her husband, except that she'd been widowed for four years. Unless she was suffering a delayed reaction, he had every reason to suppose her period of mourning was long past.

"Understand this," he told her, putting an end to her ranting by striding from the office to the rear of the main hall, and claiming the suitcases still at the foot of the stairs. "I will tolerate none of your nonsense toward Cassandra. Accept that she is my wife."

"Never!" Elvira vowed, trailing after him. "You were meant to marry Giovanna."

"That was your dream, Elvira, not mine."

His mother's voice inched a notch closer to outright hysteria. "You do not love this American! There is no passion in your eyes when you look at her! You are a red-blooded man, Benedict—a Constantino—and she will never succeed in filling your needs!"

No? Recalling the night before, he had to curb a smile.

Taking his silence to mean he agreed, Elvira continued her harangue. "Why have you shackled yourself to a woman so pale and uninteresting?"

He debated telling her about the pregnancy, and decided to stick with his first instinct to keep the news for a more auspicious time. He and Cassandra were there for only a short while. Why cause more friction than already existed? It would be different if they planned to move permanently to Italy.

"You see?" his mother gloated. "You can't answer, because you know I speak the truth. You've married an adventuress who will bring you nothing but grief, when you could have taken for your wife a fine Calabrian woman who adores you and understands the role required of her. What sort of sense does that make?"

"Relationships don't have to make sense in order to work, Mother," he said, starting up the stairs with the luggage. "Let it be enough that Cassandra and I are committed to one another. If you can't deal with that, at least have the good grace to put up a pleasant front for the time we're here, otherwise you'll leave me with no choice but to take my wife back to the United States immediately—which I'm perfectly prepared to do, and which will then leave you and Francesca to sort out, on your own, the mess you've made of things here."

With a stunning reversal, she latched onto his arm. "When did you become so cruel that you'd speak to me so coldly? You were never this way before. What's changed you?"

"I might ask you the same question."

"I am your mother," she said, and for a moment, with her tone and demeanor, she was. "Benedict, I beg you, in the name of your dead father, do not humiliate me by leaving, when you are so badly needed here!"

Despite all her earlier, irrational raving, this last plea

at least made sense. The Calabrian operation was in a shambles and all because his mother had mismanaged the land and its workers to the point of revolt and sabotage, something unheard of in his father's time. Now, her pride in taking over where her late husband had left off was on the line—and heaven knew, when it came to pride, Elvira's was unequaled. The Constantino name had been revered in Calabria for centuries; she'd walk over burning coals before she'd allow herself to go down in history as the one who brought dishonor to it.

"I've stated my terms, Elvira," he said, torn between pity and anger. "Treat my wife with respect, and I'll do what I can to put things right on the labor front."

"But of course I will," she almost moaned, pressing her fingertips to her temple and squeezing her eyes closed as if to ward off a clamor of voices only she could hear. "She will become my beloved daughter-in-law."

Really? We'll see, he thought grimly, continuing up the two flights of stairs to the third floor and letting himself into the suite. According to Bianca, their mother's mood swings were becoming both more unpredictable and more extreme, which made her sudden acquiescence to his demands highly suspect.

He found Cassandra taking a nap. She lay on her side on the bed, with one hand tucked beneath her ear, and her legs drawn up as if she were cold. He hadn't dared respond to her touch last night, for fear of where it would have led him. Hadn't dared so much as look at her. But now, with her magical hands and tongue at rest and therefore unable to drive him over the edge, he allowed himself the luxury of examining her, inch by inch, and imagining how it would be, when the danger of her miscarrying was past.

In sleep, her face appeared almost childlike and very

vulnerable. Her mouth was soft and innocent; her brow smooth and untroubled. Carefully, he bent down to sweep a strand of hair from her cheek, and marveled at the texture of both. Silky and golden, just like the soft northern California sunshine of her homeland.

As for her body...his gaze slipped lower, to the even rise and fall of her breasts beneath the loose-fitting top, the sweet curve of her hips and elegant length of leg. Ah, the body was that of a woman, ripe with early pregnancy!

He had never seen her fully naked—not even on the night they'd conceived their child—but the lush contours her clothes couldn't hide offered a tempting preview of all he'd so far missed, and his mouth went dry.

He wanted her. Badly. So much that he was hard and aching, just from looking at her. He wanted to kiss her, touch her, taste her, until her eyes were glazed with passion, and she entreated him, in breathless little sighs, to join his body with hers, and put an end to the madness he'd invoked in her.

He wanted all that and more; had from the second he first set eyes on her. No point in asking himself what it was that made her different from other women he'd known. She simply *was,* that's all, and if he were less the hardheaded businessman and more given to self-delusion, he'd have said that fate, and not Nuncio Zanetti, had had a hand in bringing them together.

She stirred and made a little murmur. Stretched her legs and turned onto her back. Braided her hands over her belly where his child lay sleeping.

Would the baby be a girl who'd grow up beautiful, like her mother? Or a boy, tall like his father, and her willing slave from the moment he took his first breath?

Would there be other babies, conceived at leisure and with love?

As if the intensity of his stare penetrated her sleep, her lashes fluttered, then lifted to reveal fading dreams in her deep blue eyes. Slowly, she rolled her head from side to side, taking in the bedroom's dark, brooding furniture, and as the real world swam back into focus, her brow furrowed and the restful innocence of sleep fled, chased away by an almost fearful uncertainty.

"How long have you been standing here?" she asked in a husky voice.

Gently, he stroked the back of his hand down her cheek. "But a moment or two only, *cara*," he assured her, again questioning his decision to bring her to the palazzo. Coping with a high-risk pregnancy was enough; she didn't need the added burden of dealing with a mother he was beginning to fear was edging disturbingly close to madness.

Cassandra ran her tongue over her lips and swept another glance around the room, this time noticing the shadows of early dusk clouding the tall windows. "What time is it?"

"Almost six o'clock."

"That late? Why didn't you wake me sooner? I was supposed to freshen up and meet you downstairs almost an hour ago!" She sat up and swung her legs over the side of the bed. "I bet your mother's fit to be tied."

"Not at all," he said, steadying her when she lurched to her feet too quickly and swayed dizzily against him. Her skin, where it had been pressed against the pillow, wore the soft, faintly crinkled blush of a newly opened rose, she smelled of warm, lightly perfumed sleep, and it was all he could do not to kiss her. "My mother will understand."

Cassandra flung him an incredulous stare. "Your mother understands nothing about me," she said, pushing him away and clinging to the edge of the bed for support. "I'm an affront to everything she holds dear. She made up her mind to hate me before she ever laid eyes on me."

Turning his mind away from temptation, he took refuge in platitudes which rang hollow even to his ears. "She's set in her ways, that's all. She never expected I'd marry an American, but that's not to say she has anything against you personally."

"Save your breath, Benedict," Cassandra scoffed. "I saw the expression on her face when you introduced us. If it were up to her, she'd have the ground open and swallow me whole."

"But it isn't up to her," he said soothingly, "nor does she make my decisions for me. I married you of my own free will, Cassandra, and while I admit the suddenness of our wedding came as something of a shock to her, now that she's had time to get used to the idea, I think you'll find her more hospitable." He pushed her toward the bathroom. "Take a few minutes to splash some water on your face before we join her in the *salone*. Then you'll see for yourself that what I'm telling you isn't just wishful thinking on my part."

Dubiously, she inspected her sleep-wrinkled clothing and grimaced. "Do you dress for dinner here?"

"As a rule, yes."

"Then it'll take me more than a few minutes to get ready. I'm not showing up looking like a dog's breakfast, and giving her one more reason to despise me."

Given Elvira's often-extraordinary reactions to perfectly ordinary events of late, he couldn't very well argue the point. "Take as long as you like. This is your home away from home, Cassandra. And if my mother has a problem with that, I'll deal with it—and her."

She looked troubled. "I'm already causing discord between you and her, Benedict. I don't want to create more."

"The discord," he told her, "started long before you entered the picture, *cara*. These days, it seems my mother can't get along with anyone." He gave her a gentle push toward the bathroom. "Go. Do what you have to."

She ran her fingers over her hair. "Is the luggage here yet?"

"*Si*. I brought it up myself. It's in the other room."

"Would you mind going through my suitcase and picking an outfit that you think will serve, while I run a bath?"

"Of course. One of your long skirts and a pretty top will be perfectly acceptable."

She smiled, and he thought that he'd give a very great deal to see her do so more often. "Thank you, Benedict."

"For what? Helping my wife unpack?"

"That, and for being so understanding." She paused in the bathroom doorway. "I'll be quick."

"There's not great rush, *cara*," he said, concerned lest she slip and hurt herself as she climbed in and out of the deep bathtub.

He wished he could stay there to help her; to scrub her back and, when she was all flushed and relaxed, and sweet-smelling from head to toe, to wrap her in a bath sheet. He wished they could bathe together, with her spine resting against his chest and his arms around her. That he could cradle her breasts, slide his hand possessively over the faint swell of her belly, touch her between her legs and make her gasp with pleasure—!

"Benedict," she said, regarding him curiously, "is there something wrong?"

Hell, yes, there was something wrong! He was in acute pain. Again!

"Not a thing, *cara*," he said smoothly. "Enjoy your bath. We usually spend an hour over antipasto and wine before the main meal anyway, but because my mother and I spent longer than planned discussing business, even she won't be her usual punctual self tonight." He checked his watch. "I'll lay out your clothes on the bed and come back for you in, say, half an hour?"

"Come back?" An expression of alarm chased over her face. "Why? Where are you going?"

"I'll shower in my old bachelor suite." *And it will, of necessity, be a very cold shower! Again!* "You'll have the bathroom here all to yourself."

"You know," she said, another her smile dimpling her cheeks bewitchingly, "if you keep spoiling me like this, I'm going to wind up being very glad I married you."

Deciding he'd better put some distance between them before rampant hormones got the better of him, he said with mock severity, "Save the flattery for another occasion, Cassandra, and hop in the tub. We're wasting time."

Oblivious to his discomfort, she flung him a last impish smile, and disappeared into the bathroom.

Elvira Constantino, splendid in a straight black, ankle-length gown whose severity was relieved only by a heavy gold cross and chain, was not alone when Benedict ushered Cassie into the ornate *salone*. A younger woman waited with Elvira, one so closely resembling Benedict and Bianca that Cassie guessed she must be the younger sister, Francesca.

"Well," his mother remarked, coming forward and pressing another of her frigid kisses to Cassie's cheek. "Here you are at last."

"Yes. I'm sorry if we've kept you waiting," Cassie said. "I'm afraid I fell asleep."

"No need to apologize. You've endured an arduous few days, traveling halfway around the world to meet us." The words clinked out of Elvira's mouth as hard as little round pebbles hitting granite, "A siesta is acceptable, under the circumstances."

Sure it is! Cassie thought, containing a shiver. *About as acceptable as if I'd brought the bubonic plague into your house!*

Benedict slipped an arm around her waist and steered her toward the other woman. "Come and meet the baby of the family, *cara.* Francesca, this is my wife, Cassandra. I expect you to take her under your wing and make her feel at home here."

Francesca glanced nervously at her mother, as if requesting direction on how to respond. Elvira replied for her. "Francesca is as busy as you'll be, Benedict. I'm afraid your little bride will have to learn to fend for herself."

"In that case, I'll have to beg off some of the chores you've laid out for me, Mother, and devote my attention to my wife, because I certainly don't intend for her to be neglected."

Although he spoke amicably enough, there was in his tone an undercurrent of steel which persuaded Elvira to take a softer approach. "Of course not, my son. We will all see to it that she is properly entertained."

"I'm perfectly capable of looking out for myself," Cassie said, tired of being batted back and forth like a ball between Benedict and his mother. "I've known from the start that this is a working honeymoon for my husband, and certainly don't expect anyone to baby-sit me while he's taking care of business." Then, since Francesca still seemed uncertain of how she was supposed to behave, Cassie took her hand and, with a smile, put to use the little bit of Italian she'd practiced earlier. *"Lieto di conoscerla, Francesca!"*

Francesca smiled with delight, but Elvira let out a squawk of unkind laughter. "As you said, Benedict, your wife does not speak Italian!"

Cassie heard the hiss of his indrawn breath, saw the angry throbbing of the pulse at his temple, and knew he'd have leaped to her defense again, had she not beaten him to it. "But I'm willing to try," she said, fixing her mother-in-law in a forthright stare. "Shouldn't that count for something?"

For a moment, Elvira stared right back, the contempt in her eyes so apparent that a person would have had to be blind to miss it. Then she dropped her gaze and said, *"Si.* Of course. It counts." She waved her garnet-tipped fingers to the windows at the far end of the room. "Francesca, show our guest the view, and I will ring for Speranza to bring in the antipasto and wine."

"I'm very happy to meet you," Francesca whispered, leading Cassie to a quartet of chairs facing a breathtaking panorama of sea and sky painted in varying shades of purple now that the sun had slipped below the horizon. "And please, Cassandra, do not take to heart the things my mother sometimes says. Calabrian women are very possessive of their sons, you see, and she had other hopes for Benedict."

Before Cassie could ask what they were, the door opened and she received her answer as another young woman entered the room. Cooing as sweetly as a dove, even if she looked more like a marauding crow, Elvira swooped over and enfolded her in a warm embrace.

"Her name is Giovanna," Francesca murmured, under cover of the ensuing babble of conversation.

"And she's the 'other hope'?"

"*Si.* I'm afraid so."

"Is she in love with Benedict?" Cassie asked, watching as the woman turned to greet him continental style, with a kiss on both cheeks.

"I think most unmarried women in Calabria are a little in love with Benedict," Francesca said with a laugh, "and some of the married ones, as well, if truth be told. But Giovanna will not try to encroach on your relationship with him. She is a good woman."

She was a very pretty woman, too, with a sweet face and gently voluptuous body, and her smile, as she came to where Cassie and Francesca sat, seemed sincere. "You are Benedict's Cassandra, and I am Giovanna," she said, her English even more polished than Elvira's. "It is a pleasure to welcome you to Calabria."

She sat in the chair next to Cassie's and asked about the flight over, how she'd liked the little she'd seen of Milan, and what she thought of Italy so far. "If you'd like a tour guide while you're in Calabria, please call on me," she said. "I'd be honored to show you the sights."

Francesca was right, Cassie soon realized. This woman posed no threat to the marriage. The danger came from the mother, and feeling Elvira's inimical gaze on her, Cassie drew her silk shawl more snugly around her shoulders.

After a few minutes, Speranza shuffled into the room,

pushing a carved wooden trolley bearing a carafe of wine, and a heavy platter containing a selection of smoked fish, olives, marinated vegetables, and tiny rounds of sausage.

"All local specialties," Francesca explained. "In fact, the olives come from our own land."

And no doubt they were all delicious. But the spicy smell of the sausage and the sight of the pimento-stuffed olives glistening under a light coat of oil, left Cassie fighting a sudden wave of nausea.

Noticing what she perceived to be her guest's distaste, Elvira inquired archly, "You do not care for our food, Cassandra?"

"Not right now," she managed to say, dabbing at the perspiration dotting her forehead.

Benedict, bless his heart, realized her distress and came forward with a glass of sparkling water to which he'd added a sliver of lime. "Here, *cara,*" he said quietly. "Sip this. It will help."

Elvira's sharp gaze missed not a thing. "You do not care for our wine, either? What a shame!"

"It's not your wine in particular," Cassie replied. "It's any sort of wine."

"Ah, *cara,* you have a problem with alcohol!" Elvira could barely contain her glee at uncovering what she deemed to be yet another fatal flaw in the woman her son had claimed for a wife.

"I'm not a recovering addict, if that's what you're implying," Cassie said, rallying to her own defense. "I'm just avoiding all alcohol right now, and I'd have thought you'd understand the reason for it."

"How is that possible?" Elvira tilted one shoulder in a dismissive shrug. "You are a stranger to me. Until a few days ago, I knew nothing of your existence. How can I be expected to know the reason behind your likes and dislikes, unless you explain them to me?''

"Stop pressuring her, Mother! Cassandra said 'no' to wine. Be content with that, and find something else to talk about!''

The speed with which he intervened on her behalf, not to mention the sharpness with which he uttered his rebuke, would have warmed Cassie's heart, had it not been for her sudden suspicion that Benedict had been very selective in what he'd told his mother. Unless Cassie was totally misreading the situation, Elvira might have been informed of her son's marriage, but she hadn't a clue his bride was pregnant.

Even more startling, though, was the effect his words had on his mother. Thoroughly subdued, she sank into the nearest chair, and when she spoke again, her intonation flowed like music, instead of snapping with malice. "I hope your suite of rooms is to your liking, child. The third floor isn't used very much anymore, but I thought that, as a new bride, you would enjoy the privacy it affords.''

"That's...very considerate of you,'' Cassie said, taken aback by the sudden about-face.

"But how else should I be? You are *la mia nuora*—how do you say in English? My daughter-by-law?''

"Daughter-in-law,'' Francesca supplied.

"Just so.'' Elvira sipped her wine and subjected Cassie to such a long scrutiny that Cassie began to squirm "It's a big adjustment, coming to a country where you don't speak the language or understand local customs,'' she finally decreed. "And then, there is the fact that we're almost nine hours ahead of California time. You've come a long way to meet us, and I can see that it's left you very weary. I should have arranged for you to eat a light supper in your suite and make an early night of it.''

Deciding this was as good a time as any to mention her pregnancy, Cassie began, ''Well, it's not just the travel or jet lag that's wiping me out. It's—''

But Benedict, catching her eye and realizing her intent, gave the merest shake of his head. ''It was all the running around she had to do before she left San Francisco that's left her so exhausted,'' he cut in deftly. ''Cassandra runs a very successful business and had to make sure it would operate smoothly during her absence.''

If steering the conversation into a different channel had been his intent, he succeeded. Throughout the remainder of the cocktail hour, Cassie was peppered with questions from Francesca and Giovanna, who wanted to know everything about her life in California.

Dusk was well on its way to night before the evening meal was served in a dining hall resembling something out of the sixteenth century, with massive furniture elaborately carved like that in the *salone,* and rich velvet tapestries on the walls. Easily capable of seating twenty, the table was set with engraved sterling and cut crystal so heavy, it could have knocked a grown man senseless. Taking her assigned place, Cassie thought the only thing missing were ladies in period costume and a troubadour playing a mandolin in the minstrel's gallery.

Conversation was lively enough, although Elvira, for the most part, leaned back in her chair and appeared totally oblivious to her surroundings. Once or twice, her glance fell on Cassie and lingered there, and if her brief show of kindness was gone, so was her hostility. If anything, she looked puzzled, as if she couldn't recall the reason this stranger was at her table. Finally, just before coffee was served, she abruptly got up from her chair and, without a word of explanation, wandered to the door.

Obviously irritated, Benedict said, "Where are you going, Mother?"

"To bed," she said, pressing a hand to her temple. "I have a headache and need to lie down."

"She's complained often of headaches in the last little while," Francesca explained, after the door had closed behind her mother. "Usually, they're preceded by a terrible burst of temper over something quite trivial."

"Has she seen a doctor?" he asked.

"No, although I've suggested it more than once. But she claims stress is the cause, and Benedict, we all know she's got plenty of that. The situation here goes from bad to worse on a daily basis."

"Bianca already filled me in," he said, flinging her a quelling glance, "but Cassandra doesn't need to burdened with the details."

"I don't see why not, if I'm now part of the family," Cassie said.

"Because you have enough to deal with, *cara*. Bad enough that my mother's feeling the strain, without it infecting you, too."

"But perhaps I can help."

"No." Not for a second did he consider the possibility.

"Please stop treating me as I'm made of glass, Benedict," she said, covering up her annoyance with a laugh. "You said yourself, I'm an experienced businesswoman, so don't be so ready to dismiss my offer to help, either—at least not without giving me a reason."

"You're my wife," he said brusquely. "And as your

husband, I'm saying I don't want you involved. That's reason enough."

Her mouth fell open in shock, and it took her a moment to recover enough to say, "I *beg* your pardon?"

"This is not America, Cassandra," he declared. "Here, a wife knows her place—"

"Knows her place?" She stared at him, unable to believe her ears or his arrogance.

"Exactly," he said calmly. "And it is not necessarily at her husband's side where business is concerned."

"Really? What a pity you didn't choose to tell me before we were married that your idea of how to treat a wife is keeping her barefoot, pregnant, and tied to the kitchen sink. If you had, I can assure you, it would have made all the difference in the world to how I'd have received your proposal."

"It's a little late in the day for that, wouldn't you say?"

"Trust me, Benedict, it's never too late!"

Giovanna cleared her throat and muttered, "Come, Francesca, let's take our coffee in the *salone.*"

Cassie shoved back her chair and flung down her napkin. "No need," she fumed, so furious she could have choked Benedict on the spot. "I'm more than happy to be the one to leave."

"But you're on your honeymoon...!" Distressed, Francesca appealed to her brother. "Benedict, please say something!"

"It's okay, Francesca," Cassie said. "He's said enough and frankly, I've had about as much of the Constantino brand of hospitality as I can stomach for one day! The lord and master's all yours, ladies, and I wish you both the joy of him!"

CHAPTER EIGHT

HE SHOWED up in the suite some fifteen minutes later. By then, she'd changed and was buttoned up to the throat in the longest, most concealing nightgown she'd brought with her, and sat at the old-fashioned dressing table, furiously brushing her hair.

"We need to talk," he announced, coming up behind her and attempting to take the brush from her hand. "I realize you found my manner downstairs to be somewhat abrupt—"

She yanked the brush out of his reach and briefly debated swatting him with it. *"Abrupt?"* she repeated, trying very hard not to screech with the rage consuming her. "Try 'overbearing, high-handed, rude and obnoxious' on for size. I think you'll find any, or all descriptions, will fit!"

He looked pained. "You know, Cassandra," he said, "you're not the only one who's had enough grief for one day. I'm about at the end of my rope, too, and in no mood to deal with yet another temperamental woman. That being so, please shut up long enough to hear me out. Then, if you still feel like raking your nails down my face—"

"Hardly!" she scoffed. "That might be the only way the women around here can vent their frustration when it comes to dealing with deranged chauvinists, but where I come from, we choose more sophisticated methods of getting even."

"I can hardly wait to experience them firsthand," he

118

said drily. "In the meantime, however, allow me clarify what I started to say before you left the dining room."

"I didn't *leave* the dining room, Benedict," she informed him waspishly. "I stormed out in high dudgeon, and if you were one-tenth as perceptive as you like to think you are, you'd recognize how thoroughly ticked off I had to be, to do that in front of people I've only just met, and you'd modify your attitude accordingly—always assuming, of course, that you're the least bit interested in keeping me around as your wife."

"Don't threaten me, Cassandra," he warned her. "We are married and will remain so, at least as long as you're carrying my child."

Refusing to acknowledge the sliver of unease *that* revealing little slip of the tongue produced, she said rashly, "And after that, do you plan to ship me off to a nunnery?"

He shrugged. "Maybe even *before* then, if I deem it necessary."

"Well, at least that would spare you having to explain to your mother that I'm pregnant, wouldn't it? Why so reluctant to spread the good news, Benedict? Could it be that you're ashamed to have her know you're not quite as perfect as she'd like to believe?"

"I'm protecting you, Cassandra. There'll be time enough to broadcast word of the baby once my mother's become reconciled to the fact of our marriage. You're too intelligent not to have noticed that she's hardly overjoyed by it, and I see no point in exacerbating an already delicate situation, particularly not if you're the one who'll bear the brunt of it."

"Why just me? Conceiving our child was a joint endeavor, in case you've forgotten."

"I've forgotten nothing," he said sharply, "nor do I

wish to become further embroiled in argument with you, so kindly be still and pay attention to what I'm about to tell you.''

Oh! *Ohh!* Seething, she said, ''Stop treating me as if I'm some medieval...*wench!*''

That stopped him short! ''I don't know this word, 'wench.' What does it mean?''

''An inferior female designed for your pleasure, however you choose to take it.''

''What a novel concept,'' he remarked thoughtfully. ''I shall keep it in mind for future reference. For now, however, I prefer to focus on the immediate present, which brings me back to what I was trying to explain, before you went flying off at a tangent.''

She'd have repudiated that allegation, too, if she'd had the chance, but he steamrolled right over her and launched into part two of his lecture. ''This is not San Francisco, Cassandra. It isn't even *Roma* or *Milano* or *Firenze.* It is a small, ancient part of Italy with customs which go back centuries and which, in many respects, lags decades behind the rest of the country in its attitudes and outlook. Calabrian women do not, as a rule, enjoy the kind of professional prominence their counterparts in America take for granted—particularly not in family-run enterprises like ours, with international connections. They stick instead to more traditional roles.''

''Really?'' She flung him a blistering glare through the warped glass of the mirror. ''I guess someone forgot to tell your mother that.''

''My mother wasn't active in any of our business dealings until she became widowed. Had there been another son, or if Francesca had a husband, *he* would have been the one to take over where my father left off. But there was neither, and because she's more familiar with the local end of our industry than anyone else in the area, my mother tried to step into my father's shoes.''

"Which you find perfectly acceptable, as long as your wife doesn't—''

"I found it acceptable at first, because our workers had been with us for generations and were very loyal to our family name,'' he said, drowning her out in a tone of voice she was quickly learning to hate. "With their cooperation, I had every reason to believe the operation here would continue to run smoothly.''

"But Mother's taken on more than she can handle, right?''

Before answering, he hesitated just long enough to make her suspect he was choosing his next words with extreme care. Not lying, exactly, but *laundering* the truth. "It would appear so. Over the last several months, our most prized product, the bergamot, has not yielded as expected. Even more disturbing, our orchards and olive groves have been severely vandalized, thereby endangering next year's crops. I surely don't need to spell out for you the ramifications of such action.''

That he was worried was apparent, and she could understand why. "No, you don't,'' she said. "Wilful destruction of property is a serious matter on more than just a monetary front. It speaks of criminal intent and poses a very real danger to anyone attempting to put an end to it.''

"Precisely. I'm not anxious for my own safety, Cassandra, but for yours, and that's why I don't want you assuming any sort of public profile while we're here. The less attention drawn to you, the better I'll like it.''

Her annoyance softening under the warmth of his obvious concern, she said, "Do you know who's responsible for the vandalism?''

"I suspect it's retaliation from certain unscrupulous and dissatisfied employees."

"What do you propose to do about it?"

"Reestablish the old order of things." He glanced at her almost apologetically. "It might mean extending our time here."

A horrifying thought struck her. "You're not hinting at relocating here permanently and taking your mother's place, are you?" she asked with unvarnished dismay.

"No," he said, firmly enough to reassure her. "You know how, as a family, we've divided responsibility among us. My place is not here at the local level. But if production of our fundamental resources cannot be implemented, we'll all be looking for other ways to make a living."

"My goodness, I had no idea things were as bad as this." She chewed her lip thoughtfully. "If cash flow's a problem, I might be able to help. No one but you and I would need to know."

"Not as long as I have breath in my body, Cassandra! I no more married you for your money, than you married me for mine."

"Well, of course you didn't, because you didn't know exactly how much I'm worth, but it just so happens that my grandmother left me a sizable inheritance."

"I don't care if she left you the Hope Diamond," he said flatly. "This is not your problem, and I won't have you involved in trying to resolve it."

"So who *will* you call on, then? The police?"

"No." He picked up her brush and began stroking it through her hair. "We are a small community. Everyone here is related, either directly or through marriage, to his neighbor. Even if it were possible to identify those responsible for causing the damage, we'd gain nothing but ill will by pressing formal charges. A man behind bars cannot provide for his family, and family in this part of the world is paramount. Punish one member, and you punish them all.''

Appalled, she said, "So you're letting felons go free? That doesn't make much sense! You're just encouraging more trouble.''

"The Constantinos have a reputation to uphold, and they do it with their own brand of justice, not one imposed by the state. Until this recent crisis, our employees have known they could depend on us to treat them fairly and with respect. I must prove to them that such a tradition has not been abandoned.''

"What makes you think they'll believe you?''

"I grew up here. I understand the people and they understand me. In the past, we have enjoyed a mutual trust, and my first task is to reestablish it. Once that is done, I'll deal with anyone still inclined toward inflicting damage to our property.''

"I don't much like the sound of that! What about the risks you'd be taking?''

"They'd be no worse than facing your wrath, *cara*,'' he said lightly.

Too lightly! He might be unspeakably bossy and annoying on occasion, but he was her husband and she realized that, in a remarkably short space of time, she'd grown very fond of the idea. The thought of him putting himself in the line of fire filled her with dismay.

Wishing she hadn't been so quick to lose her temper with him, she said, "You should have told me all this sooner.''

"I'd have preferred never to have mentioned it at all.'' He returned the hairbrush to the dressing table and rested his hands on her shoulders. "Our honeymoon's facing enough hurdles, without burdening it further with my problems.''

She leaned back and rested against him, loving the sense of security it gave her. Small wonder his field hands trusted him. He exuded a strength and integrity that inspired confidence, and made anything seem possible.

''Sharing problems is what being married's all about, Benedict,'' she murmured, closing her eyes.

For the space of a minute or two, he massaged her shoulders gently. And then, almost imperceptibly, his fingers slid to the base of her throat and grew still. ''It's about more than that, *cara mia*,'' he said hoarsely.

She heard the tortured desire behind his words, and her blood raced. ''I know,'' she said, and drew his hand down to her breast.

It remained there, shaping her so possessively, so sensuously, that her flesh ached and a bolt of sensation shot the length of her, to settle between her legs.

With a soft gasp of pleasure, she opened her eyes and looked in the mirror. She saw his gaze fixed on her reflection, mesmerized by her rapid breathing, the heightened color in her cheeks, the wild flutter of the pulse below her jaw. She saw the dark fire in his eyes and knew that hers was not the only heart leaping to win a race it had already lost.

Her glance dropped. As she watched, his hands inched deliberately to the buttons at her throat, undid them, and pushed the nightgown over her shoulders and down her arms, until it fell to her waist. And all the time, he stared at her in the mirror, gauging her response, knowing he was driving her mad.

''Don't stop, Benedict!'' she begged, on a broken sigh.

In answer, he lowered his head to kiss the side of her neck, then whispered in her ear, and she didn't need to understand Italian to know that he was speaking the language of love—of making love—in very explicit terms.

He leaned farther over her and she, cradled against his hips, reveled in the urgent thrust of his arousal between her shoulder blades. His lips trailed over the upper slope of one breast, delineating the blue veins marking her skin, before his mouth found her nipple and tugged at it gently.

Saliva pooled under her tongue, and a tiny cry escaped her. She squirmed on the padded bench. Felt the heat tracing arcs of lightning at her core.

She tried to turn but he held her imprisoned against his erection, pushed her nightgown lower, and spread his palms over her belly.

"Benedict...!" she implored, and reaching behind, slid her hands up the back of his spread thighs to their apex, and caressed the masculine configuration clustered there.

This time, he was the one who groaned, a feral, primitive sound. The sound of a warrior facing insurmountable odds.

He lifted his head again to look at her. His eyes smoldered like embers, and his chest heaved. But tonight he was not a man to submit to her wiles, no matter how powerful they might be. Instead, he fought back.

He pushed her gown lower and slipped his hand between her legs. No more able to resist his invasion than any other part of her, they fell slackly apart and gave him access. He delved deep between the moist, silken folds of her flesh and found the spot quivering at her center.

He touched it. Just once.

It was enough.

She convulsed.

Prisms of color swirled through her mind, suffused her senses. Hot, blinding. Her body clenched, released. Clenched again. And again and again, until she thought she'd faint from the sublime torture of it.

But he was horrified at what he'd effected. Withdrawing his hand, he wrapped his arms around her and held her tight, as if afraid she might fly apart if he didn't contain her.

"Don't worry, Benedict," she whispered, sensing his fear and wanting to reassure him. Wanting, if truth be told, for more—for him to lose himself inside her. "I'm fine."

"No," he said, his face a mask of misery. "I had no right to do that."

"You had every right," she breathed, reaching up to touch his cheek. "I'm your wife. What just happened between us is perfectly natural."

"No," he said again, releasing her and stepping safely out of temptation's way. "It was unwise. You could miscarry—"

"I'm not going to miscarry. We're going to have a healthy baby."

Unconvinced, he paced about the room. "Do you feel...anything?"

She'd have smiled at the question, except she knew that he was in no mood for levity. "I feel cherished."

"No cramping or discomfort?"

"Just the ache of fulfillment, and I think that's allowed."

"I didn't marry you for sex," he reminded her grimly. "I married you because you're expecting my child. If, because of something I've done, you should lose the baby…''

"What?'' she said, a bleak chill replacing the warm and lovely sensations of a moment ago. "You'd apply for an annulment the very next day?''

"I'd never forgive myself.''

"Well, Benedict,'' she said, pulling her nightgown back where it belonged and doing up the buttons, "I have a feeling it's really not in your hands. Nature has a way of taking care of itself where pregnancy's concerned. Just because we have to be careful for the next little while doesn't mean you have to behave as if I'm made of porcelain, liable to shatter at the slightest touch.''

"I'm not prepared to take the chance. There'll be no more incidents like this, Cassandra, until your doctor gives the word.''

There might just as well never have been an incident like that to begin with! The passion he'd barely been able to hold in check had metamorphosed into a reserve so cool that it reminded her of the sea fog, slinking up from San Francisco Bay to leave its clammy imprint on every room in her town house.

Depressed, she pushed back the bench and went into the bathroom. She was willing to give him everything of herself, and she wanted the same from him. But he was determined to allow her only a little, and while it was, in itself, overwhelming and magnificent, it wasn't enough.

Was she asking too much, she wondered, as she brushed her teeth. Was the outpouring of emotional generosity she felt, simply a woman thing, which men didn't understand and couldn't emulate?

She had no answers, nor was he forthcoming with any

because, when she returned to the bedroom, it was to find him gone. Her one consolation at being once more abandoned for the night was the realization that, however much it might irk him, he knew the only way he could keep a lid on the sexual attraction sizzling between them, was for him to stay away from her.

They were just finishing a breakfast of fruit, sweet rolls and coffee the next morning, when Cassie mentioned her intention to walk into the village to do some shopping. With the threat of so much idle time on her hands, she wanted to start making items for the baby's layette, but needed to buy supplies.

"No," Benedict said.

"What do you mean, *no?*" Taken aback by his instant and adamant veto, she stared at him indignantly.

"I mean, absolutely not," he said. "In fact, I forbid it."

Was this the same man who, with a single touch, had reduced her to incoherent ecstasy last night? Who, for a few stolen moments, had shown such a caring side to his nature that she'd all but fallen in love with him?

"Benedict," she said, articulating each word slowly and distinctly, just to make sure he received the message she was determined to convey, "first of all, I won't allow you to forbid me to do anything. And second, there's nothing here to keep me occupied."

Nor was there, unless rattling around in the gloomy old palazzo was considered entertainment. Francesca and Elvira had left a few minutes before for the office, to do whatever it was they did there—the latter again bestowing a puzzled glance at Cassie as if she hadn't the foggiest idea who she was—and Benedict was about to go off for a meeting with those men still willing to work the estate.

"It's too far for you to walk to the village," he said, not sparing her even a glance, so busy was he perusing a computer printout. "And even if it weren't, I doubt you'd find what you're looking for there."

"Then I'll take your car and drive to the nearest town."

"No."

Doing her best to hang on to her temper, she said curtly, "Are you afraid I might dent its precious fender? Get stopped for speeding? Trade it in for a Vespa and go whizzing all over the countryside, leaving a trail of destruction in my wake?"

Oblivious to her mounting irritation, he calmly flipped over a page, and took a mouthful of coffee before saying, yet again, "No."

"Damn it, Benedict!" Totally out of patience, she slammed her hand down on the table hard enough to make him look up. "Is that your answer for everything this morning?"

"If you want to go shopping, Cassandra," he said mildly, "I will take you, as soon as I can spare the time."

"I don't need to be *taken* anywhere," she snapped, surreptitiously stroking her other hand over her stinging palm. "I'm perfectly capable of following a map and I have an international driver's license, so what's your real objection?"

"I don't want you wandering around by yourself outside the palazzo."

"Why ever not?"

"I thought I explained my reasons, last night."

"On the workfront, yes, you did, but this goes beyond

that. For heaven's sake, on the street among other people, I could pass for just another tourist.''

"It's too early in the season for tourists, and you're too blond and foreign-looking to pass unnoticed, even in a crowd.''

"But—!''

Exasperated, he slapped the computer sheets on the table. "But nothing! The plain fact of the matter is, I'm concerned for your safety, Cassandra. I don't want you to become the target of…mischief.''

"What kind of mischief? You think a disgruntled former employee might make off with me?''

"Yes,'' he said levelly. "That's exactly what I'm afraid might happen.''

Swallowing the incredulous laugh rising in her throat, because there was no mistaking how utterly serious he was, she said, "You think I could be *kidnapped?*''

"It's a distinct possibility, and a risk I'm not willing to take.''

"So I'm to stay cooped up inside this place?''

"If you find the idea so distasteful, there are acres of walled garden for you to enjoy, and a private beach, inaccessible to outsiders, where you can swim or sunbathe.'' He drained his cup, set it down with a decisive clink, and rose from his chair. "I have to go. Please, Cassandra, don't defy me on this. Stay within the palazzo grounds. I've got enough on my mind, without having to worry about you.''

"Is worrying about my being held for ransom the reason you decided not to sleep in our suite last night?'' she said bitterly.

He stopped on his way to the door, and flung her a hunted look. "Your safety here is not an issue. The palazzo is secure. And you know very well why I didn't sleep with you last night."

In truth, he didn't look as if he'd slept at all. Grooves of weariness bracketed his mouth, and she felt suddenly ashamed for plaguing him, when he clearly had very pressing matters weighing on his mind.

Contrite, she said, "Yes, I do know why. But I wish you'd reconsider, Benedict. We might not be able to make love, but if we could at least spend the nights together, I'd find it much easier to accept your not being with me during the day."

"Sleeping beside his wife, knowing he can't make love to her, demands superhuman control of a man, and I'm far from sure I'm up to the challenge. But if it's that important to you, we can give it a try. Meanwhile, please accept that I'm not trying to come across as the heavy-handed husband, just to make you miserable."

"I realize that. I can see that you're concerned."

He brushed a kiss over her mouth. "Then please, for your own sake, stay put here until I'm free to escort you elsewhere. All other considerations apart, you saw for yourself, yesterday, how brutal the roads are around here."

"Oh, yes!" She gave a shudder of mock horror. "I was white-knuckled with nerves every time you stepped on the gas. And I almost had a heart attack when we rounded that one corner, and came nose to nose with a donkey pulling a cart and leaving no room for us to pass."

"Which is why I can't see you being comfortable driving an unfamiliar car in such unforgiving, unfamiliar territory. Trust me on this, Cassandra. I really do have your best interests at heart."

She tucked her hand under his arm and walked with

him to the door. That morning, he wore jeans, a white T-shirt, and sturdy work boots, yet even in such casual garb, he still managed to look like royalty. "I do trust you," she said softly. "And you can trust me. I won't stray from the property, Benedict, I promise."

"Thank you!" For a moment, she thought he was going to kiss her again. His hands came up to frame her face. Then, at the last moment, he backed away. "I'll see you tonight at dinner."

"Not before? What about lunch?"

"I'll eat with the field hands. But if I'm able to get enough accomplished in the next couple of days, we'll spend the weekend at my summer place in Sicily."

It didn't happen. Not only was the Sicilian trip put on hold, but their supposed two-week stay drifted into three, then four. Knowing from the comments he let slip, that a mountain of work still lay ahead before the orchards and groves were restored to full operating capacity, Cassie refrained from pestering him any more than she could help, about when they'd be going back to the US.

For his part, to relieve the tedium and give her something to occupy the long hours she spent alone, Benedict arranged for Bianca to mail her a layette package containing sewing and knitting supplies, with patterns for little jackets and hats, and directions for making a lovely hand-quilted crib cover. Cassie had to work on them in secret, of course, so as not to give away the fact of her pregnancy, but at least they gave her a sense of purpose.

They also saved her sanity, because in the days after that, she saw so little of Benedict that she began to wonder if he was deliberately avoiding her. Those times they were together, he was so preoccupied and distant that although he'd given in to her request that they sleep together, she felt no real sense of connection between them.

Oh, he provided for her well enough. She had a roof over her head, food on the table, a perfunctory peck on the cheek each night and morning. But a warm body to curl up against at night? She might as well have been lying next to one of his mother's precious marble statues!

It wasn't that she expected him to break their agreement, but did their not making love mean they couldn't show each other normal affection? It appeared so. In many ways, he was now more a stranger than he had been the night she conceived his child.

If Cassie didn't see much of her husband, though, she saw more than enough of Elvira. The minute she stepped out of the suite, the woman emerged from the shadows, a silent, disapproving figure on constant surveillance.

What did she think—that her son's wife might try to steal the family silver? Deface the paintings on the walls? Take her manicure scissors to the tapestries?

To escape the oppressive atmosphere, Cassie spent as much time as possible on the beach. It became her haven, the one place she found peace and a temporary sense of freedom. Down there, out of sight of the house, she could sit in the shade of an umbrella and work on her baby's layette, laze on the pale gold scimitar of sand, or swim in the clear blue sea, without fear of censure.

As April slipped into May, however, the temperature soared and to avoid the worst of the heat, she was forced to spend more time in the palazzo where she took refuge upstairs, on the sitting room balcony overlooking the shadowed courtyard. It was then, hemmed in by the claustrophobic atmosphere, that she missed her own home and her own friends so acutely.

Her occasional phone calls to Trish did help, but the only telephone in the residential part of the palazzo was in the entrance hall. Trying to conduct a private conversation there was near impossible, with Elvira frequently lurking in the background.

"Having fun?" Trish would ask.

"Hardly," Cassie would mutter, peering furtively over her shoulder. "Much more of this, and I'll be crawling around on my hands and knees, barking at the moon."

"Still not getting along with the mother-in-law?"

"Not a chance. Most of the time, she's got the temperament of a pit viper. The rest, she's so spaced out, it's enough to make a person wonder if she's on drugs."

"And she still hasn't clued in to the reason you're wandering around the place wearing tent dresses?"

"Apparently not."

"What about the sister?"

"Oh, Francesca's a darling, and so is Giovanna. If it weren't for the two of them acting as a buffer between me and Elvira, it'd be open war around here. But they're both as caught up in the family business as Benedict, so I don't see much more of them than I do of him."

"Well, hang in there, kiddo! With everyone working around the clock to put things in order, this can't go on much longer. And don't worry about a thing at this end. Although everyone here misses you, we're coping, and business is booming."

Yes—booming without her!

Then, as if all that weren't misery enough, Benedict sought her out one day and said, "I'm going to have to leave you here alone for a few days, Cassandra. There's a matter to be dealt with elsewhere."

Her heart plummeted with fear. She knew immediately, from his somber expression, that the "matter" had to do with meting out to those responsible for the vandalism, the Constantino brand of justice he'd spoken of weeks before.

"I can't do this anymore!" she cried brokenly. "I can't, Benedict! I've had enough. You married me and brought me here, for the baby's sake and because you believe family should come first, yet here I am, growing bigger by the day, and to maintain peace with your benighted mother, I have to keep my pregnancy secret. And now, on top of that, I have to worry that you're going to get yourself killed by a bunch of thugs, because you're too proud to enlist police help?"

"It's the way it has to be," he said, attempting to corral her in his arms.

She fought him off and dashed the angry tears from her eyes. "*No!* I won't do it. I won't wait here for them to bring your broken body back, and be left a widow before I've known what's it like to become a real wife."

He hitched one hip on the edge of the bedroom dresser and, overcoming her resistance, drew her into the vee of his thighs, close enough that she could feel the heat of his body, and smell the residue of sun-baked earth on his skin.

"Don't give up on us now, *cara,*" he begged. "Once this last matter is settled, I'll be finished here, and will take you home again. You'll be back with your own kind long before the baby's born, I promise."

"But can you promise that you'll be there, as well?"

"Of course. This is my child, too."

If only he'd said, *Of course, because I love you!* she would have agreed to anything. But what was the point in wishing for the moon when, from the outset, he'd been very clear that love didn't enter the equation?

Pressing her lips together hard to prevent herself from bursting into tears, she said "Let go of me, Benedict."

But he wouldn't release her. "No," he said. "It's been too long since I held you in my arms." His gaze fell to her mouth and remained there. "Too long since I kissed you," he said, and let his own mouth following his glance.

One kiss was all it took. Just that swiftly, that helplessly, she capitulated. She knew she'd hate them both afterward—him for being such a masterful lover, and herself for being too spineless to resist him—but for now, all that emblazoned itself on her consciousness was easing the desperate hunger which had beset her for so long.

To have him hold her as if she were the most precious creature in the world, to feel his mouth claiming hers with such unrestrained passion, was all that counted. Time enough tomorrow, when he'd have left her again, to dwell on regret and to despise them both.

CHAPTER NINE

HE LEFT the following morning, and for the next three days and nights, she was so consumed with fear for his safety that she thought she'd go mad. Finally, on the afternoon of the fourth day, and unable to stand her own company a moment longer, Cassie picked up her phrase book and made her way to the kitchen in search of Speranza, the one person who, from the very beginning, had always treated her with kindness.

Although equipped with enough modern appliances to make it reasonably efficient, the kitchen bore many reminders of an earlier era. Braids of garlic and dried peppers decorated the walls, an open-fire brick oven filled one corner, and iron pots and pans hung from hooks above the stove. In Cassie's opinion, it was by far the most cheerful room in the house and she wished she'd found it sooner.

Speranza was rolling out dough at a big scrubbed table in the middle of the floor, but she dusted off her hands when she saw she had a visitor.

"La disturbo?" Cassie asked.

"No!" The dear old soul broke into a welcoming smile, and with much effusive gesturing, led her to a rocking chair beside the oven. *"Avanti, e si accomodi, per favore!"*

Wishing she had a better grasp of the language, Cassie flipped through her phrase book, searching for the words to explain her presence, but couldn't find anything appropriate. "I'm afraid I don't speak much Italian—*non parlo italiano*."

Speranza nodded enthusiastically and waited, her wrinkled face alive with curiosity.

Feeling decidedly foolish, Cassie waved her hands and said, "I came to see you because it's lonely upstairs, all by myself—*sola*."

"*Sola. Si!*" Another smile, this one full of sympathy.

"I thought we might have coffee together." She touched her fingertips to her heart, then gestured at Speranza. "*Caffe*—you and me?"

"*Non caffe!*" Tutting with disapproval, the old woman bustled to the refrigerator, and took out a pottery jug. "*Latte—per bambino,*" she said, pouring a glass of milk and handing it to Cassie.

Startled, Cassie splayed her hands across her middle. "Benedict told you about the *bambino?*"

Speranza knew enough English to understand the question, but not enough to reply with words. Instead, she shook her head, and tapped her temple with a work-gnarled forefinger.

Taken aback, Cassie exclaimed, "You *guessed?*"

More nodding, and the widest, warmest smile yet.

"Oh…" Overcome with emotion, Cassie fought a rush of tears. "You don't know how good it feels to be able to talk openly about it. No one else knows, you see. Benedict's reluctant to say anything. Perhaps, he's embarrassed." She hunted through her phrase book, and found the word she was looking for. "Benedict *è imbarazzato*."

Aghast at the suggestion, Speranza held out a peremptory hand for the book and riffled through the vocabulary section at the back. After much concentration, she spoke, and if the pronunciation was a bit garbled, there was no mistaking her meaning. "No, *signora*. Signor Benedict, he is proud."

"I don't know, Speranza." Cassie stroked her hand over her midriff again, then touched her wedding ring. "He only married me because of the *bambino*."

This time, her message went astray, and it was pretty obvious from Speranza's knowing smile that her reply had more to do with Benedict's sperm count than his sense of honor. "*Si*. Signor Benedict *è molto virile!*"

"He's all that and then some," Cassie agreed ruefully. "The trouble is, I can never tell whether he's simply being kind and decent because he got me pregnant, or if he really cares about me, regardless of the baby."

She knew she was she was pouring out her heart to someone who hadn't the faintest idea what she was running on about, but the relief of being able to give voice to feelings she'd kept bottled up for so long felt wonderful. What Speranza made of it all, though, was impossible to tell. She clucked to herself, regarded Cassie thoughtfully when the spate of words came to an end, then took her hand and, turning it over, carefully inspected the palm.

Finally, she pushed the untouched milk closer, flexed the muscles in her skinny, wrinkled arms, and announced, "Is *figlio*. Drink, *signora, per bambino*. For boy baby to be *forte* like Papa."

Whether it was the lively delight in Speranza's dark eyes, or the sight of her surprisingly firm little round biceps that had Cassie bursting into giggles, hardly mattered. It was enough that, for what seemed like the first time in forever, *something* was truly funny.

"Oh, Speranza," she spluttered, almost choking on the milk, "you can't begin to know how good it feels to laugh again!"

But the merriment died as swiftly as it had arisen when a voice, sharp as a knife blade, cut through the cheerful atmosphere to inquire, "So what is it you find so amusing, Cassandra, that you take my servant away from her duties in this fashion?"

Wiping her eyes, Cassie looked over her shoulder. Elvira stood in the doorway, her face livid with controlled rage and her fury-filled breathing stripping every vestige of lightheartedness from the room.

How long had she been hovering there, like a big black vulture come to wreak vengeance on heaven knew what? Had she heard them talking about the baby? And what sort of price was Speranza going to have to pay for fraternizing with the enemy? Because that this was one of those days when Cassie had once again been cast in the role of adversary in her mother-in-law's eyes, was pretty hard to miss.

"Please don't blame Speranza," she blurted out, leaping from the rocking chair so suddenly that her stomach churned. "I came here uninvited, looking for a cup of coffee, and didn't mean to distract her."

Speranza, though, didn't seem the least bit fazed by her employer's annoyance. She favored Elvira with a stream of unintelligible Italian, raised one hand and gave a minikarate chop to the crook of her other elbow in a universally understood gesture of disrespect, and went unhurriedly about her chores, slapping and shaping the dough on the table as unconcernedly as if such confrontations were all in a day's work.

Ignoring her, Elvira pounced on the glass of milk Cassie was sneakily trying to pour into the sink. "What is that for? Is your constitution so delicate that you cannot tolerate good Italian espresso, like the rest of us?"

So she *hadn't* heard about the baby! Cassie almost sagged with relief, but it quickly turned to dismay when Elvira tossed the same question at Speranza, this time in Italian. Without a moment's hesitation, the old servant flung back a reply, and among the words she spat at her employer, *bambino* rang loud and all too clear through the room.

As the import of what she heard sank home, Elvira grew so still and quiet, she might have been turned to stone. Outwardly, Cassie pretty much did the same, although her heart was flopping around behind her ribs like a landed fish. Otherwise, not a sound disturbed the utter silence, except for the ticking of the big old clock on the wall, and the rhythmic thump and slap of the dough hitting the tabletop.

Finally, Cassie could stand the tension no longer. "Well, now you know what Benedict and I have been trying to hide from you, though why we ever bothered is beyond me," she said, and went to leave, even though that meant stepping closer to Elvira than she'd have liked.

She wasn't normally given to wild imaginings, but there was something about the woman that made her skin crawl. Even at her best, Elvira was strange. At her worst, as now, she was outright chilling.

"*Sciatonna!*" she hissed, making no attempt to move out of the doorway as Cassie approached. "*Slut!*"

Heart still hammering, Cassie brushed by her, intending to go to the suite. Its heavy furniture and gloomy draperies might not make it her favorite place, but at least it offered some sort of sanctuary. Elvira never ventured up there, instead preferring to confine herself to the two lower floors.

Today, however, she seemed as anxious for Cassie's

company as Cassie was to be rid of hers, and kept pace with her as she climbed the stairs. Exasperated, Cassie stopped on the first landing and spun around to face her.

"Leave me alone!" she cried, past caring about keeping the peace a moment longer. "I've got nothing more to say to you."

"But I have much to say to you," Elvira taunted, her eyes blazing. "You think to trap my son with this child you claim is his, but it will take more than such a ploy to tie him to you."

"I'm not tying him against his will, Elvira. He *chooses* to be with me."

She tried to push past, but Elvira blocked her passage. "He longs to be free of you! Why else do you think he spends as much time as possible away from this house? He cannot wait to escape your incessant neediness."

"I have never once tried to keep him from attending to business."

"No?" Elvira clutched both fists to her chest in a melodramatic gesture of pleading. "Oh, Benedict," she chanted, her voice rising from its usual contralto to a maddening parody of Cassie's lighter tone, "I'd so love to spend an afternoon with you at the Museo Nazionale in Reggio Calabria.... Benedict, your sister tells me there are some marvelous Byzantine ruins in the area. When are you going to take me to see them...? Show me where you went to school, Benedict...where you played with other boys your age."

She dropped her hands and assumed her usual tone. "And so it goes," she sneered, "day after day, hour after hour!"

"Did it never occur to you that I'm merely showing an interest in my husband's birthplace, and trying to learn something of his life before he met me?"

"Rubbish! It is all about you. You want to be catered to, you spoilt child. But Benedict does not need a child for a wife. He needs a woman."

"Does he really! Someone like Giovanna, I suppose?"

"Not someone *like* her." Elvira's direct look was honest in its enmity. "Simply *her*."

"But Giovanna doesn't want to be with him. Unlike you, she respects our marriage."

"She understands him. She *knows* him, in ways you never will. She completes him. But you...you pull him apart."

Was it true? Did she whine and complain all the time? Ask too much? Perhaps give too little?

Suddenly uncertain, Cassie said haltingly, "It's never been my intention to do that. I just want—"

Elvira advanced on her, mouth pulled back in a horrible facsimile of a smile. "You want everything, all the time! You want him all to yourself, but he is not yours to have. He never will be!"

"Stop it!" Cassie cried, chilled to the bone by that manic stare, that poisonous, implacable hatred. "If Benedict knew the things you're saying—"

Elvira loomed closer. "Yes?" She planted both hands squarely against Cassie's shoulders and gave a sharp push. "What then, *americana?*"

Stumbling from the unexpected contact, Cassie reached behind to steady herself on the banister. But she'd stepped too close to the edge of the landing and instead found herself clutching at thin air.

In horrific slow motion, she felt her body tilt off balance and swing backward down the stairs. She heard a scream and thought it must be hers because, above her on the landing, Elvira stood with her mouth closed, watching composedly.

The stone banister lacerated her knuckles as Cassie fought to retain her balance. Her groin stretched painfully as one leg became hooked between two balusters, while the other continued its perilous downward slide. But, merciful heaven, it slowed her fall enough that she managed to grab hold of another baluster, and come to rest in an ungainly heap about a quarter of the way down the staircase.

Shaken to the core, she whispered, "*Good grief*, Elvira, you could have killed me!"

Face expressionless and eyes frighteningly blank, Elvira started down the stairs toward her, and for the space of a horror-filled second, Cassie thought the woman intended to finish off what she'd started.

She did not. She stared straight ahead, stepped over Cassie with the casual disregard any sane person might display toward an ant, and disappeared into her office at the rear of the lower hall.

Shivering all over, Cassie remained with her arms wrapped around the baluster, afraid to move in case she did herself more harm than good—and terrified for the well-being of her baby.

At last, and mostly because she was even more afraid that Elvira might return, she eased herself to her feet. Despite a lingering soreness at her ribs and the throbbing ache in her groin, she appeared little the worse for wear. But the baby...?

A fresh wave of horror washed over her, fueled by shock and fear of the unknown. How susceptible to injury was a fetus at this stage of pregnancy? Could a sharp blow cause brain damage? Spinal deformity?

"Oh, Benedict!" she mourned, feeling so alone that

the tears poured down her face as reaction to the whole ghastly incident set in. "Why aren't you here when I need you so badly?"

But the fact remained, he wasn't, which meant it was up to her to protect their child. And the only way to do that, she realized sorrowfully, was to remove herself permanently from a situation which had deteriorated from unpleasant, to downright dangerous.

Even though it broke her heart to leave Benedict after she'd promised him she'd stay, the baby mattered more. And that being so, she had to get herself out of this hell house and seek medical advice. She needed to find a doctor skilled enough to assess the progress of her pregnancy, and determine whether she was fit enough to make the long journey back home—and with the ability to communicate his findings to her in English.

Then, once assured that it was safe for her to travel, she'd be on the first flight back to the U.S., half a world away from her deranged mother-in-law. Enough was enough! She'd had all she could take of Elvira Constantino.

To carry out her plan, though, she had to get herself to Reggio Calabria, and there was only one way she could do that. Making her way up the second set of stairs, she let herself into the suite, made sure her passport and wallet were in her handbag, then opened the top drawer of Benedict's dresser, praying that she'd find there what she desperately needed, to carry out her plans.

Dusty and tired, Benedict drew up to the low arch leading to what had once been the Constantino stables. They'd been converted long ago to a vast garage for housing the farm vehicles, with a section at one end reserved for the family autos.

Nudging the truck into its customary spot beside the east wall, he jumped down from the cab. The sound of the door slamming closed boomed through the empty building like a cannon shot, then faded into silence.

Although the air of desertion about the place did not at first strike him as unusual—his mother and Francesca were probably still at work in the office wing, and Cassandra was most likely down on the beach enjoying the afternoon sun—still, as he turned to leave, something tugged at his brain, begging for attention. Something about the garage that wasn't quite the way it should be....

He slowed on his way out, waiting for whatever was amiss to register more fully, but when it did not, he shrugged and headed for the house. If it was a matter of importance, it would come to him later.

He'd been gone four days. Most of that time he'd spent in mountainous *la 'ndrangheta* territory, trying to broker an agreement with Angelo Menghi, leader of a gang of outlaws who hid out in the network of caves found in the area. Angelo's younger brother, Darius, was the man Elvira hired when the foreman who'd worked for the family for nearly twenty years decided he'd had enough of her misguided rule.

Darius, though, had been an unwise choice from the first. Sly, shiftless and without conscience, he'd undermined what little stability remained with the rest of the Constantino employees, and when Elvira fired him for insurrection, his swift and malevolent retaliation had been a foregone conclusion.

Benedict had no doubt that Darius was behind the vandalism which had taken such a toll on the fruit orchards, and was equally certain he'd been aided and abetted by Angelo and his lawless affiliates.

Having to negotiate with such scum had left a very sour taste in Benedict's mouth, but he knew there was only one way to put an end to the situation, and that was through negotiation. So he'd held his nose, metaphorically speaking, and done what had to be done. Now, having succeeded, all he wanted was a long, cleansing shower, a bottle of good wine, a meal, and an evening spent with Cassandra.

He had missed her, not so much during the day, when tracking down Angelo Menghi and effecting some sort of armistice had been uppermost in his mind. But at night, lying under the bright stars, he'd thought of her soft, warm body and her sweet generous mouth, and been glad of the cold mountain air stealing inside his sleeping bag.

He'd heard her voice in the murmur of the wind, smelled the perfume of her skin in the wild flowers clustered in rocky ridges of the lower slopes. He was impatient to see her again; to hold her, however tame the embrace had to be, and bury his face in her hair. To feel the mound of their growing child pressing against his belly.

But when he emerged fresh from his shower, the third-floor suite was still empty, and so, as he went down to the main floor, was the rest of the palazzo. At least, it appeared so, at first glance. And that's when it struck him that the atmosphere was *too* still, *too* silent.

He wasn't a man prone to superstition. Dealing in tangibles as he did—contracts, shipments, excise duties, import restrictions, all defined by cold, hard facts and figures—he couldn't afford to be. But, at that moment of awareness, an irrational sense of foreboding stole over him.

Suddenly, he was striding from room to room, calling

out—Cassandra's name, Francesca's, his mother's—and hearing only the echo of his own voice responding.

He came across Elvira in the salon, purely by accident. She sat stiffly in one of the high-backed chairs facing the sea, and appeared completely oblivious of her surroundings, or him.

"Mother?" He approached her cautiously; touched her hand where it rested on the carved wooden arm of the chair. "Can you hear me?"

She didn't respond, instead remaining so immobile that, for a shocking moment, he thought she might be dead. Then her eyelids fluttered in a blink, and he saw the rise and fall of her chest as she drew in a faint, trembling breath.

So quietly that he had to stoop to hear her, she said, "I am afraid of growing old and becoming useless, Benedict."

"You're fifty-nine," he told her. "Hardly in your dotage yet!"

She pinched the bridge of her nose. Spread her fingers, fanlike, across her brow and buried their tips in her hair. "But inside my head here, my mind doesn't always work. Sometimes, it seems not to know…things it should know."

His uneasiness grew. He'd never heard her sound so defeated, so utterly unsure. "Are you ill, Mother?"

"Not I. Cassandra, though…!" She covered her mouth with shaking fingers, but not soon enough to stop a little moan of anguish. "I think she's hurt, Benedict. She fell down the stairs. I think I pushed her."

His heart jolted laboriously and when he spoke, his voice seemed to roar from a great distance. "For the love of God, *why?*"

"I can't remember," she said, lifting piteous eyes to his.

Hanging on to his sanity by a thread, he tried to speak more calmly. "Where is she now, Mother?"

Elvira lifted her shoulders in a ghost of shrug. Of what? Indifference? Ignorance?

Neither was tolerable, and in a sudden overwhelming rush of fury, he grabbed her by the shoulders. Only by dint of extraordinary self-control did he restrain himself from shaking the truth out of her. "Answer me, Elvira! *Where is my wife?*"

"I looked and couldn't find her," she replied vaguely. "She's not here."

Not here…!

Like a camera lens clicking sharply into focus, his mother's words gave shape to his earlier niggling sense of something being amiss. *The place where he always parked the Lamborghini had stood empty when he rolled the truck into the garage!*

Sweat prickled his skin and he turned cold all over. If Cassandra, hurt and distraught, had driven the powerful car over the treacherous, unfamiliar coastal roads, she could be lying at the bottom of a cliff, broken or burned beyond recognition.

Anguished, desperate, he turned again to his mother. "Where's Francesca? Could she have taken Cassandra to the village to see a doctor?"

Before Elvira could answer, a door opened somewhere in the main hall and Francesca called out cheerfully, "Hello? Anyone home?"

A moment later, she appeared at the threshold of the salon. "Uh-oh," she muttered, taking in the scene in one sweeping glance, "now what's happened?"

He knew how it must look—their mother slumped in

a chair with him towering over her, so consumed with anxiety and rage that he was practically frothing at the mouth. Controlling himself with an effort, he turned away and addressed his next remark to his sister.

"Elvira claims she pushed Cassandra down the stairs," he said tightly. "Can you, by any chance, shed some light on this?"

He didn't need a verbal response. Francesca's open-mouthed shock spoke volumes, and pain clutched at his heart—a dry, bloodless, self-inflicted wound. As easily as he'd found Cassandra, he'd lost her. He'd brought her here against his better judgment, then kept her at a distance when he should have held her close. And it might have cost her her life.

Spinning on his heel, he made for the door.

Francesca found her voice. "Benedict, wait! Where are you going?"

"Where do you think? To look for my wife—and I pray to God that I find her and our child alive."

"*Child?*" Francesca did a double-take. "Cassandra's pregnant, and you never said anything?"

"Don't start in on me," he warned, brushing past her. "Right now, I'm in no mood to justify anything to anyone. I've got bigger things to worry about."

"Such as rampaging through the countryside like a madman?" She caught his arm. "Stop and think for a minute! Cassandra might not have gone anywhere. She might be resting upstairs."

"She's not. She's nowhere in this house, and my car's gone from the garage."

Francesca paled, but clung to reason regardless. "Then we start by phoning the police. There aren't too many red Lamborghini Diablos in the area. If she's driving around out there, she'll be easy enough to spot."

"And if she's not?" He cast a savage glance at his mother, who sat with her head pressed against the back of the chair, and her eyes closed. As if, by her refusing to look, what she'd done would miraculously cease to exist!

"We'll call the local clinic, and Dr. Vieri's office," Francesca said. "Stop expecting the worst and think about it, Benedict! If she'd been in an accident, we'd have heard about it before now. It's just a matter of alerting the authorities and waiting for them to track her down. But if she decides to come back on her own, I think she'd feel a lot safer if she found you here waiting for her."

It was no more in his nature to hand over control of his affairs to someone else, than he'd thought it was in his mother's to physically attack his wife. Yet what Francesca said made sense. Better to cast as wide an official search net as possible while some daylight remained. Because if he didn't have news of Cassandra by sunset, he didn't know how he'd face the coming night.

Cassie stepped out into the late-afternoon clamor of the city, and inhaled deeply and luxuriously. For the first time in hours, her lungs were unconstricted by fear and, despite the stench of exhaust fumes, the air smelled incomparably sweet.

Her baby was alive and well. She had heard his heart beat; seen it on the ultrasound screen.

Behind her stood the hospital, no longer a site of potential threat to everything she held dear, but a benign, comforting presence designed to protect her. After compiling a thorough case history, and taking a battery of tests including a sonogram, the chief obstetrician on staff had told her, "*Signora*, your baby is in excellent health, as are you. The fall has left you with a bruise or two, but the pregnancy is not in danger.''

''And my cervix?''

''Is entirely as it should be at this stage. You and your husband may relax.'' Eyes twinkling, he'd patted her hand. ''He will be happy to hear this, yes?''

''Yes.''

But Benedict was out of touch, somewhere in the mountains of the interior, and much though she wished it could be otherwise, she had no intention of going back to the palazzo to wait for his return. If Elvira wanted a second shot at disposing of her daughter-in-law, she'd have to travel to San Francisco to get it.

As it turned out, the earliest Cassie could book a flight home was the following afternoon, but even that didn't cast a cloud on her spirits. For the first time in weeks, she was free of the looming, gloomy presence of the Constantino estate and only now, with the bustle and noise of traffic and people swirling around her, did she realize how much she'd missed them.

Reggio Calabria might be the provincial capital, but a major earthquake early in the twentieth century had destroyed much of its antiquity, and the conglomeration of newer buildings offered little in the way of interest or beauty. Yet it possessed the sort of vitality and pulse only to be found in a city, and she relished it.

Consulting the tourist map she'd purchased, she located a hotel on a quiet side street. Though not ostentatious, it nevertheless had a certain charm. The room she was shown was clean, comfortable, had its own bathroom and a telephone, and looked out over a small rear garden set with umbrella-shaded tables. Furthermore, there was parking at the side of the building for the Lamborghini.

She sat at one of the outdoor tables, and with the help of her phrase book, ordered a vanilla milkshake. Afterward, since she had nothing with her but a small cosmetic kit and the clothes she stood up in, she drove in search of a place to buy such basics as shampoo and toothpaste, and a change of underwear.

After making her purchases, she followed a different route on the way back to the hotel, and passed by a little boutique specializing in maternity wear. Confident now that she'd carry her baby to term, and free to let the whole world know it, she went inside and bought two outfits. One was a dress in silk the color of almond blossom, the other a royal-blue cotton two-piece.

By the time she returned to her room, the sun lay low in the west and kerosene lamps flared in the garden to ward off the shadows of dusk. Relaxed for the first time in what seemed like forever, she bathed, put on her new blue outfit and, lured by the tempting aromas rising from the kitchen below her open window, went down for dinner.

Ravenous, she dined on wonderful olives, and bread warm from the oven; on swordfish and pasta stuffed with eggplant; on local cheese and fruit. The only thing missing was not having Benedict there to share the experience, and she missed him dreadfully.

She saw the moon rise and listened to someone nearby playing a violin. She watched two lovers at another table—how they gazed at one another, and held hands. And again, the ache of missing Benedict took hold.

At twenty-two minutes past three the next morning, she awoke to a sensation in her womb as if a butterfly had swept open its wings. A moment later, it happened again, and she realized her baby was moving.

She wished Benedict was there to share the moment

with her. But he was not, so she settled for the next best thing. Sitting up, she reached for the phone on the bedside table and called Trish.

It was six o'clock the next morning—more than fourteen hours since he'd learned she'd gone missing—before the phone rang and released Benedict from the confines of hell.

"She's been found," the local police chief informed him. "She's registered at a hotel in Reggio Calabria. We were able to track her down through the car. Just as well you provided us with a full description, otherwise we'd still be looking."

He was on the road within fifteen minutes, the hotel name and address scribbled on a slip of paper beside him on the seat. Traffic was light and he made good time, arriving in the provincial capital before the morning rush began.

The hotel stood on a quiet side street. The desk clerk confirmed that Cassandra had taken a room and had not yet checked out. Benedict did a quick sweep of the lobby, locating the stairs, the dining room, and the door to the courtyard, to be sure he had all points of entry and exit covered, then took up his post in a corner near the front desk which commanded a clear view of the entire lobby.

She didn't show up until almost half-past nine, by which time he was beginning to worry that she'd somehow slipped through his fingers again, or else was too indisposed to make it out of bed. Just as he was about to demand a key to her room, however, she came down the stairs, dog-eared phrase book in hand.

She looked rested and lovely and reassuringly pregnant. Glowing on the outside from the sun, and on the inside with a serenity he found hard to understand, given her trauma of the previous day. He knew without having to ask, that the baby was fine.

Unaware that she was being observed, she made straight for the garden. Not about to let her out of his sight, Benedict followed and watched as she chose a table in the corner, next to a small wall fountain, popped a pair of sunglasses on her nose, and studied the menu.

The tables on either side were unoccupied. Unobtrusively sliding onto the chair directly behind hers, he leaned back and said over his shoulder, "You seem familiar with the hotel, *signorina*. What do you recommend I order for breakfast?"

She let out a sighing little squeak of recognition, a captivating sound reminiscent of the one she made when she approached orgasm, then recovered enough to say primly, "I'm a *signora*. A married lady."

"And I," he said, "am a married man in dire straits. My wife, you see, has run off, and I'm desperate to find her."

"What did you do to drive her away?"

"I'm afraid I neglected her shamefully, and in doing so, exposed her to danger in the one place she ought to have been safe. Should something untoward happen to her, I don't know how I'll live with myself."

"Does she know how strongly you feel?"

"I'm not sure. I've never actually said so, mostly because I didn't fully realize it myself until yesterday, when I lost her."

"Women need to be told, *signor*. They need to hear the words."

"Have I left it too late to convince her?"

She didn't reply and he, in a wave of uncertainty as demoralizing as it was foreign, dropped his arm to his side and reached back his hand toward her. He knew she couldn't see the gesture; knew it was a puny, even cowardly way to try to mend what was broken between them. Because she was right: actions didn't always speak louder than words; sometimes, it was the other way around.

"Is she planning to come back to me, do you think?" he asked. "Or is her plan to keep on going, and make a life without me?"

The seconds dragged by, an eternity punctuated by an avalanche of regret for the mistakes he'd made. She'd shown him in a hundred different ways that she could love him if only he would let her, but because he hadn't been able to keep his rampant testosterone under control, he'd rebuffed her overtures.

Now, unable to tolerate the suspense, he was on the verge of accepting that the distance between them had grown too vast to bridge when, as lightly as a breath of wind, the tips of her fingers brushed against his and caught hold.

"I think she'd far rather be with her husband," she said.

CHAPTER TEN

"IT'S NOT that I wanted to leave you, Benedict. It's that I didn't feel I had a choice," she said, when she could speak past the emotion clogging her throat. "Not that I blame you for what happened yesterday," she added quickly. "You're not responsible for your mother's actions."

Without letting go of her hand, he left his seat and took the empty chair at her table. He wore his navy slacks and a white sports shirt with the casual elegance so typical of everything he did. Just then, though, there was nothing casual or typical about his manner. The self-possession she'd thought impregnable lay in tatters, as evidenced by the haunted shadows in his eyes.

"But I'm responsible for you," he said urgently. "I'm responsible for my child."

"You can't always be there to intercede between me and perceived danger. No one can. And in case you haven't noticed, I'm capable of looking out for myself."

"Obviously," he said drily. "A lot more so than I realized, judging by the way you escaped under your own steam. How'd you find the drive, by the way?"

"Horrendous, especially once I got here. The traffic congestion in this city is a nightmare. But the worst part was wondering if I'd be able to find your car keys at the palazzo. I knew where you usually kept them, but was so afraid you might have taken them with you when you left for the mountains. If you had, I don't know how I'd have got away." She shot him an amused glance. "But

157

if it's the Lamborghini you're really worried about, don't be. It doesn't have a scratch on it.''

"I don't give a damn about the car, Cassandra! There are plenty more where it came from, but you...!'' He expelled a heartfelt breath. "*You* are irreplaceable, and I never again want to come so close to losing you.''

"I already told you, Benedict, that what happened wasn't your fault.''

"Indirectly, it was,'' he insisted gravely. "I could have acknowledged sooner that having you live under my mother's roof was a mistake. God knows, you tried to tell me, often enough. I could have sent you to Bianca. You'd have been safe with her. She'd have taken good care of you and the baby.''

"I wouldn't have gone. I wanted to be with you—at least, I did until yesterday. Then, I'm afraid, it all just became too much.'' She leaned across the table and cupped his jaw, wanting very much to erase the worry marking his features. "But I'm so glad you came after me. I have wonderful news.''

He shook his head in disbelief, and almost smiled. "How can you possibly mine something wonderful out of near-tragedy?''

"Easily,'' she said. "I checked into the hospital here yesterday, just to be sure everything was as it should be with my pregnancy.''

He turned his mouth to her palm and pressed a kiss there. "And?''

"And I heard and saw our baby's heart beating. Then, last night, I felt him move.'' Reaching into her bag, she drew out the prints from the ultrasound and passed them to him. "Here are the first pictures of your son, Benedict.''

"We have a boy?'' His hand shook as he took them,

and she almost started crying at the look of wonder on his face as he examined the blurry images. "And he's perfect?"

"He's perfect!"

He stroked his fingertip over the glossy paper. "We're so lucky, *cara!* So blessed!"

"Yes," she said softly. "And that's not all. The problem with my cervix...well, it turned out not to be a problem, after all. The doctor gave me a clean bill of health."

"And you trust his opinion?"

"He's a specialist, Benedict. I think it's safe to assume he knows what he's talking about."

"So I have a healthy wife, as well as a healthy baby?"

"Yes."

"I wish that was enough to make me a completely happy man," he said, the joy which had illuminated his face fading into solemnity.

Her heart sank a little. "And it's not?"

"How can it be, considering everything that happened with my mother?" For the first time since she'd known him, the candor and pride always so predominant in his gaze was tinged with shame. "I hardly know what to say, Cassandra. I wish I could offer some insight into her actions, but frankly, I'm at a loss. I questioned her, of course, but she was able to give no rational explanation for her behavior. Have you any idea what possessed her?"

"I suppose I might have provoked her." Trying to be fair, Cassie explained the sequence of events. "I think finding out about the baby the way she did was what really set her off. But what shook me was that she'd willingly endanger the life of her unborn grandchild. I know she's your mother, Benedict, but I'm sorry to say I find what she did unforgivable."

"Don't apologize," he said grimly. "I never thought to see the day that I'd say this, but she is not the mother I've always known, nor even a woman. She is a monster and while I've thought for some time that she might be mentally ill, I'm now beginning to wonder if she's not criminally insane!"

He spoke with fire, but Cassie could see what it cost him. The pain in his eyes was impossible to miss, and she hated having to add to it. But he had to know that there was no going back to the way things had been.

"I wish I could disagree with you, but I can't," she said sadly. "I'm afraid I can't ever go back to the palazzo. Nor do I don't want your mother anywhere near me or my baby, ever again."

"I understand. And I wouldn't dream of asking you to return. But I am begging you not to go back to the States, not yet. Please, Cassandra, come with me instead to La Posada, my home in Sicily. We'll be alone, there, and you'll be safe. We can start over again, the way a married couple should, with a proper honeymoon."

"I'm hardly equipped to go off on a honeymoon," she protested, laughing. "I left in such a hurry that, except for a few items I bought yesterday, all my things are still at the palazzo."

"Then as soon as we've finished breakfast, we'll shop some more."

"Well, not that it doesn't sound wonderful, but what about work? You can't just walk away when your entire family is depending on you."

"Yes, I can," he said, gripping her hands so firmly, she almost winced. "You and our baby are my family, now. I won't say I don't care about my sisters and, yes, even my mother. But I'm through with putting other people, other things, ahead of you and me, Cassandra. From here on, our marriage comes first.''

He spoke with feeling. With controlled desire. The atmosphere shimmered with the promise of unfettered passion waiting to be allayed, of a future suddenly bright with promise of the happy-ever-after she'd always longed for.

And if all that didn't quite add up to the same as *I love you, Cassandra,* it came close and, after the tumult and trauma of the last twenty-four hours, for now, for Cassie, it was enough.

He took her to shops she'd never have discovered on her own. Overrode her protests and spent extravagant amounts on her: an entire wardrobe of silk lingerie, shoes, perfume, and maternity dresses so pretty she could have stayed pregnant forever, just for the pleasure of wearing them.

They ate stuffed calamari and preserved figs for lunch, drank fragrant *caffe latte,* talked about his journey inland and the progress he'd made in putting the Calabrian end of the family enterprise in order again.

''I've persuaded our old foreman to come back,'' he told her. ''Given him full control of operations. He's well respected in the village. He'll have no trouble enlisting hired hands. Many who'd defected are ready to return and start working the orchards again.''

They arrived at his Sicilian hideaway late in the afternoon, and Cassie fell in love with the place on sight. If the Constantino palazzo hulked at the top of the cliff, all ancient stone and somber, brooding confinement, Benedict's home, situated on a gentle slope of land running down to the shore, flowed in a graceful curve of white stucco walls and blue tiled roof around a turquoise swimming pool.

Brilliant flowering shrubs filled every nook and cranny of the garden. Fountains splashed and little streams ran under rocks to form tiny hidden pools where brightly colored fish darted back and forth.

He led her on a tour of the place. The windows and doors were wide, allowing the breeze to sweep the house with the scent of the jasmine growing in a planter beside the front entrance. The rooms were spacious and airy and, during the day, filled with the rippling reflection of sunlight glimmering on the sea.

Marble, smooth as silk, covered the floors. Instead of stiff, uncomfortable carved chairs and sofas upholstered in heavy plush, leather couches, puffy and soft as marshmallows, graced the salon. The dining table was a sheet of beveled glass supported on a finely wrought iron base, the chairs pale wood with seats covered in white linen.

The master suite was huge, with floor-to-ceiling windows opening onto a private terrace, a charming sitting area at one end and, oddly, two enormous bathrooms accessed by dressing rooms.

"If you're wondering how many other women I've brought here," Benedict said, noticing her surprise at the convenient his-and-hers arrangement, "you're the first— and last. I didn't design this house, Cassandra. I bought it three years ago, for the location and view, from a couple who moved to an apartment in Roma to be near their grandchildren. That it happens to be designed for a man and his wife is purely and conveniently coincidental."

Embarrassed that he'd picked up on her thoughts with such uncanny accuracy, she replied, "You didn't have to tell me that."

"Yes, I did," he said. "There've been enough clouds hanging over us. I won't allow there to be any more. You're my lady, *cara,* and the only mistress, ever, of my house."

As the sun set, he left her to bathe and dress at leisure, his parting glance telling her that soon, very soon, there would be nothing keeping them apart. Not the walls of her bathroom, not the clothes on her body, and never again the sullen, forbidding presence of his mother tainting the atmosphere. The knowledge left her quivering with anticipation.

That night, they dined by candlelight on a terrace overlooking the sea, with the murmur of the waves falling in soft cadence against the shore, and the moon riding low on the horizon. Music drifted from the house, old songs from the 1940s, full of lost love found again and two hearts beating as one. Carmine, the chef, served veal Parmigiano and rollentini, with a light salad to start and chilled *zabaglione* for dessert.

And throughout, with every word, every glance, every touch, undercurrents of expectancy rippled between her and Benedict, an unseen but insistent third party refusing to go denied.

Sipping a small flute of celebratory champagne, Cassie sat across from her husband, conscious of time ticking toward the sexual finale of a union now nearly four and a half months old. The flicker of candle flames showcased his high cheekbones and swathed his dark eyes in mystery. Weeks of strenuous physical labor had sculpted his already well-toned body to hard perfection and deepened his olive skin to bronze.

He looked handsome as a god, and she wished she could fast-freeze the perfection of the moment—of him—and keep them as a talisman against future assaults on their marriage. Because for all Cassie's stated intention to remain as far away from his mother as possible, the reality was that as long as Elvira was alive, the specter of her destructive potential remained a dark cloud on the horizon.

"What are you thinking about, *cara?*" Benedict asked, eyeing her lazily over the rim of his wineglass.

"I'm wondering how you can bear to leave such a place. It's exquisite here."

He smiled, and pulling her to her feet, led her over the flagstones in a dreamy waltz. "I'm happy you think so because it's *my* favorite retreat, also. The Manhattan apartment is comfortable and works well as a base for North American business, and those in Paris, London and Hong Kong serve me well enough. But this is where I come when I need to unwind."

Stunned by the casual way he rattled off his real estate holdings, as if having *pieds à terre* scattered over three continents was standard for any man, she lost the rhythm of the waltz and almost stepped on his foot. "Exactly how many homes do you own?"

"Just four," he said, not missing a beat. "My work involves a fair bit of travel, and I don't care for hotels."

Apparently not! "And boats?"

"Two—the motor launch that brought us here from the mainland, and a fifty-four foot sailing sloop I keep in the Caribbean."

She swallowed. "Um… at the risk of sounding incredibly crass, are you *very* rich, Benedict?"

"I suppose." He shrugged carelessly and stroked his hand up her spine. "Why? Does it matter?"

"Only insofar as I feel like a fool," she said, staring, mortified, over his shoulder. "You must have laughed yourself silly when I offered you money to help cover the losses brought on by your mother's business mis-haps. I thought, when you talked of having to find an-other way to make a living, that you were in financial straits.''

"I didn't laugh, Cassandra," he murmured. "I was very touched by your generosity."

"Even so, it shows how much we still don't know about each other."

Slowing to the point that they were doing little more than sway in each other's arms, he brushed his mouth over the crown of her head and pulled her close enough that she could feel every line of his torso delineated against hers. "But we have the rest of our lives to learn, yes?"

"Yes," she agreed, his nearness creating alarming re-percussions within her. To an onlooker, he might have appeared completely relaxed and in control, but up this close, his body told a different story.

"Perhaps," he said, not sounding quite so composed, after all, "we should start this journey of discovery very soon. I have waited a very long time to be a proper husband to you, Cassandra, and I am not known for my patience."

The smoky timbre of his voice sent a flash of heat streaking through her that left her trembling. "Then per-haps," she suggested, "you should take me to bed, be-fore we make a public display of ourselves out here, in front of your house staff."

He needed no second urging. Sweeping her into his arms, he strode across the terrace and through the house to the master suite. "I like a woman who speaks her mind plainly," he said. "I like *you,* my Cassandra. I like you very much."

CHAPTER ELEVEN

HE'D orchestrated the entire night with such strict attention to detail that he actually thought it would happen exactly as planned—that he could tame his body and bring to this, the real start of their marriage, the subtlety and restraint that would allow both Cassandra and himself to savor every second.

It did not happen so. He was too hungry and she was too fine, too lovely and too giving. Barely had they reached the bedroom before raw need vanquished any notions of finesse. The way she breathed his name in his ear, the whisper of satiny underthings shifting against her skin, the soft, full curves of her pregnancy, her hand playing over his chest...there were too many temptations. Assaulted on every front, he was ready to burst.

Kicking closed the door behind him, he brought his mouth down on hers in the kind of kiss he hadn't dared allow before because it imitated too closely the act of love. The way she welcomed him, opening her mouth to his tongue, and moaning softly, should have staved off the wild craving long enough for him to carry her as far as the bed.

It did not.

Driven wild by the scent and taste of her, and with his mouth still fastened to hers, he lowered her to the floor, slowly enough that there wasn't an inch of her that didn't slither provocatively over him. Half-blind with need, he worked the buttons of her dress open, pushed it aside, and dragged his lips lower. To her throat, where her pulse beat as frantically as the wings of a trapped bird. To her breasts, barely contained by her lacy bra.

She whimpered when he took her nipple lightly between his teeth and rolled his tongue around it. And whimpered again, more helplessly, when he slid her dress high up her thighs. She wore no stockings underneath, just panties, and the patch of fabric between her legs was damp.

Edging it aside, he buried his finger in her soft, warm flesh. She quivered at his touch, so ready for him, so hot and moist and tight, that he almost came.

Wanting to prolong the pleasure, he attempted to put a little distance between them, but she arched against him, and clenched her thighs together, hard, to imprison his hand. Ran both of hers down his chest to his waist, and his belt. Tore open the buckle, unzipped his fly, and boldly thrust inside to cup the pulsing, heavy weight of his erection in her palm.

It was game over then. Within seconds, they were tearing at each other's clothing until they stood naked. The bed lay only five meters away, but it might as well have been a kilometer or more. There was no way he could cover the distance. No way he could hold back the encroaching tide long enough to allow the mattress to accommodate them.

Spinning her around, he pinned her against the wall, hooked his hands beneath her buttocks, and lifted her. She wrapped her legs around his waist and rested the mound of their unborn child against his belly.

"Are you sure...it's safe to do this?" Teetering on the point of no return, he fought his way past the passion smoking through his body, and dragged the question from his tortured lungs.

Her fingers gouged at his shoulders; urged him to completion. "Very sure," she whispered.

It was as well. He was, after all, but a man, as subject to human weakness as the next. And she was temptation personified.

For a breathtaking nanosecond of sheer, exquisite torment, he allowed his aroused flesh to tease hers, nudging and retreating from the eager folds of her femininity until she was begging him, in broken little cries, to put an end to her misery.

Then, at last…at long last…he was inside her. Moving with her. Thrusting in rhythm, back and forth. Feeling her close around him, strong and silken and hot. And for all that he wanted to take her in long, easy strokes, it was not to be. Responsive to every nuance of his seduction, she clutched handfuls of his hair, and burst into tears as the climax she tried so hard to delay swept over her in wracking spasms no man could withstand.

Sweat blurring his vision, he braced one hand against the door and, with a mighty groan, gave himself up to an explosion of sensation so intense, he thought it would kill him.

It robbed him of his soul.

Left him shaking and depleted.

Left him so strung out and defenseless that, with the aftershocks of orgasm still rumbling through his body, he uttered words he'd never before said to any woman. *"Ah, Cassandra, mi tesoro, te amo!"*

"What did you say?" she panted, raising dazed eyes to his.

"I love you," he said. "You are my life, and I will never again put any other ahead of you."

She wept again then, not with volatile sobs which had shaken her before, but with quiet containment. Tears filmed her lovely blue eyes and trembled from her lashes. "Oh, Benedict!" she sighed brokenly. "I've waited so long to hear you say those words. Waited so long to say them to you. Because I have loved you for a long time now, and I was so afraid you'd never love me back."

"Don't be afraid, *mi amore,*" he told her. "The bad times are behind us, and I give you my word there will be nothing but golden days ahead."

For five days, she believed him. For five days and nights, he devoted himself to pleasing her. The utter perfection of that time made the long wait for their honeymoon worth every painful second which had preceded it.

He made love to her often. With tenderness, and with unrestrained passion. Playfully, with laughter, and soberly, with heartfelt, murmured endearments. They came together in the swimming pool early in the day, with the sun just high enough to tint La Posada's white stucco walls pink; and on the beach at midnight, with only the stars to witness their pleasure.

Waking before him one morning, she watched him sleeping, all long, loose-limbed elegance, with his dark hair falling in disarray over his brow. Unable to help herself, she leaned over and pressed a featherlight kiss to his shoulder. Just enough to steal the taste of him, but not enough to disturb him.

But when she raised her head, his eyes were open and full of lazy laughter. He crooked a finger at her, and in a sleep-gravelly voice said, "Come here, wench."

"Yes, master," she purred, sliding on top of him.

"Buon giorno, mi amore," he murmured, thrusting up to meet her.

* * *

He showed her Sicily. Took her to Palermo, to little, out-of-the-way *trattorias,* and introduced her to traditional Sicilian foods like cuttlefish served in its own black ink, and the best veal Marsala she'd ever eaten. Tempted her with Sicilian *gelato* and almond marzipan pastries colored and shaped to resemble fruit. Showed her palatial homes, Byzantine and Romanesque Gothic churches.

One day, when they were out in the country, they met the family and friends of a bride escorting her in a procession from her parents' home to the village church, where the groom waited with his mother and other witnesses. This led to Benedict's explaining the phenomenon of *Mammismo,* common throughout Italy but especially prevalent in Sicily, in which men maintained such close ties to their mothers that their first loyalty, always, was to *Mammina* instead of their own wives.

"But not in your case," Cassie said, secure in his love. "You'd never put your mother first."

"No, never," he replied, grabbing her in a fierce hug. "I am Italian by birth, but North American in outlook."

It all came to an end on the sixth day, beginning with a phone call from Francesca. She was so beside herself that, even though Benedict took the call, Cassie could hear her sister-in-law's distressed voice from clear across the room. Benedict's expression was thunderous when he finally hung up the phone, and that Elvira was at the root of whatever crisis had arisen came as no surprise to Cassie.

"You have to go back there, don't you?" she said hollowly, a leaden dismay sinking to the pit of her stomach, and leaving her shivering despite the day's brilliant heat.

"Si!" He practically spat out the word. "But this time, I promise you, Cassandra, I will put a stop to the

nonsense, once and for all. I will not allow Elvira to continue creating upheaval in all our lives.''

''I don't know how you'll stop her. She doesn't live by other people's rules.''

''I'll find a way,'' he said, framing her face between his hands, and scouring her features with his gaze. ''One way or another, I promise you this will end. If I have to, I'll have her committed. God knows, she's giving every indication she's losing her mind!''

''Even if you do, I won't come with you, Benedict. I sympathize with your dilemma. I even recognize this isn't something Francesca can manage alone. But I *absolutely refuse* to expose myself or our baby to further jeopardy.''

''Nor will I ask you to.'' He pulled her hard against him, close enough that she could feel the furious thud of his heart. ''I will send you to Bianca, instead.''

''No,'' she said. ''There's no telling how long you'll be tied up this time, and I've already stayed away from my business interests weeks longer than I originally intended. If I can't be with you—and it would seem, yet again, that I cannot—then I'm going home.''

He held her tighter and drew in a savage breath. ''I can't bear to think of you being so far away!''

''I don't consider it an ideal solution, either. But all other considerations apart, I'm not being fair to Trish, leaving her to handle my workload, as well as her own. Much though I like Bianca and her family, my life isn't with them, nor is it here, in this country.''

Releasing her, he paced the length of the room and stared out of the window, his spine rigid, his shoulders tense. ''You're my wife, Cassandra!'' he finally burst out, spinning back to face her. ''You belong with me! This shouldn't be happening to us, not now, not when we've just given our marriage a fighting chance to succeed. Can we not arrive at some sort of compromise that will allow us to remain together?''

His misery tore at her, but not enough to weaken her resolve. "I refuse to subject myself to more of your mother's abuse. I'm sorry, Benedict, really I am, but she crossed a line with me when she pushed me down the stairs. There's no going back on something like that.''

"Then how about this? Tomorrow, let me put you on a flight to *Milano*. Stay with Bianca and give me until the weekend to clean up this latest mess. Three days I'm asking for, *cara*. You can give me that, can't you?''

"And what if you can't work things out that soon? How long, Benedict, do I put *my* interests on hold while you take care of yours?''

"Three more days only.'' Picking up the phone, he punched in a number and carried out a rapid-fire conversation with whoever answered. "So," he said, hanging up finally and turning again to her, "we have tickets on a flight leaving *Milano* at three on Friday afternoon. I'll meet you in the departure lounge two hours before that. By Saturday, you'll be home again.''

He made it seem possible, easy. Yet nothing involving Elvira was ever simple. She thrived on complications.

Seeing her doubt, he took her hand and crushed it to his heart. "I promise you, Cassandra, nothing will prevent me from being beside you on that jet. On Saturday night, we'll be dining on Fisherman's Wharf. On Monday, I'll be looking for office space in San Francisco, and you'll be back among the friends you've missed, among people who love you almost as much as I do. I swear on my life, I will not allow my mother to derail our marriage a second time.''

She heard the conviction in his deep, sexy voice; saw

it in the dark, fervent glow of his eyes. And because she loved him and wanted very much to believe him, she buried her reservations and agreed to his terms. "Three days then. But if you let me down..."

He touched his finger to her mouth. "It isn't going to happen."

They left Sicily the next morning, and by midafternoon on Tuesday, she was once again in Milan. Bianca and Enrico took her into their arms, and into their hearts, with the kind of warmth she hadn't known from family since her mother's death.

"We'll make this a holiday for you," they said. "Before you know it, Friday will have arrived and so will Benedict. Never doubt him, Cassandra. He is a man of his word."

That night, he phoned to make sure she'd arrived safely and to give her a progress report. He'd arranged for Elvira to be admitted to hospital in Reggio Calabria the next day, for a full physical and psychiatric assessment.

Regardless of the outcome, her reign of terror was over because Pasquale Renaldo, Francesca's high school sweetheart, had asked her to marry him. He was a good man. He'd worked his own family's bergamot orchards since graduating from college and was well able to take over the running of the Constantino estate.

"Te amo, Cassandra," Benedict told Cassie, at the end of the call. "I'll see you on Friday."

On Wednesday, he phoned with another update. He'd be arriving in Milan at ten-thirty on Friday morning, leaving him plenty of time to make the international flight. He was meeting with Elvira's doctors tomorrow, to learn of their findings, and was determined to enforce whatever treatment they prescribed for her.

Before hanging up, he said again, *"Te amo, cara mia. Only two more nights apart, and then we're together forever."*

On Thursday, he didn't phone, but Cassie tried to accept Bianca's explanation that turning over the family operation to Pasquale would be a long and complicated process, particularly in light of Elvira's mishandling of so many aspects of the business. Still, the hours dragged and no matter how hard Cassie tried, little tendrils of uneasiness uncurled inside her like evil snakes eating away at her optimism. Not until Benedict was by her side and they were miles away, would she really believe the nightmare was over.

At last, Friday arrived. Simmering with pent-up anxiety, she arrived at Malpensa airport in time to meet his flight from Calabria. But although the commuter jet disgorged a vast number of passengers, Benedict was not among them.

"We must not have noticed him," Bianca said, slipping an encouraging arm around Cassie's shoulders. "Don't forget, he was expecting to meet you in the international departure lounge, not here. Because he's in transit, he might have gone there by a different route, and is already waiting for you."

But he was not. Nor did anyone answer when Bianca phoned the palazzo to find out if he had, in fact, been on the flight in the first place. "But that's a good sign," she insisted, steadfastly refusing to admit the unthinkable—that he simply wasn't going to show. "Francesca's probably helping Pasquale get used to his new job, and Benedict's already here, probably buying you something exquisite in the duty-free shop. Either that, or he's missed his flight. But if he has, he'll be on the next one, and you've still got four hours before you leave—plenty of time, Cassandra, really!''

"Why don't I believe you?" Cassie said, so miserably furious that she could barely speak.

Ever the loyal twin, Bianca said staunchly, "I know he won't let you down. Trust him, Cassandra."

She *had* trusted him, time and again. She'd married him, on trust; let him spirit her halfway around the world, on trust. Against her better judgment, she'd remained in his crazy mother's home when every instinct told her she should leave. She'd entrusted him with her life, and with her child's.

Most of all, she'd trusted him to keep his last promise to her. But he had not, and when the final boarding call came over the loudspeakers for passengers traveling on Delta Airlines Flight 7602, to New York JFK, she knew what she had to do.

"Leave for America without him?" Bianca was aghast. "But he's your husband, Cassandra! You must be here when he comes. He will expect it. It is the Italian way!"

"I don't care about the Italian way," she cried. "I'm an American and from now on, I'm doing what's best for me."

"But there will be an explanation for his actions!"

"There always is, Bianca," she said wearily. "And the trouble is, there always will be. Benedict can't separate himself from this family's problems. He makes them his own. Every time something goes wrong, he feels he has to fix it." She picked up her carry-on bag. "Either he shows up here in the next five minutes, or this marriage, such as it was, is over."

He did not. When the Boeing 767-300 took off some fifteen minutes later, the seat beside her remained unoccupied.

He arrived at the international departure gate in time to see the aircraft carrying his wife lift off and head toward the west. Frustrated, breathless, exhausted, he raked weary fingers through his hair and swore softly.

"That's not going to help any," a familiar voice informed him, and he turned to find Bianca behind him, her face crumpled with misery.

The faint, unreasonable hope that Cassandra might not have boarded the jet died. "So she's gone," he said.

"She's gone." His sister, normally so calm, gave vent to her annoyance by rapping him smartly on the arm. "How could you let her down like this, Benedict, when you knew how much was riding on keeping your promise to her?"

He caught her hands. Held them firmly, knowing he was about to deal a blow she couldn't possibly be prepared for. "It couldn't be helped," he said, and related what had happened.

For a moment, she looked at him uncomprehendingly, then fell against him with a cry. "Our mother had a brain tumor?" she said, when she could control her tears. "Oh, Benedict! Is that the reason for her headaches, and her odd behavior?"

"It would appear so." He led her to a row of unoccupied seats, and waited until she'd composed herself a little before going into the details. "Fortunately, the tumor itself was benign. Removing it, though, involved delicate, potentially life-threatening surgery too complex to be performed in Calabria. She had to be flown to Rome where a team of neurosurgeons performed the operation last night."

"You're saying she underwent surgery yesterday, and I'm only now hearing about it? For pity's sake, Benedict, why? You had no right to keep this from me. Elvira is my mother, too!"

"Once we had a diagnosis, everything happened too quickly. Her headaches were warnings of a time bomb waiting to go off. If we'd waited another week to seek a medical opinion—perhaps even another day—we might have left it too late."

"Even so, a phone call to let me know—"

"Bianca, there was no time for you to get to her beforehand, so what was the point? You'd have done nothing but pace the floor all night, and fret at being too far away to be of any help. I decided it was best to wait until we knew the outcome of the operation."

"And Cassandra? She didn't deserve to be kept informed of the reason you didn't show up when you said you would?"

"I'd have told her once we were headed back to the U.S."

"Except you didn't get here in time to do that. She was very angry, and very hurt. I don't know how you're going to make this up to her."

"I do." He checked his watch and saw that nearly an hour had passed since he'd arrived in Milan. He had no time to lose, if the plan he'd conceived during the flight from Rome was to succeed. "As her only son, it was my duty to see that our mother received the treatment she needed, but I've done my part here, Bianca. The rest is up to you and Francesca. Elvira's facing a long road to recovery and needs her family's support, but I can't be the one she leans on. I have a marriage to look after, and a wife and child to care for. From now on, my first responsibility is to them."

"Of course. I understand completely." She reached up and kissed his cheek. "I can see you're impatient to be off so I'll get out of your hair. Call me with good news soon, and don't worry about a thing at this end. Francesca and I will cope."

He watched her leave, regretting having to lay such a heavy burden on her shoulders when she already had a family of her own to care for and he, in the past, had always been the one to step in when help was needed. Yet, what else could he do this time? At what point did he reclaim the right to live his own life?

He smelled of hospitals, of antiseptic chemicals; could even taste them. He needed a shower, a shave, a change of clothes, and, God knew, he needed sleep. But attending to those needs lay far down on his list of priorities. Eyes gritty with fatigue, he expelled a long breath and took out his cell phone.

"It's Benedict Constantino," he said, when the call went through. "I have to be in San Francisco before tonight. How soon can you get me there?"

He had another two hours to kill before the private jet was cleared for takeoff. Long enough to claim his luggage and take advantage of the amenities in the charter company's executive lounge. Long enough to call Cassandra's friend Trish, and enlist her help.

CHAPTER TWELVE

THROUGHOUT the long, endless journey home, Cassie tried to come to grips with her situation and decide how she was going to proceed, once she was back in familiar territory. But weariness, while not allowing her to sleep, seemed to have robbed her mind of its ability to reason. She existed in a vacuum, totally removed from everything and everyone around her.

She wished she could remain there forever. It was, in a strange, out-of-this-world sort of way, very peaceful, except for those moments when, without warning, Benedict wandered into her thoughts. Then the pain and loss besieged her on all sides.

She felt wounded. Betrayed. Robbed of joy. For a brief, lovely time, he had loved her. But not enough. Never enough. And her mind, clicking into gear, recognized that it all had to end. She couldn't keep putting herself through the mill this way. It was too destructive, too debilitating, too humiliating.

Her flight touched down in San Francisco just after seven that night, nearly an hour later than scheduled because of air traffic delays leaving JFK in New York. No one was there to meet her because she hadn't let her friends know she was returning. She was too fragile to tolerate their sympathy. All she wanted was to go home and surround herself with the things she loved—her grandmother's china, her bombé chest, her paintings, her rugs. *Things* didn't hurt. Only people could do that.

She took a taxi from the airport, paid the driver, then

stood a moment on the sidewalk and let the fact that she was home at last seep into every pore. *Now,* she could take charge of her life again.

Leaving her bags inside the lower lobby, she climbed the stairs and let herself into the town house. The place had been closed up for nearly four months, yet the moment she opened her front door, the fragrance of flowers—of freesias—assailed her.

She had always been susceptible to the memories evoked by scents. A whiff of Chanel No.5 brought her mother to mind as vividly as if she sat next to her in the quiet living room. A good Cuban cigar took her back to childhood, and Aspen at Christmas with Trish whose father lit up after dinner, and filled the house with the rich smell of expensive tobacco.

And now the intoxicating perfume of freesias swept over her in waves and brought Benedict alive in her mind more thoroughly than if he'd been standing there in person.

Dazed, she walked into her living room and found it full of flowers. Of freesias in glorious shades of purple and burgundy and yellow, in vases on the mantelpiece, and the coffee table. On the window ledges and the desk. Then, belatedly, she realized other things: the music coming from her stereo—songs from the forties about lost love found again, and two hearts beating as one; the windows open to the soft evening air; the aroma of bread warming in the oven.

As if drawn by invisible threads, she wandered through the other rooms. Came upon more freesias in the bedroom, and a sinfully seductive nightgown laid out on the bed. Discovered candles burning in her bathroom.

Finally, with her pulse fluttering and her spirit caught midway between hope and despair, she made her way to the terrace where she found the glass patio table set for dinner for two—and Benedict.

"Welcome home, *mi adorata*," he said, his voice embracing her like velvet.

"This is not possible!" she exclaimed, clutching the edge of the French door for fear she might faint with shock. "You're not really here!"

To prove her wrong, he came to her and swept her into his arms, and the feel of them closing firmly around her was very real indeed. "I am here," he said, "because this is where I belong. With you, my *bella* wife. Always with you."

"No," she protested, struggling to free herself because the temptation to forgive him was too overpowering to resist, and she knew she shouldn't give in to it. "You didn't meet me in Milan. You didn't keep your word."

"No," he admitted, releasing her just far enough that he could look into her eyes. "I did not, and for that I will always be sorry. But if you'll let me explain, perhaps you'll find it in yourself to forgive me one more time."

"I don't know that I can," she said, but allowed him to draw her down beside him on the padded cushions of the love seat under the eaves.

"Then at least agree to listen, before you pass judgment."

Well, she could hardly refuse to do that. And in all truth, as her shock dissipated, she found herself agog with curiosity. "How long have you been here?" she asked, sinking against him despite her best intentions to remain at a distance. "When did you have time to go to all this trouble?" Then, as another thought occurred,

"And how did you get inside my house? You don't have a key!"

"But Trish does," he said. "And Trish is a true romantic. Thank her for setting the scene, and thank me for having enough sense to turn to her when I needed help. Otherwise, you'd have found me sitting on the doorstep when you came home."

"But why, Benedict? Why put me through so much needless heartbreak?"

"Because I had no choice," he said, and told her the whole story.

"You could have phoned and warned me," she said, when he was done.

"And said what? That I was putting my mother ahead of my wife yet again, after promising it would never happen again? Should I have preyed on your sense of decency and fair play to blackmail you into staying in Italy when you were desperate to come home?" He shook his head. "No, it was better to tell you everything *after* the fact, when we were together again. Unfortunately, I arrived too late to make that happen in Milano, but I did my best, *cara*. I missed you by only a few minutes, and for the rest of my life, I will regret what that must have cost you."

She looked at him and saw that she was not the only one who'd suffered. Indeed, to be fair, he'd paid by far the greater price. Worry and exhaustion were painted on his face in equal measure.

"Well?" He returned her glance candidly, ready to accept whatever decision she meted out to him.

All her anger and pain dissolved. Overwhelmed, she pulled his head down to her breast and stroked her fingers through his hair. "You did what you had to do, my darling," she said softly. "And you're not the only one with regrets. As your wife, I should have been there to help you through such a very difficult time. I know how much it hurts to lose a mother. For your sake, I hope Elvira makes a good recovery.''

''I hope so, too. I would like you to know her as she used to be, instead of as she was these last few months. But what matters most is that you and I are together again.'' A tremor shook him. ''I could not face losing you, Cassandra. You are more than my wife, you are my life.''

Courtesy of Trish, there was crab fresh from Fisherman's Wharf for dinner, and sourdough bread, and salad, and delicious little pastry shells filled with fresh strawberries. But it all had to wait until much later, when the moon had risen and the air had turned too cool to eat outdoors. Because there was more important business needing attention, and that took place in the bedroom.

''Te amo, Cassandra,'' he said, after they'd made love with the quiet intensity of two people who'd come too close to losing everything that mattered to them.

''Te amo, Benedict,'' she replied, lifting her face for his kiss.

November, four months later.

Even from the road, it was plain to see that the Constantino property was well-cared for, that order had been restored. The orchards stood lush with fruit. Huge padded baskets hung from the tree branches, slowly being filled with the precious hand-picked harvest of bergamot.

At the palazzo, a different Elvira waited. Still chic and sophisticated, still loving her ornately formal home, but with a softer edge to her voice, a warm albeit nervous welcome in her smile.

"I've brought your grandson to meet you," Cassie said, placing Michael Vincenzo in her mother-in-law's arms. "He is so much a Constantino that I think it's time the two of you met."

"*Grazie,*" she replied, clearly on the verge of tears. "*Grazie tante,* Cassandra. It is more than I deserve. They tell me I treated you very poorly, *cara.* I hope you'll allow me to make it up to you and embrace you into my family as you deserve."

With a warmth she'd never have thought possible six months ago, Cassie enveloped both her son and his grandmother in a swift hug. "Of course! We all deserve nothing but good things from here on, Elvira. I'm very happy to see you looking so well."

"And I," she said, regaining her composure with difficulty, "am so grateful to you. I have only to look at my son to know that you are a good wife who makes him very happy, and to look at your son to know that you are also a very good mother. So, now we will go into the house. The rest of the family is anxious to meet this little one, and Speranza has been preparing for his visit for days."

Crooning softly to the baby, she led the way through the cavernous front hall to the salon at the back of the palazzo. Yet somehow, the gloom of the place seemed less oppressive, the cold of the ancient stone less pervasive.

Perhaps it had to do with Benedict's arm around her waist, and the secure knowledge that he would always be there, whether or not she needed him. Or perhaps it was much simpler than that, and merely had everything to do with love.

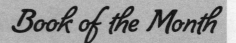

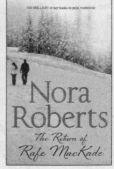

What will you treat yourself to next?

*Ignite your imagination,
step into the past...*
6 new stories every month

INTRIGUE...

Breathtaking romantic suspense
Up to 8 new stories every month

Medical Romance

*Captivating medical drama –
with heart*
6 new stories every month

MODERN™

*International affairs,
seduction & passion guaranteed*
9 new stories every month

nocturne™

*Deliciously wicked
paranormal romance*
Up to 4 new stories every month

RIVA™

*Live life to the full –
give in to temptation*
3 new stories every month available
exclusively via our Book Club

You can also buy Mills & Boon eBooks at
www.millsandboon.co.uk

*Visit us
Online*

M&B/WORLD2